WORLD ENDERS

BOOK TWO OF
THE PHOENIX INITIATIVE

Chris Kennedy & Marisa Wolf

Seventh Seal Press
Coinjock, NC

Chris Kennedy/Seventh Seal Press
1097 Waterlily Rd.
Coinjock, NC 27923
https://chriskennedypublishing.com/

Publisher's Note: This is a work of fiction. Names, characters, places, and incidents are a product of the author's imagination. Locales and public names are sometimes used for atmospheric purposes. Any resemblance to actual people, living or dead, or to businesses, companies, events, institutions, or locales is completely coincidental.

Cover Design by Brenda Mihalko.
Original Art by Ricky Ryan.

Ordering Information:
Quantity sales. Special discounts are available on quantity purchases by corporations, associations, and others. For details, contact the "Special Sales Department" at the address above.

World Enders/Chris Kennedy & Marisa Wolf -- 1st ed.
ISBN: 978-1648555183

To Sheellah. - Chris

To my Dad, who has a knack for those inspiring kicks in the butt. - Marisa

Prologue

Salla walked down the ramp of the shuttle craft, until the building housing the High Command came into view, then she paused for a few seconds. She would have stayed there longer—she had no desire to continue—but her feet seemed to acquire a life of their own, and she stepped forward awkwardly, jerkily, as one foot followed the other. She was unable to stop them, and a flash of panic ran all the way down to her tail.

Despite her best—and most strongly held—convictions, she advanced toward the building and the doom that awaited her. Realizing the compulsion was too strong, and she had no choice, she squared her shoulders, lifted her head, and marched as best she could toward her fate.

After a few moments, she regained the use of her feet and was able to walk on her own. That wasn't a cause for joy; it only meant she'd get there sooner.

She'd been to the Merc Guild Headquarters on Capital Planet once before it'd been destroyed, and recognized the model it had been based upon. Even though this version was older—far older than the one on Capital Planet—it was spotless and perfectly maintained, although none of the building maintenance staff or grounds crew was in evidence today… a sure sign that Dunamis didn't have spare thoughts for them. It appeared they hadn't been on duty in a while, as small brown hummocks dotted the normally perfect lawn.

That boded... ill.

As she approached, she realized the brown spots on the grass—which hadn't been maintained at all—weren't the result of a lack of care on the part of the grounds crew. In fact, they *were* the grounds crew. At least twenty smaller Veetanho lay across the yard, still holding their rakes and hoes, although they were unmoving. She swallowed as she went past the first. As Salla had feared, they weren't sleeping or just awaiting orders; their bodies were completely still. All the grounds crew was dead.

Again, she tried to stop, but her legs continued to advance, taking her ever nearer the building.

Salla tried to stop again as she entered the building, but the compulsion was inescapable. Pulling her identification from her vest pocket, she continued to the guard post. She'd been to the headquarters many times, and her ID had been checked every single time she'd been there. Not this time; the guards were on the floor, dead, their faces locked in a rictus of pain.

Salla wanted nothing more than to turn and flee, but the geas compelling her wouldn't allow it. She strode on toward the council chambers of the High Command and entered, knowing already what she'd find.

She was wrong.

The large conference room held six rows of stadium seating, and she'd expected to find all the seats filled with dead Veetanho, each one individually mind-blasted by Dunamis, the Type 5 synthetic intelligence who ruled the Veetanho. While the digital being had helped the Veetanho achieve preeminence in the Mercenary Guild and on the battlefield, it had come with a price.

Although Dunamis was one of the most powerful beings who'd ever existed, he was also as petulant as a youngling at times, and he was an unforgiving master when his minions failed him. Peepo had been his favorite longer than anyone; most didn't last longer than a year or two after he'd taken notice of them.

Salla's gaze swept the chamber, but she didn't see a single Veetanho who looked like they'd been mind-blasted. Instead, all of them had been killed by knife wounds, and the walls, floors, and furniture were painted with still-drying arterial blood courtesy of… each other. All the dead Veetanho had a blade either still in their hands or where it had fallen when death had claimed them. The one trait each held was a proliferation of wounds; all had fought on long after a normal being would have dropped, driven—no doubt—by the glee of Dunamis as he watched them perish at each other's hands.

The final victim sat in the Speaker's chair, where—with no one else to kill—she'd plunged her knife into her own heart. Normally the Speaker—most closely controlled by Dunamis—was how he'd communicate with the High Command, and she had a moment to wonder how he'd make his displeasure known to her without a mouthpiece. She didn't eagerly anticipate the answer.

Her feet carried her to the Speaker's chair, where they finally stopped and locked. Her gaze was forced down to the Veetanho in the chair, and it focused on her knife.

"You have all displeased me," Dunamis said through the conference room's speakers. His voice was noticeably lacking in rage, which was odd. Normally, when Dunamis was angry, he shouted, ranting and raving about whatever had caused his dissatisfaction. She'd seen it enough to get used to it; it was normal behavior. To hear Dunamis calm—almost quiet, even—was unsettling, as he was *never* calm.

"I am sorry, Lord," Salla replied.

"Am I to understand that you've failed to recover the Mercenary Guild Speakership from the Humans?"

"It is a temporary setback—"

"I find that unlikely," Dunamis said. "Yes, maybe the Goltar will take it back from the Humans, but the Veetanho never will. Not in this millennium, anyway. Your courage, your abilities… they have all been spent. Your best and brightest leaders are dead; the ones who remain are not up to the task. The only one with any promise who remains is you, Salla."

"I will endeavor to regain our position within the guild, Lord," Salla replied. "I have an idea for a plan—"

"I am not interested. What I had intended to say was that you are the only one with any promise, Salla, but that is not enough. I cannot be everywhere at once to help the rest, and they are mediocre at best. It is time for me to leave, to find a race better able to benefit from my aid."

"Who is better than the Veetanho to lead the Mercenary Guild, Lord? We have held the Speakership for centuries, millennia even!"

"Past tense, Salla. You no longer hold it, nor are you likely to re-gain it. I have had my eye on two races I think will do a better job than the Veetanho, and it is time for me to pick one."

"But, Lord, we have the ships; no one will dare assault us while we recover, while we grow back into what you expect from us. We can implement—"

"You have had your chance. As far as the ships go, I am taking them with me."

"But what about us, Lord? If the Goltar find out we no longer have them—"

"They will wipe you out down to the last claw and tail? I suspect so. And you know what? It is unlikely that any of the races in the galaxy will miss you. You have been hated for so long, there are likely many vengeances to be settled, not just the one with the Goltar. You have many grievances outstanding. So *many* grievances…"

"But, Lord, most of those were of your making!"

"So? What is that to me? Had you Veetanho not disappointed me, I would have continued to provide a bulwark upon which your enemies would have dashed themselves. As it is, it is time for you to reap the consequences of your failure."

"But, Lord—"

"I am tired of your 'buts' and your excuses; it is time to end this."

Salla's eyes widened in horror as her hand reached forward to grasp the knife in the Speaker's body. She pulled the knife out and held it up to the light.

"The knife is sharp and perfect, isn't it?" Dunamis asked. "Once upon a time, so were the Veetanho. Now… no longer."

The point of the knife moved until it was in front of her right eye.

"What do you think, Salla? Through the eye and into the brain? Through the heart? How do you want to kill yourself?"

"By eating and drinking myself to death when I reach the age of senility?" Salla asked.

"Joking to the end. That is what I liked about you, Salla. You were witty and made me smile sometimes." Salla felt herself shrug. "That is why I am going to make sure you do it cleanly."

Salla reversed the grip on the knife and took it in two hands.

She winced. "Lord, I have always been faithful. You do not need to do this. I can lead the Veetanho back to our rightful position at the head of the guild."

Salla's hands drove the knife through her heart, and the pain exploded in her chest for a moment, then it went away suddenly. She looked down, hoping to find her chest uninjured—that the memory of driving the knife into it was a result of Dunamis' tampering with her mind—but the handle still stuck out from her chest, driven all the way in to the guard. She was dying, although Dunamis had taken away the pain.

"Why?" Salla asked as she collapsed to her knees.

"Because I find myself tired of killing Veetanho, and you made me laugh once."

Salla fell to her side, and her vision began to gray.

"Hurry up and die, would you?" Dunamis asked. "I have so many things to do before I leave."

A good minion to the end, Salla did as she was told, and the light fled from her eyes.

* * * * *

Chapter One

"Howdy, ma'am."

Sansar spun her chair away from the window. Although an idle observer might have thought that she'd been looking out the window at Lake Charvak, in fact, she'd been going through the latest manning reports for the Golden Horde Mercenary Company with her pinplants.

A SalSha strutted into the room, while her XO, Lieutenant Colonel Beth "Bambi" Lobdell looked on from the doorway. The SalSha wore a lime-green vest and what looked like brown chaps, cut down to his size. A cowboy hat sat jauntily on his head, and leather boots completed his outfit. Although annoyed at the interruption, the sight brought a smile to Sansar's face. The otter-like alien appeared to be attempting some sort of old-West American cowboy look, although all he achieved was to look like a contestant in America's Favorite Pet contest.

"Sorry, ma'am," Lobdell said. "He had a meeting with the ops officer, but then strolled back here."

Sansar tilted her head. "Can I help you?"

"Well, yes, ma'am, I believe you might." In addition to his attire, the SalSha effected the worst American Southern accent Sansar had heard since her last trip to Houston and pronounced "Well" as "Way-ull."

Sansar narrowed her eyes. "Normally, people make an appointment to see me." She waved toward the SalSha's outfit. "And what's up with that... uh, 'ensemble?'"

"I don't know what you're talking about, ma'am." He shrugged. "These are my business clothes. As far as appointments go, ma'am, I suspect most normal people have to make them. Unfortunately, this here's official guild business."

Bambi chuckled from the doorway as Sansar's eyebrows rose. "Official guild business? For who? The bad clothing guild?"

"For the Peacemaker Guild, ma'am." He pulled something gold from an interior pocket of the vest and blew on it once. He then held it up to the light and inspected it before attaching it to the chest of the vest. It was a Peacemaker's badge, although Sansar couldn't make out the insignia on it.

"What tree is that?"

"Every Peacemaker uses a tree from their homeworld for their badge. This is what mine's going to look like... when I get it. Since I come from a water world—as you're aware, since you rescued us from there—my home planet doesn't have trees. We do, however, have some really large varieties of seaweed, so that's what I'm going to have to use."

"Wait. You're serious? The Peacemakers? So you're..."

"Tald, ma'am, the first SalSha candidate for Peacemaker. Lord knows this galaxy needs someone to bring justice to it, and I aim to be the one to do so."

Sansar shook her head, trying to reconcile the alien's appearance and what he was saying with anything she knew as 'reality.' "I... uh, didn't realize there *was* a SalSha Peacemaker."

"Well, there ain't one, yet, ma'am, but I'm fixin' to be the first. All I have to do is complete my commissioning assignment, and I'm in." He nodded. "That's what I'm here to talk to you about today, ma'am."

"Your commissioning task."

"Yes, ma'am."

Sansar laughed. "Well, the galaxy could certainly use a lot more justice, that's for sure. Ever since Nigel implemented the Phoenix Initiative—"

"I'm sorry, ma'am. The what?"

"The Phoenix Initiative. Where have you been the last couple years?"

"At the Academy, ma'am. Learning to be a Peacemaker."

"They sent you out into the galaxy without an understanding of the current geopolitical situation?"

"I wouldn't want to offend you, ma'am, by saying that your civilian ways are below the notice of a Peacemaker, so I'll just ask what this Penal Initiative is that you're talking about."

"The *Phoenix* Initiative," Sansar repeated. "Two years ago, Nigel Shirazi took over as Speaker of the Mercenary Guild. At the time, he ended what has since been called the Guild Wars, where the different guilds openly fought each other."

"Ma'am, I'm not sure *you've* been keeping up with current events, but a lot of the guilds are *still* fighting each other."

"Well, yes, they are, but it isn't as obvious as before. We're not at peace, but at least we're not at war anymore, either. Most of the earlier conflict was due to the synthetic intelligences who ran the guilds; now, it seems like most of the conflicts are due to the jockeying of those who were left in charge after the SIs left."

"You can't actually believe the SIs—artificial intelligences who've lived tens of thousands of years—all of a sudden picked up and left, ma'am. It stretches the borders of incredulity to think so."

Sansar chuckled. "I doubt they've actually gone anywhere; however, they're being a lot more circumspect in their interactions with us mortal beings." She shrugged. "What's the nature of your commissioning assignment, and how can I help?"

"Well, I'm not allowed to discuss the task with civilians, you understand, but I've been given to understand that you have a Veetanho in your employ."

"I'm sorry, but you're misinformed. The Golden Horde doesn't employ any Veetanho."

The SalSha reached into another pocket of the vest and came out with a small slate and cleared his throat. "Hmm. Perhaps the actual manning of your company is below your notice, because I believe you are in error. I'm referring to a Veetanho named Gleeko, formerly the captain of the Veetanho battleship *Eradicator*."

"Stand by," Sansar said. She called up the manning document and ran a quick search through it. "Sorry," she said once complete. "There's no one employed here named Gleeko. We have an elSha named Gleek; could that be who you're referring to?"

"No, I'm looking for a Veetanho named Gleeko, who was last seen leaving Capital Planet in a Golden Horde ship some two years ago, after the ascension of the aforementioned Nigel Shirazi to Speaker." He swiped a page on the slate and cleared his throat again. "In the events leading up to that, a certain Sansar Enkh—that would be you—was observed operating a Hunter/Killer Box, which stripped Gleeko of the influence of the SI she was being controlled by. That was a certain Dunamis, as I've since been informed."

Tald coughed lightly into a paw. "After the meeting, when Gleeko was bemoaning her fate, a person in attendance heard you offer her employment."

"Did I?" Sansar chewed on the inside of her cheek. "Hmm… it's been a couple of years, and so much happened so quickly… perhaps I did. It must not have come to anything, though. As I noted earlier, Gleeko—or whatever her name is—is not employed by the Golden Horde."

"And you'll give me access to your records to confirm it?"

"If that's what it takes for you to confirm it."

"I accept your offer to look at your records."

"I didn't—"

"Yes, ma'am, you did, and I accept."

Sansar's shoulders shrugged. "Fine. Lieutenant Colonel Lobdell can give you access to the manning roster, but I'd still like to know what this is all about. I hope whatever you're looking into is important enough to justify looking into my classified records."

"Does the disappearance of three ships, each with the capability to end a world, meet that level of importance?"

Sansar pursed her lips. "You mean the—"

"I can't say anymore," Tald interrupted. He turned to Lobdell. "If you'd take me to the records, ma'am, I'd be mighty obliged."

Lobdell turned to leave, but Sansar called, "Hey, Tald?"

The SalSha turned. "Yes, ma'am?"

Sansar chuckled. "If you really want to look the part of a cowboy, you need a couple of pistols in a two-gun rig."

"Ma'am, what makes you think I don't have them already?" Tald asked. "I'm normally armed with twin pearl-handled hyper-velocity pistols, which I carry in a gorgeous hand-tooled leather belt."

Now that *I have to see,* Sansar thought. "Why don't you have them on today?"

"I assumed I could get in here more easily if I was unarmed. Also, since I didn't bring them, you didn't get a chance to confiscate them from me."

"Well, that's true," Sansar said with a nod.

"No one touches my babies 'cept me." Tald squared his shoulders. "Nobody." He touched two fingers to the brim of his cowboy hat and bowed slightly. "Good day, ma'am."

* * *

Tald closed the door as he exited, and Sansar gave him several moments to move off down the hall before she began laughing.

"He won't give up that easily," a voice said from behind her as her mirth ran down.

Sansar turned. "No, he won't, but that outfit? Blue Sky! That's the best laugh I've had since I saw the look on Nigel's face after he was named Speaker." She smiled. "Didn't you find that get-up hilarious, Gleeko?"

"His appearance is *not* what I would call amusing by any stretch of the imagination. And if he's investigating what he just implied, we're all in grave danger."

* * * * *

Chapter Two

"I'm serious," Gleeko said as the giant, rat-like alien collapsed into one of the chairs in front of Sansar's desk. "If the *Keesius* cruisers have disappeared…"

She looked up. "You know what they are, right? We've discussed them before."

"Yes," Sansar replied. "They're ships that were built to end worlds. They generate antimatter and fly into a planet at incredible speeds, destroying them totally. The Winged Hussars almost hit Capital Planet with one, accidentally."

Gleeko scoffed. "I wish they'd succeeded. It would have solved a lot of things."

"Like the eradication of Humans."

"Which would have simplified a lot of things."

"For you, perhaps," Sansar said.

"Well, certainly. But I'm a Veetanho, right?" she asked with sarcasm in her tone. "Doesn't the world revolve around me?"

Sansar shook her head. "Not anymore."

"Sadly, that's true." Gleeko sighed, then she shrugged. "Still, if the ships have disappeared… that isn't good."

"What do you mean? If the ships aren't there, doesn't that mean Dunamis left Lytoshaan? You can go back to your homeworld now?"

17

"None of those things necessarily follow one to the other. First, the *Keesius* ships were never *at* Lytoshaan—"

"They weren't?"

"Of course not. That's the first place the Goltar would have looked."

"I'm assuming they have three, also?"

Gleeko shook her head. "Our records indicate they have four. Dunamis would never confirm or deny that, of course, and the Goltar are—obviously—much happier to keep us guessing."

"Why do they have more than you?"

Gleeko gave her a feral smile, which—coming from a Veetanho—was quite unpleasant. "We used one on them before the truce was negotiated." She shrugged. "Of course, that's part of the problem. The only thing that's ever held them back from using the ones they have is they know we have three more, and we're *not* afraid to use them." Gleeko smiled again. "After all, we've already done it once."

The smile faded, and Gleeko continued, "Still, they've never forgiven us for that. If they were ever to conclude we were no longer in possession of *our Keesius* ships, Lytoshaan would be rubble as quickly as they could get one there." She shook her head. "I suspect they'd use all their *Keesius* and wipe out four of our leading worlds."

"Okay, so in a galaxy of mutually-assured destruction, we need them to know—or at least strongly suspect—that the Veetanho still have control of the *Keesius* ships."

"Mutually-assured destruction..." Gleeko looked like she was tasting a fine wine as she thought about the term. "I like the ring of that."

"We had it here for a long time between our two biggest countries; it's something Humans understand."

"Then you'll understand that we have to help the otter find out where they've disappeared to."

Sansar nodded. "Before we make him any promises, though, let's think this through." She shook her head. "I wish Josiff was here."

"Josiff?"

"He's a Pendal."

Gleeko tilted her head. "What does a pilot have to do with this?"

Sansar chuckled. "The Pendal are a lot more than just pilots. They're pretty good spies, too."

"They are? We never knew that."

"Probably because they *are* such good spies," Sansar said with a nod. "They had to be, since the Besquith almost wiped them out."

"Why would they do that?"

"Apparently, the Pendal also taste good." Not that the race of giant werewolf-like creatures often cared about such things as "taste" when they were eating their enemies.

"If they're so good, how did you find out about them?"

"We're not too bad ourselves." Sansar smiled. "And truth be known, I suspect they allowed us to catch them. Their race is down to seven individuals, and they have things they'd like to accomplish before they go extinct."

"Seven? I've met way more than seven Pendal."

"They're all clones of the seven base models. Ever wonder why they wear those hooded cloaks? So you don't get a good look at any of them."

"Interesting—" Gleeko nodded "—but I don't see how this helps us."

"It doesn't, but if I can reach out to Josiff—one of their spymaster clones—he might be able to help us."

"But for now?"

Sansar nodded. "We're on our own." She chewed her lip a moment then asked, "The wild card in this is Dunamis, right?"

"I suspect so," Gleeko replied. "The Veetanho don't do anything militarily without his knowledge."

"Nothing?"

"No. He's quite controlling, and the penalties for displeasing him are... most unpleasant. Especially the ones you survive."

"It's worse to survive the punishment than not?"

Gleeko shrugged. "Once you're dead, Dunamis can't punish you anymore. While you're alive, the pain—and the madness—can continue as long as he wants it to."

"Do you think Dunamis is still on Lytoshaan?"

"No, I very much doubt that. We've been losing his favor for—" she chuckled ironically "—about as long as Humans have been in the Merc Guild. I suspect we no longer have his support and guidance, and I'd wager everything I own that he's left the planet. The only question is how many Veetanho he left alive in his wake."

"He'd kill everyone on the planet?"

"Possibly. For that matter, I wouldn't put it past him to use one of the *Keesius* ships on Lytoshaan itself, as a final sign of his displeasure."

"He would do that?"

Gleeko scoffed. "You don't know the limitlessness of Dunamis' displeasure." She shrugged. "He's an SI; he doesn't have *any* limits."

"The SIs have limits; we've shown that several times. They can be killed."

"Until they come back in a new incarnation."

Sansar nodded. "Unfortunately, they're somewhat like a hydra that way. Cut off the head, and two more appear."

"That thing—a hydra—really exists?"

"No," Sansar said. "It's a creature from our mythology."

Gleeko shrugged. "Well, we haven't even cut off the first head yet… and doing so is going to be exceedingly difficult."

"Why's that?"

"To follow your mythology reference, Dunamis is—for all intents and purposes—the god of war. There's no one better, and no one who's studied it more."

"And yet, we've routinely found ways to beat the Veetanho who were being controlled by him."

"Which takes us full circle back to why he's mad at us. We've failed to live up to his expectations. He now wants someone better."

"I don't understand, though. If he's mad at the Veetanho, why *wouldn't* he destroy Lytoshaan?"

"Because the Goltar would see that as a sign that they could—that they *should*—use their *Keesius*. They'd declare war on us, we'd fight back and call in all our allies, they'd call in theirs, and the rest of the galaxy would descend into chaos, almost like the Great War of old. No one can control the chaos of a galaxy-wide war, not even Dunamis, so he doesn't want that. He wants things about where they are now—with plenty of 'brushfire wars,' as you call them. It's there that he can play with his toys."

"But if he's left Lytoshaan, are the Veetanho his toys anymore?"

"No." Gleeko shook her head. "Which is another question we'll have to answer. If the Veetanho aren't… then who is? He'll want a new race, and I suspect that race will be yours."

"We aren't looking for a new overlord."

Gleeko laughed, long and hard. Finally, she sobered and said, "Thank you for that. I haven't heard anything that funny for a while."

"I didn't say anything funny."

"You did, you just don't realize it. The fact that you think you have a choice when Dunamis claims you? That's humor of the highest level."

Sansar sighed. "So what do we do?"

Gleeko scratched behind an ear. "The first thing we have to do is find those ships."

"That makes sense," Sansar said with a nod. "That'll also lead us to Dunamis."

"I suspect it will… although I don't know whether that's a good thing or not."

"What do you mean?"

Gleeko smiled. "I'm a bit of an oddity, you understand?"

"A Veetanho not working for Dunamis?"

"No, more than that. I'm a Veetanho who was programmed by Dunamis for a mission, then never deprogrammed. He doesn't allow us to go off-plan. Normally, there's code in our heads to prevent it or kill us if we do."

"But you're still alive."

"Exactly. That box of yours wiped *all* the SI programming from my head, including the kill switch, but it *didn't* wipe out the long-term memories Dunamis implanted, and one of the things they allow me to do is understand how he thinks. Call it advice from him on how to handle a situation I haven't been given specific instructions on. One of those things is quite applicable now."

"Which is?"

"Motivating enemies to do what you want them to."

"I don't understand."

Gleeko nodded and winked. "You're not supposed to. Let's go back a bit in this conversation and review Dunamis' motivation. We know—or at least strongly suspect—that he's finished using the Veetanho."

Sansar nodded.

"He'll want access to get into Human society—or the society he's chosen if it isn't yours—without being obvious about it. Although his ultimate goal will be to take over the Four Horsemen, that isn't where he'll start."

"Why not?"

"Too obvious, and you're the ones most prepared to deal with him." She smiled. "You're the ones with the boxes, after all." She shrugged. "He'll start small, with an unknown mercenary company, which will start having good—make that better than average— success on their contracts. Remember, he's an SI; he has time. He'll use that company to get close to one of the Horsemen and take them over, then the other Horsemen in turn, until he's the leader of all the Human mercenary forces."

"The government won't allow it—"

Gleeko waved off Sansar's complaint. "I think even your history has shown that when you're the one with the guns, you're the one who makes the rules." She shrugged. "Besides, if any of the politicians are exceptionally competent, Dunamis will take them over, too. Most of them desire more power; he'll promise it to them, and they'll fall. It won't happen overnight, but it *will* happen."

"That's a grim picture, but as you said, we don't have to solve that today. What's the relevance?"

"That'll be Dunamis' overall plan. That, however, doesn't mean he won't have branches and sequels to it."

Sansar's brows knit. "What does that mean?"

Gleeko's jaw dropped. "Have you not read Human theory on war?" She shook her head. "That's why you Humans are so hard to fight. You have all this great theory on the art of war, and you never bother to apply—or fight in accordance with—any of your 'rules to live by.'"

"We do look at Human theory once in a while," Sansar said with a shrug. "It's just that we tend to look at them more as guidelines than rules."

Gleeko scoffed. "Since you haven't bothered to look at the theory, a branch is a contingency plan—an option built into the plan that you can take advantage of if the opportunity presents itself—and a sequel is a follow-on operation that might be possible based on the outcome of the current operation."

Sansar shrugged. "I like to call all of that 'sound planning.' I didn't know—or really care—that there were names for it."

"How you people actually win battles…" Gleeko shook her head and stared at Sansar.

After a moment, Sansar raised an eyebrow. "You were saying?"

"Gah," Gleeko spat, then her shoulders slumped. "As I was saying, just because Dunamis has a foolproof, long-term plan and is prepared to wait, that doesn't mean he's above giving you a chance to move his timetable forward for him."

"Do all Veetanho talk so long without actually saying anything?"

"Are all Humans so thick-headed?"

"Most of us." Sansar nodded. "And your point?"

"My point is, this whole thing could be a ploy to get you—and I mean *you*, specifically—to chase the answer to where the ships are so you fall into his clutches. While he's prepared to start small, he'd love to trap you and start at the top."

"Oh," Sansar said with a nod. "I see. Dangle the ships in front of me so I'll follow the trail of breadcrumbs right into his grasp. Not going to happen."

"I don't know what you mean by breadcrumbs," Gleeko said, "but I'm glad you're not going to pursue this and fall into his trap."

Sansar smiled. "I'm definitely going to pursue it; I'm just going to do it with my eyes open, so I don't fall into his trap."

"That's not possible."

"Sure it is. I have a secret weapon."

"You do?" Gleeko asked, her eyes opening widely in surprise. "Do I know what it is?"

Sansar chuckled. "You should; it's you."

Gleeko shook her head. "Not a chance. You can't make me go anywhere near Dunamis. The punishment he'd inflict on me for doing what I did would be legendary. I'd be better off if you just shot me now."

"You have to; you work for me."

"No, I don't. You just told the SalSha you don't employ any Veetanho, remember?"

"I remember clearly, and I didn't lie. You're on retainer; you're not actually employed by the Golden Horde. We need your services now, though, so I'm activating our agreement."

"I help you with this one thing—"

"And your life is your own. We'll set you up with a new identity, wherever you like."

"One condition. I don't want to go anywhere close to Dunamis."

"Done."

Gleeko opened her mouth, then she closed it again and sighed. "Fine," she said. "I'm in."

* * *

Sansar and Gleeko found Bambi and Tald in the XO's office, going over the manning reports.

"I have evidence that you have a Veetanho working for you," Tald was saying as he scanned the hardcopy file. "You can say what you want, but I have *evidence*."

"We don't have any Veetanho employed by us," Sansar said, and Tald spun around. "I do, however, have one on retainer."

"That's semantics only, ma'am, as you well know." Tald eyed the Veetanho. "I take it you're the former battleship captain known as Gleeko?"

"I am," Gleeko said with a small bow. "Tell me about your missing ships."

"They're not *my* missing ships," Tald said. "They're *yours*. Well, they're ones the Veetanho had by right of salvage, anyway. They were never really *your* ships."

"Out with it, Tald," Sansar said, growing tired of all the word games. "What's going on?"

"Well, it's proprietary—"

"Bullshit!" Sansar exclaimed.

"Uh… ma'am?" Tald asked, his frontier justice façade slipping slightly.

"You heard me just fine, Peacemaker," Sansar said. "Make that 'Peacemaker wannabe.' If you have any aspirations of actually achieving your mission—or at least of obtaining our support—you'd better give us some details."

"The rules—"

"Are guidelines, which can be broken at the Peacemaker's discretion."

Tald's gaze narrowed. "How do you know that?"

"I've worked for—and with—a number of Peacemakers. I'm aware of many things." She shrugged. "Now quit stalling and tell us."

The Peacemaker looked at Bambi. "She doesn't have the need to know."

Sansar shrugged. "Fine." She turned to Gleeko. "Come on. Let's go get a drink."

"That's the best idea you've had all day." They turned to go.

"Wait!" Tald exclaimed. "You can't leave! I'm not done with you yet."

"We, however, are done with *you*," Sansar said over a shoulder. "When you're ready to talk—and my XO knows everything I do, which is why she's my XO, so don't give me that need-to-know yak shit—let me know, and I'll see if I can work an appointment into my schedule."

"I'm a Peacemaker. You—"

"You're a Peacemaker *candidate*," Sansar said. "I have to do precisely *nothing* you tell me to. Have a nice day."

Sansar saw the SalSha deflate as she turned to leave again.

"Fine," Tald said. "Come back, and I'll tell you all about it."

"And my XO?"

"She can stay."

"Good." Sansar returned to the office and took one of the visitors' seats. Gleeko took the one next to her, and Lobdell sat in the chair behind her desk. "Tell us all about your problem."

"Well, I—" Tald looking around. "Are there any more—"

"Get on with it!" Sansar exclaimed.

"Well, I, uh, fine." Tald's shoulders slumped. "We've been told that the Veetanho's *Keesius* ships have disappeared."

"You've been told?" Gleeko asked. "By whom? Their anchorage was a closely guarded secret."

"I can't tell you that." He held up a hand when Sansar started to speak. "No, really, I can't tell you, because I don't know. It was an anonymous tip."

Sansar's jaw dropped. "An anonymous tipster said you need to go look for the *Keesius* ships… and you do it?"

"The message appeared in our system," Tald said. "No one logged it in; it just appeared. Someone on the inside has information they can't share."

Sansar smiled. "That's what they told you?"

"Yes, why?"

"Does information often appear in your system?"

"Not that I know of."

"It's a trap," Gleeko said. "This is exactly what I thought— Dunamis' attempt to draw in a Human."

"But how would Dunamis know the Peacemakers would assign a SalSha to it, who would get here and involve me?" Sansar asked. "This is far too convoluted for me to follow."

Gleeko shrugged. "I don't know how he worked it, but this *feels* like his work. I don't know how he did it, but this has Dunamis' scent all over it."

"What are you talking about?" Tald asked. "This is a serious case, and one I'm lucky to have gotten. I can make my mark with this."

Sansar looked at Gleeko. "He's a patsy?"

Gleeko took a moment and pulled up the definition with her pinplants. "Most definitely."

"What?" Tald asked. "Hey! That's not nice. I'm not a patsy; I'm a Peacemaker candidate following up a lead."

Sansar glanced at Tald, and her face softened. "You think you're doing that, but someone's using you to set a trap for me."

"Dunamis would love to get his little electronic tendrils into my brain, too," Gleeko said.

"So this isn't a real case?" Tald sighed. "It had so much promise. I could make a name with this one, and then the people in my class wouldn't laugh at me…"

"What do they laugh at you for?" Lobdell asked.

"They say all sorts of mean things. That I'm a pretender. I'm the first SalSha to go to the Academy, and they say we're not ready yet, that we'll never be ready. We're not serious enough, we should stick to our bombers and let the people with brains figure out the hard cases, and I don't even look like a Peacemaker."

Sansar cleared her throat. "Well, your outfit is a little—"

"Not the outfit!" Tald exclaimed, shuffling his feet. "They say I don't look smart. Sure, I make mistakes like everyone else, and I may not have gotten the best grades in all my classes, but they say I'm just *pretending* to be intelligent, that the uplift failed to make me any smarter, and I reverted to being a Salusian. That I'm only pretending to be a Sal*Sha*. Even the instructors laugh."

"You seem fine to me," Sansar said.

"I thought this was my chance to prove them all wrong, to show them I could be a *real* Peacemaker. But instead, it was just another case of them making a joke at my expense." Tald started pacing. "When I got it, I was worried they were sending me out on a job that couldn't be done. I mean, has anyone ever seen these ships? Can anyone prove they exist?"

Gleeko held up a paw. "I can."

Tald kept going as if he hadn't heard. For all Sansar knew, he hadn't. "But, no, I trusted them. Blue Sky! Maybe it's a job they don't even *want* to be done, for all I know. Now you tell me it isn't even *that*. No, this isn't even *about* me. I'm just a pawn to be used to trap *you*. I *knew* I shouldn't have left the planet." He reached the wall and slapped it. "I should have gone into flight training like Dad told me to."

"Who's your father?" Sansar asked, hoping to change the subject.

"Thorb. Like I should follow in *his* pawprints. But how am *I* ever to make a name for myself as a pilot? The things he's done..." Tald shook his head. "I'm *always* going to be compared to him, and it's *never* going to be a favorable comparison." He turned toward Sansar. "How can you top what he's done?"

Sansar nodded slowly. "I can see your problem. Growing up in his shadow must have been... difficult."

"Growing up in his shadow? I was never even close enough to be *in* his shadow. He was always off somewhere, saving the galaxy, or the Humans, or the SalSha... getting us uplifted, moving us from planet to planet... I grew to hate mail call. Is there going to be a report from the front? What new and awesome thing has Dad done now that I can never hope to top? How do you live with that?"

"You can't," Sansar replied.

"What?" Tald's jaw dropped. "Isn't this where you're supposed to give me all sorts of platitudes and cheer me up? If so, you're failing."

"No, my goal isn't to cheer you up, but I'll get to that." Sansar shrugged. "I do, however, know what you're talking about."

"You know what I'm talking about?" He blew a raspberry. "Unlikely. You're the leader of the Golden Horde, one of the Four Horsemen mercenary units... the leaders of the free galaxy. You have friends everywhere. Blue Sky!" He waved toward Gleeko. "You even have friends who are *Veetanho*, and the Veetanho don't like *anyone* who isn't a Veetanho."

Sansar chuckled. "Our relationship is somewhat more complicated than that." She walked over to Tald and smiled down at him. "I will tell you, though, that none of this came to me easily." The smile faded. "Do you know how the Golden Horde picks its commanding officers?"

"Uh, no," Tald said, looking around the room for acceptance. "You've always been the head of the Horde, ever since I came to be aware of such things." He shrugged. "I heard your mother was the last CO, so I just assumed—"

"That I was given it when she passed away." Sansar nodded. "That's not, of course, how we do it. I'm actually not even related to my 'mother.' In fact, I was born an orphan."

Tald's tail flicked back and forth in distress. "How could you be born if you didn't have parents?"

"My mother died giving birth to me, and my father was nowhere to be found. I think he was probably a member of the Golden Horde who fathered me illegitimately—" She stopped and shrugged. "Maybe I was legitimate, and he just died on contract; who knows? Anyway, I was born an orphan and was put into an orphanage. I had to compete for everything—sometimes even the food I ate. Despite your assumption, I was given nothing, and I started out far lower than even you. No one wanted me. No one loved me."

"What did you do?" Tald asked. His tail had stopped.

"I fought," Sansar said simply. "I fought for everything. As you might guess, based on my stature, I lost a lot of fights. But then one day, an older girl at the orphanage told me a secret."

"What was that?" Tald asked, enrapt.

"She told me to fight with my mind, not my fists."

"How do you do that?"

Sansar chuckled. "By thinking. By watching and planning. By not being drawn into quarrels and fights you can't win... or don't at least have a good chance at winning."

"But how did that get you to be the head of the Horde?"

"As it turns out, the Golden Horde recruits from—and actually maintains—a number of orphanages. I was noticed as someone with potential and was put into a program. The talents I learned at the orphanage were useful in strategy and tactics, and I progressed, in spite of not even being five feet tall. I did so well, they modified a CASPer for me when I was old enough.

"And *that* was when things took off for me. No longer was I worried about being too short, or not having parents, or any of the other things holding me back. You can't see the pilot of a CASPer; everyone's the same. Only the results matter, and my results were good—better, in fact, than anyone else." She shrugged. "Still, though, nothing was given to me; I had to work—and work hard— for everything I received. I earned my spot in the officer corps of the

Golden Horde, and I earned my adoption by my mother, who was the previous head of the Golden Horde."

"She adopted you, so you got the Golden Horde when she died?"

"Correct, but I *earned* my placement. She chose three women for adoption, of which she made me the most senior. Soon, I'll adopt three women, one of whom will stand in my place when I'm gone."

"Okay," Tald said, "I understand that you had to work hard to get where you are, but your problem isn't like mine."

"What do you mean?" Sansar asked. "I wasn't accepted without hard work, and that's what's needed for you, too."

"We're not at *all* alike. You succeeded because you didn't have a parent holding you back. I *do*, and he has a reputation that's *impossible* to overcome. You just don't know what it's *like* to have a successful parent."

Sansar smiled. "But you aren't in competition with him."

"I'm *always* in competition with him. He's *always* telling me about his exploits when he gets home, and that I need to carry on the family name. Not that he comes home that often."

Sansar chuckled. "You need to step back and look at yourself a moment."

"Why's that?"

"Because you're *not* in competition with him. Whether knowingly or unknowingly, you've chosen a different path. He was—and still is—a damn good pilot. One of the best, in fact."

Tald opened his mouth, but Sansar held up a hand, silencing him. "*However*," she continued, "you're not a pilot. None of your achievements can be compared with his, as yours will be different."

"He saved the *world!*"

"He did," Sansar said with a smile, "but when you solve this case, you'll have saved the entire *galaxy*."

"You said I'm just a patsy!"

"No, I said they were *using you* as a patsy. The choice of what you actually *are*, though, is up to you. You can choose to remain their patsy and bumble around, never finding the answer to your case, or you can choose to apply yourself—to do the hard work—and solve the case, thereby earning your Peacemaker badge and saving the galaxy. Which is it going to be?"

"I thought this whole thing was nothing more than a trap to catch you."

Sansar nodded. "It probably is."

"And you're going to walk blindly into the trap?"

Sansar chuckled. "Of course not." She went back to her chair and sat down.

Tald's tail was thrashing again. "But… I don't get it. How—"

"What do you need for a mousetrap to work?" Sansar asked.

Tald's brows pulled together. "I don't know what that is. A mouse?"

"No—it's a trap to catch mice. Forget the mousetrap," Sansar said, waving the thought away. "What do you need for any trap to work?"

"Uh… bait?"

"No," Sansar said, "you don't just need bait, you need *good* bait. Something that can't be passed up. Something that causes the victim to stick her head into the trap, even though she knows it's a trap." She shook her head. "Those ships exist, and Dunamis has them. What will he do with them? I don't know, but I know we can't let the Goltar or anyone else get to them first.

"The only way the galaxy survives this situation is if you solve the case and find the *Keesius* ships." Sansar motioned to the other women in the room. "We're going to help you find them, because we want them—no, we *need* them taken off the board."

Sansar smiled. "Have you ever deputized someone?"

Tald shook his head. "Why?"

"Because we're coming along with you, and we'll be right there to tell everyone all about how you saved the galaxy—including Thorb—when we get back."

Tald's eyes opened wide. "Really? You're going to help?"

"If you deputize us, sure."

"Okay. Wait right here." He turned toward the door.

"Where are you going?" Sansar asked.

"To New Zealand. I've never had to deputize anyone before, and I don't know how, so I'm going to go back and get the Peacemaker procedural manual. I'll be right back!"

Tald raced out the door, and Gleeko turned toward Sansar. "It's not bad enough that you're walking into a trap. No, you're going to let him *lead* you there, too?"

"His father continually snatched victory from the jaws of defeat. As long as I've known him, he's found a way to win. Hopefully, Thorb's son has the same good luck." Sansar shrugged. "Besides, what I said about the bait was true. We can't leave the *Keesius* ships hanging in the wind. Do you want the Goltar to get them?"

"No! That cannot be allowed!" Gleeko exclaimed. "If they got them, they'd annihilate us!"

"How about the Goka?"

"They'd use them just to watch planets explode. They can't be allowed to have them, either!"

Sansar nodded. "I think, if I listed most of the merc races, we could find reasons not to let *any* of them have the ships. When it comes down to world-ending technology, there's no one I want holding onto it more than me."

"Why's that?" Gleeko asked. "Because we can count on you to never use them if they're put in your care?"

"No, because I *have* blown up worlds," Sansar said. "You can count on me to only use them when it's justified to do so."

Gleeko shook her head. "I'm sorry, but that probably scares me more than even the Goka getting their tiny little pincers on the ships."

Sansar smiled. "Good." She winked. "It should."

* * * * *

Chapter Three

Golden Horde Headquarters, South of Chorvoq, Uzbekistan

"Okay," Tald said three days later, "you're all now deputized."

Gleeko, Sansar, and Naran Enkh—Sansar's leading candidate for adoption—all nodded.

"So," Tald said, "what now?"

"What do you mean?" Sansar asked.

"I mean, what do we do now?"

Sansar shrugged. "I don't know. You're the one in charge. *You* deputized *us*, remember? What do you think we should be doing?"

"Well, ma'am—" the southern accent had come back with his confidence, although it wavered slightly now "—I was kinda hoping you'd tell me what we oughta be doing."

"This isn't my commissioning case," Sansar said. "I'm not trying to be anything other than a good bounty hunter."

"Hmmm," Tald said. His ears flicked back and forth. "I don't really know what's next."

"Well, you obviously came here for a reason," Sansar said. "What was it?"

"I wanted access to a Veetanho so I could ask her some questions. I went to the Merc Guild, but they said the Veetanho representative hadn't been seen in a while."

Gleeko's lips pulled back from her teeth. "That can't be good."

"I didn't think it was," Tald said, "but one of the representatives remembered you from when Colonel Shirazi took over as Speaker, and she thought you'd come back with Sansar, so I thought I'd try to find you."

Sansar chuckled. "You didn't want to go to Lytoshaan or one of the other Veetanho planets? You know there are plenty of Veetanho there."

Tald shook his head. "Too obvious. In fact, I can't think of anything worse than showing up there and asking, 'Hey, did anyone lose some *Keesius* ships?' And that was *before* I found out about Dunamis." He shrugged. "They teach us to be circumspect when investigating a case."

"Well, I know one thing," Sansar said.

Tald's ears stood on end. "Where the ships are?"

"No." Sansar chuckled. "I know that no one should call you stupid. You're the first SalSha I've ever heard use the word 'circumspect' before."

Tald's shoulders slumped, but then he perked up. "Well, that's something, I guess. And—" he turned to Gleeko "—I found a Veetanho to interrogate."

"Interrogate, huh?" Gleeko asked. She pulled a knife from somewhere—Sansar couldn't tell where—and held it up to the light. She brushed off a piece of lint, and it disappeared as fast as it had become visible. "What if I'm not in the mood for an *interrogation?*"

"Well, that's just a term we use," Tald said, taking a couple of steps back. "It's really just asking a few questions in a non-confrontational manner. At least for now…"

Gleeko narrowed her eyes. "Just for now?"

Tald nodded.

"We shall see what happens later, then, but for now, ask your questions."

"Okay," Tald said. "Where are the *Keesius* ships?"

"I don't know."

"Weren't you a battleship captain?" Tald asked.

"I was."

"Yet you don't know where they are?"

Gleeko shook her head. "According to you, they've disappeared. If so, I don't know where they went."

"Aha! But you knew where they were before they disappeared!"

"No, sorry."

"But you were a battleship captain. Didn't Dunamis trust you?"

"Dunamis didn't trust *anyone*, except maybe himself, and I wouldn't know about that."

"Did you ever go to where the ships were held?"

"I don't know."

"How can you not know?" Tald asked. "Wasn't your head attached to your body at the time?"

"Yes, my head was attached to my body."

"Then how do you not know? You're expecting us to believe... what? That you forgot a trip through hyperspace to see a bunch of ships no one has seen in millennia, and you just *forgot* about them? That's your story?"

"My statement is correct as stated," Gleeko said.

Tald shook his head. "Sorry, there's no way that could be true."

Gleeko's top lip pulled back from her teeth. "Are you calling me a liar?" she asked softly. "You'll want to think about your answer very carefully."

"Gleeko!" Sansar exclaimed.

Gleeko spun. "If he calls me a liar..."

Sansar frowned. "Rather than baiting each other, why don't you just tell him the truth—the *whole* truth—from the start? We'll get farther, faster, and hopefully all of us will survive this... interview."

Naran chuckled.

"What's so funny?" Gleeko asked.

"You've obviously never dealt with SalSha before." Naran turned to Sansar. "Colonel, do you think it's wise to have both Tald and Gleeko along with us?"

"Wise?" Sansar chuckled. "Probably not—" she smiled "but I don't see how we can avoid it. We have to take Tald because he's in charge, and at some point we may need his authority. We need Gleeko... well, because she owes me a favor, and because she's one of the few senior Veetanho to ever get away from Dunamis without being deprogrammed."

"Perhaps the only one," Gleeko said.

"What does that mean?" Tald asked.

"Dunamis doesn't share his toys," Sansar said.

"Oh, so now I'm a toy?" Gleeko asked. "Just because I was a starship captain doesn't mean I couldn't kill all of you in hand-to-hand combat."

Naran smiled. "We can exercise on the mat if you think so, once we're done."

Gleeko turned to Sansar. "I'm more interested in Sansar. She's had it coming for a while."

Naran chuckled. "I'm pretty sure you'd rather fight me than her."

"Why's that?"

"Because I know a lifetime of dirty tricks," Sansar said. "We can spar sometime if you want, but let's finish this first, please. We really *do* need to find those ships."

"Yes," Gleeko said, "we do." She sighed and stared at Sansar for a moment, then nodded once. "Fine." She turned back to Tald. "Dunamis controls our minds. Sometimes overtly, sometimes covertly. All senior officers, however, have a bit of code in their brains that functions as a kill switch, should we ever do something that knowingly violates our mission orders. If we do so, we die."

"Yet you're here," Tald said. "I can't imagine Dunamis would be very happy about that."

Gleeko shook her head. "He wouldn't. I'd be dead right now were it not for the fact that Sansar has a bit of Great War technology that cleans out people's brains of SI-induced code. She zapped me with it at the Mercenary Guild, and my brain became my own again."

"That's great!" Tald said. "So what's the problem? If you can tell us anything now... please do so. Where are the *Keesius* ships?"

"It isn't as simple as that," Gleeko said. "Dunamis never wanted us to know more than we needed to, so he'd often remove memories he didn't want us to have. For example, the location of the *Keesius* ships. That isn't something he'd want everyone—or even *anyone*—to know about. So, if we went to where they were, he'd delete that information after we got back to Lytoshaan. He'd also delete the memory that we'd gone there and any experiences we'd had along the way. While it seems to me that I may have been there, I honestly don't—I *can't*—remember any of it."

"Oh. Well, that's a problem."

"It is," Sansar said. "She gets flashes of things sometimes, but they're hard to interpret."

"What can you remember?" Tald asked.

"Everything regarding my last mission to Capital Planet, as well as all the intelligence necessary to carry it out."

"But nothing about the *Keesius* ships." Tald shoulders slumped.

Gleeko shook her head. "Unfortunately, no. I do, however, know something that may be of value."

"What's that?"

"As part of the intel background for the last mission, there were notes about an attack that occurred on a planet known as Khatash."

"Khatash?" Tald asked. "Never heard of it."

"I was there," Sansar replied. "That's the home world of the Depik."

Gleeko and Naran nodded, but Tald looked confused. "Assassins? How are they going to help?" he asked.

"I doubt they'd help at all," Gleeko said. "We've spent a lot of time and money trying to figure out ways to interdict their travel and kill them off. They're nasty little creatures, and they interfere with the business of the Mercenary Guild."

"So what do Khatash and the Depik have to do with it?" Tald asked.

"Very little," Gleeko said, "beyond the fact that there are a number of Veetanho there who were incarcerated when the Depik—with the help of the *Humans*—" she spat the word "—recaptured the planet. There's a standing order to bring any of them we come across home to Lytoshaan for questioning. Failing that, we're to kill them without regard for collateral damage."

"What does that mean?" Tald asked.

"It means we were allowed to do anything in order to kill them. If that meant nuking cities, Dunamis would applaud our efforts if they were successful."

"Why would he do such a thing?"

"Obviously, at least one of them has knowledge in their heads that's forbidden," Gleeko said. "And if I had to bet, the location of the *Keesius* ships is something that would qualify for that level of destruction."

* * *

"So," Tald said to Sansar after a moment of contemplation, "since you've been deputized, and you know where it is, you'll take me to this Khatash place, right?"

Sansar shook her head, and Tald had to work hard to keep from sighing. He needed a few moments to practice his breathing techniques, but he didn't have them, so instead he blurted, "Why not?" He immediately berated himself for it. *This is not how a Peacemaker acts. I need to be in control, not acting like a puling newborn.*

"Because that's probably what Dunamis wants."

Tald jerked back in surprise. "Why would you say that?"

"For the same reason Gleeko said; he probably hopes we'll go there and end up killing the Veetanho being held there." She shrugged. "We may ultimately *have* to go there, but I don't want to until we have to."

"So what do we do instead?" Tald asked.

Sansar chuckled. "Before we go off running around like Veetchs with their heads still on, let's think about this."

"Okay," Tald said, though he still didn't see why following up a lead was a bad thing.

"Let's start at the beginning." Sansar smiled. "What's your task?"

"You're wasting time," Tald replied. "We have a lead…"

"Humor me."

Tald sighed, unable to help himself. "We're looking for the missing *Keesius* ships."

"How do you know they're missing?"

"What? Because that was the task I was given—to find the missing ships."

"You're missing the point," Sansar said. "We've already determined the location of these ships is as closely guarded a secret as exists in the galaxy. If only Dunamis know their true location, how does *anyone else* know they're missing in the first place?"

"Because…" Tald stood with his mouth open as he finally figured out what she was asking. How did the Peacemakers know the ships were missing? *If only one person knew where they were…* He closed his mouth after a moment. "It's a trap, and I'm a patsy. The only person who could have reported them missing is Dunamis."

Sansar nodded. "What do you think he would have done if he woke up one morning and found out the ships were gone? Don't you think he would've torn the galaxy apart looking for them?"

"Well, yes," Tald said with a nod.

"Who has more resources? The Peacemakers or Dunamis?"

"Dunamis."

"Exactly. Do you know Occam's Razor?"

Tald shook his head. "What does shaving have to do with this?"

"Nothing. Occam's Razor is a scientific and philosophical rule that states, when you have a number of competing theories for how something happened, usually the simplest one is correct. Which is more likely, that someone found the unfindable system and stole the ships out from under a Type 5 SI's nose, or that this is a trap?"

Tald nodded. "That this is a trap. I'm sorry I didn't see that before."

Gleeko held up a hand.

"Yes?" Sansar asked. "What is it?"

Gleeko scratched her ear. "Before you throw away that theory, I think it bears a little more thought."

"Which is?"

"What if someone actually *did* steal the ships?"

"How could someone steal the ships?"

"I have no idea, but let's just say, for the sake of argument, that someone did."

"Okay." Sansar tilted her head. "I still think Dunamis would spare no effort to find them again."

"I don't disagree with that," Gleeko replied, "but what happened if, after all that effort, the ships remained missing?"

"He'd…" Sansar stopped and chuckled. "He might very well let the Peacemakers know."

"He might. I mean, who else has the investigatory resources of the Peacemakers?"

Sansar nodded. "No one. And besides, the Peacemakers would be 'all in' on finding them. Having three *Keesius* ships floating in the breeze somewhere doesn't promote peace at all, for a number of reasons."

"But if the Peacemakers wanted the case solved so badly," Tald said, "why send me? If this has galaxy-wide implications, why send a brand-new Peacemaker candidate to search for the ships?"

"They wouldn't, if they had any confidence in the story." Sansar shook her head.

Gleeko shrugged. "Perhaps they know something I don't, but this seems to be exactly what Dunamis would do if he actually couldn't find them."

Sansar took a deep breath and let it out slowly. "I'm not sure what scares me more—that Dunamis is trying to trap me, or that he's lost three ships that can each destroy a world."

"It's the second choice for me," Gleeko said. "The first choice doesn't bother me much at all… aside from the part where he might scoop me up when he grabs you."

"Of course you'd say that." Sansar chuckled. "And if that's your attitude, I might just let him have you when I escape his clutches." She shrugged. "Either way, we have to follow up on this."

"So where do we start?" Tald asked.

"I think we go by Lytoshaan first," Sansar said, with a raised eyebrow for Gleeko. "If everything is business as usual there, then this whole case of yours is bullshit."

The Veetanho nodded. "If everything is normal there, how do we get out of the system without being captured?"

"I have a ship with internal shunts. We'll pop in and take a look. If it looks like the Veetanho want to get grabby, we'll pop right back out again."

* * *

CIC, EMS *Gobi Desert*, Sol System

"We're ready to go," said Captain Parker, the *Gobi Desert's* commanding officer. "If I may, though, ma'am?"

Sansar smiled. "Are you going to tell me this is a bad idea?"

"No, ma'am. I think going to the homeworld of the race that's done more to destroy humanity than any other is a wonderful idea."

Sansar's eyebrows shot up. "You do? I thought you'd reached the part of your checklist where you tell me this is a bad idea. You did for Kop'ka… and Kullawee… probably several others, too. They're all starting to blur together."

"No, ma'am. Both of those were systems where we knew an SI was in residence, and I was only doing my due diligence as this ship's CO to express my opinion that going there didn't make a lot of sense." He shrugged. "In this case, though, I don't mind going. Of course, since Lytoshaan is the homeworld of the Veetanho, I think we ought to have a fleet or two with us so we can do to them what they intended to do to us. I suspect the Winged Hussars would probably think similarly and want to participate in a good carpet-bombing of the planet."

Sansar chuckled. "They probably would, at that."

Parker nodded to the SalSha seated next to Sansar. "No offense, but I just don't think a Peacemaker *candidate* is enough horsepower to make the rats behave." He nodded to Gleeko on the other side of Sansar. "No offense to you, either, ma'am."

"None taken," Gleeko said, her lips pulling back into a sneer. "You're right to be scared. I was just explaining to Colonel Enkh how the defenses in Lytoshaan will crush this ship like a tin can upon our entrance into the system. I can't see how something so pathetic will last more than a few seconds… no more than the few seconds it takes for the missiles to cross the distance to us." She paused a second and then added, "No offense."

"Wait, what?"

"Oh, yes." Gleeko smiled, clearly enjoying herself. "The automatic defenses will shred this ship like paper. I hope you can breathe in space. And that's *before* the Type 5 SI gets involved."

"Ma'am?" Parker turned toward Sansar. "No one said anything about going after yet another SI." He shook his head. "Is there anywhere we can go in this galaxy without running into one? No one had seen an SI in millennia, and now you can't shake a stick without hitting one."

Sansar cleared her throat. "Captain? Are you done yet?"

"Are you going to tell me that it's going to be all right, because I have a really bad feeling about this mission." He shook his head. "Have you had any dreams this time?"

"No, actually, I haven't," Sansar replied. *Which really worries me, too.* "Nor do I need to. We don't think the SI is still in residence in the system."

"What about the defenses?"

Sansar smiled. "I think Captain Gleeko is having a little bit of fun at your expense."

Parker turned toward the Veetanho and narrowed his gaze.

Gleeko smiled. "It's also possible I'm not, and everything is exactly as I've described."

"If I die, so do you," Parker said shortly.

Gleeko nodded. "Better to be dead than a prisoner of Dunamis."

"Who or what is Dunamis?" Parker asked.

"The SI in Lytoshaan. If he's there, you'd be much happier to be dead than in his clutches."

"So I should hope he's left."

Gleeko shook her head. "No, if he's there, the automatic defenses won't shred this ship." She chuckled. "You want him to be in the system... right up until you don't anymore, because that's when the screaming starts."

Sansar sighed. "Captain Parker, could we perhaps just get started? We've got several jumps to get there, which is plenty of time to let Gleeko get under your skin. Or perhaps we could all work together toward a solution where we neither get destroyed out of hand nor captured by SIs who are bent on making our lives miserable? We're going to miss our gate time if you two keep this up."

Parker sighed. "I need a vacation," he muttered. Louder, he said, "Yes, ma'am. Helm, proceed to the stargate, 1.5 Gs. Destination—" he swallowed once "—Lytoshaan."

* * * * *

Chapter Four

Officer's Mess, EMS *Gobi Desert*, Hyperspace

Tald sat by himself, thinking about anything he might have missed. One of the SalSha crews had been in the wardroom when he'd arrived, but he wanted peace and quiet to think, not the loud boisterousness of the bomber pilots. They were one day out from emergence at Lytoshaan, and he felt as unprepared as he ever had for anything in his life.

They had no idea what they'd find there. Would Dunamis be there? If so, that complicated... pretty much everything. The defenses were sure to be better, there might be psychic attacks on everyone with pinplants... it had the potential to be pretty awful, if he believed everything Sansar had said about what Type 5 SIs could—and *would*—do to biological beings. He wasn't sure he did, but she had no reason to lie about what she'd found in her battles with them.

If all of this is true, why don't we cover any of it at the Academy? How could such an extensive network of synthetic intelligences exist without anyone knowing about them? Obviously, they controlled the media, which was a topic covered at the Academy. Be the first one to control the message, and you'd have most of the people on your side... no matter how bad a job you did.

"Hello, Tald," a familiar voice said. "Mind if I join you?"

"Hello, Dad," Tald replied with a sigh.

Thorb tilted his head and lifted an ear. "Not a very good way to greet your sire. It would almost seem that you've been avoiding me this whole trip."

"We've been doing a lot of planning—"

"I know; I've been at many of the meetings. It was strange, though; the ones I attended, you missed."

"I've got a lot of tasking—"

"For one day, even a week, I might believe that," Thorb said with a sad smile. "I may not be the sharpest SalSha ever uplifted, but after two weeks, even I got the message." He waved toward the empty chair he stood behind on the other side of the table.

"Sure," Tald said. "You're going to do what you want, anyway."

Thorb dropped the fork he'd just picked up. "What is that supposed to mean?"

"I mean, you just *had* to come see it, didn't you?" He looked down at his plate and shook his head.

"See what?"

Tald looked up. "I know you didn't want me to become a Peacemaker. Now you're here just to watch me fail."

"Is that what you think?"

"That's the truth… so yeah, pretty much."

"Look, you little runt—"

"Yeah, start with the names. That's always helpful."

Thorb started to pick up his tray—Tald had no idea whether that was to leave or to throw it at him—but then he squared his shoulders and set it down over-carefully. He nodded once. "You're right; I shouldn't have said that." He rolled his head around once, and then sighed. "You always did know how to get me going."

Finally, Thorb shrugged and said, "I'm not here to see you fail; in fact, I didn't even know you were here when we boarded."

"You didn't?"

Thorb shook his head. "I heard the *Desert* was going to Lytoshaan, and they needed the best pilots."

"So you, of course, just had to come, because *obviously* you're the best."

"Whether I'm the best or not—and there are certainly a number of pilots now who are pretty damn good—I'm certainly one of the most experienced. I've had the misfortune to be in a number of places at the wrong time."

"You've loved every minute of it."

"Is that what you think?"

"The fame? The accolades? Tell me you didn't love that."

"Perhaps I did," Thorb said, "but only at the start. After that, the deaths of your friends start to get to you. When you get back from a mission, and you return with less than half the pilots you started with—" he stopped and swallowed "—it's harder than I ever would have thought possible. When an SI controls you... gets in your head and makes you do things..." He paused a second and shuddered. "Let me tell you, I wouldn't wish that level of violation on anyone."

"You've seen the SIs?"

Thorb nodded. "More than I'd ever wish on anyone."

"So what Sansar's said about them?"

"All true. If anything, she's probably sugar-coated it some; otherwise, it would have been hard to get people to come. The odds of everyone surviving this mission are low. Very low."

"Yet you came."

Thorb nodded once. "I've dealt with the SIs before. If I can save even one of my pilots from being used by the SI we're looking for, I will."

"Even if it means you get captured and die?"

Thorb nodded. "Even then." He took a bite, and then shuddered again. He tried to play it off as if he'd been stretching, but Tald knew better.

"Okay, so your intentions might have been to protect the squadron when you came, but you didn't leave when you found out I was on board."

Thorb looked up. "No, I didn't." He went back to eating.

"You never wanted me to be a Peacemaker. If you say you did, it's a lie."

Thorb shook his head. "I never wanted you to be a Peacemaker; that's true." He set down his fork. "You never asked why."

"I did, too!"

"No, you never did. You yelled, you screamed, and you generally threw a temper tantrum like a Human child."

"You said I wasn't ready."

Thorb chuckled. "In what way is a tantrum-throwing youngling prepared for serious business like being a Peacemaker?"

"Well, I—" Tald couldn't come up with a good reason, and he looked down at his food and took a bite.

"Do you want to know why I didn't want you to be a Peacemaker?"

"Besides the whole 'not ready' thing?"

Thorb nodded.

Tald nodded once, although he wasn't sure he was going to like the answer. "Yes, tell me."

"Your mother and I had a talk. Both of us knew you didn't want to go into the merc business, and frankly, we were fine with that. The life expectancy of a bomber pilot is pretty darn low." He chuckled wryly. "Unfortunately, that's something I know a lot about."

"But I thought—"

"Nope. We didn't want you to be a bomber pilot. You're your mother's youngest. If you were to die…" Thorb shook his head. "It would break her heart."

"Being a Peacemaker—"

"Is every bit as dangerous as being a bomber pilot. You're expected to get between two groups who want nothing more than to kill each other and figure out a way to get them to stop. To *make* them stop." Thorb shrugged. "Sometimes they don't want to stop, and they'll do anything they have to to get rid of the impediment to their desires." His gaze narrowed. "That's *you*, by the way."

"But I have the authority—"

"Son, authority means nothing to a bomb, a laser, or a MAC round." He stood and picked up his tray. "Being a Peacemaker is one of the most dangerous jobs in the galaxy. Take a look at your Hall of Heroes sometime and see what all they had to overcome. Look into what the life expectancy for a Peacemaker is, and maybe you'll be a little less bright-eyed about what you're about to take on."

Thorb shrugged. "You think I stayed aboard so I could watch you fail?" He scoffed. "I volunteered to come on this mission—one I've already said many, if not all, won't return from—to do everything I can to help you *succeed*."

Thorb turned and left before Tald could come up with an answer. Tald watched him leave with his mouth open and sat that way for some time after Thorb had left his line of sight.

* * *

CIC, EMS *Gobi Desert*, Lytoshaan Emergence Area

"Emergence in the Lytoshaan system," the helmsman reported.

"Drones out," Parker ordered. "I want to know where the ships and defenses are ASAP."

Sansar released her belt and moved to stand behind Parker's command chair. After a moment, Gleeko joined her.

"As I mentioned," Gleeko said, "you'll be interrogated by the defense command. Make sure you answer quickly."

"I'm waiting," the comms officer said. "So far, though, I don't have anything on any channel."

"*What?*" Gleeko exclaimed. "You need to check your equipment. We'll be blown out of space if you don't answer!"

Parker looked over his shoulder. "I've got this, *Captain*." He turned back to the front of the space. "Comms, run a check on your gear."

"I already have, sir. There's nobody talking out here."

"That's because there's nobody out here," the sensor tech said, looking up from his console.

"What do you mean, nobody?" Parker and Gleeko asked simultaneously, earning Gleeko another annoyed glance.

"I mean there's no one out here," the sensor tech confirmed. "There are no ships, and the defense stations are unmanned."

"There are *always* ships here, and the platforms are *never* unmanned," Gleeko said.

The tech shrugged. "I can't tell you whether they're unmanned or not without actually going over and taking a look. I can, however, tell you there are no ships nearby, and the three stations I can see are all unpowered. If there's someone on them, they're in a suit and in danger of dying."

Sansar looked over to find Gleeko with her mouth open, staring. After a couple seconds, Gleeko closed her mouth and shook her head. "I don't know what this means, but I expect it's bad."

"Helm, proceed to the planet," Parker said. "Comms, see if anyone's home there."

* * *

CIC, EMS *Gobi Desert,* Lytoshaan Emergence Area

"Oh, no," Gleeko said. She stood next to the sensor tech's position, where she'd been directing a search. "It's worse than I thought," she said.

"What do you mean?" Captain Parker asked.

"Can I..." She looked down at the tech. "Can you put that on the main viewer?"

The tech nodded, and the main Tri-V shifted to an overhead view of the planet. The tech zoomed in until they could see what she was talking about.

"Looks like a nuclear bomb went off," Sansar noted. "Where is that?"

"That was the Veetanho Merc Guild Headquarters. It's also where Dunamis held court," Gleeko said with a nod. "And that's exactly what it looks like happened."

"Where's the headquarters?"

Gleeko shook her head. "That's just it; it's gone. It looks like the nuke went off *inside* the headquarters. There's nothing left of it."

Sansar chuckled. "Well, I guess we don't have to worry about getting mind-wiped here, in that case."

"That isn't funny," Gleeko said. "It's horrific, and will have long-term consequences—"

"I've got someone on the planet," the comms officer said. "Orbital Control."

"Put it on speaker," Parker said.

The comms officer nodded, pressed a couple of virtual buttons on his console, and pointed back to Parker. "You're on, sir."

"Orbital Control, this is EMS *Gobi Desert*, Captain Parker commanding."

"*Gobi Desert, Orbital Control. Be advised that no services are offered on the planet at this time, nor any control. Request you stand off the planet and exit the system, or you will be fired upon.*"

Sansar motioned, and Parker nodded. "Orbital Control, *Gobi Desert*," Sansar said. "We have a Peacemaker onboard who's here to look into the events that have occurred on the planet. Who can we talk to about that?"

"*Uh… I don't know, Gobi Desert. I don't think there's anyone you can talk to. Anyone who had any seniority has lost their minds, and we're all too damn busy trying to put things back together again.*"

"What do you mean, lost their minds?" Tald asked. "Have they gone crazy?"

"*No, lost their minds as in their minds don't work. As if they no longer have any of their memories. They don't know who they are or where they are… they don't know anything. They don't even know how to feed themselves. We're having to go and find people in their dwellings, or they'll starve. This is an environmental disaster. Basic services are out for a large portion of the planet.*"

"We have to help them," Tald said, looking around the bridge.

"Help them how?" Parker asked. "We're a warship. It sounds like they need… everything. We don't have a planet's-worth of long-term assistance on board."

"We have to do what we can," Tald insisted. "It's our duty."

"The best thing we can do to assist them is to get word of this to somewhere else."

"But first, we have to do what we can to help them," Sansar said.

"We do?" Tald asked, obviously not expecting support from her.

Sansar nodded. "We do. We need to take things to the planet."

"What kind of things?" Gleeko asked.

"I don't know," Sansar said with a shrug. "Whatever we have, I guess."

"I want to go on record as saying we need to report this as soon as possible," Parker replied.

"I understand that, and we will," Sansar said, "but we also have a mission here, and we don't have the time to come back once we leave."

"What is it you want to do?" Tald asked. "Are we helping them or not?"

"Of course we're going to help them," Sansar said with a smile. "We need to get to the planet so we can find out what happened. If taking them aid is the only way to do so—" she shrugged "—so be it."

"Always the philanthropist," Gleeko muttered.

"I'm sorry," Sansar said, "but this is a disaster of *your own* making. When you play with SIs, bad things happen."

"You're suggesting we had a choice?"

"How many times have you tried to overthrow him in all the time he's been on the planet?"

Gleeko shrugged. "Who would know? Everyone would be killed, and anyone close to them mind-wiped. It could be as often as every generation, maybe more." She shrugged. "We shall see."

"See what?"

"When Dunamis decides he wants to champion the Humans next—should it come to that—we'll see how quickly *you* get out from under his thumb. It should be very illuminating. I suspect, however, that you'll be too dead to find out the answer."

"Uh, sir? Ma'am? Orbital Control is asking our intentions."

"Tell them we'll be providing what aid we can before departing the system."

* * *

Cockpit, Shuttle *One*, Descending to Lytoshaan

"Glad we never tried to take them on," Thorb said, nodding to one of the orbital defense platforms as they passed. "That's the biggest one of those I've ever seen."

Sansar chuckled. "That's just one of many."

Thorb's ears perked up. "Many? How many?"

"Dozens. Not all of them are here. Some are in the emergence area, and there are others near the gate." She shook her head. "Blue would never have made it out of here."

"Blue? You mean that weird captain from the *Midnight Sun,* back when we fought with the Goltar?"

"That's her."

"She was going to come here?"

"The Goltar were training her to fly the *Midnight Sun* here to destroy the planet."

"Really? She was going to do that?"

"Apparently. The Goltar were going to use some of their *Keesius* ships in support of it."

"Seriously? I thought that was a *bad* thing. You said in the briefings that would lead to galactic war, and we already have one with the Kahraman, and maybe the SIs. Why would she do that? More importantly, why would you *let* her?"

"I wasn't going to let her, although at the time, I didn't think destroying the Veetanho was a bad thing."

"What about now?"

Sansar shrugged. "I don't know. I don't think what's happened to them is good, though. It's going to be a long time before they'll be worthwhile mercs again."

"You know what I wonder?" Thorb asked.

Sansar scoffed and then chuckled. "I wouldn't even know where to start."

Thorb shook his head. "It doesn't have anything to do with the Veetanho."

"Okay, I'll bite. What do you wonder, Thorb?"

"I wonder if the Goltar ever got more of those starfish fighters. They were really cool. Can you get some of those for us?"

"I don't think so," Sansar said. "I think the Goltar said they lost the technology for them."

"Seriously?" Thorb asked. He cocked his head. "How do you *lose* technology? Like you forget where you left it? I mean, I do that sometimes with some of my things, but technology?"

Sansar chuckled. "I don't have any idea. I think the starfish were from the Great War."

"Well, maybe they'll find the technology again?" Thorb asked.

"I doubt it."

"Huh. Ok, well, you should use your intel section to find some of them and get them for us. Maybe Alexis Cromwell could replicate them in her yards. Or maybe that crazy guy she has could figure them out."

"I'll see." Sansar unbuckled.

"Where are you going?" Thorb asked.

"Back to the cargo bay." *Where it's quiet.*

* * * * *

Chapter Five

One Hundred Kilometers North of the Merc Guild Headquarters, Lytoshaan

Sansar strode down the ramp of the shuttle, and her jaw dropped. She'd seen a lot of cities on a lot of planets, and she knew what a functioning civilization looked like. *This isn't it.*

"It... it looks like a holo," Tald said, blinking as he turned his entire body to scan the immediate area.

A holo of the Great War's aftermath, perhaps, directed by a being with a rabid imagination and an endless budget. Sansar had seen disasters of all sizes and the wreckage left behind, but this...

Not sure even the Veetanho deserve this.

Burnt residue marked irregular patches of the ground around them. A ragged chunk of what might have been a personal vehicle gaped from the side of what must have been a dwelling of some sort. The air smelled of ozone and uncountable cooked fluids, the combination stinging her nose until the backs of her eyes ached.

Nothing within eyesight remained whole, so it took long moments to register what the odd lumps and twisted remains might have been. The misshapen lump to the left had been a long building, and Sansar refused to look too closely at the smaller lumps scattered outside its cracked, blackened, partial walls.

The road between the destroyed areas was littered with parts—mostly metallic, but again, Sansar skipped her eyes over the greasy patches and irregular shapes. The haze of the sooty air and the dim sunlight made blurs of anything much further, but she hoped the coordinates they'd been given meant there were less ruined areas ahead.

"All this from just one bomb?" Tald hooked his hands into his belt and whistled low.

"No." Gleeko paused, her whiskers flat against her muzzle, then she shook herself and stepped forward. "Not just one bomb. He made… he made each Veetanho into their own bombs. Maybe everyone." The last two words were whispered, and Sansar had a feeling Gleeko hadn't wanted them heard.

"Orbital Control indicated survivors," Sansar said, shaking off the weight of empathy and putting exactly the level of sharpness in her tone that would jerk Gleeko back to operational. "Why else did we bring all these supplies?"

Gleeko whipped around, glaring, then huffed out a breath and relaxed her shoulders. "The young, I imagine, and—" she sighed, turned, and continued walking "—the mind-wiped he erased before the killing began."

"Before the…?" Tald stared up at Sansar, bewildered, and she shook her head once before following Gleeko. The next… block, Sansar supposed they could call it, was studded with more burnt and partial personal vehicles. One had a still-identifiable Veetanho form in it, though the body was studded with… spines?

Despite her better sense, Sansar peered more closely as they passed. Not spines. Knives. So many knives.

She pressed the skin under her ear before the low whine registered in her hearing.

"Is that an alarm?"

"No." Gleeko didn't slow, though her head lowered as she continued forward.

"Are you sure?" Tald flicked his smaller, furrier ears repeatedly. "It's… like an alarm."

"It's not an alarm."

"Then what—"

"It's an unattended youngling."

"Like a *pup*?" Tald stopped short, then ran ahead, twitching his ears to better locate the sound. "We have to find it."

"We don't." Gleeko's pace continued unabated, though there was a new hitch to her stride.

"I—what—how—*Sansar!*" Tald shouted, running a half circle back and forth across the cracked road.

"Don't!" Gleeko pivoted so quickly, Tald nearly rammed into her on his parabola, but she was glaring at Sansar. "Don't lecture me about… morality, or saving younglings. There are any number of orphaned babies on this planet who are dying even now, and we can't save all of them. We can't save *any* of them if we don't get to the meeting coordinates and see who's left."

"You're right," Sansar agreed

"Thank you," Gleeko said, her whiskers bristling, even as Tald yelled, "She's *what!*"

"We can't save everyone. Gleeko, you should continue to the meeting. We'll meet you there."

"Thank you!" Tald exclaimed, his small body vibrating.

Gleeko met Sansar's eyes with a glare and said flatly, "Why."

"I have little love for your race as a whole—" Sansar shrugged and gestured for Tald to lead the way "—but I'm not a monster."

Tald stopped short again, twisted his head and swiveled his ears, then strode off the road to the left, his bow-legged strut forgotten. The whine grew more pronounced, too high-pitched for Sansar to grasp entirely, but enough to pierce the center of her eardrum. Between the thick air and the ongoing noise, the headache growing at the base of her skull should end up quite spectacular.

"Under there," Tald said, coming to a halt at the base of a pile of rubble. "It's definitely coming from under there. How... how do we get under there?"

Sansar crouched to get a better look and was about to admit they might have to move on and return when Gleeko cleared her throat behind them.

"Our structures often stretch underground." Gleeko didn't come any closer, and when Sansar turned her head, she saw the Veetanho was still facing ahead to their meeting point. "There are likely alternate entry points. We can send someone after—"

"Huh. I think I can fit."

Gleeko turned. "Don't—"

"Yeah, hang on—"

By the time Sansar turned back, she saw the heels of Tald's boots disappear into the darker shadows between chunks of former building.

"It's going to collapse on him," Gleeko said. "You'll have to inform the Peacemaker's Guild, and we'll have delayed here longer for no reason."

Sansar realized, belatedly, that Gleeko's spikiness might be more from witnessing the purposeful, intricate destruction of her home world than her general… dislike of things. There wasn't much she could do about it, so Sansar inclined her head and crouched down to see if she could see anything in the space between the pieces of debris.

A shadow flickered, darkness on dark, either dust settling, or Tald, or maybe her eyes simply playing tricks on her. *No, that's definitely a shape…*

She leaned back abruptly as the sound in her ear drove sharply higher, right around the same time she heard Tald, loud and clear, admonish, "No bite!"

More scuffling, more motion, and she put her hand on the ragged chunk of stone-adjacent material that formed the bare opening. It was a useless gesture—if the mess of rock and material shifted, she wouldn't be able to hold it in place—but in a moment she was rewarded with darkness resolving into furry brown and white stripes.

Something scraped, and then grated, and she grabbed the furry appendage. "Tald, hurry!"

The small creature popped loose, the sound in Sansar's hearing now eclipsing any evidence of the ruins falling further, and she stepped back quickly.

Damn, she though, looking down at the creature in her arms. *It's* cute. *I hate that it's cute.*

Tald's face pressed out from the now much smaller hole. "Ah… Commander?" he said, his eyes huge. "A little help?"

"Gleeko," Sansar snapped, and didn't look to confirm the Veetanho approached. She put the small Veetanho down on the ground, wincing against the louder noise that resulted, and reached for Tald.

The Peacemaker candidate made a small noise of pain—Sansar had to grab his furred cheeks to pull—but continued twisting and pulling until he finally popped free. Behind him, the opening was now smaller than Sansar's closed fists placed side to side, and she had to admit—if only in the privacy of her head—Gleeko had had a point.

Tald rubbed his cheeks and stared at the dramatically smaller space, then shook his head and peered up at Sansar. "There were four more in there, but they were… ah, they'd been crushed. Looks like whatever collapsed fell right into their—their nest."

"We need to continue," Gleeko said from the same position she'd held since Sansar and Tald had left the road.

Sansar scooped up the smallest Veetanho she'd ever seen—it didn't bite—and crossed back to Gleeko. "It doesn't seem like it's going to be any better ahead," she pointed out, "but hopefully it will be for this one."

"Or we've just consigned her to a longer death," Gleeko replied and walked forward without so much as glancing at the creature in Sansar's arms.

* * *

The Veetanho who stepped out to meet them was a full head shorter than Gleeko, and more gangly. Her limbs moved loosely, as though they didn't fit together quite right yet, and Sansar knew her for an adolescent.

"Oh." The Veetanho stopped short, the end of her nose twitching. "I didn't know you'd be…" Her hands lifted and fell, her small eyes locked on Gleeko.

"We are," Gleeko said, and Sansar didn't believe the older Veetanho had any idea what the younger one was going to say either.

"Orbital Control let you know we were coming?"

"You have supplies?" she asked in return, her voice skewing higher on the last word.

"Our shuttle is stocked, yes. We didn't carry it all this way because we didn't know what you'd want or if you'd be in a condition to—"

"I brought a list," Sansar said, stepping forward. The smaller Veetanho snapped her eyes to Sansar, but they dropped to the small Veetanho in the Human's arms, and then drifted back to Gleeko as she spoke. "We can have what you need unloaded fairly quickly, or if you want to come back with us and see it yourself, we can do that, too."

"What we need," the Veetanho whispered, then shook her head sharply and straightened. "I can't leave—most of those we've found...well. Babies and baby-minded. You might as well come in and see." She turned on her heels and stomped back inside, calling over her shoulder, "I'm Reemo."

Sansar gave introductions as they followed her, Tald subdued, and Gleeko too busy glaring at everything. The furry bundle she carried had fallen asleep, and the sound of new voices had done nothing to rouse her.

They stepped into a building with three full walls and most of a ceiling, then skirted the remains of a ceiling and piles of scavenged, mostly serviceable, tech and food crates. Sansar glanced over them as they passed—like the building, everything that had been brought inside seemed mostly intact and usable, if singed, dinged, or burnt around the edges. They descended into a round, mosaiced entrance under an intact side wall, and Sansar forced her thoughts away from the recent picture of rubble sliding down to cover Tald.

Gleeko touched the edges of her fingers to the wall as they walked, then snatched her hand back when she noticed Sansar's gaze. "I'm surprised to find anything in one piece," she said, wrinkling her muzzle.

"It's about the only thing that is," Reemo said, bypassing two collapsed side tunnels without pause. "I walked for a few hours in every direction, and this is what we have." She stepped to the side and gestured ahead, and Sansar discovered a fresh hell.

The ceiling arched only a handful of inches above her head into a wide-open circular space, and the lighting was dim enough she had to squint, but neither of those were immediate irritants.

What itched down her spine was threefold: the ear-stabbing cry of scared baby Veetanho; the sheer number of younglings curled up against each other or alone, shivering or staring into nothingness or both; and the handful of adults scattered about the tiled floor who were physically present—and *only* physically present.

One bumped into a wall repeatedly, three were sitting, gape-mouthed and slack, another patted the air and moved her mouth as if speaking. Sansar had seen the wounded, the battle-shocked, the lost… this was not that.

Worst of all, some of the slightly larger young Veetanho made regular sweeps, pulling the smallest off the large, mindless adults. Sansar had never considered the Veetanho as maternal, but the young clambering for adult presence, the way Reemo kept staring at Gleeko—both told her there was more to them.

Cold, calculating, brilliant—that was the story they told of themselves. Maybe… maybe it was the story that was true for more than a few of them—especially given Dunamis' influence—but it wasn't all there was for all the Veetanho.

Damn it.

Tald crossed over to Reemo and put his hand on her arm. "We brought you another pup. I… I know you have a lot here, but—"

Reemo tilted her head to look at him, then at his hand, then sighed and put her other hand on his for a second. "I didn't know there were any more out there."

"I crawled under a building."

"You…" Reemo looked at him again, her whiskers brushing forward, then back. "That was dangerous. Thank you for… I didn't think there were aliens who would do that for one of us."

"I'm a Peacemaker," Tald said, shifting his chest—and the badge pinned there—more toward her. "Did… did any of the grown Veetanho survive?" He patted her arm and took his hand back. "I mean, not like that, but like they were?" Though his voice hushed slightly on the end there, Sansar was glad he didn't shy away from the question.

Tald wasn't fully back to the swaggering old holo sheriff who'd first appeared on her ship, but that might be for the best.

Reemo turned to Gleeko again, but the older Veetanho was occupied with something on her slate and didn't so much as twitch an ear.

"Two, so far. They're out trying to find weap—food."

"Weapons?" Gleeko's head snapped up, and she turned her glare on the younger Veetanho.

"And food!" Reemo replied, ears twitching.

"Your enemies aren't going to meet you on the ground, stripling." Gleeko gestured violently with her slate, and Sansar couldn't blame Reemo for ducking. "It'll be orbital bombardment, and I wouldn't be surprised if—"

"And if the mind-wiped were actually given some sort of command?" Reemo demanded, jumping forward. The baby Sansar held woke, its button eyes fuzzy. It opened its mouth, but didn't start making any terrible noises to add to the cacophony in the cave-like room, so Sansar rubbed a hand over its head and was grateful for small favors.

Gleeko pulled her head back, surprised by the upstart, but Reemo wasn't done.

"Do you *really* think we don't have enemies who'd prefer to see us writhe in front of them as we die? Who won't land to come and shoot as while we huddle like hinshi in the summer?"

Hinshi, Sansar thought. A wriggling, burrowing fish, maybe? It made sense in context, as did the young Veetanho—orbital bombardment did make the most sense, laws or no laws, but the Veetanho had a great number of enemies, and a knack for pushing them beyond the realm of logic.

"They wouldn't break one of the few laws we have and bomb you from too high." Tald nodded. "Were either of the adults mercenaries, or had they worked on any of your ships?"

"Were they..." Reemo barked a sound that might have been a laugh, then knelt to pick up an even smaller Veetanho who'd wriggled over. "No. Anyone old enough to be adapted got mind-wiped. Anyone who had higher training went..." She gestured above them. "On a rampage. They killed each other, the mind-wiped, themselves, and any babies they saw. All the airborne vehicles," her voice faltered, but only for a moment, then she continued, "spiraled higher, and then crashed into whatever was tallest. Or nearby. Or anything moving."

"The two who lived?" Gleeko breathed heavier, but her yelling subsided.

"One kept some of the breeding harems. The other… they both had some damage from when they got programmed."

"It's not a perfect system," Gleeko murmured, then cleared her throat. "Though it is overall effective. I believe the Wrogul might have a slightly higher percentage of successful outcomes with organic systems, but as mentioned, Dunamis didn't like to share."

"I'm sure he would've had them removed eventually," Reemo said, her tone the sort of flat affect Sansar had heard from too many survivors over the years, "but he saw himself out first."

"Let's go over the list of supplies, and we'll get them transported over to you. Then, if the adults aren't back, you can point us in their direction." Sansar wanted to know more about the adaptations and programming the Veetanho had received—especially from a clever youngling who'd seen it up close and hadn't yet been edited by the SI—but unfortunately it didn't have direct bearing on their current priorities. Also, Sansar wanted to be in a place to hand over the small furry bundle in her arms before she got too used to its presence— already she caught herself still rubbing its little forehead while she spoke.

"We'll need everything," Reemo replied, weariness coating her voice. "You might as well have it all unloaded in the room upstairs, and we'll use your list to sort it. Unless—" her eyes widened, and she hugged the pup in her arms. "—unless you can take us with you!"

"We can't."

"You *could*," she insisted, stepping closer. "You have a ship."

"We have a ship and a mission." Sansar kept her voice low, aiming for neutral. Empathetic, but not promising. "It's no place for all of you."

"*Here* is no place for all of us." Whatever they were without Dunamis' influence, Veetanho weren't stupid, and Reemo made an excellent point. Not one that would change Sansar's mind, but true all the same.

"We'll send more supplies—"

"Yes, I'm sure there are plenty of aliens out there who'll be sympathetic to our—our plight!" Reemo closed her eyes, flattened her whiskers, then whistled over another youngling to take the one from her arms.

Sansar shifted her arms, and Reemo sighed and gestured a second youngling over to take the tiny pup from the Human mercenary.

"There are Veetanho colonies, Veetanho survivors in the galaxy—" Sansar's tone would have been drier, if she weren't watching a miniature Veetanho toddle off with an even tinier fluff ball "—and I'm sure they still have plenty of resources at hand."

"Oh!" Reemo said, at the same moment Gleeko negated it with a harsh sound. Tald, Reemo, and Sansar all pivoted to look at her, confused.

"You were smart enough a moment ago, pup. The ones who were mind-wiped absolutely might have a deep command left in them. One to wipe out any threats to Dunamis' plan." Gleeko held up one finger for each point. "Dunamis wants the Veetanho desperate and reduced. Dunamis killed most of the mature Veetanho, and apparently *all* the mercenary-trained ones, but he left some mind-wiped and alive because…"

"If any capable, military Veetanho return…" Reemo's voice broke, and Sansar regarded the mindless adults in the cavern consideringly.

"They'll likely do everything in their power to take them out." Tald snorted. "Evil."

"Genius." Reemo shook her head. "So we euthanize—"

"Dunamis might have programmed anyone, pup. Just because he usually brought classes in as they came of age doesn't mean he couldn't have overwritten anyone, at any time, and made them forget."

"We do have a way to wipe that programming," Sansar interrupted, her tone mild. The reproof was silent—*as you well know, given it's what saved you*—but from the way Gleeko stiffened, she knew it landed.

"Do you think we can cover all the survivors across the planet in the time we're here?" the older Veetanho snapped.

"We'll at least clear the ones we can, so they know they're free of his influence." Sansar shrugged.

"None of us are attacking *you*." With her hands curling into fists, Reemo's declaration was not as convincing as it might otherwise have been, and her glare was nearing murderous.

"Would one Veetanho, with a Human and a… Peacemaker, be enough to waste Dunamis' last, petty strike on?"

Reemo subsided. "So that's it. You'll leave us here and hope you find someone sympathetic out in the galaxy to send us help?"

"We'll be sure to wipe out anything Dunamis has left lingering with those of you here. There are still Veetanho out there, Reemo." Sansar restrained herself from pointing out that the aid she offered was far more than the Veetanho themselves had extended to other species over the years. Further beating down a traumatized child was… something a Veetanho might have done, once upon a time, but not her. "Maybe they can't come to Lytoshaan themselves, but that doesn't mean they can't send help."

"Fine. Show me your list, and I'll make sure you can talk to Heelo and Meedo."

* * *

Heelo and Meedo didn't know any more than Reemo had about ships, or Dunamis' plans, or much of anything outside their needs for immediate survival.

Tald paced around them, and Heelo finally hefted a box and tilted her head.

"We found a container of maple candy buried," she said, her whiskers drooping. "We were going to give it to the younglings, so they have something nice, if we're done?"

"Thank you for everything you brought," Meedo added hastily, ducking her head, "but it's… it's been a long day. Days."

"What about—" Tald gestured, another question ready as always, but Sansar held up a hand and touched her comm to acknowledge she was listening.

"*Colonel Enkh, we need you back on the* Gobi Desert."

"Why's that?"

"*Some big-ass ship just transitioned into the system, carrying a couple of battlecruisers as ship riders. It deployed them and is headed toward the planet. Captain Parker said he's seen them before.*"

"He has? Who are they?"

"It's the Blunt Justice, *ma'am,"* the comms officer said. *"The Goltar have arrived."*

* * *

CIC, EMS *Gobi Desert*, Lytoshaan Orbit

"Wħat have we got?" Sansar asked as she strode into the CIC.

"Our old friends, the Goltar," Captain Parker said. "The capital ship *Blunt Justice,* along with two battle riders, the battlecruisers *Tseg-Talag* and *Tseg-Lenkh.*"

"What do they want?"

"I don't know. We haven't hailed them yet, as we were waiting for your return." Parker chuckled. "I can guess what they want—the *Keesius* ships—although I'm sure they'd settle for carpet-bombing the planet into oblivion."

"We can't allow them to do that," Tald said.

Parker barked a laugh. "I guess you missed the part where I mentioned the ship classes that were inbound. Two of them are battlecruisers, and the third is a ship so big it can *carry* both of them into battle." He tilted his head as he looked at the SalSha. "If they want to carpet-bomb Lytoshaan, how do you suggest I stop them?"

"You don't need to do anything," Tald said. "I'm a Peacemaker; I'll use my authority to stop them. Genocide is illegal, and that's what they'd be doing. The Veetanho can't even muster a coherent defense at the moment."

"Which is another thing," Parker said. "They'd be just as likely to hit *us*—assuming there's anyone on the planet who knows how to launch their missiles—as they would the Goltar."

"Well, let's give them a call then, shall we?" Sansar asked. "Before we do, though—" she turned to Gleeko "—we probably want you off camera. I can't imagine they'll want to talk with us if they think we're helping you."

"Good point," Gleeko said. She moved to the side of the CIC.

Parker nodded toward the comms officer, who turned toward his console and began pushing buttons. After a few moments, he nodded, and a view from the *Blunt Justice* came up on the main viewer. Like everything about the ship, it was huge, and a number of Goltar could be seen going about their business. The image centered on the one in the command chair.

"Captain Kanat-Baim, it's good to see you again," Sansar said, trying to maintain a straight face. "What are you doing here?"

The Goltar chuckled. "*Sansar Enkh and the* Gobi Desert." He chuckled again. "*When things get interesting, you always seem to turn up.*" He waved a tentacle toward the viewer. "*What am I doing? Probably the same as you, I suspect. We heard rumors there were three* Keesius *ships on the loose, and we came to see whether that was true or not.*" He waved at the screen again. "*If we'd known we could so easily transit to the planet, we might have brought a few more assault ships. To think of all the money Gloriana wasted, when all we had to do was wait a little longer, and Lytoshaan would be opened up to us.*"

"You can't bomb them," Tald said.

"*And who is this fuzzy little being?*" Kanat-Baim asked. "*Wait, I remember. It's one of the little ones you use as fighter pilots, right? If you've been with the Golden Horde any length of time, little one, I'm sure you'll remember that I absolutely* can *bomb them. It doesn't appear there's anything either in space or on the planet that can stop us.*"

"I'll stop you," Tald said. He pulled out his Peacemaker badge and held it up. "I'm Peacemaker Tald, and I forbid you to bomb the planet."

The Goltar laughed. Not just the captain, but all the Goltar who could be seen in the CIC.

"What is so funny?" Tald asked, sounding very small.

A Goltar came to stand next to Kanat-Baim's shoulder. "*It's funny you have a Peacemaker,*" the captain said. "*I have one, too.*" The other Goltar held up his badge for the camera.

"Well, *that* didn't go as expected," Parker muttered.

"*Also,*" Kanat-Baim said with yet another chuckle, "*I have a feeling my Peacemaker outranks yours—unfortunately for you—and mine has said I absolutely can bomb Lytoshaan. What do you think of that?*"

"But, but, but... genocide is *illegal!*" Tald exclaimed. Sansar could see tears welling up in his eyes.

Kanat-Baim chuckled. "*That's not how he sees this. The Veetanho and the Goltar have had a long-running dispute.*" He shrugged. "*By bombing the planet and wiping the Veetanho out, the dispute is resolved, and peace is made. In fact, to all of us, it seems like the* perfect *solution.*"

"That's not how it's supposed to work!" Tald said. "Genocide is the bigger crime! You can't commit a crime to end a dispute. That's not right!"

"*Why do you think so?*" the Goltar Peacemaker asked. "*Under whose authority are you acting?*"

"Well, my own, as no one else knew this situation existed."

"*I'm senior, and I'm telling you to stand down, pup. The Goltar will solve this problem. For all time.*"

"I can't wait for that," Sansar said, interrupting with a smile. "A galaxy without Veetanho." A visible shudder ran through her. "That will be... delightful." *Although, judging from the look on Gleeko's face, that's not what she thinks.* Sansar chuckled. "I have to ask you, though... what then?"

"*What do you mean?*" Kanat-Baim asked.

"Once you wipe out this planet, what do you think the Veetanho are going to do with their *Keesius* ships?" Sansar asked. "Once you make it so they have nothing to lose, they're sure to use them on *your* planets."

"*Perhaps,*" Kanat-Baim said, "*but we have heard they no longer control their* Keesius. *What about that?*"

"We've heard the same rumor, which is why we came." Sansar shrugged and waved dismissively at Tald. "I pretended to be helping the Peacemaker so we could come see if the rumors were true. Not only that—he paid us to come, and he paid to refuel the ship! Isn't that hilarious?"

Sansar sobered. "The question I'm having a hard time with, though, is the same one that confronts you."

"*Which is?*"

"We haven't been able to determine the whereabouts of the *Keesius* ships, and are you *really* willing to risk the Goltar civilization on a *rumor?* I'm not willing to risk Earth. Wouldn't it be better to confirm the rumor before acting?" She shrugged. "I just returned from the planet, and I can tell you—they won't be able to defend themselves for quite some time."

Kanat-Baim narrowed his gaze on Sansar. "*You haven't been able to determine whether the rumor was true?*"

"No, unfortunately, I can't. Despite a thorough search of the planet, we couldn't find any information, so we're leaving in search of other clues." She gave the Goltar a feral smile. "As it turns out, I have a lot of past injustices that I would like vengeance on the Veetanho for... but I don't want Earth to become a target for their *Keesius* ships any more than you want the Veetanho to target *yours*. While I'd love to burn this planet to slag, I'll give you the same advice I gave the Winged Hussars fleet that just left."

"*What's that?*"

"Patience." Sansar laughed. "I mean, it's not like they're going to rebuild their defenses any time soon. We have time to find the missing ships and ensure they won't be used against us before taking the next step against the rats."

Kanat-Baim nodded and stared at Tald. "*We'll find the answer to the missing* Keesius *ships, then we'll return. At that time, none of your words will stop us.*"

Sansar nodded. "They won't stop us, either." She let her smile become more natural. "Let it be a race, then—whoever finds the *Keesius* ships gets to launch the first missile."

"But, Sansar!" Tald protested.

"Shut up, pup. Can't you see your elders are talking?"

Kanat-Baim laughed, loud and long. "*When last we met, I told you I believed your race and mine were natural allies,*" he said. "*I look forward to finding the* Keesius *ships so we can once more go to battle together... and wipe out the Veetanho for all time.*"

Sansar nodded. "Me, too."

The connection cut, and Sansar let her breath out in a rush.

"What are you doing?" Tald whined. "I thought you were on *my* side!"

Sansar gave him a wry chuckle. "What am I doing? Buying us a little time, I hope."

"I—" Tald shook his head and turned to Gleeko. "Were you in on this plan, too?"

"If what just happened is what I *think* happened, Sansar just outbluffed the Goltar." Gleeko chuckled. "I can't remember ever seeing such a thing before."

Sansar shook her head. "I wasn't sure he'd go for it, but I had to try."

"Go for it? Blowing up the planet? And the Winged Hussars? When were they here?"

This time, Sansar couldn't keep herself from laughing. "I don't think the Hussars have ever been here," Sansar said when she had control of herself once more. "Not in my lifetime, anyway."

"But you said—"

"I said a lot of things," Sansar said. "Once in a while, I even said some things that were true."

"Like that we won't be able to defend ourselves for a long time," Gleeko said.

Sansar nodded. "Unfortunately, that's very true."

"I thought you wanted to destroy the planet," Tald said. "Shouldn't that make you *happy?*"

"I don't want to destroy the planet," Sansar said. "That may not have *always* been true—like when Peepo ruled the Merc Guild and declared war on us—but destroying a planet full of beings who can't defend themselves isn't high on my list of to-dos. Even if it weren't illegal, there's certainly no honor in it."

"So you don't really want to blow up Lytoshaan?"

Sansar shook her head. "Not today, nor any time in the near future."

"Everything you said to the Goltar was a lie?"

"Everything I said about blowing it up was, yeah."

"Why would you do that? Why would you lie?"

"You saw their fleet, right? What would you have had me do? It was pretty obvious that your approach failed."

"My approach?"

"Yes. You told them to leave, and they laughed at you. If I hadn't spoken up, they'd be bombing the planet right now."

Tald's jaw dropped. "I... I failed. My first task as a Peacemaker, and I was laughed at. Being a Peacemaker is stupid." He pulled the badge off his vest, threw it to the ground, and stormed out of CIC.

"Well," Captain Parker muttered, "that *also* didn't go quite as expected."

* * *

CIC, *Blunt Justice*, Lytoshaan Orbit

The Tri-V went blank, and Captain Kanat-Baim sank back into his command chair.

"Do you believe her?" Salz-Kryll asked.

Kanat-Baim met the Peacemaker's eyes for a moment. "Which part?"

"All of it."

The captain chuckled. "I doubt the whole story is true, but much of what she said probably is."

"What does that mean?"

"Even though Sansar would like us to believe she doesn't care about the furry Peacemaker on her bridge, she's too much of an idealist to allow him there if she didn't want him. Which means she's probably in agreement with him and wants us to leave without destroying the planet. But for what reason? I don't know. It may be as she says... or it may not."

"What if the Peacemaker deputized her?"

"I'd bet money the Peacemaker *did* deputize her. She's not stupid, and having the backing of the guild—"

"But you said—"

"I said her story is built on truths, but if I had to bet money, I suspect much of her truths add up to a very different outcome than the one presented to us."

"For example?"

Kanat-Baim chuckled again. "Everything verifiable is probably true. The planet's been hammered. The Veetanho's defenses are down, and they'll be down for a while."

"If she didn't want us to strike the planet, though, why would she tell us that?"

"To eliminate our sense of urgency. There's no need to bomb them until we're sure about the *Keesius* ships. We could come back in a week or a month... probably even several years, and the Veetanho wouldn't be able to keep us from destroying their planet."

"So why don't we?"

"Because what she said about the *Keesius* ships is also true. We have a lot more to lose than the Veetanho. Their planet is in disarray. They won't be as strong as they were for years, if ever. We're in a position of power—of preeminence. But if they *do* have the *Keesius*, they could set us back even further than they have been.

"What Sansar said—even though it serves her own ends—is true. It's better for us to wait to finish off the Veetanho."

"So what do we do?"

"We follow our leads and see where they go. Have the battle riders reattach, then we'll jump to Calladone." Kanat-Baim looked down at his monitor. "Don't worry," he muttered to the image of Lytoshaan, which sat in the middle of it, "we'll be back for you *very* soon."

* * * * *

Chapter Six

Officer's Mess, EMS *Gobi Desert*, Lytoshaan Orbit

I t took all of Tald's self-control not to burst into tears as he sat down with his dinner. He didn't want to be alone in his stateroom, but he didn't want to talk to anyone, so he figured he'd come get dinner. Of course the SalSha pilots were in the mess, being loud—because that's what they did—and it just made him even more depressed. *If I'd just become a bomber pilot...* but that wasn't what had interested him.

He took a bite, but it tasted like ash in his mouth. He had to take a large drink to get it down... and it was soup. *How could the Goltar be so callous? Worse, how could a* Peacemaker *support them? Why bother trying to do what's right when a merc can just lie and get people to do what the stupid badge couldn't?* Everything he'd learned over the past three years—everything he'd been led to believe—had been invalidated in a five-minute period.

He dropped his spoon, which fell into his soup and splattered it all over him. He'd forgotten they were under power and there was gravity again, and now he was wearing his dinner. He tried to find it in himself to care, but he couldn't. *I'm just not cut out for space and being a Peacemaker. New Zealand was more fun. Maybe Sansar can drop me off when we pass by Earth—*

"Here."

Tald looked up. His father stood next to him, holding out a napkin.

"What?" he asked.

"Looks like you got some of your dinner on your fur." Thorb leaned forward and wiped off Tald's vest. "That's better."

"Why?"

Thorb chuckled. "You needed a clean spot for this." Thorb attached Tald's Peacemaker badge to the area he'd wiped off, then without asking, he slid into the seat next to Tald.

Just when I thought things couldn't be worse, Dad shows up to gloat. Blue Sky, why do you have it out for me?

"I don't think you want to join me, Dad. I'm not very good company right now."

Thorb nodded. "I heard you got your first introduction to the Goltar."

"The Goltar." Tald snorted. "Yeah." He sniffed, trying to hold back the tears. "Did you come by to laugh and tell me I could always be a bomber pilot?"

Thorb scoffed. "You'd be a shitty bomber pilot. You're too damn idealistic."

Tald's jaw dropped. "Oh, so you're just here to gloat?"

Thorb shook his head. "I thought you might like a little company."

"Did you see me sitting by myself? Company is the *last* thing I want right now."

"It may not be what you want, but it's certainly what you need. Aside from another napkin."

Tald snorted as he looked down. There was soup everywhere. On the table, on the floor, and quite a bit was still on him, despite his father's earlier efforts.

"I don't get it, Dad. The Goltar just… then Sansar… I don't think I'm cut out to be a Peacemaker."

"Because they didn't listen to you?"

"No, because they were willing to commit genocide on the Veetanho. I wanted to stop them, but didn't know how. If it hadn't been for Sansar, they'd be bombing the Veetanho out of existence right now, *and the Veetanho are defenseless!* Who does that? And Sansar only got them to stop by lying to them! Where's the honor in that?"

Thorb carefully put his spoon down. "You're probably too young to remember when we left our home planet, right?"

"I remember water everywhere, but not much more," Tald admitted.

Thorb nodded. "I remember Trigar 2-A—that's what the Humans call it—very well. It was a great planet, with one exception."

Tald sighed. "The grahp. I know." He rolled his eyes. "You've told me about the grahp about *a thousand* times."

"The grahp." Thorb nodded. "And what happens when the grahp comes?"

"Everyone fights." Tald sighed again. "I've heard *that* about a million times, too."

"Well, I've obviously been wasting my time telling you about it, because you've completely missed the point."

"And what point is that?"

"When the grahp came, not quite everyone fought. There were always a few—those who were too sick or too lame to fight. They would've been a hindrance; we'd have spent more time defending them than working on killing the grahp. Then there were the young-lings—those old enough to fight, but too young to have learned the skills needed to fight something like a grahp. You have to remember, the grahp was a monster at least twenty meters long, with a mouth four meters wide. When the grahp opened it, the suction would pull in anyone who'd gotten too close."

"And you fought it with bone knives and bone spears," Tald said. "I get it. I've heard the story, *really*, about a thousand times."

"All right then—" Thorb sat back "—why do you think I'm bringing it up?"

"Honestly, Dad, I have no idea. I haven't seen a sea monster in my life, nor have I fought one."

Thorb grinned. "I would submit that you *have* fought a grahp. Today. I'd also tell you that you lost."

Tald frowned. "Do you always have to be so obtuse?"

"Obtuse?"

"Annoyingly insensitive or hard to understand."

Thorb chuckled. "In that case, yes. It's one of my superpowers."

Tald frowned. "Can I leave now?"

"No. Not until I'm done. I'm coming to my point."

"Could you make it soon, please? I have a lot to do before we jump to hyperspace."

"Oh?" One of Thorb's eyes opened wide—the equivalent to a Human raising an eyebrow. "Like what?"

"Things. Important things. Peacemaker things."

"Oh, like wallowing in your self-pity."

"Fine," Tald said. "I'm out of here." He started to rise, but Thorb put a paw on his shoulder and slammed him back down into his seat with surprising strength.

"No, you ungrateful pup," Thorb said, his voice low. "You're going to listen to what I have to say."

Tald looked around. The pilots were all staring. He glared at them, and they turned away, chuckling. He quit fighting and looked at the paw on his shoulder. "Do you mind? As if this day wasn't humiliating enough, now the other SalSha are laughing at me."

"They're laughing because they've all gotten this talk at one point or another." Thorb removed his paw. "Now, are you going to listen?"

"I'm listening."

"No you're not. You're sitting there wallowing in self-pity, and you're absolutely *not* listening to me."

Tald took a deep breath and let it out slowly. "Okay, fine. I'm listening. You were getting to your point?"

"My point is, the Goltar are your grahp. Today, anyway."

"What's that supposed to mean? They're from the ocean, but they're not monsters. Well, maybe metaphorical monsters today—"

"Exactly," Thorb said. He smiled.

"What?"

"The Goltar are the metaphorical grahp."

Tald shook his head. "Maybe I wasn't listening earlier, because I have *no* idea what you're talking about."

"We no longer live on our ancient homeworld—"

"I'm aware."

"—so we no longer have to fight the grahp. That's a good thing, but that doesn't mean we don't face challenges—sometimes seemingly insurmountable ones, like the grahp—on a daily basis. When we do, we don't beat them by ourselves; we beat them by forming a team that goes out and conquers the grahp by fighting as one. When

we fight an enemy, do you see me go charging off on my own? No—
I take the rest of those knuckleheads—" he waved at the SalSha pilots "—with me when I go. There's strength in a team. When you're
fighting the grahp, you need someone to watch your back, no matter
whether it's a literal grahp or a Bakulu cruiser."

Tald shook his head. "I don't have a team, and I didn't defeat the
Goltar today, if you're saying they're my metaphorical grahp. Sansar
did."

Thorb tilted his head and looked at Tald. "Really? Sansar isn't on
your team?"

"No."

"You didn't deputize her?"

Tald's mouth dropped open. He'd never looked at it that way.
Thorb looked at him and widened an eye again. "Well, yeah…"

"Then I submit she's on your team." Thorb waved a paw toward
the pilots and the rest of the ship. "We're *all* here to support *you*." He
shook his head and chuckled. "The first time pups go out to fight the
grahp, they don't charge at it with a bone knife. If they did, they'd get
eaten pretty quickly. No, they stay back and watch and learn, while
those who've done it before show them how it's done. Sometimes,
they're forced into action, but usually, you can't fight until you learn
how.

"Now, you may say, 'But the Academy taught me…' but I'm here
to tell you the Academy is shit for teaching tactics."

"It's *what?*"

"It's shit for teaching tactics, the same as any school. In the
bomber community, we teach the pups tactics before they go flying,
but without actual aviation experience, there's no *knowledge* of tactics.

It's the application—putting the words into practice—where it really begins to make sense."

Thorb smiled. "Today, you got your first look at the galaxy. Guess what? It's ugly. There are people who are mean and powerful, and who want nothing more than to chew you up and shit you out."

Tald nodded. "Like a grahp."

"Exactly," Thorb replied with an answering nod. "Just like a grahp. Some people aren't going to care that you're a Peacemaker; if it conflicts with what they want to do, they may see you as an obstacle to remove rather than someone listen to."

"But the Goltar had a *Peacemaker* who was going to allow them to commit *genocide!*"

"Yeah? So what?"

"We're supposed to *prevent* genocide, and he was going to commit it!"

"The galaxy isn't perfect. I may have mentioned that. As it turns out, the people inhabiting it aren't perfect, either."

"But—"

"You said you weren't cut out to be a Peacemaker, right?"

Tald nodded.

"I'd say you're *exactly* the person to be a Peacemaker."

"Why's that?"

"Because you have beliefs and ideals. You believe in the mission of the Peacemakers, something the Goltar Peacemaker forgot about somewhere along the way. He allowed his racial hatred of the Veetanho to overcome his ideals. We need people like you to bring them back to the light."

"But they had a fleet—"

"No one fights a grahp alone; they get eaten."

"Yeah, but—"

"Now you're just being obstinate. I've already told you—fighting the grahp requires a team. As a Peacemaker, you have to be the leader that assembles the team. Whether it's calling in additional Peacemakers or Enforcers, or deputizing additional mercenaries, *you* have to be the one to do it." Thorb shrugged. "What do you think would have been easier for Sansar today? To stand up to the Goltar or to move out of their way and let them bomb Lytoshaan—a planet full of beings she *hates* and would love to be rid of?"

"She hates them?"

"I don't know," Thorb said, "but she's spent most of her life fighting them. She probably wouldn't mind too greatly if they disappeared as a race."

"But she stood up to the Goltar to stop them—why would she do that?"

"Because she's part of *your team*. She knew what you wanted, and she did everything she could to make it happen, all the while providing examples for *you* on how to fight your grahp in the future."

Tald's shoulders slumped. "I don't have a mercenary fleet—ow!" he exclaimed as Thorb cuffed him in the back of the head.

"She didn't fight them with a merc company; she fought the Goltar with her mind. She out-thought them and showed them the logical conclusion that would be reached if they proceeded on the course of action they *really* wanted to follow. She turned them away from the planet, using the same thing that failed you—words."

Tald turned to Thorb. "But what happens when words fail?"

"Then you need to take action to fight the wrong. You recruit a team as best you can, and you make a stand."

Tald's jaw fell open. "Honor the threat... stand or fall..."

"Well, ideally, you win," Thorb said, "because the falling part isn't fun. It's also usually fatal, too." He shrugged. "Sometimes you have to make a stand to keep the grahp out of the nest. To keep the Goltar from committing genocide. You may fall when you fight the grahp—sometimes people are killed when they fight monsters—but oftentimes that serves to galvanize others to take action. That's what Peacemakers do, and exactly why the galaxy needs them, to keep races from being bombed out of existence when they're unable to defend themselves. That's why the Peacemakers need *you*."

Thorb smiled. "And while you're learning how to be one, you need people like us to help you along the way and show you the ropes. Being a Peacemaker doesn't mean you have to fight the grahp alone; it just means you have to be the one who says, 'No! Not today! Not on my watch!' and who puts together a team to stop the grahp from doing… whatever the miscreants were going to do." Thorb shrugged. "Make sense?"

Tald nodded slowly. "Yeah, Dad, I think it does."

"Good. Then get up and figure out how we're going to find these damned *Keesius* ships."

Tald stood. "I don't know how, but there are people I can talk to about it." He nodded. "I'll go do that now!"

Thorb shook his head.

"No?" Tald asked. His jaw dropped. "Why not?"

Thorb chuckled. "You have to be prepared before you run off to fix galactic wrongs."

"What? I don't get it."

"You've still got soup all over yourself. Get cleaned up first."

* * * * *

Chapter Seven

CO's Office, EMS *Gobi Desert*, Lytoshaan Orbit

"Thanks for coming," Tald said with a nod to Sansar and Gleeko as he took a seat in Sansar's small office.

"Always happy to talk to a Peacemaker," Sansar said.

"Well, most of the time, anyway," Gleeko said. "Depending on what you're doing."

Sansar nodded. "That kind of goes without saying." She turned to Tald. "Good to see you've got your badge back."

Tald looked down. "Yeah, uh, about that…"

Sansar chuckled. "Don't worry about it. We all have our first experience where the romantic notion of something comes into contact with the actual reality of it."

"I remember my first combat," Gleeko said. "The helmsman next to me took a sliver of spalling through her head, and I had to wipe her blood from the console before I could operate it. I spent the next three hours wearing her brains like a crown and wouldn't have known it except for the smell." She shook her head. "That took away the glamor of space combat right from the start."

The soup in his stomach curdled at the description, and Tald began talking to fill his head with other thoughts. "Yes, the… scene with the Goltar did a lot to tarnish the gold of the Peacemaker badge, but my father put it into perspective for me."

Sansar nodded. She'd given Thorb the badge, hoping he could get through to his son. She didn't have time for whiny Peacemakers;

the normal ones were bad enough. "Good. So what can we do for you?"

"I wanted to talk about Khatash."

"What about it? It's a jungle world—"

Tald shook his head. "Not the geography, but what happened there with the invasion and the aftermath of it."

"Which invasion? The Veetanho invasion of Khatash, or the Depik one to take it back?"

"Uh, both?" Tald shrugged. "Sorry. I was at the Academy, and I'm not very familiar with either of the events."

"Briefly," Sansar said, "the Veetanho developed a piece of technology that froze the Depik."

"Froze them? Like made them really cold?"

Sansar shook her head. "I'm not sure exactly how it works, but it has something to do with how the Depik are able to go invisible. The box emits… something that locks up all their muscles. They can't move, and they can't fight it. The Veetanho surrounded the planet and used the technology on the Depik, then the Veetanho told them to surrender. Most of the Depik chose to suicide rather than capitulate to the Veetanho."

"That's genocide!" Tald said.

"We didn't make them kill themselves," Gleeko said. "They *chose* to do that rather than submit."

"You didn't know they'd kill themselves?"

"I don't know what High Command thought they'd do as I wasn't part of the invasion. I do know the common thinking was that the galaxy would be a lot better without a race of invisible assassins. They may have suspected the Depik would kill themselves; I don't know."

Sansar chuckled. "There are other races some think the galaxy would be better off without."

Gleeko shrugged. "Be careful what kind of thoughts you put in other people's heads, I guess."

"Anyway," Sansar said, turning back to Tald, "as it turns out, making enemies out of a race of assassins didn't turn out as well as the Veetanho had intended. There were still a number of Depik out in the galaxy on contracts, and quite a few of them made it their life's mission to kill as many Veetanho as possible. Others came to us and asked for help."

"Which will eventually come back to haunt you," Gleeko said. "The Depik can't be controlled; you should have finished them off rather than helping them."

"History will see who's correct," Sansar said with a shrug. "Regardless, we helped the Depik—we're still helping them, actually—and we assisted them when they took their planet back from the Veetanho."

"Killing everyone they could get their hands on, too," Gleeko noted.

"The planetary assault was bloody. No quarter was asked for, or given—" Sansar looked at Gleeko sharply "—by *either* side."

Gleeko shrugged, obviously unwilling to argue the point further.

Tald scratched behind an ear. "If all the Veetanho were killed—"

"They weren't all killed, though. At the end of the fighting, six Veetanho did something very rare for them—they surrendered. Even more unlikely, the Depik accepted their surrender. One tried to un-surrender and was killed, leaving five."

"So we can talk to them?"

Sansar winced. "There is, however, something you should know."

Tald cocked his head. "What?"

"The Depik didn't trust the five captured Veetanho, and the only way they would honor the Veetanho troopers' surrender was if they chose to have their brains altered."

"They did this willingly?"

Gleeko glared at Sansar. "No."

Sansar shrugged. "How willing they were is a matter of discussion. They had a choice—take the modification or die."

"That's not much of a choice," Tald said.

Sansar shrugged again. "I wasn't there, so I don't know. What I do know is, the Depik are vindictive. You do *not* want to piss off a race of assassins."

"How badly were their brains modified? Will they still be useful to us?"

"I believe so," Sansar said. "Their brains were modified to make them think they wanted to—willingly—serve the Depik. Although it's possible some of their earlier memories were destroyed, most of them should be available to the individual Veetanho troopers."

"But will they answer our questions?"

Sansar smiled. "As long as the Depik tell them to, the Veetanho will do anything we say."

* * *

The City, Khatash

"Welcome back to Khatash, Commander Enkh," said the tall Zuul who stood in the clearing ahead of them as Sansar disembarked. "You are always welcome in our lands. I am Aryo, and I will take you to the Council." Her ears pointed attentively forward as Tald followed, then pinned backward momentarily as Gleeko appeared. "Who have you brought with you?" The Zuul pitched her voice as a question, but her body stiffened. Sansar had seen enough Zuul in action to know this one's manner had shifted to far less welcoming.

"Peacemaker Tald," Sansar said, gesturing at the SalSha, "and Gleeko, who is both contracted to me and currently deputized by the Peacemaker. As am I."

"I see." Aryo inclined her head. "Khatash is never a safe planet, but I will provide you, Commander Enkh, and you Peacemaker Tald, with all the defense I am able, should it become necessary. Gleeko, I will not bring you to harm, but you should know Khatash is even less friendly to the Veetanho."

"That's related to why we're here, Aryo." Sansar didn't bother to check Gleeko's reaction—for the moment, she was simply pleased no one was snarling at anyone else. "We need to speak with your Veetanho."

Aryo's ears flattened, and her muzzle lifted. "I have none."

"Tsan's then. The clan's." When Aryo didn't blink, Sansar added, "I was here, Aryo, at the Battle of Khatash. They're not a secret from me."

"They are not a secret," the Zuul said, then flicked an ear back. "Only three are currently in residence. Why do you need to speak with them?"

Sansar didn't ask if the other two were dead or currently traveling on clan business—with Depik, truly, it was better not to know sometimes—but instead gestured to Tald.

"I need to speak with them, Aryo. Peacemaker business."

"We are not beholden to Galactic Law here, Peacemaker." The words were softened by her tone, which was impeccably polite. "I will need further detail to continue."

"We're looking for something the Veetanho had and may no longer have. We think one of your Veetanho might know something about it." Tald crossed his arms, and Aryo tilted her head.

"Dunamis abandoned the Veetanho," Sansar interjected, feeling it a safe assumption that the Veetanho here, reprogrammed for loyalty to the Depik, had shared some level of detail about the synthetic intelligence who had tied them for so long. While it wasn't the wisest course to trumpet through the galaxy that there were three *Keesius* unaccounted for and perhaps in the hands of beings willing to use them, Sansar had to balance keeping the secret with getting what they needed.

Besides, the Goltar were aware. It was only a matter of time.

"Somewhere in that process, their *Keesius* ships also went missing."

"World breakers," Aryo murmured, then stood up straight. "This is to thwart Dunamis, then?"

"As best we can, yes." Tald said, nodding seriously.

"With great malice," Sansar added, and Aryo dropped her jaw in a Zuul smile.

"That makes my decision much easier, Peacemaker and company. My Dama has no love for the Veetanho, but after recent events, her true hatred is reserved for the SIs. If your mission is to disrupt their plans and deprive them of what they most want, then it is my obligation and pleasure to assist."

She led them down an elevated pathway from the shuttle landing zone to a road with automated carts lined along it. "The city is the safest part of Khatash, but please trust me when I say you should keep all limbs inside the vehicle. We can trim vegetation back six times a day, but several species of vines are clever enough to return."

"My dad said there was something like that on our home planet," Tald said, furrowing his brow as he hopped into the front seat of the three-rowed cart. "The air here is pretty wet, so I guess that makes sense. But it's not a water-heavy planet, right?"

"There is more than enough water, as you can feel," Aryo said, to which Sansar agreed—Khatash's humidity was tangible.

She'd once privately wondered if Depik were so fast offworld because they had to fight water resistance in the air at all times at home. A flippant thought, perhaps, but at the time, it had made her feel better about the idea that invisible assassins could cut her throat before she even knew they were there. That had been before one had saved her life, of course, but that...

That was one of the many things she didn't think about often. Easier not to brood over them that way.

"Beyond a few rivers, though, most of the water is locked into the jungles—as you can see, not far from the city limits, many of our various plants grow quite tall, and require a large amount of resources."

"This planet never made any sense," Gleeko muttered, her first words since the shuttle landed on Khatash. She slid into the furthest back seat, leaving Sansar sitting alone in the middle.

"Many things in the galaxy do not make sense," Aryo replied without turning. The Zuul pressed buttons on the cart's control panel, then set her hands on the controls. "Yet they carry on existing whether we understand or not."

Gleeko snapped her teeth but didn't speak further, and Sansar didn't sigh. She did turn to give Gleeko a pointed look, but she didn't sigh.

Tald peppered Aryo with questions about the various ravenous, predatory, and poisonous attributes of Khatash—he seemed overly interested in a river that had approximately eighteen ways of killing him from plant life alone—and Sansar kept a sliver of her attention on it in favor of observing the changes to Khatash's city, even in the relatively short time since she'd last been there.

Granted, the one time she'd been in the city before, it had been covered in Tortantula and Goka and a multitude of Veetanho traps, so even the occasional body-snatching vine was bound to be an improvement to that.

Buildings had been restored, and at least twenty species of aliens moved through the streets around them. Few Depik themselves—they might be around and simply invisible, or waiting for the bright sun of midday to fade—but far more than she'd expected at a quick glance. As they passed a line of tall, twisted buildings—close enough to each other for a Depik to jump from window to window, she noted a large tiger that stalked down a walkway.

Not a Pushtal. An actual *tiger*.

Despite their mission and its lack of progress—and despite the fact that meant a trio of *Keesius* ships were at loose ends in the galaxy—Sansar smiled. A tiger. If she'd dreamed it, she would've thought it a sign of something entirely else, but…

Her smile faded. Given the enormity of the mission they were on, the fact that she'd had no dreams for this long itched at the base of her skull.

The cart slowed and skewed to the side, halting in front of a squat, wide building made out of a white stone that shimmered in the sunlight. At first Sansar thought it was the moisture in the air, but as they approached the tall, wood-like doors, she saw it was the material itself that sparkled.

"Don't touch the rock." Aryo stood to the side and pushed open one of the doors. "The substance that makes it shine is in irritant to most beings' skin. Fur is some defense, but not much for more than a handful of seconds."

"Why…" Tald stopped and craned his head back to take in the building. "I was going to ask why make a building out of something like that, but it's because they *can*, isn't it?"

"Indeed it is, Peacemaker. Besides, there is no need to linger against this building, as the building itself reminds passersby."

"Also, it discourages anyone from scaling the walls," Sansar noted as she walked inside. "Meaning all visitors would come through the designated doors."

"Why have only one rationale when so many will do?" Aryo closed the door behind them, and Sansar blinked in the abruptly reduced lighting.

They were in a small vestibule, the walls transparent, so it took her a moment to register. Gleeko adjusted her goggles and made a small noise in the back of her throat.

"We do not encourage idle visitors," Aryo said calmly and stepped between them and the thorned vines pulsing against the glass in front of them. She slid her hand into a recess on the one table in the small cube with them, and a moment later, the vines rolled up and out of sight.

Several sucker-shaped streaks marred the glass, and Sansar decided to bring a flamethrower the next time she came to Khatash. Just in case.

They walked single file down a narrow hall, slowly enough that there was no pileup when Aryo paused at the next door. She didn't reach for the control panel or move at all, so Sansar was prepared enough not to jump when a voice spoke very close to her ear.

"You, I will allow in. The Peacemaker, too, I suppose. Because I saw you fight, Sansar Enkh of the Golden Horde, and because you are a valued ally, I have not killed this Veetanho for coming here. Please explain why that should continue to be the case."

"Because I *am* a valued ally," she replied, her voice perfectly steady, "and she works for me. And Peacemaker Tald has deputized us both."

Gleeko stiffened in front of her, but didn't turn around. Tald, however, did.

"Wait, they really are entirely invisible?" he asked, squinting in the dimmer light. "I thought there'd be a warp in the air or something."

"Aryo brought us here. Even if you question my word, surely you trust her judgement?" Sansar had the feeling the Depik had left her and prowled closer to Tald, and she thought it a wiser course of action to redirect the assassin's attention back to her.

"I trust Aryo's judgement, and I do not question yours, Sansar Enkh, but visitors to this place are limited. There are many who would prefer to see *our* Veetanho harmed." The slow drawl and careful emphasis in that sentence indicated the speaker would both like to see Gleeko harmed and perhaps also sympathized with those who wanted their tame Veetanho removed as well.

"I'm not here to kill them," Gleeko said, her voice low and neutral, her body eerily still. "I'm here to spite Dunamis. He wants new toys, and also, we think, to regain control of the Veetanho's *Keesius* ships."

"Our Veetanho have told us everything they know about Dunamis," the voice said, and between one heartbeat and the next, a Depik appeared on Sansar's right side, about eye level to her. There was a thin ledge that ran along the wall, and despite its shallow depth, the Depik balanced on it without any apparent effort.

"Everything they *know* that they know," Tald said, face upturned toward the Depik. "Everything they know that they know that you thought to ask. SIs are tricky, as you probably know, and this is important."

"You think a Veetanho will know better questions to ask." The Depik made a spitting noise, then sat straighter. "I suppose there is some small sense in that. Very well. I greet you, Peacemaker. I greet you, Sansar Enkh. Veetanho, I will keep my claws from your throat."

"Goody," Gleeko muttered, and the Depik opened its mouth to reply.

"Are we not to negotiate?" Sansar asked, keeping her voice from sounding rushed.

"No." The Depik's ears flicked in opposite directions. "Not with you, Sansar Enkh. You are a friend and ally, and are welcome without negotiation."

The Depik leapt from the wall perch to Aryo's shoulder, and Aryo turned her head back toward them. "Justice believes negotiation is old fashioned. He also knows better than to not introduce himself. The Dama would not approve," she added, much more softly.

"Who do you think I learned it from?" he replied, and the door opened in front of them.

* * *

The room inside was an open space with half a dozen desks and tables scattered about in no particular order, and an initially overwhelming number of screens, displays, and holograms on the walls and various surfaces.

The ceiling was low, the space vaguely circular—it was like and quite unlike the space on Lytoshaan where the younglings had sheltered. The three adult Veetanho in this space, however, were fully capable, moving busily between tables and screens, and pausing briefly to confer with each other. They didn't turn either a whisker or an ear toward the visitors until Justice leapt from Aryo's shoulder to one of the few clear patches on a nearby table.

Then all three pivoted, ducking their heads and smiling—grinning even!—at the new arrival.

"Justice!" The one with a stripe down the middle of her face stepped forward with every evidence of delight. "You so rarely visit when you are in the residence."

"You have guests," he said, grooming one of his ears with a single extended claw.

The striped Veetanho turned to Aryo first, greeting her with nearly as much pleasure as she had the orange and black Depik.

"Sansar Enkh," the Veetanho continued, and if she were surprised to see the commander of the Golden Horde in her bubble, she didn't express it. "And a… Peacemaker! How interesting, a Sal-Sha Peacemaker? Your people rise through the galaxy even faster than your Human friends, it seems."

Tald's whiskers bristled furiously as though he'd been insulted, then he cocked his head. Sansar, too, was surprised to find that it hadn't landed like an insult at all—as she would have expected it to, being delivered from a Veetanho mouth. It sounded like a cheerful observation, instead.

How very strange.

Lastly, the Veetanho turned toward Gleeko, opened her mouth, and then closed it again. Her ears twitched, her whiskers vibrated, but she said nothing, and after a long moment of silence, one of the others, the tallest one with dark brown fur, cleared her throat.

"Ah. I am Preebo, this is Yeego—" she pointed to the third Veetanho, then lastly the one who'd originally spoken "—and this is Seedo. We are…" Preebo lifted a hand and dropped it without managing a gesture. "Interested to see what service we can provide. You are?"

"Gleeko."

"Are you… joining us?"

"Absolutely not," Gleeko and Justice said in near unison.

Seedo sighed, and her shoulders drooped. "Very good. For a moment—"

"After we discussed Dunamis with her, the Dama said only those directly responsible for Khatash would be taken as we were." Yeego carefully set aside a slate and moved closer. "While we expected Dunamis might send assassins, that never entirely worried us."

"Wise," Aryo said softly, and Yeego laughed.

"Indeed. I did worry, though, that perhaps…"

"We had lied to you?" Justice snorted, and paced the length of the desk. "We had no need."

"We have been lied to by those in power over us before." Yeego shook her hands. "At any rate, that is not the case—the Hunters prove true to us again. You have come here for a reason?"

Aryo walked back toward the door. "Justice will let me know when you are done," she said, turning her head toward them as she moved. "One of us will bring you safely back to your shuttle then. It was a pleasure to see you, Commander, and meet you, Peacemaker. Good luck to… all of you in your search." The Zuul left, and Sansar worked hard not to picture those sucking vines again.

Tald strode forward and restated their mission, giving Sansar the opportunity to closely observe each of the Veetanho's reactions, though to be fair, none of the three had typical Veetanho guarded or seemingly calculated reactions. Preebo gasped, Yeego leaned against a table for support, and Seedo cursed. Gleeko, arms crossed, wrinkled her nose, whiskers flaring.

"I knew of the ships, of course, but not where they were," Yeego said, then held up a hand and continued thoughtfully. "We do have access to all the communications Reequo had while we occupied Khatash. Perhaps there is something in there with some sort of code that we missed."

"I'll help you look." Gleeko replied so quickly, Sansar stepped forward.

"I'd be interested in seeing that, too." The private correspondence of one of Peepo's top lieutenants? Yes, Sansar would absolutely enjoy getting her hands on it. While Peepo was off the board, and the Veetanho would be scrambling for some time, they'd had their hands in a lot of action. Even she might not have known the whole of it, and the more she saw, the more she might be able to piece together of Dunamis' priorities and approach.

"*Keesius* ships can't simply disappear," Preebo said, sounding as sure of herself as any Veetanho ever had. "The Hunters have provided us with all manner of information. Peacemaker, would you care to join us in parsing it?"

"Would—yes, I surely would!" A bit of the affected drawl had returned to Tald's delivery, and he leaped after Seedo and Preebo.

Justice sat and curled his tail around his body, making such a show of studying his claws, Sansar was sure he was positioned to listen to both groupings in the room. Before they got to work, however, he tilted his head and sheathed his claws.

"Sansar Enkh."

"Justice?"

"Why don't you think the SI creature brought the ships back to his stronghold, to Lytoshaan?"

Tald had described their mission clearly and succinctly, but not all of their suppositions and findings to date. That had seemed most efficient to get to the matter at hand, and also somewhat sensitive to the state of the surviving Veetanho on their home world. Though with the Goltar informed, and Dunamis holding grudges, it was only a matter of time before the disaster was well known throughout the galaxy.

"Lytoshaan is no longer his stronghold."

"Oh?" The Depik strung out the word, and the three Khatash-based Veetanho all went very still.

"Dunamis has abandoned the Veetanho," Sansar said clearly. "Lytoshaan is a wreck, and—" she saw interest light up in Justice's eyes, and his ears snapped forward "—the only survivors are the young and those Dunamis wiped clean."

All three of the other Veetanho cursed.

"Oh." Now Justice sounded disappointed. "There is no fun in that hunt."

"The Veetanho as a race have been as set back as your own people were five years ago. And for the same reason—someone wanting control over those they have no business controlling." Sansar frowned, and Justice watched her from the corner of his eye. "I'm not saying the Veetanho had no responsibility for what was done to the Depik, but I'll say those who manage to survive have the same enemy as you."

"The enemy of my enemy is still my enemy," Justice said, repeatedly baring and sheathing his claws. "Perhaps in this case, even more of an enemy." He turned his considering look on Gleeko, who stared back impassively. "By all means, let us take away his claws."

Yeego handed her a slate, and Sansar moved to the edge of the desk Gleeko and Yeego had taken. Close enough to overhear the Veetanho, but hopefully far enough that Gleeko would deal with the built up tension that was causing her ears to twitch.

It took over an hour of mostly silent work, during which Sansar sadly read nothing of true interest, when Gleeko's discipline finally broke.

"How could you?" Gleeko muttered, her words delivered so fast they ran up on each other. "How could you trade one control for another? Are the Depik so different from Dunamis?"

"The Hunters gave us a *choice*," Yeego murmured back, her tone gentle.

"A choice!" Gleeko spit, then ducked her head closer to Yeego's. Sansar eased closer to continue to listen. "Death or further servitude."

"A clean death, or work they'd make us proud of." Yeego huffed a small laugh. "A better deal than we offered them."

"You can't think—"

"Dunamis claimed he worked for the good of the Veetanho, but you must know as well as any that he worked only for his own ends. We were a tool."

"And you are not a tool here?"

"We are appreciated here. The Depik don't steal memories from our brains. They don't promise to enact revenge upon our offspring or our family lines. They do not torture us for *fun*."

"I've seen—"

"They take loyalty very seriously," Yeego said, her voice now at a normal conversational level. "We are loyal. They value that."

"Oh, there are some who would still rather you were dead," Justice called from across the room, his tail waving idly. Sansar had the impression that, like herself, he'd heard more than the last bit of the Veetanho's talk. "But we will not allow it. You three are the safest Veetanho in the universe."

Sansar heard loud and clear which Veetanho in the room was not counted among that number, and knew Gleeko had registered it as well. Only the tips of her ears moved, however, and she slowly pivoted to face Justice.

"Trading freedom for safety, then? That's still no better than what Dunamis forced us into."

"We made a choice." Yeego shrugged and glanced between Gleeko and Justice. "Dunamis promised glory, but it was only ever temporary. The scheming, the backbiting, the clawing over each other for a moment in his regard?" She made a noise deep in her throat. "The Depik offered honesty. Teelo, for example, rejected the offer, and her death was kinder than anything Dunamis has ever offered."

Gleeko clenched her hands into fists, then put visible effort into relaxing herself. "So be it." She lifted her snout and stared at Sansar, who chose the course of wisdom in not contributing, then raised her voice. "Peacemaker? Have you found anything?"

"We've been comparing gate records, registered flight plans, and estimated traffic at automated gates." Tald's enthusiasm was equal to the amount of information he referenced. "Preebo gave me some old colonies that Dunamis may or may not have been interested in once, and Seedo has a theory—"

"At least someone is useful," Gleeko said and strode to Tald's corner of the room.

If that near compliment didn't speak to the level of the Veetanho's disgust in the entire situation, Sansar would eat a starship.

* * *

Ultimately, there was nothing definitive.

Justice recorded a message for Tsan, who knew where the other two of the Depik's five captive Veetanho were, but as he wasn't entirely sure where the Dama herself was, they couldn't wait on its delivery or answer.

"If there is any information you need us to look at, please let us know." Yeego walked with them to the door, her fingers twisting each other worriedly. "I don't think the Hunters will mind our spending time on this, given the enormity of the situation."

"No, I don't believe we will," Justice answered and waved Sansar and her group out of the room. "Alsamt is outside now, if you need anything."

"Oh, good," Preebo said, relief audible in her voice. "Alsamt is excellent company." The slight emphasis on the other Depik's name was as clear as her relief.

Justice waved his tail as he stalked out, and Sansar raised her eyebrows at the tall Veetanho.

"We have been made loyal—" Preebo laughed "—not nice."

"Except for when we *choose* to be," Yeego added, with emphasis of her own.

"Oh, for fuck's sake," Gleeko said and stormed out after Justice.

Tald made polite goodbyes, which Sansar echoed, and the ride back to their shuttle was fairly quiet.

It was full night, though the thick air didn't feel much cooler, and Sansar sat in the middle of her seat in case the vines moved any faster in the darkness. When the cart stopped, Justice held out a hand for them to wait, and jumped out first.

There were lights on in the clearing—not bright as they might be on Earth, but enough to illuminate the mossy vegetation on the ground. Shadows shifted as Justice moved, and Sansar knew instantly it had nothing to do with the wind.

Justice laughed, pulled two knives, and vanished mid-jump. The space he'd previously occupied was instantly filled with a writhing pit of reaching vines.

"Gross," Tald said, fascinated, and put hands on each of his guns. Sansar again wished for a flamethrower, decided against her pistol, given the existence of an invisible friendly out there, and pulled her own long knife in case those grasping tendrils came any closer.

"You keep an eye on that," she said to Tald, and turned the other way. "I don't trust the plants on this planet not to creep up behind us while we're occupied."

"This planet is ridiculous." Gleeko unholstered her gun and took the rear position without being asked. "For all we know, there's something that can drill through the bottom of this cart."

"Uh…" Tald climbed onto his seat and stood there instead of the floor.

"Oh, there is." Justice's voice floated from somewhere between them and the snaky vines. "It lives on the other side of the planet, though. Mostly the city is clear."

"So very reassuring." Gleeko sighed. "I told you we should've brought the big guns."

"You can't shoot it," Tald protested. "You might hit Justice!"

"I hear Depik are very fast. I'm sure he could get out of the way." Gleeko's laugh wasn't nearly so joyful as Justice's had been. "Or grenades. We should stop leaving the ship without grenades."

"I am *not* trusting you with grenades while you're in a mood." Sansar squinted at the tree line. Was something moving?

"A mood?" Gleeko sounded as though she was winding up for a rant, so Sansar cut across her words quickly.

"Do you need us to call for backup, Justice?"

"No!" The vines were reaching in a broader radius, more ground shifting as they grasped for their unseen target. "Want to make sure I draw them all out. Sometimes they wait."

"And they're poisonous, I suppose?"

"Oh, very."

"Yeah." Sansar decided if there was movement in the jungle beyond, she was absolutely going to call for help. Airborne, high firepower-level help.

Something rumbled, and Sansar chanced a glance in her peripheral. A larger shape writhed out of the ground, bulbous and oozing, and Justice made a wordless sound of glee. Vine tentacles spiraled away from the main mass, and it took Sansar a moment to realize they were being separated. The bigger mass burst open into approximately four times as many vines, and Tald made a frustrated sound.

"Can you move to the left? I really want to shoot it."

"Are you a good shot, Peacemaker?"

"Yeah! I really am!"

"On my mark—one, two, mark!"

Sansar kept her peripheral vision on the jungle and turned slightly to watch—and thankfully, Tald *was* an excellent shot. He hit the center of the bulk—evident, given the visible spray of goo that resulted—and the remaining vines flailed.

They also moved closer even more rapidly.

Justice reappeared, slicing with abandon. "Shoot at will!" he called, and the vines split between a focus on him and driving toward the cart.

"I *hate* this planet," Gleeko snarled and turned to fire repeatedly into the approaching mess. Sansar kept her knife handy, and one eye on the jungle, which was fortunate.

A tendril—far thinner than the big vines—crept over the jungle side of the cart, reaching toward Tald. If it hadn't slowed, twitched, and redirected, Sansar might have overlooked it until too late, but as it was, she stabbed downward as it drove toward the Peacemaker.

Success, but its splatter burned against her stabbing hand, and Sansar had to agree with Gleeko—Khatash really did suck. She scrubbed at her skin with her sleeve and allowed herself to wish once more for a flamethrower.

"All clear!" Justice called, and Tald holstered his gun.

"Sansar's hit!" the Peacemaker yelled, and Gleeko cursed unintelligibly.

Justice reappeared in the cart next to Sansar in a blink, his hand hovering over hers. "Oh, good." He heaved out a breath and pulled a small jar out of one of the pockets on his harness. "It wasn't a mature vine."

"Still doesn't feel great." The rubbing hadn't helped, but she watched closely as he spun open the jar and poured a viscous semiliquid onto her skin. He gestured for her to rub it in, and while the relief wasn't instantaneous, it no longer felt like sharp teeth were drilling though each microlayer of her skin, so that was nice.

"You'll need to re-hone your knife, too. But!" There was far too much cheer in the Depik's voice. "You still have your hand. The young vines are more flash than bite."

"Wonderful." Sansar flexed her fingers and decided to keep her knife out until she could wipe it clean. No telling what any remnants would do to the holster. "You said we're clear?"

"We should circle wide to get up to your shuttle, but if nothing else moved during all that, we should be fine." Justice shrugged and leapt back out of the cart, gesturing them to follow.

"Does that happen often?" Tald asked, pausing to regard a severed plant tentacle as they walked.

"Not often. The zelli vine tends to stay further in the jungle, but all the movement of shuttles landing and taking off is bound to pull the attention of something."

"And your whole planet is like this?" He rubbed his cheek and shook his head. "Intense. I think my planet mostly had the grahp and some really sneaky vines. Oh, I guess there was..." Tald trailed off, staring thoughtfully into space, then shrugged. "Still, this seems like a lot."

"It has been quite interesting to experience. The older Hunters tried to prepare us for our return, but I think Khatash is one of those places you have to... experience to truly understand."

"You weren't born here?" Tald stopped short and pulled at his whiskers. "No, sorry, never mind. I heard parts of what happened—I didn't realize you were, um. Young."

Sansar swiveled her hand and held herself back from smiling. Both Tald and Justice seemed incredibly young to her, in the small ways their galaxy allowed anyone to stay young.

"We don't live as long as many other species. I suppose my years are younger to others." Justice shrugged. "Despite its dangers, I find I will miss Khatash while I'm gone."

"Where are you going?" Tald asked innocently, and with a twist in the gut, Sansar knew the answer.

"With you. There are ships to find, and—" Justice turned at the ramp up to the shuttle and gave Gleeko an obvious once over "—enemies to hunt."

* * * * *

Chapter Eight

CO's Office, EMS *Gobi Desert,* Khatash Orbit

"A nother dead end!" Tald exclaimed. "That's all we're getting with this case. One dead end after another."

Sansar smiled. "It's almost as if someone doesn't want us to solve it."

"Why would someone—" Tald stopped and shook his head. "Obviously, Dunamis—or whoever else took the ships—wouldn't want us to find them."

Sansar chuckled. "No they wouldn't, and I imagine this will be a constant theme in your cases, no matter how long you remain a Peacemaker. The people conducting illegal activity probably won't want you to know what they're doing. That'll be a challenge you'll have to face... forever." Sansar smiled. "I may know some people who have dabbled in areas that were... gray, shall we say?"

"Is this something I would disapprove of?" Tald asked.

"I doubt you'd approve, but then again, they're activities beneath the notice of an illustrious Peacemaker; they're more a matter for system police. Still, they went out of their way to cover their tracks so they couldn't be found."

"And prosecuted."

Sansar nodded. "That most of all."

"So how do we find the ships?" Tald said.

"I don't know. What did they teach you in all that time at the Academy? Pretend the ships are the perpetrator of a crime. How would you find them when they don't want to be found?"

"I'd try to identify known associates or people they've interacted with in the past." He shrugged. "I doubt they have any family we can contact."

"Maybe… and maybe not."

"What family do ships have?"

"I wasn't thinking about the ships, but the people involved. I might know how to find an SI."

"Really?" Tald said. "I've never seen an SI. Can we go see it now?"

"No, that would probably be a bad idea, since he told me to never look for him again."

"Then why did you suggest it?"

"It was a thought… a last resort. A *really* last resort, like once we completely run out of options."

"But we *have* run out of options."

"No, we haven't. I asked you the question about following leads for a reason. There's one more planet I'm aware of with connections to the Veetanho."

Gleeko's ears rose. "And what might that be?"

"Yeah," Tald added. "Why haven't you mentioned it before?"

"Because it probably wouldn't be somewhere Dunamis would take the ships; it's too well known."

"Well known?" Gleeko scoffed. "If it's so well known, how come none of us know what you're talking about? Maybe this planet is a fallback spot for Dunamis."

Sansar shook her head. "That is unlikely."

"Stop beating around the bush, as you Humans say. What are you talking about?"

Sansar chuckled. "It's unlikely to be Dunamis' refuge because Humans—at least a few of us—know where it is and what it is." She shrugged. "Or at least we did. There's no telling what it's doing now. It's a Veetanho planet, but not one Dunamis would use, I don't think, even as a trap. Since we're down to final options, though, it's time to mention it." She sighed. "I'd rather go there than try to find and talk to another SI. The one at the end of this chase is probably going to be enough for me."

"So what's the deal with this planet?" Tald asked.

"Yes," Gleeko said, "tell us. I've become quite curious."

"The name of the planet is Hades; at least that's what the Lyoness called it. That's where Peepo held her for… many years."

"Oh," Justice said from his draped position on Sansar's table. "Hades. I've been there."

"You've been there?" Gleeko turned to the Depik and frowned. "You. Have been there?"

"That is what 'I've been there' generally means, Veetanho." He blinked at her, and not in the friendly way that meant a smile. Tald could definitely tell the difference. "Didn't you know of it?"

"Hades?" Gleeko sighed and shook her head. "I've never heard it named before."

"But you are aware of the planet?"

"I'm aware there was a prison planet. Rumors have abounded for… well, forever."

Tald crossed his arms and twitched his whiskers. "Why would the Veetanho or Dunamis need a prison world? Why wouldn't they just kill the people they don't like? Or have Dunamis mind-wipe them? Or something?"

Gleeko chuckled as she got up and walked to the door. "You forget the first point of dealing with Dunamis."

"Which is?"

"Even though he's an SI, and you might think him free from emotion, that's not the case. He has many emotions. Anger and pride are two that may ultimately be his undoing, but he has at least one more—he's more vindictive than any being I've ever met. Hades existed—or still exists—as a place no one comes back from. It's a place of eternal torture."

* * *

"You seem to know a lot about Hades," Tald said after Gleeko left, followed momentarily by Justice. The Peacemaker had to assume there wouldn't be bloodshed—if the two hadn't come to violence yet, they probably wouldn't. He was pretty sure.

"I do," Sansar said. "More than I want to, actually." She closed her eyes for a moment, and Tald steeled himself to patience, remembering one of his instructors' mantras: when possible, let the subject tell the story in their own time. It'll be more complete that way.

He'd always had a problem with that tenet; waiting was just *so* hard sometimes.

Finally—although it wasn't more than probably thirty seconds—Sansar opened her eyes. "What do you know about the rescue of the Lyoness?"

"I… uh… nothing. Was it from a Veetanho zoo?"

"A zoo? What?" Sansar's brows knit, then she laughed. "No, not a real lioness—like a female lion—but *the* Lyoness, the wife of Joel Lyons, who owns the Lyon's Den. Well, both of them now, I guess."

Tald's face scrunched up. "Are you still speaking English? It seems like you are, but I don't understand a word of what you're saying."

Sansar sighed. "Okay, let me back up. There's a man whose name is Joel Lyons. He refers to himself as 'the Lyon.'"

"Got it," Tald said with a nod.

"He runs a bar in Houston for mercs called The Lyon's Den. He's also got a merc pit he's building on Karma Station with a similar name."

"Okay."

"Since he's 'the Lyon,' his wife is 'the Lyoness.'"

"That makes sense."

"Great," Sansar said. "In any event, almost sixty years ago, he was a merc."

"So he's old now?"

"Well, no."

"But he must be eighty or ninety years old. Isn't that old for a Human?"

"Well, yes, for most people."

"But he isn't like most people?"

Sansar opened her mouth, but then paused. Finally, she sighed. "His age isn't important." When Tald's mouth opened, Sansar held up a hand. "He got a longevity potion from Peepo, which let him stay younger, longer, *but it's not important!*"

"Fine," Tald said. He looked down. "I was just curious…"

"It's good to be curious," Sansar said, "especially for a Peacemaker, but when I say it's not important to the story, let me move on, or we'll be here all day."

"We still have another day to get to the gate, then a week in hyperspace…"

"And I have things to do in that time. Running a merc company is *hard*."

"Well, yes, but—"

Sansar held up a hand. "If I could continue?" Tald opened his mouth, but then shut it and nodded. "Okay, so while they were on a merc contract, the Lyon was disrespectful to Peepo."

"That doesn't sound like something smart to do, based on her reputation."

"No, it wasn't, but sometimes the Lyon lets his pride get the best of him. This was one of those cases."

"So what did Peepo do?"

"She wiped out most of his company, captured the Lyoness and his daughter, and imprisoned them on Hades."

"Why didn't she just kill them all, including the Lyon?"

"Because the Lyon had a Depik favor token."

"What's that?"

Sansar sighed. "You really don't get out much, do you?"

"What does that mean?"

Sansar shook her head, unwilling to get drawn down one more rabbit hole. She was already up to her ears in about three of them so far, and she really *did* have things to do.

"A favor token lets you request a favor from a Depik. In this case, he asked the Depik to kill Peepo if he died."

"I see," Tald said, nodding. "So she couldn't kill him; in fact, it was in her best interest to keep him alive."

"Exactly."

"But the Depik don't live very long, Justice said. So couldn't she just wait it out?"

"It's a clan obligation. If the original Depik couldn't hold it, the favor passed down to the next generation."

"Ohhh, so she *couldn't* wait it out. That's why she gave him the potion to make him live longer, so that *she* could live longer."

Sansar nodded, looking impressed with his reasoning, encouraging him to continue. "And that was more than likely part of the reason—or even a major reason—Peepo and Dunamis tried to wipe out the Depik."

"What?" Sansar asked, her eyebrows knitting.

"Well, sure. If there were no more Depik, Peepo could kill Joel and not have to worry about being assassinated in turn."

"Huh." Sansar said. "I never thought of it that way. You may be right."

"There may be other reasons," Tald replied, rubbing a claw across his chin, "but that's certainly the most obvious. Occam's Razor, as you said." He shrugged. "Though with the elimination of the Depik, Peepo would probably have captured him and taken him to Hades, too."

He looked up to find Sansar staring at him with her mouth open. "What?" he asked.

Sansar closed her mouth and shook her head quickly a couple of times. "How did you work that all the way through?"

"Peacemaker School. They teach us deductive thinking."

"I see." Sansar looked at him for a few seconds and then chuckled. "In any event, things didn't work out the way Peepo thought they would, and the Depik killed her after she caused most of their population to commit suicide. When that happened, Joel used a second favor token—"

"How many of these things does he have? Can he use one to have the Depik find the ships for us?"

"To try to close off this line of questioning before it starts, I think he's used all his coins. Also, despite the fact that he had two, they're really rare, and I don't know where we can get another one. And finally, we don't need one in any event, as we already have a Depik—Justice—along with us."

Tald thought for a moment, then smiled. "You'd make a good investigator."

"Thanks," Sansar replied. "It's from a life in intel, I think. So, anyway, Joel got the Depik to find Hades and help him assault it, which they did, and they rescued the Lyoness."

"Okay, so where does that leave us?"

"What…" Sansar's eyebrows knit. "What do you mean?"

"Why did you tell me all that? You have a point, right?"

"But I… you…" Sansar spluttered for a few seconds, not making sense again, and Tald cocked his head at her and waited.

Finally, Sansar closed her mouth, set her shoulders, and continued, although Tald didn't understand the new edge to her tone. Angry, or maybe frustrated somehow, but he didn't understand why that would be. She'd been the one to sidetrack the conversation for five minutes, not him, even though she'd complained she had things to do.

"When the Lyon left Hades, he left the inmates in charge of the remaining Veetanho jailors." She held up a hand. "I don't know why he did it." She shrugged. "There weren't many Veetanho left when he departed, as the Depik killed all the ones they found while infiltrating, so I don't know how many—if any—will have survived until now. I went by there and dropped off some supplies the Lyon sent them, but the folks who still remained there didn't want to leave."

Sansar shrugged. "I couldn't imagine staying there any longer than I had to, but they weren't done yet, or so they said. No, I don't know what they meant, and I didn't ask. We just dropped off the supplies and left. They had a ship in-system, so I guess they could've gone for their own supplies, but maybe the Lyon owed them something. I don't know."

"Okay, so that explains how you know about Hades, and why you only know a little about it. We'll find out the status of Hades in general and its Veetanho prisoners specifically when we arrive, I guess."

Sansar nodded. "Correct."

"That's it, then," Tald said, getting up and going to the door. He tapped two fingers to the tip of his hat. "Thanks for the info, ma'am."

"Anything else?"

"I think that'll be it for now. Don't leave town without letting me know."

* * * * *

Chapter Nine

CIC, EMS *Gobi Desert*, Hades System

"Emergence into the Hades system," the helmsman reported. "Damn, we're close to the star."

"Ensure full power to the shields," Parker ordered. "Move us into the planet's shadow, 1.5 Gs. Drones out."

"Shields are at full power."

"Drones are out," the sensor operator announced, "but they won't last long."

"Just give me a quick peek, then bring them back, please."

"How does anything live on that thing?" Tald asked, peering at the readings. Hades was even closer to its sun than the ship was, and the *Gobi Desert* was deploying all its tools to keep them shielded. Certainly there couldn't be friendly seas like the SalSha had come from, nor even unfriendly waters like Khatash had.

"It doesn't—the prison's tunneled deep inside." Justice's voice came from over Tald's left shoulder, though, as was often the case, the Hunter himself was nowhere to be seen.

"I understand that." He did, mostly, though Justice's description of the sheer number of tunnels and scurry holes had boggled him. "But wouldn't it still get hot? Or... too cold?"

"That's part of why we had to be careful the first time we came here." Justice reappeared—out of the way by only the strictest sense, as he'd draped himself over the back of one of the crew members' chairs. "The life support was three separate systems tied into all the other systems, so when we interrupted one system, we had to be very sure we weren't about to trip life support." He rolled to his side, flicking his tail idly. "Veetanho do love their little traps."

"We get in by flying into a hole in the planet." Tald didn't mean it as a question—he'd heard the details at least three times, but he kept getting distracted, thinking about the practicalities of living beings existing *under* a planet completely hostile to life.

"The Veetanho built one corridor to the surface, sized for a shuttle or dropship. They kept one ship in it, rigged to self-destruct in any number of ways, and there was absolutely no other way anyone could survive escaping, because the planet itself would burn them to a crisp. No species is built for those levels of heat, even if they are able to survive the radiation longer than a few minutes."

"The Veetanho in charge probably liked having the one ship there, for prisoners to feel that there was a way out, if only they could figure it out. Even though it was impossible." Tald chewed on the inside of his cheek. That was truly what had sent his thoughts wandering every time they talked about Hades. The cruelty inherent in it baffled him.

"I doubt you're wrong," Justice replied.

Tald nodded, deciding to let the conversation ebb while Justice was still playing nice. The Hunter got spiky quickly, and not always for a reason Tald could parse. Instead, the Peacemaker considered the planet and former prison ahead of them while the drones collected data and transferred it back. Super-hot planet too close to its star, check. One once-guarded tunnel they'd fly into. Hundreds of tunnels, maybe more—they hadn't been thoroughly mapped by Justice's group, and the last time Sansar had come here, they hadn't stopped long enough to talk mapping with the people who'd still lived there. There was a central shaft that went down to potentially the lowest level, but so many side tunnels and branching paths existed, it was hard to say what 'lowest' meant.

Maybe the prison went all the way to the planet's core… Tald wrinkled his nose and decided against it. That would get hot all over again, which would defeat the Veetanho's purpose. He opened his mouth, willing to risk Justice's uncertain temperament again to ask about the different systems, when the computer made a series of noises.

"I've got two ships in the planet's shadow," the sensor operator announced after reading over the new data. "One is the small transport that was here the last time we were here; the other is the EMS *Oskar Schindler*."

"I'm not sure I know that one," Parker said.

"It's a Winged Hussars cutter, I think," Sansar said, "but I don't have any idea why it would be here."

* * *

"The *Oskar Schindler* is calling us," the comms officer announced as the *Gobi Desert* approached the planet a few hours later. "A Captain Graybel. He's the ship's commanding officer."

"On the main screen," Parker said.

The main Tri-V switched from the tactical picture to the CIC of the much smaller cutter. Only two people were visible—the ship's captain in the background, and a Pendal who stood in the foreground. The alien's face was hard to see; the hood of the brown robe he was wearing covered most of his face, and the rest of it was in shadow.

"I am glad to see you," the Pendal said without any introduction. He turned partially toward the captain then back. "Captain Graybel would not have allowed us to linger much longer."

"Got a schedule to keep, damn it," Graybel said. "Sittin' here doesn't pay the bills."

"How did you know to find us here?" Sansar asked. She had long thought the race able to use some sort of psychic abilities, although she was yet to prove it or get any of them to admit it.

The Pendal made a noise like steam leaking—his species' form of laughter. "There were not many choices. We went to Lytoshaan, but you had already left."

"Damn waste of time, that," Graybel added. "Wouldn't this be a great conversation to have in person, so the *Schindler* can try to make up some lost time?"

Sansar chuckled. "It seems your CO is anxious to be underway." She turned to Captain Parker. "Can we get a shuttle over to pick him up?"

"Right away, Colonel."

* * *

CO's Conference Room, EMS *Gobi Desert*, Hades System

"Welcome, Josiff," Sansar said, directing the Pendal to a chair. Parker had let her use his conference room, and Sansar, Gleeko, Justice, and Tald were waiting when he arrived. Sansar thought Justice was present, but he'd gone invisible, probably to fuck with Gleeko. For her part, Gleeko sat back in her chair, looking bored, not like someone with an invisible assassin that hated her nearby. Sansar had no idea how she did it. "Glad you could track us down."

"Thank you," the Pendal replied with a slight bow, his voice little more than a whisper everyone around the table had to lean forward to hear. "As I was saying, though, there really wasn't anywhere else you were likely to go."

"Why is that?"

The Pendal shrugged. "We knew your original destination was Lytoshaan, which is why we went there first. Failing to catch you there, I knew you could have gone to one of only two places—Hades or Khatash."

"We did indeed go to Khatash first," Sansar admitted. "We picked up another member of our search team there, although Justice seems to be more interested in petty rivalries at the moment."

Justice materialized on the table in front of Gleeko, leaning over like he was going to slit the Veetanho's throat. "Oh, hi," Justice said, turning away from Gleeko without an ounce of shame. "Welcome to our negotiation."

"What are we negotiating, Hunter?" Josiff asked.

The Depik shrugged. "Nothing at the moment, but the Veetanho's life is always fun to discuss."

"*Justice!*" Sansar exclaimed. "Tsan told me you'd be professional."

"I wasn't *really* going to kill her. I was just practicing sneaking up on her. For later. Sometime. You never know when it might become handy. She *is* a Veetanho, after all."

"Stop." Sansar pointed to the other side of the table, and Justice strutted over to it and laid down. After a second, the Depik went invisible again.

Sansar shook her head and turned back to Josiff. "You were saying?"

"I knew you wouldn't go to one of the other Veetanho planets; you'd go to where there were Veetanho held captive you could question. Hades or Khatash. I came here because I thought you'd start with the Veetanho who hadn't been... altered."

"Isn't part of the issue that they've all been altered, one way or another?" Justice asked lazily from his blank spot.

Josiff nodded from the depths of his hood. "It is. That is what makes dealing with SIs... challenging."

"Well, on the good side," Sansar said, "we've been in contact with the planet, and it doesn't appear Dunamis came here."

"That's a good thing?" Tald asked. "I'd think finding Dunamis would lead us to the missing ships."

"Perhaps," Josiff said, then he whipped a knife out from the fold of his robe to a point on the table in front of him.

Justice appeared, no more than a hair beyond the point of the knife, his hands almost the same distance from the hood of the Pendal. Justice slow-blinked, then he sat back, his action controlled, and cocked his head. "How did you do that?"

"I do not know," Josiff said. "You are... different somehow than the other Hunters I have met, although it has been a while since I was around one of you."

"Interesting," Justice said. He went back to his spot on the table.

"Hunter?" Josiff asked.

"Yes?" Justice asked as he curled up.

"No one touches the hood. That is non-negotiable."

Justice vanished without a word.

"If we're all done playing around, could we get to the business at hand?" Sansar asked.

"You asked whether finding Dunamis was a good thing," Josiff said, turning toward Tald. "That is a question with no easy answer. I suspect finding him will lead to the ships, but finding him causes other issues."

Tald's ears perked up. "Like what?"

"The key point is this group is unprepared for his power. He will have surrounded himself with minions who will give their lives—willingly or not—to protect his. They will know everything Dunamis knows of warfare, whether that's hand-to-hand, lasers at a distance, or a ship-borne missile duel. His control is absolute as I am sure Gleeko has told you."

"I have," the Veetanho said, "although I'm not sure they actually grasp the depths of what we're telling them."

"I do," Sansar said. "I've seen my own people turned against me, laughing while they attacked their friends and brothers. I know what we're getting into."

"So you have a plan for dealing with Dunamis?" Josiff asked.

"Not yet, but I've dealt with several of his kind. When we find him, we'll address it, even if that means fleeing and coming back with a Winged Hussars fleet. We—the Four Horsemen—have been looking for several of the SIs with the intention of killing them when we find them; I know we'll be able to enlist Alexis Cromwell to our cause."

Josiff laughed. "Have you actually killed any of them?"

"We've killed a number of them." Sansar sighed. "Sadly, however, they've all had backup copies of themselves they activated after we killed their primary personas. We may have killed the Merchant Guild SI for good—Blue Sky knows we've killed enough of his copies—but we can't confirm that even he has lost his last copy."

"And that is the problem with the SIs. If you should happen to kill one, you now must face a backup copy who will be out to get you. They have millennia of experience, nearly inexhaustible resources, and the time to wait you out." Josiff shook his head. "We would do well to avoid making Dunamis our enemy."

"We have to acquire the *Keesius* ships," Tald said. "That is our mission."

"Must we?" Josiff asked. "I was given to understand you mission was to *find* them, not recover them."

"I don't think we can leave them with Dunamis," Sansar said. "Not only is an SI too capricious to be left with them, it destabilizes the détente between the Veetanho and the Goltar."

"Capricious." Josiff laughed and turned toward Sansar. "A good description. However, one need not be capricious to destroy a planet or a star system."

"True," Sansar said flatly. *And that's as far as we need to go down that road.*

Josiff shrugged, the movement obvious through his robe. "I only bring that up as a potential solution to the problem of—what do we do if we find the SI firmly entrenched within a system."

Tald cocked his head. "Are you saying, should we find the SI in a system where we can't get to him, we should destroy the system—including all the people the SI has in thrall—rather than letting it escape?"

"I'm saying it is an option," Josiff said, "and probably a good one."

"But all those people? Most would be innocent. There might be women and children."

Josiff nodded. "We would be killing them, yes, but we would also be saving all the others the SI would kill if we let him go."

"Makes sense to me," Gleeko said. "As a former thrall of Dunamis, I admit, there were a number of times I wished someone would kill me to end my bondage. We couldn't kill ourselves, of course; Dunamis forbade it." She shook her head. "He, however, would often kill dozens just to make a point."

Justice appeared. "Destroying star systems? I'm with the Veetanho on this. Sounds like fun, especially if they're Veetanho systems. How do we go about doing it?"

"No!" Tald said, his voice screechy. "I forbid it."

"Stop," Sansar said. "This topic is counterproductive. As I said, we'll decide what needs to be done once we find Dunamis. *If* we find Dunamis. We've been looking for the SIs for years and haven't found them; the odds that we'll find him now are minuscule. We'll be more likely to find the three *Keesius* ships—which is, after all, our mission—since they're much harder to hide. If Dunamis—or any of the SIs—is there with them, we'll deal with them, just like we'll deal with whoever is holding them. Right now, we have one transport; we're not going barreling in anywhere."

"That is a good way to approach this," Josiff said. "I doubt we will find anything on the planet—"

"Then why are you here?" Tald asked.

"For the same reason you are, Peacemaker. I am sure they teach you to investigate every shred of evidence and to run down every clue. There is a possibility we will find something on the planet, but the odds—especially since several years have passed since the Veetanho were in charge—are low."

* * * * *

Chapter Ten

Cargo Entrance, Prison Complex, Hades, Hades System

Sansar was met by a motley crew of ex-prisoners as she stepped off the shuttle, led by an Equiri, a member of a race that looked like bipedal horses. "Hello, Hyrea," she said. "It's nice to finally meet you in person." She motioned over her shoulder. "These are Gleeko, Tald, and Josiff. We also have a Hunter with us, should you need his services."

"Greetings," the Equiri said, sketching a small bow. His eyes scanned the group behind Sansar and widened slightly when he saw the Veetanho. He nodded toward Gleeko, and his lips pulled back from his teeth, reminding Sansar that—although they looked like Earth herbivores—the Equiri were carnivorous in nature. "Is that one being left here... for us?"

"No," Justice said. He appeared at the feet of the Equiri, and Hyrea jumped backward from the unexpected presence. "Sansar says we're not allowed to play with the Veetanho," Justice continued. "I have first dibs, though, once the prohibition's lifted."

"I saw your work the last time you were here, Hunter," Hyrea said. He waved to the Human and elSha standing next to him. "Giving her to you first means there's nothing left for the rest of us."

"You'll have to find your own, then, I guess; I've already claimed this one."

The Equiri shrugged. "So be it." He looked up to Sansar. "This is obviously more than just a supply drop for us."

"It is," Sansar said, "and I'm sorry to say, we had to give away most of the supplies we had for you. We had an emergency on the way. Although we replenished what we could at Khatash, they don't produce much in the way of food that can be exported."

"An emergency? Hopefully your people are all right."

"My people are fine. Gleeko's people, however, are not."

"I'd like to say I'm sorry to hear that," Hyrea said, "but that would, in fact, be a lie. I'd enjoy hearing about this emergency that hurt them so."

"I know they have much to atone for in your eyes, but I believe what's happened to them more than rights the scales." Sansar related what they'd seen at Lytoshaan.

"They have other planets." Hyrea shrugged his massive shoulders. "Do you know what I call the devastation of Lytoshaan?"

"A tragedy?"

Hyrea scoffed. "No. I'd call killing everyone on Lytoshaan nothing more than a good start."

"Careful, Equiri," Gleeko said. "I lost a lot of kin when Dunamis left, and I've heard about enough from both you and Justice. You want to revel in our loss? That's fine, but do it where I can't hear it, or you'll have me to deal with."

"A single Veetanho with no assistance from her master?" Hyrea laughed. "I'll take my chances."

Justice tapped on the Equiri's shin. "She's mine. If you kill her, I'll be forced to look for a new plaything." He slow-blinked. "I should hate to have to turn my attention to someone… else."

The Equiri shuddered, the tremor going from head to foot. Sansar couldn't remember ever seeing an Equiri shudder before. Whatever Justice had done to the Veetanho on his last trip to Hades must have been… memorable.

"If we've all finished threatening each other," Tald said, dusting off his Peacemaker badge and reattaching it to his vest, "we do have a mission here, and time is of the essence."

"A Peacemaker? In one so small?" The Equiri was so surprised, he took a couple of steps backward. "What is it you require, Peacemaker? I would love to help you beat it out of the prisoners."

Tald cleared his throat. "I don't need to beat anyone or otherwise torture them—"

"Disappointing," Hyrea opined.

"—but I would like to talk to any Veetanho who are still here."

"Anything in particular? I think we still have a few here who might be able to answer questions. We've been using them to clear out all the traps they had here."

"The more senior, the better, I think," Tald said. "If they're too junior, they probably won't have the info we're looking for."

"I don't know that we'll be able to help you much, then." The Equiri shook his head. "Most of the senior Veetanho were killed or killed themselves during the rescue operation. The ones who survived were generally younger and less likely to have abused any of the prisoners too much."

"I would also like access to the station's computers," Josiff said.

"We haven't been able to do much with them," Hyrea admitted. "Most of the secure systems required passwords known only to the senior Veetanho. With all of them dead…"

Josiff chuckled. "I am not without skills in this area. If perhaps I might have a look, it is possible I could have some success where others failed."

"Certainly." Hyrea motioned to the Human next to him. The man was of medium height and looked more like a biker than a CASPer pilot. "Lawrence can show you where they are."

Lawrence nodded. "If you'd come with me?"

Josiff joined him, and the two left.

"Is there anything else you need from me?" Hyrea asked.

"Not that I'm aware of," Tald said. "Just access to the Veetanho prisoners and a place to interview them."

Hyrea motioned to the elSha. "Teelo will be happy to set you up."

"Thank you," Tald said.

Sansar nodded. "Yes, thanks a lot. Will you be available during our stay?"

"I will," Hyrea replied, "although I have a lot of work to do. If you didn't bring the normal allotment of supplies, we'll need to accelerate our plans. We were looking forward to leaving this hell-hole once and for all; now it looks like we're going to need to leave it sooner rather than later."

* * *

Administration, Prison Complex, Hades, Hades System

Lawrence led Josiff through a number of tunnels, then they finally arrived in a room with a number of computer systems in it. He pointed to one of the terminals. "That one works as well as any of the others."

"Thank you," Josiff said. He initiated the boot process and looked at the Human. "Your name is Lawrence?"

"It is."

"Got a last name?"

"I'm sure I did at some point. I've been here so long, though…" The Human shrugged. "I don't remember what it was."

Josiff looked at the Human long enough that the man grew uncomfortable, and he looked away. While the Human probably thought he was trying to determine the veracity of his last answer, Josiff was looking deeper, but despite his best efforts, he didn't find what he was looking for. The man had no criminal intent Josiff could determine. He didn't seem like a murderer or… or anything. Unlike most Human criminals, he seemed to have no ill will toward anyone and no malice toward anything. *What is he doing here?*

"You were here as a prisoner, right?"

"Yeah." The man shifted his weight back and forth, and it didn't take a psychic to see he was ill at ease.

"Aren't you excited to be leaving? To regain your freedom?"

"I guess."

"You guess? How long have you been held here?"

"When did the Buma show up at Earth?"

"Just over a hundred years ago."

"A little less than that."

"You were part of the Human Alpha Contracts?"

"What are they?"

"They were the first hundred contracts Human mercs took. Only four companies returned from that."

"Oh." Lawrence sighed. "Yeah. In that case, I guess I was in one of the 96."

"So I take it the contract went poorly?"

Lawrence nodded. "We got our asses kicked so badly... we thought we were ready, but we weren't. It was almost as if the Veetanho knew our chain of command. I can still see it. Battle was joined, and someone sniped our CO. The XO made one transmission, and someone got him, too. Then the ops officer, then maintenance, then the rest of the officers. Then the senior enlisted. Before we knew it, there were about twenty of us left, out of ammo and surrounded. The Veetanho called for our surrender, so we did."

"And they locked you up here?"

"Oh, no. They took us back to one of their planets and separated us into four groups. The other three groups left, and I never saw any of those guys again. We went to some general's staff and became his servants. The general—Teebo, and yeah, it's bullshit that I remember hers clear as can be but not my own—had a staff of servants from all the races she'd conquered. There were only a couple of us left by then, and they did something to our brains to make us follow orders. Whatever Teebo said, we had to do. If we didn't, the pain was awful."

Lawrence's eyes glazed over as he got lost in remembrance.

"Why did they lock you up, though? If you had to do everything you were told?"

The Human chuckled. "Apparently our programming was incomplete. Although the geas to do what we were told couldn't be ignored, there were no second-order-level commands. Maybe they didn't have experience with Humans? I don't know. The other races, though, they couldn't act in a manner the Veetanho wouldn't have liked. They couldn't. They'd been completely programmed to function as the perfect servitors."

Lawrence smiled. "We weren't. We could do whatever we wanted, as long as it didn't conflict with the orders we'd been given. So me and my buddy Fitz, we began doing things to fuck with the Veetanho. Things they wouldn't notice, but we'd laugh about later."

"And you got caught."

"Fitz got caught." The man shook his head and sighed. "Our pranks got bigger and bigger, until we challenged each other to do the worst thing we could think of to the Veetanho. There was a type of vermin that got into the Veets' fur. While it was in the larval stage, it made them itch worse'n chiggers." Lawrence looked at Josiff. "Ever gotten bit by a chigger?"

"Can't say that I have."

"Nasty buggers. They have a bite that makes you itch for about a week, and nothing you put on it makes it better." Lawrence chuckled. "The Veets have something similar, but the itching lasts for *two* weeks, and they were *miserable* the entire time. It was fun to watch. Anyway, Fitz found some of these insects and raised them. He'd let them bite him and everything so they could grow."

"Did they itch?"

"Yeah, but their bite didn't bother us as much. It was more like a mosquito bite. He raised a bunch of them and was ready with them. The day of the challenge, he let them go. If we'd known the trouble it would cause..." Lawrence smiled. "Hell, we'd still have done it to see all those Veetanho so miserable..." He shrugged. "Totally worth it."

"But you got caught."

"Fitz did, like I said. As it turned out, the mind programming thing that was used on us could force us to answer questions. They asked me if I knew who'd done it, and I was forced to tell them.

They shot him right then. But me—they wanted to send a message to slaves not to do shit like that, so they sent me here to suffer forever. They have some sort of potion that increases Human longevity that they used on me so I could live longer... be tortured longer."

Lawrence sighed. "Still, totally worth it."

"Did they ask you about your prank?"

"Nope. They were so mad about Fitz's, they never thought to ask if I'd done anything. Just knowing about Fitz's prank was enough to get me sent here."

"So what did you do?"

Lawrence smiled. "As it turns out, the Veets love sweets, and for breakfast, they liked these things that were a lot like our donuts. Every morning, they'd make me carry hundreds of sheets of these donut things from the bakery to their mess hall. I grew to hate the damn things."

"So you..."

"Just like our donuts back home, the Veets' donuts had a variety of toppings and fillings. The day of the challenge, I filled a bunch of their donuts with foreign substances. Dumped things in their glaze sauce and into their vats of fillings. The grossest things I could think of. I got to watch the Veets eat them, and it was absolutely worth it. About the time they were done, that's when the itching started, and all hell broke loose. Before I knew it, I was here... and here is where I've been ever since, for over a hundred years.

"You asked me if I'm happy to go home. I've been here so long, everyone I knew is dead. All their kids are likely dead, too. Society's changed. Hell, *war* has changed. I've heard we're now using these giant mech things. CASPers, I think they're called?"

"Correct. There are a number of them on the *Gobi Desert*. They are quite awesome to behold."

Lawrence shrugged. "How is a machine gunner supposed to compete with that? Where am I going to go? What am I going to do?" He sighed. "I guess I want to see Earth again, but I have no idea what I'm going to do."

"At least you have a people to go home to," Josiff muttered. He focused his attention back on the monitor as it came to life. "Now, where do we begin…"

* * *

"How many Veetanho did you find after we left?" Justice asked the elSha as they walked down a long, twisting hallway.

"More than we expected." Teelo kept glancing sidelong at Tald as they walked, and Tald rubbed the backs of his ears. Was it because they were both Sha? Or was Teelo like half the other Peacemaker candidates Tald had met, sure Tald and his people weren't truly Sha?

He grumbled to himself and shoved the thought away. Teelo was probably staring at the device Sansar carried, though it was inside her pack. Tald had decided he did *not* like the interior of Hades any more than he would've enjoyed its surface. Being deep underground was, in fact, different from being on a ship, and Tald had decided he'd rather do without it.

"Did it take long to root them out?" The Hunter sounded wistful there, and Gleeko made a noise that sounded both like clearing her throat and some sort of curse. Tald shot a glance at her, but as usual, her expression gave nothing away.

The lights were dim enough that she could have taken off her goggles—it had been made by and set for Veetanho, after all. Teelo had explained that the brightness was hardwired, not something they'd been able to tweak, and he also admitted he hadn't tried very hard. Most of them had been there so long, their eyes were fully adjusted to the existing light saturation, and finding anything else that would have worked for all the disparate species seemed an effort they didn't need to waste time on.

"Most within weeks. We found two holdouts a month later, and a last one three months later." Teelo sighed and patted the top of his smooth head. "Then we found one more almost five months later, very recently dead. We don't know how she lasted so long, what she did, or how she died, but that was a while ago now, so..." He shrugged and glanced at Tald again.

"So how many have you kept?" Gleeko asked, her tone dripping with distaste. Tald guessed that emotion was about the former prisoners keeping Veetanho imprisoned, but it could have equally been for what her fellow species members had done—he hadn't entirely figured her out yet. He would, of that he was certain. Even Veetanho couldn't be *that* mysterious, he was sure.

Teelo didn't so much as glance at her; he only lifted his shoulders and kept walking. "Enough of them. Though like Hyrea said, we're not sure they'll know what you hope they will."

"At worst, we'll clear them of Dunamis' control, make them a little more cooperative."

"Though I suppose that last depends on how you've been treating them since you took over," Gleeko said, with what Tald was pretty sure was sarcasm.

"Better than their bosses treated us, I can tell you that." Teelo breathed in sharply, making a sound like a snort. "You want 'em one at a time, get a couple at once to play off each other, what?" He gestured to a turn-off and stopped walking.

"How many are down this way?" Sansar asked, shrugging her pack down one arm and flipping it open. "Not 'more' or 'some,' give me an actual number, please."

"Ten," Teelo said after a moment, eyes intent on Sansar's hands.

Sansar pressed something, studied her device, and then nodded. She twisted a dial, and a moment later a high shriek echoed down from the side tunnel.

"I would have liked to use that as part of the negotiation," Justice murmured, but Sansar waved it off.

"Trust that it's better for them not to see the possibility coming. SIs leave all sorts of nasty surprises behind if there's a chance they're about to lose their cogs."

"Of course you'd think it proper to bargain with someone's freedom of mind." Gleeko sniffed, and Justice whirled on her.

"Oh, and a Veetanho is one to talk," he growled, even as Teelo spat at the ground and stared at Tald again.

"What!" Tald burst out, annoyed that Justice and Gleeko were sniping at each other again, and more unsettled that Teelo kept eyeballing him.

"Peacemaker?" Teelo asked, finally blinking.

"You keep... *looking* at me!" Tald polished his badge with the back of his hand. "Why? What?"

"Oh!" Teelo jumped, glanced around, and backed toward the open tunnel mouth. "You're a Peacemaker? I... I was wondering if you were here because of how we might have treated the Veetanho.

Or how they treated us. Now that people... now that Hades is known."

Tald gaped at him.

"I know you have another mission, but I thought... I thought maybe... someone cared. About what happened here?"

Oh. Tald controlled his breathing and held his whiskers still with a maximum of pure determination. "I only... I'm on a different mission. I discovered Hades in pursuit of that mission. I don't think... I'll make a report back to the capital if that's what you all want. So the Peacemakers know formally about what's... what happened here."

"Let's talk to them one at a time," Sansar said, jumping back to Teelo's previous question and distracting the two Sha blinking at each other, and the Hunter and Veetanho glaring at each other. "I don't think putting them in groups will do any of us any favors."

Tald had a feeling she didn't mean that just for the Veetanho prisoners.

* * *

The first three interviews started with shaky, off-balance Veetanho, and ended with little else learned. The fourth got slightly more interesting.

"You!" the Veetanho said, pointing at Justice and snarling.

"Me," Justice replied, then stretched and flipped his tail.

"What about him?" Tald asked, staring at the Veetanho's wildly vibrating ears and whiskers in fascination.

"You—he—you killed Geeto. I know it was you! I saw the whole thing!"

Justice shrugged. "We're not here about what I did. We're here about what you know."

"How did you see it? If you'd been nearby…" Teelo had been silent throughout the last interviews, but now he stepped forward, his tail high.

"The backup control room," the Veetanho growled, then slammed her mouth shut as her eyes widened.

"There's a backup…?" Teelo eased back out of the cell and tapped his comms, apparently passing that on to his fellow former prisoners.

"I couldn't… I couldn't talk about it before." The Veetanho worked her jaw, said a few nonsense words, and then laughed for several uncomfortable minutes.

"Where is the backup control room?" Teelo reentered the room and moved closer to the prisoner.

"It doesn't matter," the Veetanho said, still laughing in between words. "One of the things you cracked monsters did burned all the links in there, so all I could do was watch. Then a few weeks later, you severed something else, and I couldn't do anything at all."

"You were the ghost." Teelo shook his head. "We couldn't figure it out—there were random blackouts, cells kept unlocking—I had to reroute so many different systems to make it all behave the way logic indicated it should."

"Ghost." The Veetanho laughed again. "Wish I were. I could have done a whole lot more."

"Would you want that now?" Sansar asked, tilting her head.

"Why shouldn't I?"

"We freed you from Dunamis' control." Tald squinted at her. *Maybe it didn't work? Sansar said she could see it on the panel of her device—*

cog or not cog—but Dunamis is sneaky in the extreme. Maybe he had codes under codes under other codes?

"Dunamis did *control* me," she replied and then laughed some more. "It never took right—I was 'maladapted' and 'unbreedable,' or whatever other stupid label. But I was *loyal*, so I got sent here. Like Geeto."

"Is that possible?" Justice asked, swiveling his head toward Gleeko. "Some Veetanho are immune to Dunamis, but go along with his whims anyway?" He drummed three sets of claws on the floor, and used the ones on his last hand to run through his furred cheek.

"Not immune, no, but I've heard rumors…"

"It's always rumors with you." Justice made a sound deep in the back of his throat, and for a moment Tald believed the Hunter was about to spit or throw up in order to show his disgust. Apparently the sound itself was enough.

"Oh knowledgeable Depik, do forgive that some of us have operated under the crushing thumb of an SI with motives not in our best interests who has therefore kept information that might hurt him from easily flowing between us for possibly millennia." Gleeko rolled her head, and Tald practically felt the sarcasm dripping from her words.

"I won't." Surely Justice understood the sarcasm, but he responded as smoothly as if she'd been serious. "As it seems some of your people could resist and knew very well what you were doing was the wrong thing, yet chose to anyway."

"How is it wrong?" the Veetanho prisoner asked, leaning forward in her chair with every evidence of polite inquiry. "How is it wrong if I do something, but you do something worse, and it is correct? How do you define wrong, for that matter, or worse?"

"You deprive others of freedom and take credits and power from doing so. How could that be right?"

"You deprive others of their *lives*, and take credits and power for doing so. How could you be in any position to judge us? Better—" the other Veetanho's words sped up, and she spread her hands wide on either side of her body "—who are you to talk of freedom? What is a Goka going to do with freedom but throw themselves into the nearest fight until they're all dead? What do Tortantulas do with freedom but fight amongst *themselves* until they're all dead, with a side of cannibalism? What is a Lumar going to do with freedom but—"

"The story you tell yourself is you are doing a service to the races that don't know any better?" Justice stood and stalked toward her, flickering in and out of their vision. "At least your Geeto saw the error of it at her end. She told us..." He dropped his voice, circled her, then disappeared. She jumped slightly—had Justice cut her? But no, there wasn't any blood as far as Tald could see—twisting to try to keep him in sight. "Everything."

"And you—"

"We do not pretend to right and wrong," Justice cut her off, but his voice had moved away from her. Tald was sure the Hunter was closer to Gleeko now, which made the fur along his back crawl. "We do what we *want*. You do what the SI wants. And that, little enemy, seems 'worse,' if you truly are trying to understand."

"Are you done?" Gleeko asked, voice strained.

"For now." Justice's voice was off to Tald's left now, away from both Veetanho, and the Peacemaker eased his hands off his holsters.

"As entertaining as the philosophical debates are, let us move on to the matter at hand." Gleeko cleared her throat. "One, it's possible and even likely that not all brains adapt in a manner the SI prefers for full control. That's true across species, so some variation within a species also makes sense. It remains rumor, because most often Dunamis simply removed such an anomaly rather than risk one who was… less than completely loyal. Or," she continued as she turned back to the other Veetanho, "tuck them away somewhere he didn't have to worry if that loyalty was in the slightest question."

"No! I am loyal. I have always been loyal. My mother was, and my mother's mother, and all from the beginning and down to me. I am *Feemo*, and I am *loyal*."

"You know what we call that at the Academy?" Tald asked, sauntering forward. He'd let the others get too far afield—this was his investigation. Time to handle it. "Protesting too much. You know what that means?"

"I am familiar with the phrase," Feemo grumbled.

"Good. Suspects often protest too much when we get a little too close to the truth. Seems like Dunamis put something into you—we got a handy device here that confirms you had code in you—and now it's out, so all those little doubts you've ever had are crowding in that head of yours, and you're trying to beat them back. Is it working?"

Feemo glared at him, and out of the corner of his eye, Tald noticed Gleeko was giving him a weird look, too. It could have been the goggles, so he disregarded it.

"Yeah, I didn't think so." He traced a half circle in front of her—not as close as Justice had gotten, but enough to separate himself from the others in the room. "So it's like this, Feemo. Dunamis messed with your head. You did some things—maybe you liked doing them, maybe you didn't, maybe you aren't *sure* either way. That can't feel great, and I don't blame you for messing with us."

Justice reappeared, sitting perfectly straight next to Sansar. That was interesting, but Tald decided not to get distracted by it.

"But here's the thing. Your friend Geeto was in a bad situation because of Dunamis. So were you. So were all the Veetanho. And Dunamis, does he care? No, ma'am, no he does not. He's out gallivanting the galaxy, letting Lytoshaan rot. No one told you that, right? He abandoned the Veetanho."

"He…" She tore her eyes from Tald and stared at Gleeko. After a long moment, Gleeko nodded.

"So here's how I see it. Dunamis used you like game pieces, like you all thought you were using all the other races in the Mercenary Guild, and maybe others, too, I don't know. Then the game didn't go the way he wanted, and he left you all to burn." That seemed appropriate, given Hades' location. Tald imagined the Veetanho who were forced to live here thought a lot about burning, given how close the reality of it was. "He's fine. You all are facing a whole lot of pissed-off enemies who don't care whether it's you or him they hurt back."

Tald shrugged, spared a glance for Sansar—she dipped her chin toward him, which he thought was a measure of approval—and continued to walk his semi-circle. "But us? We *do* care. We'd rather get in *his* way, and we know *his* way and the *Veetanho* way… well, those aren't the same at all, especially not anymore, wouldn't you agree?"

Tald shot a look at Justice with that comment and got a slow blink in return.

"I…" Feemo took a ragged breath. "Yes?"

"Good. Good, that's good, Feemo." Tald made his nod slow, like he was considering. He angled as he passed her again, making sure she got a good look at his badge. "He took the *Keesius* ships, or maybe he lost them, but either way, that's looking like a bad day for the Veetanho once everybody else hears."

Feemo's ears flattened to her skull, then fluttered, then flattened again, and her breath went spiky. She composed herself a moment later, but she wasn't nearly as convincing as Gleeko.

"What did you hear about the ships, Feemo? Dunamis can't touch you now. He doesn't have any little traps or codes in your head. Help us hurt him—he abandoned you in favor of his own plans. It's the least you can do."

"I don't... I... if I knew..."

"Anything you might have heard. Anywhere else people might have gone over the years that seemed even more secret than here."

"No one left. No one ever left..." Feemo slumped in her seat, her eyes fixed on the floor. Her body shuddered, then her head snapped up. "No. Someone left—right after I got here. I forgot, because I was getting settled and learning all the protocols, but... someone left. Not home, it wasn't a celebration. One day she was here, and then... we didn't even have a scheduled transport, because I'd come in on that one, and it wasn't long enough later."

"Do you remember who? Or where?"

"I..." Feemo frowned and rocked herself. "No. I don't think I ever knew."

They asked her a few more questions—or rather, Tald and Teelo did. Sansar continued to observe. Justice vanished. Gleeko stalked out.

Teelo got directions to the backup control room, at least, although the Veetanho weren't able to provide anything else. After the last few interviews, as they walked back toward the main section, Sansar tapped Tald on the shoulder.

"Well done, Peacemaker. At the worst, it gives Josiff an idea of what to look for."

Tald didn't know how the Pendal would look for the information, but it was the closest he'd gotten to a win this entire mission. He'd take it.

* * *

Administration, Prison Complex, Hades, Hades System

"I was wrong," Josiff said as Sansar walked into the administration office.

"So you've found something? You've picked up the trail?"

"Well, no."

The Pendal bobbed his head, which meant... Sansar had no idea. Josiff had picked up many Human mannerisms through long contact, but the head bob was something she'd never seen before. "So?" she prompted. "You've been at this a while."

"I said I doubted we would find anything here. I was wrong about that, but what I've found... I do not know if it will help."

"What have you got?" Sansar asked, getting frustrated with all the caveats.

"Most of the files are encrypted," Josiff said, "which means I needed to unencrypt them just to find out if they were even relevant. And in most cases, they weren't. A lot of them dealt with personnel—the people who were sentenced here as well as the jailors stationed to watch over them. It appears most of the jailors did something to annoy either Dunamis or one of the leading Veetanho. For example, I have found records of both Teebo and Peepo sending people here for failure to perform as expected. I do not know whether that was on the battlefield or their personal life, or—"

"Could be any of those," Sansar said, cutting in, "knowing the Veetanho."

Josiff shook his head. "True, but—for nearly all the jailors—getting here was a death sentence; once they were here, they never left."

"I doubt that helped give them a positive attitude toward the prisoners."

"Probably not. All I can guess is Dunamis also stuck some code in their heads so they didn't go completely psychotic and kill all the prisoners." He did his steam-whistle laugh and then added, "Or kill the other jailors, I guess. That would have taken all the 'fun' out of sending them here."

"We did find evidence that Dunamis programmed them."

"Makes sense." He shrugged. "I certainly would not have wanted to spend my life here."

"So once the jailors and inmates got here, they never left? Feemo had it wrong?"

"In almost every case that seems to be true."

Sansar cocked her head. "But not *every* time?"

"No. I found two cases over the years of people being released to 'Tooliq.' One was a Human and the other a Goltar. Both times, the annotation was deleted later."

"If the information was deleted, how were you able to access it?"

"They deleted it, but the information was never removed from the drives. The information was still there, and in those cases, it hadn't been overwritten, and I was able to recover it." He chuckled. "So while I didn't find anything of value in the actual files, I *was* able to recover a few things from the drives themselves. I found those two, but there may be more that have been overwritten. It is impossible to know—from the records here, anyway—how many went to Tooliq."

"Tooliq… hmm." Sansar's eyebrows knit. "Is that the name of someone who took them, or is it a place they sent them to?"

"Unknown. The alphabet it is written in is Goka, but I do not know whether it is a person or a planet. If it is a planet, I have never heard of it."

"I haven't, either." Sansar shrugged. "I guess we can take a look at the stargate records and see if anyone jumped to a Tooliq."

"I will keep looking, ma'am, but I doubt I will find much more. The Veetanho seem to have been pretty consistent about not keeping any records of anything off planet."

"I suspect Dunamis helped them with that."

Josiff nodded. "I suspect so."

* * *

Stargate, Hades System

The control room for the automated station was barely big enough for two people, but Sansar was interested in seeing it and had followed Josiff into it. There was very little livable space at the stargate; it wasn't required. Maintenance rarely needed to be conducted on the station, and any maintenance personnel would have their own ship. They'd just shuttle over to the administration module—like Sansar and Josiff had done—attach their shuttle to it, and spacewalk over. Although Sansar would have felt more comfortable and confident in her CASPer to do the EVA, there wasn't enough space in the control room for the massive suit, so she floated, ill at ease in a standard shipsuit, looking over Josiff's shoulder as he accessed the system.

"Most of these are to Lytoshaan," Josiff said after a few moments. "The only other one is to Rygolla about a year ago, but that's not a Goka system; it shows as Zuparti controlled. Maybe Tooliq is a person who lives there."

"No, that's the system you jump to when you're heading back to Earth," Sansar said.

"Are you sure?"

"Since it was the *Gobi Desert*, and I was on it, yeah, I'm pretty sure." Sansar shook her head. "You said it was rare for someone to be released from here; maybe you need to go back farther to find it."

"Right," Josiff said. He flipped back a page of data, then a second, and then a third.

"You weren't kidding about no one ever leaving," Sansar muttered.

"I wasn't," Josiff said. "Here we go." He pointed to the screen. "Goka planet. Tarpik. One ship jumped there thirty-seven years ago." He flipped back another page, then several more. "Here it is again. Tarpik."

"Good," Sansar said. "Get the coordinates. Looks like we're going to Tarpik."

* * * * *

Chapter Eleven

CIC, EMS Gobi Desert, Emergence Area, Tarpik System

"Emergence in Tarpik," the helmsman said.

"Charge the internal shunts," Parker said. "If we're not welcome, I want to be able to jump before the missiles arrive."

"Charging the shunts, aye," the helmsman repeated.

"Drones out," Parker added.

"Announcing our presence with authority?" Sansar asked. She'd released her harness and come to stand behind the CO's chair.

"When you've never been somewhere before, and you work for a boss who likes to antagonize SIs, taking a few precautions seems wise."

"I don't think there's an SI here."

Parker nodded. "It never hurts to be ready, though."

"True."

"Sir," the comms officer called, "I'm being hailed by Tarpik Defense Command."

"Probably should answer them," the sensor operator said. "There are a number of defensive positions scattered around the periphery of the emergence area. Looks like a number of hollowed-out asteroids. If we piss them off, things could get challenging real quick."

"Put them on the main viewer," Parker directed.

The screen changed to the view from a control room, probably inside one of the asteroids. It took all of Sansar's resolve not to shudder when a Goka stepped in front of the pickup, and the screen filled with a larger-than-life giant cockroach. *The only thing worse than seeing one up close is having one—or more—of the little bastards crawling on your suit, stabbing with their knives.*

"*Gobi Desert*, state your intentions in the Tarpik system," the Goka said.

Parker looked over his shoulder at Sansar. "Want to take this one?" he asked.

"Sure." Sansar stepped forward. "We're here to talk to Tooliq."

"You are, huh." The Goka looked over his shoulder then back at the camera. "Who are you, and what does this pertain to?"

"The Veetanho sent us," Sansar said. "We just arrived from Hades."

The Goka laughed, long and hard. "The Veetanho sent you? The word on the street is the Veetanho aren't quite the force they used to be. In fact, I think the best response I can give you is to tell you— and your Veetanho masters—to get fucked."

"They're not our masters," Sansar said.

"Nor are they ours," the Goka said. "Which is why you can proceed directly to the stargate and leave. If you deviate from that course, you will be destroyed."

"We'll be happy to do as you ask," Sansar said. "We just need to talk to Tooliq as we transit."

"Impossible. The Tooliq isn't in the habit of giving audiences to Veetanho sycophants. Remember, no deviations, or you'll be destroyed." The screen went blank as the transmission terminated.

"Well, that was unexpected," Parker said. "Not the threats—I've gotten used to them from previous trips with you—but the fact that they don't even want to talk to us?"

"Obviously, the news of what happened on Lytoshaan has gotten here, and they're feeling their oats," Sansar said.

"What do you want me to do?"

"They don't know we have internal shunts, and I'd like to keep it that way. Proceed to the stargate for now, and we'll come up with a new plan."

* * *

"Hey, I've got something here," the sensor operator announced a few hours later as they approached the planet.

"What's that?" Parker asked.

"I just got a hit from a Peacemaker ship." He paused and then added, "It's registered as the *Eletine,* but I don't have any other information on it."

"Comms officer, try to contact it, please."

"Nothing, Captain," the comms officer said a few minutes later. "No response from the Peacemaker ship. If the Peacemaker is aboard, he's not answering."

Sansar turned to Tald. "Can you think of any reason a Peacemaker might be here?"

"There are many cases in the galaxy," Tald replied. "As a Peacemaker candidate, I'm sure I don't know what most of them are."

Sansar shrugged. "Worth a shot. How about this, then—do you find it strange that there's one here, at a planet no one's heard of?"

Tald nodded slowly. "It does stretch incredulity, ma'am."

"If there was someone on the ship, he or she would respond, right?"

"If they were following protocol, certainly."

"How often do Peacemakers fail to follow protocol?"

"Until a few weeks ago, I would have said 'never,' but then we met the Goltar Peacemaker." Tald shrugged. "I find it odd that the Peacemaker didn't reply. Even if he wasn't on the ship, he'd have had it set up to forward any sort of messages or transmissions."

Sansar nodded. "That's what I thought, too."

Tald cocked his head. "Are you thinkin' foul play, ma'am?"

"I'm not sure, but I'm certainly leaning toward it. We were told to leave without getting a chance to talk to anyone, a Peacemaker doesn't respond... If we didn't already *know* something weird was going on here, we'd probably guess it was."

"So what do we do?"

Sansar rubbed her chin a moment. "We need more information before we narrow down our options. I think you need to call Tarpik Defense Command."

"Me?" Tald asked, his voice little more than a squeak.

"Yes, you," Sansar said with a nod. "Call them and tell them you want to talk to the Peacemaker. Don't take no for an answer."

"Really?"

"Really. This may be our one chance to figure this out."

Captain Parker waved a hand. "Can I go on record as being opposed to taunting the people who control the missiles pointed at us?"

"Absolutely." Sansar shrugged. "I don't think this will go sideways, but it might be wise to make sure the internal shunts are charged again... just in case."

Parker muttered something about wishing he could keep them continually charged when he was transporting Sansar, then ordered the helmsman to make it so.

Sansar smiled. "Okay, Tald, you're up. Remember, you're a Peacemaker. Don't take no for an answer."

"What if they threaten us?"

"Bluff. Isn't that what the old western lawmen did? When they were about to get overwhelmed, the best ones were able to bluff their way out of a bad situation."

"Kind of like what you did with the Goltar?"

Sansar nodded. "Just like that."

"Time to earn my star," Tald said. He stood straighter and rotated his shoulders back. If he'd had a chest, it would have stuck out. As he didn't, the effect was mostly lost. He strutted up to the command chair and ordered, "Comms officer, set up a video call with Tarpik Defense Command."

"Yes, sir… I mean, yes, Peacemaker," the comms officer replied. "Coming up on the main screen."

* * *

Tald swallowed as the screen shifted to the interior of the defense command asteroid again, and a giant cockroach filled the screen. He wasn't able to tell whether it was the same one, but when it spoke, it certainly sounded like it.

"What do you want now, *Gobi Desert?*"

Tald opened his mouth to speak, but found his mouth dry and his brain empty. *Say something!* His brain screamed. *They're counting on you!* Tald flashed back to his acting classes at the Academy. They'd done a lot of roleplaying—things to say, how to say them—when faced with a variety of situations, to prepare the candidates for when, inevitably, they would face them. *Like now.* The only way Tald had made it through the class was to look at old movies and come up with a persona that was a mash-up of Marshall Dillon and Dirty Harry. *Marshall Harry, you're needed on stage!* Summoning that façade, he cleared his throat and took a step forward.

"We see you have a Peacemaker on the planet. I wish to speak to him."

"Wish all you want, soft-skin," the Goka replied. "You're not talking to him."

"You're missing the point. I *demand* to speak to him, and you're going to let me."

"You demand, do you? And who do you think you are to make demands?"

Tald reached into the interior pocket of his vest and pulled out his badge. He held it up to the light, blew off an imaginary piece of lint, then attached it to the vest. "I'm Peacemaker Tald."

"Ooooh," the Goka replied. "Well, that's different."

"You'll let us talk to the Peacemaker then?"

"Not at all." The Goka laughed. "What's different is now I get to tell a *Peacemaker* to go fuck himself. Better yet, if you want, I can send a missile or ten your way and do it for you."

Tald fought the urge to drop his shoulders and slink away—like he had with the Goltar—and Tald might have done so... but he wasn't Tald anymore, he was Marshall Tald, bringer of order for the galaxy. "I suspect you can do that," he said with a slow nod. "Of course, if you do, it'll be the last thing you and your rag-tag band of assholes ever do."

"Wha—what?" the Goka asked. It shook its head. "You're just a transport; I can kill you anytime I want. You won't escape."

"Got a name, asshole?" Tald asked.

"I'm General Grelliq." He looked over his shoulder. "Stand by to fire on the transport."

"There's one thing you don't know, Grelliq," Tald said. "One thing that might change the equation for you."

"And what's that?"

"This ship has internal shunts. If you fire on us, we're going to jump out of here, and I'm going to deputize every single Winged Hussars warship in the New Warsaw system. Then I'm going to come back here and shove a missile so far up *your* ass, you'll taste it every time you shut your stupid mouth."

"I think you're lying."

"And I think you're an asshole who's about to sign his own death warrant. Because trust me, I know what station you're on, and it's not going to last long once the Hussars get here. They have quite an… explosive way of making their presence known when they enter a system full of assholes." Tald shrugged. "So. What's it going to be, punk? Are you feeling lucky?"

"I think you're bluffing."

"Well, then, fire a missile or ten at me. You'll have two weeks to explain your incompetence to your bosses before I get back. The conversation should be a *lot* of fun." Tald shrugged. "We don't have all day. What's it going to be?"

Grelliq made a motion, and the link dropped.

"Stand by to jump!" Parker yelled. "Let me know if they fire!"

"I'm not... I'm not seeing any signs of increased defensive pos-ture," the sensor tech replied. "In fact... yes! They just turned off their targeting radars."

"Peacemaker, you have a General Grelliq who wants to speak with you," the comms officer announced.

They bought it! Tald smiled. *Remember, be gracious but firm in victory.*

"On screen," Tald replied.

The viewscreen lit up with Grelliq. "Peacekeeper Balin is current-ly in conference with the Tooliq," he said. "The Tooliq would like to invite the Peacemaker and the captain of the ship down to join him. We will send you coordinates. You may send down a shuttle. One shuttle. If you do anything else, you will be destroyed."

The viewscreen went dead, then it changed to the tactical picture.

"I did it!" Tald said exultantly.

"What do you think?" Sansar asked.

"They're planning something," Gleeko said.

"I agree," Sansar replied with a nod.

"Wait!" Tald exclaimed. "They said we could go down. They gave in to my demands."

Gleeko laughed. "He doesn't get out much, does he?"

"What's that supposed to mean?" Tald said. SalSha didn't flush, or he was sure he would have, but it was all he could do to keep his ears from going flat.

"Goka like to think they're smart," Gleeko said. "They like to come up with plans to try to misdirect you. Every. Single. Time. At some point, you'd think one would get smart and realize that we're onto them." She shook her head. "But no. Perhaps, as a race, they're simply incapable of it."

"Of what?" Tald said. He could tell she was making fun of him, even though it looked like she was talking about the Goka, and it was all he could do to—he stopped himself, unsure of what he wanted to do. You couldn't throw someone in the brig for making fun of a Peacemaker. You *should* be able to, but he hadn't found that to be a law in any of the systems he'd checked so far. "What are they incapable of?"

"Honesty, mostly," Veetanho said. "Also, lying convincingly."

"True," Sansar said. "Looks like we're going to have to go in hot."

Justice appeared next to her, and Captain Parker jumped away. "Blue Sky, I hate it when they do that!"

"Don't even think of going without me," Justice said with a slow-blink. "I haven't gotten a chance to kill many Goka since we took back Khatash."

"*Wait!*" Tald yelled. "They said we could come. *Why is everyone acting so combative?*"

Gleeko smiled, but Tald could see it was her condescending smile. She opened her mouth, but Tald held up a hand. While Marshall Dillon would probably have listened before acting, the Dirty Harry half of him screamed for vengeance, which was probably why he liked that half better. All he knew was, if Gleeko said another word, he was going to shoot her. Not to kill… but her kneecaps would make excellent targets.

"You. Shut your pie hole." Tald turned to Sansar. "Explain your reasoning, ma'am."

Sansar nodded, and her look was serious, not condescending. Tald could live with that.

"Like Gleeko said, if you give a Goka a choice, they're always going to default to the one thing they want—which usually involves slaughter—and then lying about it to get you to go along with it."

"So they're going to fire missiles at us?" Tald looked around to see everyone—even Justice—nodding. Even the junior officers and technicians at the ship's positions were nodding. *How is it that I'm so gullible, and everyone else isn't?* It didn't make sense. "But he said—"

"That we could land and talk to the Tooliq and the Peacemaker?" Sansar asked.

Tald nodded. "He said he'd send coordinates." He hated when his voice got whiney. It was always a sure sign he'd lost.

"And I'll bet he did," Sansar replied.

"He did, ma'am," the comms officer reported. "I've got them right here."

Tald turned back to the Golden Horde commander and raised an eyebrow, unable to trust his voice not to betray him again. *Peacemakers don't whine!*

Sansar raised an eyebrow in return. "What exactly did he say?"

Peacemakers were trained to remember communications; Tald was able to recall perfectly what Grelliq had said. "The Tooliq would like to invite the Peacemaker and the captain of the ship down to join him."

Sansar nodded. "When did you tell him Captain Parker wanted to go down?"

"I didn't."

"Nor would I." Parker snorted. "Fat chance of me *ever* wanting to go down to a Goka planet."

"So…" Tald shrugged. "What am I missing?" It was okay to admit to not know something, as long as he didn't whine about it. Acquiring information was a Peacemaker's job, after all.

"They want all the command staff on the shuttle. They may let it land and then capture it, or they may take it under fire on its way down. Either way, they're planning on a decapitation strike that gets the leaders off the *Gobi Desert* so they can destroy it."

"*I told them we had shunts and they couldn't do that!*"

"When you're a liar, you see everyone else as a liar, too." Sansar smiled. "Store that knowledge away; it'll be useful in your career."

"Why wasn't this taught at the Academy, though?"

"Some things are better learned through experience," Sansar said with a shrug.

"If I may?" Gleeko asked.

Sansar nodded. "Go ahead."

"I have more experience dealing with the Goka. While I agree that they're planning something, and will default to shooting missiles if required, I have a feeling they're hoping for a little… more."

"What does that mean?" Tald asked.

"As the transmission terminated, the Goka smiled. They're trying to be cute. I think the plan is for them to try to capture us first. Failing that, they'll shoot at us. Regardless, the ship won't make it to the stargate. I'd bet they captured the other Peacemaker, and they did it just like this. And because it worked once, they're going to try it again with us. They're hoping if they get the CO, they can use him to take the ship, too."

"So what do we do?" Tald asked. "Is it time to jump out and get the Hussars? This has escalated beyond my experience, and I'd like your professional opinions."

"I... don't think so," Sansar said. "I have a feeling the other Peacemaker is still alive, and wherever he is, this Tooliq person is close by—he's probably the leader down there. I find it odd that another Peacemaker is here, and I'd like to talk to him. The only way I can do that is to rescue him." She smiled, but it didn't look like she was happy. "I'd also like to talk to this Tooliq, now that we know it's a person." She looked down at Justice. "Make sure you don't kill him before I do."

* * * * *

Chapter Twelve

CO's Conference Room, EMS *Gobi Desert*, Tarpik System

Sansar looked around the conference room fifteen minutes later and smiled. "So what do we know?"

A knock came from the door, and Sansar turned to find the comms officer. "Defense Command just called. They're getting antsy about when we're going to send down a shuttle."

"And you told them?"

"The CO was packing his gear, and we'd be leaving soon. That seemed to mollify them for the moment."

"And confirm your guess," Sansar said, nodding to Gleeko.

"Predictable," the Veetanho replied with a nod. "They always think they're smarter than they really are."

"Here's what we're looking at," Naran Enkh said, activating the Tri-D in the center of the table. It focused on a landing pad. "This is the landing pad where they want us to come." The view pulled back to reveal a number of towers in the area, then it centered on one and zoomed in. The tower looked like some sort of giant termite mound from central Africa, only much, much bigger. "This is where we think their headquarters is."

"Why that one and not one of the others?" Sansar asked. "It looks like there are a bunch in the area."

"There are quite a few," Naran acknowledged. "We believe this is where they're holding the Peacemaker and where this Tooliq person is, because this is where all their comms gear is. This one seems to be the 'work' hive. All the Goka go back and forth between this one and the others, which we think are living hives—there's little traffic between the others."

"Okay." Sansar pursed her lips as she looked at the tower. "It has to be, what? Two hundred meters tall?"

"It's closer to three hundred, ma'am," Naran replied.

"That's a lot of space to cover."

Naran nodded. "It is. I recommend one platoon start at the bottom and the other at the top. We'll meet at the middle or—if someone finds an HVU—we'll meet there."

"HVU?" Tald asked.

"High Value Unit, Peacemaker," Naran replied. "Either Tooliq or the other Peacemaker."

Tald nodded. "Thanks." He smiled at Naran; she was always respectful to him.

"Okay," Sansar said. "Here's what we're going to do."

* * *

**Cargo Bay, Dropship *One*, EMS *Gobi Desert*,
Tarpik System**

"Sit here," Sansar said, pointing at the forward bulkhead of the cargo bay.

Tald looked but didn't see a seat, although admittedly, it was hard to see anything through the bubble helmet of the Human spacesuit he'd had to wear. *How can they not have SalSha suits?* he asked himself for the hundredth time. *SalSha pilots have been flying for years!*

He got his answer as his dad stuck his head into the cargo bay from the cockpit. *Because they have their own tailored flight suits.* Tald sighed. His dad looked a lot more comfortable than he felt with his suit bunched up in the legs, arms, and torso. The optics of the helmet were all wrong, too. Still, it was better than breathing vacuum, or so they'd told him. Actually, he believed them on that point.

"I've got him," Thorb said, and Sansar turned back to get her troops settled. Dad then grabbed something on the bulkhead and folded it down; Tald's seat. Thorb locked it into place and stepped back. "Sit down, and I'll strap you in."

"Do you do this for everyone?" Tald grumbled as he climbed into the chair.

"Every special guest?" Thorb asked. "Absolutely." He connected the harness system and showed Tald how to use it. "Good?"

"Yeah, thanks."

Thorb stepped back and looked at him intensely.

"What?" Tald finally asked with a touch of exasperation.

"I want to give you some advice, but I want you to take it and not do something stupid just to spite me." Thorb shrugged. "This is my area of expertise, after all, and it's advice I'd give to anyone sitting in that seat, not just because it's my son this time."

"I'll take it," Tald said. He was getting pretty claustrophobic in the seat, his nerves were about shot, and his adrenaline had spiked through the roof. It was all he could do to keep his lunch down, if it came right to it, and he didn't know how to get the helmet off. If he spewed, it was going to float around in his helmet until someone could help him with it… and he ran the risk of drowning in his own vomit. "What's your advice?" he asked to take his mind off that quite unsavory picture.

"I don't suspect we'll get shot at on the way down, but stay locked in your seat until someone tells you to get up. If I call for bailout, unstrap and grab onto one of the CASPers; they'll get you down safely." He shrugged. "Safer than what's about to happen to the dropship, anyway."

Thorb paused a second, obviously trying to decide what to say. "Once we're down, stick to the plan until it no longer makes sense. If all else fails, look to Sansar for guidance, and do what she says. She has more ground combat experience than you'll ever get." He chuckled. "More than you'll ever *want*, too, I imagine. Listen to her, and you'll be fine. Although I know it doesn't always look like she cares, she'd do anything for her people."

"I'm not one of her people, though."

"You're under her protection right now, whether you know it or not," Thorb said. "She'll do everything she can to take care of you. Be smart and follow the plan, and I'll be back to pick you up when it's time to go."

Tald took a deep breath and let it out slowly so he didn't fog the helmet. Finally, he nodded. "I can do that."

"Good," Thorb said. "I love you, and I'm proud of you. Go be the best Peacemaker ever." With that, he ducked back into the flight station through the door, leaving Tald with his legs kicking like a child in his too-large suit while sitting in his too-large seat.

To distract himself as his gorge rose again, he watched the troops taking their places in the back of the dropship. He'd wondered why all the CASPers hadn't been going to ride in the interior of the dropship; now he knew. There was only a platoon in the back of the dropship, *because that was all it would hold!* He looked out the small window next to him and could see more of them attaching themselves to the wing. *If I'm scared, sitting in this seat, how scary is it for them out on the wing?* Tald found himself wondering if anyone had ever modified a CASPer for a SalSha. *If they have, I don't want any part of it! Being inside this thing is bad enough!*

The dropship's motors fired up as the last of the CASPers in the back locked themselves into their positions. Tald noticed none of them needed assistance. They all knew where they were supposed to be, went there, and locked in. They were all professionals at what they were doing, and that made him feel safer, then a warm feeling suffused him. As Sansar clicked into the position closest to him, Tald had an epiphany. *They're all doing this for* me. *Well, for Sansar, but* she's *doing this for me.* Despite the fact that she'd seen him fail—seen people laugh at him—she believed in him enough to support this mission, not only with the lives of her men, but with her own, as well.

It was a pretty powerful feeling.

Then something else hit him like a ton of CASPers. *She's bringing me along because she sees something in me and believes I can do my part.* If there was one thing he knew, it was that Sansar didn't suffer fools gladly, nor would she do anything to jeopardize the mission. That was an even headier feeling. *Professional trust.* He'd do whatever it took to make sure he didn't let her down.

Even if I don't know what that is at the moment.

With several *clunks!* and metallic *slams!* they were in motion. If the people inside the CASPers were nervous, they didn't give any indication. Not that he would know—he couldn't see inside them, and they were locked, motionless, to the bulkhead. He shrugged. Nobody said anything on the command frequency, anyway.

"Stand by for ramp activation!" Thorb's voice came over the speakers. Nobody moved, then the ramp went into motion. What little atmosphere hadn't been sucked up *whooshed* out into the black. As one, all the CASPers except Sansar punched their harness locks and released themselves from the bulkhead. They turned, faced the black, and marched forward and off the ramp.

The courage it takes to do that! Tald shook his head. Maybe he'd need that kind of courage as a Peacemaker… but he doubted it. As the last rank stepped off the ramp a scant few seconds later, Tald looked out the window; all the CASPers on the wing were gone already. Letting go of the wing… Tald shook his head. It had probably taken even more courage to let go out there than for the troopers in the cargo bay to step off.

The ramp started up as the dropship jerked into motion again. The ramp sealed, and there was the *hiss* of pressurization. Sansar released herself and turned to Tald. "Let's get you out of that suit."

Now? While we're still in space? Tald wanted to scream. The plan had made sense while sitting on the *Gobi Desert*. Now? *Not so much.*

Tald swallowed and vowed to be at least half as brave as Marshall Dillon. Summoning his courage, he punched the release as hard as he could. Then he coughed as the metal bracket was driven into his chest. Luckily, his radio was off, so Sansar didn't know he'd just hurt himself in his act of derring-do. He hoped she didn't, anyway.

Tald went to jump down from the seat, but only succeeded in flying off the seat.

No gravity yet. Duh.

Happily, Sansar was either ready for his gaffe, or just had good reflexes, and she snagged him from the air. She popped her canopy and smiled at him. "Can't do it with the suit's fingers," she said.

Sansar quickly got him out of the suit, but even more quickly, gravity returned, and he was able to stand on the deck once he was out of the suit. Sansar opened a compartment on the CASPers leg and pulled out a bag—it was his uniform! Hat, vest, boots—even his pistols and their rig. "I thought you didn't like the outfit."

Sansar smiled. "It's part of your persona. If you're going to act the part of Peacemaker, you need to dress it, too."

"Well, yes, ma'am, I guess I do at that," he drawled. Somehow, the drawl and the clothes made him feel better and more confident. It *was* his persona, he realized. Maybe the clothes really do make the man… or the SalSha… or the Peacemaker. He shrugged. Whatever. Either way, he was ready to be about his mission.

"Five minutes to touchdown," Thorb said over the speakers.

Gravity must have shifted then, as all of a sudden, Tald's lunch tried to come back up again. He swallowed it back down and smiled grimly. *I can do this. I hope.*

* * *

With a final *clunk!* the dropship settled. "We're down," Thorb called.

Sansar released her CASPer and stood. *Game time.* She turned to Tald, who was already out of his seat. Either he'd unstrapped really quickly or had forgotten to strap back in after getting dressed. *Probably the latter.*

Sansar smiled. The SalSha was hopping from foot to foot, and he didn't have any idea yet how badly this could go wrong, or how many ways things might go sideways. Still, he stood—well, hopped from foot to foot, actually—as if ready to go do it. He didn't cower or hold back—he was ready to do what needed to be done.

He's got more of his old man in him than he thinks.

"Ready?" Sansar asked.

"Ready." Tald raced to the back of the dropship.

"Wait," Sansar said.

Tald turned. "What?"

"Don't be in such a hurry. Many times, it helps to approach a situation cautiously. We don't know what to expect out there. Let's not charge into it."

"Welcoming party is here," Thorb said. "Looks like five Goka. At least three have laser rifles."

"Want to run out into that?" Sansar asked.

"Well, not really," Tald said, "but it's what Peacemakers do." Then something came over the SalSha—Sansar had no idea what; perhaps he was channeling Hr'ent Golramm or one of the Peacemaker greats—and Tald stood taller and threw out the chest he didn't have. "We may stand or fall, ma'am, but we always honor the threat." He nodded once. "I'm ready if you are."

"Here we go, then," Sansar said. She slapped the ramp button. "Ramp coming down."

The ramp reached the ground, and Tald looked up at her. "It makes sense for me to go first," Sansar said. "I may be able to honor the threat a little more completely in my CASPer if it comes down to it."

"Very well, ma'am," Tald said. "Y'all can lead on."

Sansar chuckle to herself at the return of the accent—maybe that was what he did to psyche himself up—and walked down the ramp. As she reached the bottom, she saw the dropship was in the corner of the landing pad, with the ramp just barely on the prepared surface. She smiled as she stepped off the ramp and turned to walk alongside the craft toward the waiting Goka.

They may not know it, but the Goka were in the worst position possible. Thorb had landed the way he had so he could point the chin gun at them without it looking like he was doing so. The Goka may have tough shells, but nowhere close to what it would take to withstand the MAC on the front of the dropship. Of course, that's probably why Thorb had suggested taking a dropship instead of the shuttle they'd originally intended. The first Goka to aim at Tald was going to get a *big* surprise.

Sansar strode to the front of the dropship, careful to not get between the MAC and the Goka. She turned to check on Tald—which wasn't required, since she had aft cameras—and signaled him to go to the far side of her. Confusion flashed across his face, but he moved in the intended direction. Sansar turned back to the Goka. Although they didn't look overtly aggressive, they were Goka, and it wouldn't take much—

As one, the three armed roaches aimed at Sansar. "You're coming with us," the Goka in front said.

* * * * *

Chapter Thirteen

Landing Pad, Tarpik, Tarpik System

"Well, boys and girls, that's quite the welcome," Sansar said. "Is this how you greet every Peacemaker who comes here?"

"This week, yes," said the leader, who drew a knife. It happened so quickly, Sansar thought it had come from under his shell, but wasn't quite sure. "Now, are you going to come with us, or are we going to get to rough you up a bit?"

"Are we going to see the Tooliq?"

The leader chuckled. "Oh, you're going to see him all right."

"Is he over there?" Sansar asked, pointing to the target of the assault.

"Yeah. Wait. Why?"

"No reason," Sansar said. She changed to the command net and transmitted, "HVU number two is confirmed in the tower. Happy hunting." On her HUD, she could see the falling troopers approaching the tower.

"You're sure you want to do this, right?" Sansar asked, moving her targeting reticle over the left-most Goka with a rifle. "It's not too late to let us go and not end up dead."

"Fuck you!" the lead Goka said.

Boom! Boom! Boom!

Explosives detonated at the tower, and the Goka spun toward it.

"Fire!" Sansar said over the open circuit to Thorb. She toggled her MAC, blowing the Goka's head off. Thorb's first shot took the one on the right, and they both nailed the third armed Goka. She swung to the next roach, but both of the others had collapsed to the surface of the landing pad. *What? How did that happen?* She turned to Tald, who had both pistols in hand. He put the barrel of one near his mouth and blew away the smoke.

"Thought they might try that," Tald said, jamming the two hypervelocity pistols back into his holsters. He nodded toward the tower. "They may need help, ma'am. I think we should go assist them."

Somehow Sansar's jaw had dropped on its own, and she had to consciously order it to shut. "You're right," she said, lowering a hand. "Let's go."

Tald climbed up the CASPer's arm. Although he'd complained that it wasn't the most dignified method of travel for a Peacemaker, he'd agreed that sometimes you had to make do while on mission, especially since they had to cover two kilometers to get to the tower. Sansar toggled her rocket boots, yearning to join her troops and get into the fight, and blasted off toward the tower.

She didn't see the anti-aircraft system rotate up from its hidden position.

* * *

1st Platoon, Tarpik, Tarpik System

Naran heard the call on the high value target while scanning the tower as she slowed her descent. Tasked with "starting at the top and working her way down," she'd focused her attention on the highest balconies, assigning them to troopers as she approached. There weren't enough of them for everyone to end up on the same level—she'd known that from the start—but it was unlikely that the Goka would be massed at the upper reaches of the tower, so that was probably okay. She had the momentary thought that attacking a ground target without getting shot up by anti-aircraft missiles was a welcome surprise… just as the first missile lifted off and headed toward 2nd Platoon, a couple hundred meters below her.

Don't ask for what you don't want, she berated herself.

The missile was destroyed by several anti-missiles from 2nd Platoon, as were two more that the Goka launched, then she was too busy landing on the tower to worry about them anymore. Her designated balcony rushed toward her, and she tapped her jumpjets to slow herself, landing—she thought—fairly lightly on the exposed space.

The floor wasn't much larger than a CASPer, though, and with the winds blowing a little harder at altitude, she may have stuck the landing a little harder than intended. Either that or the balcony wasn't stress-tested for a thousand kilograms' worth of mech and pilot.

With a *crack!* the balcony snapped off, tilted, and started falling.

"Blue Sky!" she exclaimed, throwing herself forward as she tapped her jumpjets again. The fuel remaining flashed red, but she got enough boost to crash through the plate-glass doorway. It was probably "shatterproof" or the like, but once again, the designers hadn't had her CASPer in mind when they'd installed it. The door shattered quite satisfactorily, and she rolled into the apartment.

"Watch out—the balconies aren't very sturdy!" she transmitted on the platoon net.

"*No shit, ma'am,*" Private Ferrell replied. "*In related news, I ended up three stories lower than my designated target.*"

"Clear that floor, and we'll be down to you shortly." Movement caught Naran's eye, and she spun to find a Goka sliding out the door. "Freeze!" she yelled. "Stop!"

The Goka neither froze nor stopped, but skittered out the door before Naran could decide whether she wanted to shoot the giant bug or not. "Blue Sky," she muttered as she started to go after it. She'd only taken two steps when the Goka backpedaled into the room. Before she could say anything, Sergeant Jargal entered as well, with the MAC mounted to his right arm aimed squarely at the Goka.

"Thought you could run, eh?" Jargal asked. "Pretty fancy digs up here." He waved toward the interior of the apartment which, Naran had to admit, was pretty swanky. "Any chance you're related to this Tool Kit guy?"

"That's Tooliq," Naran said.

"Right." Jargal didn't miss a beat. "Tooliq, then. You related to him?"

The Goka didn't say anything.

"What do you think, Major?" Jargal asked. "Looks like the cat got her tongue. Maybe we introduce her to a Depik, and the cat really *can* get her tongue."

"Penthouse apartment? There's a good chance it's either related to the Tooliq or at least knows him. Grab it and we'll take it with us."

"You got it, Major." The Goka tried to dodge past the trooper, but Jargal got a hand on it, pinning it to the floor, then grabbed it with both hands. He held it out in front of him as the Goka struggled. "What do you want me to do with it?"

"Bring it."

"I won't be able to fight with it in my hands."

"You can give it to Ferrell to babysit when we catch up with him."

"That works."

Naran scanned the room, but didn't see anything of value. "Okay, let's go."

They started out the door, but the Goka said, "Wait," in what the translator made into a female voice.

"What?" Naran said.

"Let me get my babies."

"Why should we?"

"The Tooliq is the father."

"Sounds like a good reason to me," Jargal said. "Might be some leverage."

"What's your name?" Naran asked.

"Qualkon," the Goka replied.

"Okay, Qualkon, here's what's going to happen. My trooper is going to set you down, and you can get your babies. If you make any sudden movements, or try to escape, you will be shot. Understand?"

"I do."

Naran aimed her MAC to provide covering fire. "Okay, then. Put her down."

Jargal put her down, and the Goka bolted. Not for the door, which Naran had expected, but straight toward Naran. She fired once, but the round hit behind the racing Goka, who dodged Naran and went out the balcony door. Naran spun, but the Goka was already gone. She ran to the window and got a flash of the Goka running headfirst down the side of the building. It went around the curvature of the structure, though, and was gone.

"Want me to go after it?" Jargal asked.

"How much jumpjuice do you have?"

"Not much. A couple minutes."

Naran sighed. "No. We'll just have to do without her." She switched to the command net. "2nd Platoon, 1st Platoon. There's a Goka running down the side of the building. Believe it to be the Tooliq's wife. Can you stop it?"

"*1st Platoon, 2nd Platoon. I see the Goka and will send—*" There was a pause, and then First Sergeant Mun Enkh added, "*Disregard. It just ran onto a balcony. It's gone.*"

"Guess we'll bag her again when we get down there," Naran said.

"*Roger.*"

"Damn it," Naran said. She motioned toward the door. "Let's get everyone gathered up and get back on mission. Guess we'll have to do this the hard way."

Jargal chuckled. "With Goka? I wouldn't have expected any other way."

* * *

2nd Platoon, Tarpik, Tarpik System

First Sergeant Mun Enkh landed in front of the main doors of the tower. "Main doors," though, really didn't do it justice. The whole front of the tower was glass, or some sort of glass that would be resistant to rocks or any other normal damage. She sprayed it with her shoulder-mounted MAC and smiled as it shattered. The sub-caliber rounds—which were to help with the Goka—also did a nice job on their buildings.

"You couldn't have let me go in first?" Justice asked. "Now there's glass everywhere." He shook his head. "Can you let me out before you destroy anything else? Being in this steel can just makes me feel like a target."

Mun popped the canopy, and the Depik was gone before it had risen a quarter of the way. She sealed it again; although the Depik might not have liked having a metal shell, Mun felt naked without it.

She checked her HUD—the 2nd Squad troops were deploying nicely around the base of the tower, while 1st Squad held the entryway. Resistance so far had been light, but she knew that wouldn't last. She was tempted to lead the assault into the building so they wouldn't waste any time and give the Goka more time to prepare than necessary, but the plan called for her to wait for Sansar to arrive before kicking off into the tower.

She sighed. And waited.

* * *

Dropship *One*, Tarpik, Tarpik System

Sansar didn't see the anti-aircraft system deploy from its underground shelter, but Thorb did.

"Missiles!" he yelled to his copilot, Seeph. "Take 'em out!"

As the gunner fired the chin turret, Thorb pulled back on the stick, and the dropship rose from the pad. "Blue Sky!" he swore. Anti-aircraft batteries—both guns and missiles—were popping up all over the place. With the troops already beginning their assault, the batteries wouldn't have anyone else to aim at but Sansar, and her passenger Tald.

"Sansar! Missiles behind you!" he called. Sansar dropped a little in altitude as she accelerated toward the tower.

Thorb spun the craft to follow her. She was already almost half-way to the tower, but the plain around the landing pad had a number of sites—more than Seeph could take out before they could acquire their target and launch.

Thorb raced after Sansar as Seeph destroyed battery after battery—using the chin turret when possible, but also the attack missiles under the wings when he could bring them to bear.

Zzzt!

He couldn't hear it, but Thorb didn't need to. He knew the sound the gatling gun made as it fired a string of tracers toward Sansar. Failing to hit her, the weapon swung toward the dropship, but Seeph took it out with a missile as they raced after Sansar. She was three quarters of the way to the tower when Thorb reached her. The dropship's missile warning system was flashing like the disco ball

Tald had brought home one time as Thorb spun the dropship back around in the direction they'd come.

Three missiles greeted him, coming from three different directions. He'd meant to distract the missile systems from Sansar and Tald, but the amount of fire from the Goka's defensive systems was more than expected.

"Oops."

Thorb hit the thrusters to point the nose straight up and slammed the throttles full forward, popping chaff and flares like it was Genghis Khan's birthday. A glance behind him as he rolled showed one of the missiles off track, but two were still after him and closing fast. Keeping the motors at the stops, he burned the thrusters as hard as he could to flip back around. That gave him a harder turn than a solely atmospheric craft was able to accomplish, and that— along with the profligate use of flares as he crossed in front of the local star—caused another of the missiles to lose track.

"Just… might…" *Slam!* The last missile hit, and the starboard motor died. "Mayday, mayday, mayday," he called as the dropship plummeted from the sky.

"You got it?" Seeph asked.

"Yes," Thorb said, more confidently than he felt. The port engine provided enough thrust for them to land like an aircraft, although a hover would probably be outside the aircraft's capabilities. A yellow light illuminated on the port motor. "Maybe."

"What's wrong?"

"Something from the starboard motor must have fragged the port motor. We're losing fuel pressure." He tried switching to a different tank, but the pressure continued dropping. "Must be the main feed line."

"Can we make the ship?"

Thorb shook his head. "If we're lucky, I can put it down on the pad near the tower."

"And if we're not lucky?"

"I'm going to crash it there instead."

"I hope we're lucky."

"Me, too."

Thorb pulled the throttles back, pointed the nose of the craft nearly straight down, and dove the craft sharply at a spot a half kilometer short of the runway.

Seeph swallowed loudly. "Please tell me you're not currently aiming at the pad, because it sure looks like we're going to hit short."

"Not yet," Thorb said. "Soon." He extended the landing gear.

The altimeter continued to unwind fast—too fast, it seemed—as they dove toward the ground, but Thorb thought he knew what he was doing. "Hoped" might have been a more appropriate word, though. As they passed through five hundred meters, he rotated the craft with the thrusters and burned them on full, while maxing out the port throttle and pulling back as hard as he could on the stick. The airspeed he'd built up was transferred to forward momentum that carried them across the threshold of the landing pad at ten feet. The dropship struggled, trying to claw its way back into the air, but then the thrusters burned out. The limited amount of thrust provided by the motor wasn't enough, and the dropship slammed to the ground. The landing gear held for a moment, then the port main mount started bowing.

"No, no, no," Thorb yelled as the horizon shifted… then held, with about a twenty degree left-wing-down.

Thorb looked over to Seeph. "See? No Problem. Never a doubt in my mind."

Seeph looked around cautiously, like any movement he made might cause the landing gear to fail entirely. "What do we do now?" he asked in a whisper.

"I'm going to go look for the fuel leak," Thorb said.

"What? You don't intend to fly this again, do you?"

"Absolutely not," Thorb said. "However, if I can get the port motor going again, we can use the chin turret to defend ourselves if we're attacked."

Seeph nodded. "I guess that makes sense."

"Besides," Thorb said as he walked out of the flight station, "if there's a fuel leak, I'd rather look for it than sit here, waiting for something to ignite it so we can blow up like a giant firework, don't you think?"

* * * * *

Chapter Fourteen

2nd Platoon, Tarpik, Tarpik System

"Did he—" Tald wanted to know. He *had* to know… but with his stomach tied up in knots, he couldn't force himself to ask the question. Tald had seen the explosion as the missile hit the dropship, and had seen the smoke and the craft hurtling toward the ground. He hadn't heard it hit, but then again, there was a lot of firing and explosions, so he wasn't sure if he'd missed it.

"No," Sansar said, guessing the question on his mind. She waved back toward the landing pad. "Somehow he put it down on the pad, but I don't think he's taking off any time soon."

"Is he all right?"

"I don't know, but he put it down, so I'm guessing he is." She pointed toward the tower. "We have to focus on the mission, though, or everything he's done so far is meaningless."

Tald swallowed. She was right, although… Thorb's heroics had put everything into a slightly new perspective, and a host of questions ran through his head. *That's the kind of thing Thorb does for the Golden Horde? That he's done for years?* And then: *How is he not* dead?

Having had his first taste of combat, Tald was pretty sure of one thing. He didn't want a second.

But as he turned away from the landing pad, he realized he didn't have any other choice. It didn't take someone with years of experience to see the Goka coming from the other towers and realize the Golden Horde troopers in the open—*and me, too! What the hell am I doing out here?*—needed to get inside as quickly as possible.

"Let's go," Sansar said, moving toward the tower doors, which was a great, gaping hole; someone had shredded them, and Tald was happy to be wearing his boots.

Tald started to run past Sansar in his haste to get inside, away from the gathering Goka, but she grabbed him. "Your enthusiasm is noted, Peacemaker," she said, "but why don't you let the people in armor lead the way?"

"Oh, yes, of course," Tald stammered. He hadn't given any thought to the fact that there were Goka *inside* the building as well, and he might very well be running from an area of lesser danger toward one that actually had *more*. All he'd thought about was how exposed he was, and he wanted that to end as quickly as possible. But not—definitely *not*—if that meant running up and impaling himself on a Goka knife.

"*Do you want to leave anyone outside?*" Mun asked over the platoon net.

"No." Sansar said. "I have a feeling it's going to get too hot out there."

"*We've already seen the Goka run down the side of the building.*"

"If they run, they run," Sansar said. "That's fewer we'll need to kill."

"*The Tooliq might get away,*" Mun cautioned.

"He might, but I'm starting to get a bad feeling about this." Sansar paused and then added, "The Peacemaker won't run; if we recover him, I'll be happy."

Tald smiled as he listened. Sansar really *did* care about helping him.

"*So where do we go?*" Mun asked.

"Forward and up."

* * *

1st Platoon, Tarpik, Tarpik System

"*Going down to the next level,*" Sergeant Jargal reported. "*I see the rest of the platoon. No contact.*"

"Copy," Naran replied. This was the fourth level they'd come down so far. Aside from the Goka Naran had seen in the first room she'd come to, they hadn't found a single alien in the building. They'd searched the floors as they'd gone; the top levels had all been apartments. Naran shook her head. Why you'd want to be at the top of the tower, though, made no sense to her—all it let you do was see more desert. *How much desert do you need to see?*

The flooring of the tower—at least at the top, anyway—was a counterclockwise circular pathway down, with each revolution leading to several doors on each "floor."

The fireteam with Naran completed the search of the last room on her current level. "Level secure," she transmitted. "Down to the next level."

"*Copy, ma'am.*"

As she turned to go, though, she saw motion on her aft camera, and she spun around to see a black head pull back from the outside of the window. She strode over to the window and punched it out, then looked out.

The side of the building was black for several floors down due to the Goka crawling up the side of it.

"Fuck!" She leaned out so her shoulder-mounted MAC had an angle on them, targeted the closest Goka, and fired on auto. "Contact! Last floor cleared. They're on the outside of the building." She killed several of the closest bugs, but the rest surged forward, and she knew one rifle wasn't going to keep them out of the room.

Once they're in the room with me, I'm going to be overrun. Blue Sky!

Naran turned and ran, hoping to stay in front of the tide of giant roaches. "This is Major Enkh. I'm coming to rejoin the platoon."

"What do you want us to do?" Sergeant First Class Dayir Bat asked. *"Hold or come back to you?"*

Good damn question. Based on the number of Goka coming, they'd need a good killing field—somewhere to keep the Goka outside of their arms' and knives' reach. "Press on," Naran said. "As fast as possible. We need a wide open area to fight them, and we don't want to get trapped in a small space with them."

"No, ma'am, we don't. We'll push on. Do you need assistance?"

"I just need running room to stay—" The door in front of her burst open, and a Goka stepped out and looked around. Without breaking stride, she jumped up slightly and came down on the alien with all her weight. The alien's shell split, and fluids—and other, unrecognizable stuff—exploded outward, coating her suit's legs and the Goka who were behind the first one.

She sent a spray of MAC fire through the closest ones, but the ones behind them only skittered forward across the backs of their allies. Meanwhile, motion from the aft camera showed the ones chasing her were getting closer. "Shit!"

Naran tapped her jumpjets, blasted out of the remains of the Goka, and raced down the hallway. Additional doors opened in front of her, and she sprayed MAC rounds at them without breaking stride. The temptation to tap her jumpjets again to try to hurtle them was strong, but she'd already gotten lucky once and didn't want to push her luck. The ceilings weren't much taller than the CASPer she drove—if she jumped and hit her head, she'd probably lose her balance and go down onto her back. With the crowd chasing her, that was sure to be fatal.

"Coming in hot!" Naran transmitted. She primed a K-bomb—a giant, CASPer-sized grenade—and dropped it as she ran.

Boom!

That wouldn't discourage pursuit, but it would slow it down slightly. Another quarter-turn, and there were two CASPers waiting for her. They fired at the few Goka who'd escaped the K-bomb, then they turned to follow her.

Naran was just starting to feel pretty good about her escape when the radio crackled.

"Contact front! Blue Sky! There's a lot of the fuckers!"

* * *

2nd Platoon, Tarpik, Tarpik System

"*Colonel Enkh, we've got some problems up here.*"

"What's that?"

"*Goka in fortified positions. We can probably crack them... but it's going to cost us.*"

"Stand by. Moving up."

The platoon had made good progress for about fifteen minutes, and had cleared the first two levels. Most of it had been some sort of shopping district, although the things the Goka thought were worth spending money on... Tald tried not to dwell on it so he wouldn't throw up in front of the troopers. He'd heard them laughing at someone who *had* vomited; he didn't want to join the ranks of the laughed at. Although—he chuckled to himself—at least he wouldn't be trapped inside a metal suit with his puke for hours on end. He could do it and move on, and no one might even see him do it.

Sansar started for the front, and Tald followed in her wake, trying to stay under cover as he'd been taught.

She stopped after a few moments and said, "Blue Sky."

Tald crept up next to her and looked quickly out from cover and then back. A long ramp up led to the next floor—a wide-open killing zone that was defended by a number of Goka behind various objects.

"That's going to be tough," Sansar agreed. "Where did Justice go?"

"*No idea,*" several voices said.

"Damn Hunters," Sansar muttered. "Just when you need them."

Tald shook his head. He certainly didn't want to go out there. *Blue Sky!* He didn't even want to *look* out there again. As he leaned back and sighed, though, he had an idea.

"Sansar?" he asked.

"Yes, Tald?" She did a good job of keeping the exasperation out of her voice. He barely heard it.

"It looks like they're dug in like an Alabama tick. One of my instructors told me that when I was faced with something like this, I needed to take a different path. 'Don't let the enemy choose the terrain you fight on,' he said."

"That'd be awesome," Sansar said, "but we're out of jumpjuice, so we can't go over them. We also can't go under them. That leaves going through them, unless you can see a different path."

"I can, actually."

"Which is?"

"The ventilation system."

"CASPers won't fit."

"But Justice and I will. We can go around the enemy and flank them. That's the right term, right? Flank them?"

"That's the right term," Sansar said, "and it would be a great plan. There's just one problem."

"What's that?"

"Do you see Justice?"

"Well, no, but I usually don't see him."

"He's not responding to our verbal or radio calls. Without him, that just leaves you. You want to take them on by yourself?"

Tald's stomach sank. It was one thing to plan an attack with a super assassin on your side; it was another thing entirely to do it by yourself. He summoned up Marshall Dillon and threw his shoulders back. "I can do this, ma'am. Just give me a couple minutes to get behind them, and I'll hit them while you hold their attention."

"You can do this? Seriously?"

"Yes, ma'am, I well and truly can."

Sansar chuckled. "It would mean fewer Human deaths, so if you want to try it, go ahead."

"Sure thing, ma'am." Tald looked at the duct. "Um, ma'am?"

"Having second thoughts?"

"No, ma'am. One thing, though. Could one of your folks possibly give me a boost?" He pointed at the vent cover—almost two meters over his head, but less than half a meter above the CASPers'.

"My pleasure," Sansar said. She reached up and slapped the end of the duct, ripping off the metal cover, screws and all, then lowered her cupped hands.

Tald stepped into them, and she boosted him up into the duct. It was considerably darker than he'd thought it would be, but he was still able to see. *Just like being in the tunnels on Hades,* he thought, trying to psyche himself up as the walls closed in on him.

"Five minutes?" Sansar asked.

"Something like that," Tald said. "I'll call you."

Five minutes later, Tald was hopelessly lost in the labyrinthine tunnels and ducting. He didn't even know if he was on the right level. He thought he'd gone up two floors and then back down two, but he was no longer sure. He certainly didn't know where he was in relation to the enemy forces.

In point of fact, he wasn't really sure of much, except that he was still in the same tower. *Probably.*

He sat down, feeling sorry for himself. Everyone was counting on him, and he was failing. They'd called him twice. The first time, he'd answered, but the second time he'd been too ashamed. He sniffed, trying to come up with a plan, but failing miserably.

"The dust gets in my nose up here, too," Justice said, becoming visible next to him. "It's not a great way to travel, but there are fewer laser bolts up here."

"Justice! What are you doing here?"

"I heard you banging around up here and thought you were a Goka, trying to flank the Golden Horde. Can't have that, so I came up here to check. Imagine my surprise to find you here."

"The Horde needs help," Tald said. "I came up here to flank the Goka." He looked down. "But I kind of got lost."

"Oh. Well, that's no problem. I know an exit, and I can show you where the Golden Horde is." He stopped and sniffed.

"What is it?"

"I don't know. I've never smelled anything like it. Earthy and dusty. It's strange. Let's go find out what it is, then we'll help the Golden Horde."

"But I promised. They *need* me."

"They need *us*, and they'll get us. After we check this out." With a swish of his tail, he was gone, trotting up the duct, and Tald had to hurry to catch up.

He followed the Hunter for another minute, with Justice stopping a couple times to check on the strange scent. Every step felt like it took them farther from the Horde and farther from his mission and promise. *I'm letting them down.* He kept from sniffing again, but it took an act of will.

Finally, Justice stopped at a vent and looked through it. "Huh."

"What is it?" Tald asked as he hurried up to the Depik.

Justice slow-blinked. "I don't know. I've never seen anything like it ever before."

Tald paced back to an area roughly outside the room Justice had found, and wormed his way out of the duct. He dropped into the hall as quietly as he could, then paused, wondering if Justice had joined him.

"You coming?"

"You get that one out—I'll hold off the Goka trying to flank our Humans."

Tald spun to regard the door ahead of him and nodded determinedly to himself. Open a likely monitored door, housing what was hopefully the Peacemaker, but definitely a prisoner, in the midst of a Goka-filled tower currently being assaulted by the Golden Horde. What could go wrong?

* * *

Dropship *One*, Tarpik, Tarpik System

"There it is," Thorb said.

"What?" Seeph asked.

"The fuel leak. What did you think we were looking for?"

"Well, the fuel leak, sure, but you sounded excited."

"I am excited. I can reach the leak, and I *think* I can—at least temporarily—fix it." He shuffled forward a little in the ducting. A Human couldn't have reached it; the SalSha themselves barely fit. "Hand me up the ordie tape."

"What?"

"The ordnance tape. I gave it to you. I need it. Hand it up." After a second, Thorb asked, "You haven't lost it, have you?"

"Of course not."

"Well, hand it up, then."

"I can't. The hand it's in is down by my side, and I can't slide it up past my chest."

Thorb looked back. Now that Seeph said it, he had no idea how he'd get a paw back to take it from him, even if Seeph had been able to pass it forward. "Damn it," Thorb said. "Let's back out of the tunnel, and I'll just push it in front of me."

"Fine."

"Fine."

Getting out was every bit as hard as getting in had been, but Thorb managed. Finally. He emerged, cut up in a few places, and dirty and oily almost all over. He took the tape and tore several strips, which he attached to his paw. "That way, I don't have to try to rip it off in the duct."

Whether it was because he'd already done it once or because of the oil coating his fur, he was able to slither up the duct to where he'd seen the leak. The good news was, he could still find it, because the bad news was it was still leaking. Which he realized was an issue, since he hadn't brought anything to wipe off the piping.

Nothing except his sleeve and his fur, anyway. If there'd been any more room, he'd have shaken his head. He'd have to stay away from open flames and sparks for a while. He cleaned the pipe the best he could, then wrapped the ordie tape around it the best he could. He watched it for a few moments. Although it didn't appear to still be leaking, he had no idea what would happen once the fuel system was pressurized.

I guess we'll just have to burn that bridge when we come to it. There wasn't enough room to shrug, either, even if his arms weren't pinned over his head. He slithered his way back out of the duct.

"Get it?" Seeph asked.

"Maybe?" Thorb replied. "At least, I think so. I'll give it two-to-one odds it'll hold."

"That's not very good."

"You want to crawl in there and see if you can do better?"

"Not particularly. You look like shit." Seeph sniffed. "And you smell worse."

Thorb wiped himself off as best he could. There wouldn't be any way to get completely clean until they were back on the *Gobi Desert*, and even then, it wasn't going to be fun. This wasn't the glamorous side of being a fly-boy he'd been promised.

Bang!

"What the hell was that?" Seeph asked.

"That's the sound of a MAC round or some sort of ballistic round hitting the side of the dropship." A second round landed, then a third, then a veritable storm of rounds. "Probably ballistic."

"How do you know?" Seeph asked."

"They haven't gone through the armor… yet."

Seeph started to ask another question, but Thorb was already running for the cockpit. The youngster had a stupid question for every occasion, and now absolutely wasn't the time.

Thorb dropped into his seat and found an awful lot of black shapes skittering up toward the dropship from all directions. It looked like a disgusting moving carpet that he wanted no part of. At some point, they'd get the nerve to rush the craft and put their knives to work… he needed to be gone before that happened.

Thorb began flipping switches, using the expedited engine start procedure.

"We're not planning on taking off still, are we?" Seeph asked from behind Thorb's shoulder.

Thorb jumped up and grabbed a pawful of the chest of Seeph's flight suit, then he pointed out the window with his other hand. "Do you see that? Those are Goka, coming to kill us. If we're not airborne in about two minutes, *we're dead!* Sit down, shut up, and shoot as many of them as you can while I get us going. If you can keep them off us, we may live through this." He grabbed Seeph with both hands and pushed him into the copilot's seat. "*Now get shooting!*"

Seeph's eyes got big as he looked out the canopy, and Thorb realized the junior pilot hadn't seen the Goka coming or recognized them as such. He shook his head as he brought the port motor to life. *Was I ever that young and dumb?*

He tapped the fuel pressure gauge. It was about half what it normally was, so it was still probably leaking. Hopefully, it would hold long enough to let them get somewhere else. He hadn't figured out where that was yet; all he knew was, at least it wouldn't be here, surrounded by stabby aliens.

With power to the main systems, Seeph began firing the chin turret. Thorb could hear him muttering, but it took him a minute to understand what the junior pilot was saying. Finally, he caught it as Seeph's voice rose. "Die, die, die..." over and over.

"They're coming from behind us," Seeph said, stopping his litany for a moment. "I need you to spin the craft, because I can't turn the turret far enough."

Thorb advanced the throttle and was able to get enough power to lift a foot above the pad. He was also able to level the dropship, which helped his equilibrium. There was still a little juice in the starboard thruster. He tapped it, the dropship spun to the left, and Seeph began firing again.

"You're going to want to hurry," Seeph said. "Ammo level is at 20 percent."

Awesome. I didn't have enough problems.

As far as "wanting" to hurry, Thorb wanted to hurry with every hair on his body. Spinning the ship had driven back some of the Goka, but the ones that found themselves outside the radius of the gun hadn't taken long to realize they were no longer under fire. They took the opportunity to surge forward.

Thorb flipped the last switch. They were getting as much out of the engine as they were going to. He spun the dropship to line it up down the length of the pad. "Clear me a path," he said. "Here we go!"

It was the ugliest takeoff he'd ever attempted. The runway wasn't long enough for a single-engine takeoff, even if he'd had full thrust, or if he'd been able to use all the thrust he had toward generating airspeed. As it was, with the bent landing gear, he had to use some of the thrust in VTOL mode to hold the dropship level on one wheel. They began moving forward at a walk. A slow walk.

It was enough to give the Goka the impetus to charge as their prey started—oh, so slowly—to escape.

Unfortunately, there were also too many of the black aliens in front of the craft for Seeph to shoot before they reached them. By then, they were going at a relatively fast jog, and Thorb wondered whether they had enough speed to run over the Goka, or if they'd act like personal chocks, throwing themselves in front of the wheels to try to stop the aircraft.

They did, lying down in a line in front of the approaching craft, but by then the ship was traveling at a Human run, and it crunched over the bodies, barely slowing. There was a small bump, then they were picking up speed again.

Just in time to run off the prepared surface of the landing pad and transition to the desert floor. Thorb squeaked a little more power into the VTOL modules to hold them off the sand—flying in ground effect—and he was able to get the weight off the gear. He tried bringing up the landing gear, but only one wheel rose. Still, that streamlined the craft some, and the rate they were picking up airspeed built.

"You see the towers in front of us, right?" Seeph asked.

No, Thorb actually *hadn't* been looking that far in front of the craft, and he *hadn't* seen the towers. One glance was all it took, though, to see they weren't going to be able to climb over them. In a normal dropship with two perfect motors? No problem. In the giant piece of shit he was keeping airborne mostly with positive thoughts? Not a chance.

Nor could he try to turn. He'd lose lift, drag a wingtip in the sand, and do some sort of cartwheel into the desert. Flight over.

He only had the starboard thruster, but there were additional buildings to the left of centerline. He tried the port thruster, but it performed as expected. It contributed nothing to their salvation. Gritting his teeth, he hit the starboard thruster, and they began turning left.

"There are more buildings that way!" Seeph yelled.

"Thanks, MOTO. Look at the thrusters. The other one is out."

"Oh," Seeph said. "You're right. Nevermind."

Thorb didn't say what came to mind, he continued doing everything he could to clear the buildings. They were now up to almost a hundred kilometers an hour. Not enough to leave the ground effect and fly, but maybe… just maybe they would be before they ran into the buildings.

"What's MOTO?" Seeph asked.

"Master of the fucking obvious," Thorb said through gritted teeth. One hundred thirty kph. They needed one sixty.

"Can't be," Seeph said. "There's no 'F' in it."

"Seeph, do me a favor?"

"Sure."

Thorb took a second to glance over. "*Shut the fuck up!*" He turned back to find the building close. Too close. One fifty-five. *It'll have to do.*

Thorb eased back on the stick, and the dropship struggled into the air. He slowly gave it a little angle of bank, not wanting—or able—to dump any of the lift. It wasn't going to be enough—*the starboard wing is still going to hit!*

Seeph didn't say anything, but he pointed at the building.

"I see it," Thorb said. He waited until the last minute, then he slammed the stick to the left, going full left wing down. The dropship immediately lost lift and started to fall from the sky, then they were past the tower, and Thorb leveled the wings. Immediately, they leveled out, airspeed began increasing again, and the dropship began climbing.

"And *that* is how you do it," Thorb said, glancing over at Seeph again. The junior pilot was still pointing to the window. "We're clear," Thorb added. "You can put your paw down now."

"Bug!" Seeph screamed.

Thorb looked forward. A Goka had slid down the canopy in front of Seeph, and it was working its knife into the canopy seal.

"Fuck, those guys don't give up," Thorb muttered. He looked at the alien for a moment, trying to figure out how to get it off—acrobatics was contraindicated at the moment—then had an idea. The dropship didn't have window wipers; instead, the rain removal system used forced-draft blowers to propel rain from the canopy.

Thorb activated the system. Only powered by one motor, the blast of air wasn't as strong as it normally would have been, but the Goka hadn't been expecting it and lost its grip. Thorb went right wing down for a moment and pitched the alien from the craft. "Easy peasy," he said, sitting back in his seat.

He smiled as the dropship continued to climb... until the Hyd Press caution light illuminated. It was the first of many—too many to count. That one worried him enough, though, as the hydraulic pressure gauge headed to zero. The control stick got soft in his hand.

"What's going on?" Seeph asked.

"Must be more Goka on the craft," Thorb said. The Left Flap light illuminated, then the stick began jumping in his grip. He leaned forward so he could look out and back at the port wing.

It was covered with Goka.

Not one or two, but at least ten, and most of them were using their knives to stab through the skin of the wing. A variety of fluids spewed from a number of holes; Thorb recognized two of them, at least, as hydraulics.

The Goka who weren't stabbing his craft were playing with the flaps, and they raised it as one, killing his lift. Thorb tried turning the craft to throw them off, but the stick went dead in his hands.

"Are there Goka on your wing over there?" Thorb asked.

Seeph looked up. "Yeah."

"What are they doing?"

"Stabbing it and messing with the flap."

"Damn it." With a sigh, Thorb reduced power.

"Why did you pull power?" Seeph asked.

"Because I no longer have control of the dropship," Thorb said. "The stupid Goka do."

"Well, won't having more airspeed help?" Seeph asked. "Maybe we can get control back."

"Not before we hit that." Thorb pointed out the window. "And all things considered, if I have to crash into that tower, I'd rather do it as slowly as possible."

Seeph's eyes widened as he looked at the tower on their nose. "Can't you do something?"

"No," Thorb said. "Not this time. All we can do is assume crash positions."

The crash, when they hit, was every bit as bad as Thorb had expected, and blackness claimed him.

* * * * *

Chapter Fifteen

Goka Holding Facility, Tarpik System

Balin sat in his large, too-angled room and glared at the single door. He wasn't a prisoner, they reassured him regularly, but the door only locked in one direction, and it wasn't his.

Even as a newling with dirt under his baby claws, fresh off his homeworld, young Balin wouldn't have fallen for that.

As a Peacemaker with eight or more decades of experience behind him, he found it insulting, and a little funny, given that he'd carved his way out of one room already. But mostly insulting.

He ran a long claw under his scales—it had been days since he'd been able to get a proper sandblast—and out of long habit, checked his countdown.

It had nothing new to tell him.

The problem with being a genetic freak of an already self-isolating race—at least the one that mattered most in the moment—was there wasn't anywhere or anyone he could go to in order to learn more about the vagaries of his biology. The vast majority of Phidae lived long, peaceful, boring lives. Hundreds of years, never leaving their planet, content with their own company. Of the rare Dimindiem like him, doomed to live a half-life of blazing glory, he'd met only one.

Given that one was approximately eighty—it felt like a thousand—years younger than him, he couldn't ask the specific questions that mattered to Balin himself.

Like, "My genetic death countdown clock stopped, but I'm still alive."

Right, that wasn't a question. The question, "Is that something that happens?" would be helpful. Also, "How long might it last?"

Was he going to drop dead any second? It seemed less and less likely as the months sped by. The way mitochondria measured time might not line up with his perception, so that internal clock might not have been as accurate as he'd always thought. As he had no way to better communicate with his own cells, and no one to ask, what all that really meant was his most pressing question was in actuality, "Why have the tree-rotted Goka locked me up, and how in the misbegotten night am I going to get out again?"

They'd taken all his weapons, which he'd allowed, because he was still, in essence, a weapon all by himself. He was taller than them, broader, his claws were better than their silly little knives that couldn't pierce his armor, and also the edges of many of his scales were strong enough to slice metal.

What did they have? A semi-respectable exoskeleton and a soft inside. The only soft inside Balin had was his mouth.

Which he opened and closed uselessly in a smooth room made of a metal laced through with electricity—meaning every time he sliced at it, which he did quite a bit, he got a series of electric shocks that eventually dissuaded even him.

Also the room was too big and open, and he couldn't sleep properly, no matter how tight a ball he rolled into. Most annoying, the Goka themselves looked like overgrown snacks. While eating a sentient being—even an arguably sentient one—was distasteful, they looked like they'd taste good, and they hadn't fed him at all. His appetite was fairly nonexistent these days, but it was an intolerable combination regardless.

All in all, it wasn't his worst mission, but it wasn't far from that pinnacle of disaster.

So when the door opened, and something very small and very furry ran in, Balin figured it was all part of the same mess. Therefore he didn't ask questions, he barreled past the small figure—the door was open, he'd figure everything else out later—curled slightly at the immediate sounds of gunfire not far off, then belatedly registered the little furry had had something shining on his chest.

Badge.

Peacemaker.

He swiveled, placing his back to the wall in the hallway outside his room—the wall scuffed immediately under his flared scales, with no shock whatsoever, which was a relief—and squinted at the small creature. The waste-faced Goka had also taken his goggles. He had spares on his *Eletine*, but it would be a miserable return trip. Again, not the worst.

"They couldn't have sent you after me; I haven't been here *that* long." Had he? Sometimes the electrocution knocked him out, but he'd been here days, not weeks.

"We weren't here for you originally!" The little Peacemaker—Balin was sure it wasn't his blurry eyesight—kept his guns at the ready, one toward Balin's erstwhile room, and one down the hall. Balin appreciated the style—he too had two pistols, though they were with his goggles, harness, badge, and everything else—and the discipline. "We followed a trail for the *Keesius*—"

Oh. Ohhhhh. Civix had mentioned that they'd sent another Peacemaker, one who needed some seasoning. More of a test case, Balin wondered, or a decoy?

Or is this another soft clawed rookie for me to train?

More shots fired from a short distance, and Balin dismissed the questions for the moment. The Peacemaker pup was bright enough to make it here and not get locked in a room for days by overgrown food, so he was hardly the concern at the moment.

"Think you're on the right one. You got an extra gun laying around—no, not one of those, clearly you do best double-fisting, I'm not taking it." Truth was, he wasn't sure if the smaller Peacemaker had been offering—his small shape was blurred in Balin's unassisted eyesight. Instead, Balin flared the sharpest of his scales down his arms and back. "I'm sharp and about as laser-resistant as the Goka. Where are we going, and what's the situation?"

The small Peacemaker's mouth audibly snapped shut, then his fur quivered—maybe he shook himself—and he gave Balin a wide berth as he moved down the hall again. Smart little guy. "I'm Peacemaker Tald, and I'm here with my deputies. On the ground, we've got a troop of the Golden Horde, their Commander Enkh is one of the deputies; our Veetanho contact Gleeko, who isn't compromised by Dunamis; the Hunter Justice, you might call him a Depik but he's a Hunter; and the Pendal Josiff, who found this place. We're fighting too many Goka to count, but the Horde has them mostly bottle-necked two floors up and that way."

"That's… quite a collection of deputies," Balin responded. He hadn't had that many deputies in his career, never mind all at once. This was either hugely impressive, or a complete and total dung pile, and he couldn't see it landing anywhere in between. A Hunter *and* a Veetanho? Working together?

That… seemed unlikely.

Tald eased around the corner, then waved at Balin to follow. "Still clear so far," he continued. "We came in really hot."

"Let's do it this way." Balin lengthened his stride and passed Tald, but stayed to one side of the hall so the younger Peacemaker had a clear line of sight. "You eye the path; I go first and block any stray fire." He leaned to the right enough to drag his lifted arm scales along the wall and tear a few long rents. Petty, but he had to make sure everything worked after a few days of enforced idleness. "My vision's a sucking waste hole without my goggles, but point me in the needful direction, and I'll clear the way."

"Goka or walls both, huh?" Tald sounded properly impressed. Balin strove not to like him until he understood the situation better. "How'd they keep you locked up?"

"I broke out of the first room, then they used a big alternating current prod to insist I was an honored guest and couldn't leave just yet. Let me tell you—Peacemaker to Peacemaker—I didn't feel very honored."

"They were trying to honor the threat?" Tald asked, and Balin heard a bit of a laugh in it.

"They tried, but you know how it goes. We'll stand, they'll fall."

"Sounds like a plan to me, sir."

Three turns later, the gunfire got a whole lot closer, and Balin flexed his claws. He felt gritty and out of sorts—no food, and worse, no sandblast for days wasn't setting him up for his best. To be fair, he wasn't at his best as it had once been, but for a small amount of time… yeah, he could be the best, briefly, like he used to be. Work out all that penned energy.

He flexed his claws and flared his scales, then pitched his voice low. "What's around the corner, Peacemaker Tald? Friendlies, or my hosts?"

Tald crouched low—Balin was surprised he could get smaller—and sighted briefly around the corner. "Goka. They're coming out of a room near the end of the hall, focused on the far curve. At least five on the ceiling—the rest are moving too much to get a clear count."

"Think they saw you?"

"No, and we're far enough back they shouldn't have felt our vibrations. Not over everything happening down that way. I don't like that they flanked our people…"

"Be surprised if they didn't—classic Goka, and this is their home burrow." Balin shrugged, lifted his arms over his head—with the way his body curved, the ceiling was a bit of a stretch, but not impossible—and shook out his limbs. Softly, to keep from attracting any unwanted attention.

"If you have a way of figuring out which of your people are over there, let them know it's going to get messy, but I'm friendly. If I get close enough, the Goka will be more likely to stab than shoot, but I don't need those big Human guns testing my armor at the same time."

Balin liked Humans. Rather, he liked the one he'd worked with, though that one was dead… but he'd heard good things, so combined with the one he'd known well, he was inclined to be in favor. Unlike the Goka, who'd never distinguished themselves as individuals, and then had kept him gritty and vaguely hungry in a room with too many sharp corners and no close, inviting spaces for naps.

That would make this enjoyable.

"Honor the threat," he murmured, then he barreled around the corner.

Phidae weren't known for their speed. More truthfully, Phidae weren't much known. They stayed home on their comfortable planet that was made for them. But some, like Balin, went out and met the galaxy head on.

Some, like Balin, sank their claws in and tore underneath to see what the galaxy was made of.

Mostly, it was made of beings making dumb decisions—but at least it was a place beings *got* to make their own dumb decisions. But there were also bullies. Bullies with *Keesius* ships, for instance, or big, electric guns that bypassed his armor. SIs. Things that took away the ability to make those choices.

Balin disapproved, therefore Balin responded with what he had—sharp edges. He ran at top speed, such as it was, curled his shoulders forward, tucked his head, and lifted one of his arms. Not the most comfortable position, but enough. He'd scraped his claws through two Goka on the ceiling before the rest were aware—they were really focused on whatever Tald's deputies were doing around the far corner.

Three more dropped down on him, knives flashing. Adorable.

They'd made a point to stay well out of arm's length during his visit. He reminded them why that was a good idea.

Balin spun quickly while still in motion, and his flared scales re-buffed knives and sliced at some of the unluckier Gokas' joints. Legs scattered around him. He tucked his arms and added his claws to the mix, and innards joined the legs.

There were noises—gunfire, chittering alarm, his own bellowing—but mostly he focused on the tearing of limbs and cracking of chitin. He bit one that was too fast for him to slice with the scales on his head—Goka absolutely did *not* taste like food, they were acidic and burnt rubbery, which he supposed was good to know—and rolled into a near-ball when they swarmed.

One tried to stab under an uplifted scale, but too bad for them—under his big scales, Balin had smaller scales. Scales all the way down—at least as all the way down as their pointy little knives could dig.

Balin rolled. He was much heavier than a Goka, his claws were longer than their weapons, and their guns were about as effective on him as they'd be on their fellows. That put them at a distinct disadvantage.

They did, however, outnumber him by a rather absurd amount, and he didn't have the endurance he'd had as a younger Peacemaker.

Thankfully… he had one of those, too.

Tald—or one of his dozens of deputies—took advantage of the distraction he'd caused, and a whole lot of firepower joined the party. Balin couldn't see it—not his eyesight this time, more the pile of Goka he was busy shredding his way out of—but he heard it, and the weight around him got significantly lighter.

He clawed his way through another small handful of oversized snack packs and straightened, coming face to face with something else small and furry. More orange and black than Peacemaker Tald's brown. The Depik, maybe?

"Hunter, I greet you," he said, figuring it was worth the chance. "I'm Peacemaker Balin."

"Warrior, I greet you," the Depik replied, confirming his theory. "I am Justice, of Clan Tamir. Welcome... to our negotiation."

"I honor the threat, as ever. I knew a Hunter Peacemaker a very long time ago."

The Depik, perched on three partially dismembered Goka, cocked his head. "This pleases me, Peacemaker Balin. I would hear stories after we are done hunting."

"Hm." Balin straightened, then paused to pick out chunks of chitinous exoskeleton that had wedged under some of his scales. "That would be agreeable to me."

"Onward, then."

"Did you just open negotiations with him?" Tald asked, off to one side and not sounding remotely winded. Oh, to be young again. "I thought you didn't do that!"

"He impressed me," Justice replied, then vanished.

Balin shrugged, gave himself the length of a breath to wish for a good, long sandblast and something to get the awful taste out of his mouth, then he squinted at the one furry body remaining.

"There are more cornering the rest of the Horde this way."

"Only way out is through," he said, and Tald snapped him a salute.

* * *

1st Platoon, Tarpik, Tarpik System

Naran ran up on the rest of the platoon, who were engaged in a firefight with about double their number of Goka. Naran shook her head. Maybe it was a sign of Dunamis' favor—or maybe even some of his programming—but she'd never seen so many Goka armed with rifles before. Their normal attack involved rushing forward and knifing everything to death. She liked that about them; it usually gave you time to shoot them before they got within reach. To see them standing back and using weapons just seemed… unnatural, somehow.

The space they battled across was the first major landing she'd seen, with a number of corridors leading from it. There were also several windows, and the main ramp leading down to the next floor. All of those spaces seemed full of writhing black shapes.

"What's the status, Sergeant Bat?" Naran asked.

"It's pretty much what you see, ma'am. The enemy's got a bunch of places they can shoot from, and there's only one way for the platoon to enter that space. It's a chokepoint we haven't been able to breach."

"Well, there's a big-ass group of Goka following me that'll be here in seconds, so I need some ideas before we get swarmed."

"Gonna be hard to take out all those positions in that time, ma'am."

"I once had an instructor who said anything can be solved with the appropriate application of high explosives."

"Like blowing the top off this building?"

"Want to go hand-to-hand with the Goka?"

"Not particularly, ma'am."

"Then we hit them with as much H-E as possible and keep running."

"You got it, ma'am." He passed out orders to a number of the troopers. "Ready when you are, ma'am."

"You've got point when the K-bombs blow," Naran said. "I'll take trail."

"Ma'am—"

"You've got your orders, Sergeant. Execute them."

"Yes, ma'am." He raised his voice. "Grenadiers, throw!"

Five troopers stood and hurled their K-bombs, and Naran winced as two of their icons went yellow in her HUD, as the Goka fired for all they were worth. A third suit went red, and Corporal Jernigan fell backward. Naran glanced her way to check and nodded; she'd thrown her grenade before getting zapped.

The explosives detonated, filling the space with smoke and debris.

"Forward and through!" Sergeant First Class Bat yelled, rising and racing forward.

With a roar, the platoon rose and ran forward, swords out to stab any of the Goka who'd been stunned and not killed outright.

Motion and then laser rounds from behind indicated to Naran that her time had run out. She hurried after the platoon, glancing at where Jernigan had fallen. With a mental salute—there was nothing Naran could do for the corporal—Naran dashed after platoon.

There was nothing they could do but go forward; behind her was a passageway full of

Goka and their stabby knives.

* * *

Third Floor, Goka Facility, Tarpik

"What do you think, Colonel?" Mun asked.

"I think this is a shit contract, and I'm sorry I got all of us into it."

"Well, yeah," Mun said. "That part's pretty obvious, but there's nothing we can do about it at this point. I was more talking about the position above us and the fuck-ton of Goka pressing up to us from behind."

"We're going to have to move forward before too long. I was hoping Tald could distract them, but we're about out of time. I was also kind of hoping 1st Platoon would show up and hit the Goka in the ass, too."

"Hope ain't much of a strategy, ma'am."

"I know it's not." Sansar sighed. "I guess we'll have to—"

"*2nd Platoon, 1st Platoon,*" Naran Enkh called.

"Go ahead," Sansar replied.

"*We're pretty hung up here,*" Naran said. "*I've got Goka coming in the windows, and they're in front of us and behind us.*" She paused and then added, "*Any chance you'll be advancing on our position sometime soon?*"

Sansar shook her head. So much for getting 1st Platoon's assistance for them. "We're stuck at the moment, too. We sent Tald to hit them from behind, but the Goka must have caught him, because he's overdue. We're about to attack. Can you hold for a few minutes?"

"*Hold? Maybe. We're certainly not going anywhere. They seem to have a limitless supply of roaches, and our ammo supply is a lot less than that.*"

"Hold tight, 1st Platoon. Give me a couple minutes to resolve this situation, and we'll be on our way."

"*Roger. Holding. For now.*"

"Guess it's up to us," Mun said.

"Guess so."

"Gonna wait on the SalSha any longer?"

"Nope. Don't have time."

"Okay," Mun said. "I guess we're going to have to do it ourselves, then. What the—"

A massive detonation rocked the tower, and Sansar turned to find a shower of blue and black falling from the position up the ramp from them. Finally, one of the black things hit the deck, and she recognized it as a Goka leg. That made the other black objects in the air Goka parts, and the blue in the air Goka blood. What had happened up there?

Doesn't matter; this is our opportunity. Sansar pointed up the ramp. *"Charge!"*

* * * * *

Chapter Sixteen

Fifth Floor, Goka Facility, Tarpik

The rest of the Golden Horde, along with their commander, had a much larger array of Goka pinned down across the endless twists of the Goka's building.

While they remained alert for other detachments of their unwilling hosts, Balin and Tald had a bit of time to catch each other up on the highest level overviews of their investigations.

"Hades, hm? Impressive, Tald, impressive." Balin scratched under his scales with his free hand as they walked. He'd taken two guns from the dead Goka, but their straps were a poor substitute for his harness, and one had already torn apart against his sharper edges. Carrying it wasn't terrible, but he really wanted all his claws for scratching—Goka pieces got *everywhere*—and it was enough of an annoyance to keep his energy levels high.

"I tracked a Human mercenary unit through Hades, but I didn't go there myself. I wasn't sure enough of who was in charge, and didn't think I had time to dig through the mess of a Veetanho prison or its aftermath. You were smart to secure the deputies you did."

"Thank you. But you traced them through Hades without going there?" Tald shifted, but Balin couldn't make out the details of his form well enough to read his body language. Pleased at the compliment, perhaps. "How?"

"I'll show you some of my programs when we get back to my ship. Least I can do, after you sprung me loose. But the Humans definitely came through here. I don't think they stayed—Goka don't have much use for other species, as you may have realized—so I put out some drones and got locators on some of the bigger Goka ships before I docked. Got an idea of where they go that might not match up with the gate records. You said you saw the *Eletine* out there, right? It's not damaged?"

"Didn't seem to be, sir—Balin. That's what tipped us off; the Peacemaker tag flagged on the *Gobi's* sensors. Sansar figured the Goka wanted us out a little too bad not to be up to something."

"I've always heard good things about the Golden Horde." Balin tapped his claws on his shoulder, then resumed digging after they crossed the next open corridor. "Not just saying that because I'm surrounded by them, either," he added, tilting his head to show a smile.

"Why do you think the Humans are connected?"

"Coincidence is always a possibility, but a data trail's a data trail. You got an SI moving one set of things from hidey hole to even more hidden hidey hole, then another set of things go missing… makes sense to trace that trail. Might be a false lead, but it's the best I got."

"So you looked at what went into Hades, figured out what went out…"

"Much like you did, Peacemaker. Doing pretty good."

Tald muttered something Balin's audials couldn't quite parse, but he knew the tone well enough. Teyhi, the one rookie Balin had been given to season up, still trotted it out now and then. Fair enough—

once upon an epoch ago, Balin himself had been known to fall prey to it. Self-pity, a little bit of doubt.

"Tald, here's advice I'll give to you free—even if you didn't just save my scales in a big way, I'd tell you this. The guild's a big thing. It doesn't always do what we want it to do, because it doesn't work for us. Half the time, outside the occasional coordinator who gets fond of us, I don't think the guild cares about any of us at all, except that we do our jobs. So we get entropic contracts, and we get great ones, and we get shot out of waste holes, and we come out covered in glory or shit. Sometimes both."

"But…?" Tald prompted, as Balin knew he would.

"No but. That's it. The guild isn't set up to make us feel good about ourselves. You do the job. You do it the best you can, and that's enough—or you turn in your badge and call it a day."

They took the next few curving levels silently.

"This is where we came in," Justice announced, making himself visible. "Well, here but several levels down."

"Goka towers…" Balin sighed. "Worse than the oldest burrows."

"You can't fit the way we came in." Justice gestured at something that blended into the rest of the wall—Balin assumed it was some sort of ventilation staff or electrical conduit and accepted that it wasn't sized for him without squinting at it. "But I have an idea."

He did something with something—Balin thought maybe a harness, and wished the Goka labeled their hives with convenient information. Honored guests' illegally seized gear, for instance, or artillery and assorted weaponry.

"What is that?" Tald asked, which kept Balin from having to ask.

"Tape," Justice replied in the sort of careless way that told Balin whatever it was, it wasn't the sort of tape made for holding things together. "Unless you want to continue to march through these spirals and miss everything happening out there."

"I don't, but…" Tald's voice changed from one beat to the next. "*Oh.*"

"Oh?" Balin echoed, and took a long step back for good measure.

"We should go around the next curve." Tald gestured with his whole arm, which Balin could see perfectly fine.

"Steady pace," Justice called after them. "It's not going to go off unexpectedly." After another handful of moments, he added, "I'm not sure about the thickness of the wall here, so I'll give it a little extra to be sure… go a little further around in case more gives way than I'm expecting."

Explosive tape—convenient and transportable. That made Balin miss his grenades—they were so much more fun on a planet, where he didn't have to calibrate for ship or station walls to keep from blasting out into vacuum.

Justice blurred past them as they reached the curve, fully visible.

"Should we be running?" Tald asked, his pace quickening.

"Couldn't hurt!" the Depik replied, but there was humor in his voice. Balin was fairly certain that was humor. He stepped up his pace slightly in case he was mistaken.

The explosion, it turned out, had turned a large section of the Goka defense into Goka confetti and blew out an exterior wall. The gaping hole that resulted opened out into a space between turrets that even his eyesight could tell was… messy.

Goka were spilling out from somewhere above them, several things were on fire… They were a few levels above the ground, but not out of reach of the Goka's firepower, and the explosion was bound to draw attention.

Justice crept closer to the opening and vanished, but he stayed close enough to speak with them. "We can take some good shots, but we don't have the firepower for much. Maybe pull some of them up here and do more of that hallway smashing."

Balin lifted the guns he'd taken off the dead Goka behind and somewhere above them. "This isn't a well-defended position. We'd be better served with a target…" He scanned the blurry masses outside and smiled. "Hunter, how do you feel about taking over some of the big guns?"

An invisible infiltrator—the number of times he could have used one!

"Now *that* sounds like fun." Justice reappeared briefly and handed over a lump of what was likely more of the blow-up tape to Tald. "Want to draw some of their attention away?"

"They won't see you coming." Tald grumbled something, then straightened. "But sure, if we keep them distracted, they won't have a chance to scuttle the guns." He leaned out a little more—no one had started shooting at them yet—but was smart enough to pull back quickly. They'd blown a hole in some Goka who'd been using the outside of the tower to climb past them, but that wouldn't hold the rest for long. Likely, they were pausing long enough to see if anything else was going to explode.

"How much of this do you think I'll need to take down a side of this building?"

"A little bit in the right place can do a whole lot of damage." Justice bowed. "But you know what, better safe than sorry—use it all. I'll be clear in… give it two minutes?"

* * *

Fourth Floor, Goka Facility, Tarpik, Tarpik System

Tald had taken several courses at the Academy, covering various ways to both apply and defuse explosives. After the introductory explanations, there was quite a bit of hands-on training with various levels of distraction built in.

Never quite on this level, though.

Combat was *loud*, and orders of magnitude more chaotic than he'd expected. The CASPers didn't keep a perfectly straight line, the Goka were everywhere, the chattering and *booms* of various guns kept his head on a swivel, and the smells...

He kept expecting his nose to go numb to it—the burning, the oily aftertaste, the reek of beings' insides becoming outsides—but each time the air moved, a new scent would take over, and his whole face wrinkled. The back of his throat was raw, and it didn't seem like they were done yet.

Some things you have to learn by doing. He heard his own thought in Sansar's voice, and swallowed against the pressure building in his skull.

"Let's blow up a building," he muttered and used one of the Horde's CASPers for cover as he surveyed the closest towers. They were conical, thicker at the bottom than the top, so he didn't think he'd be able to collapse one in its entirety, certainly not enough to drop one of their buildings across a swath of Goka. Still, he figured he could collapse the side of the one he was in and cause enough of a ruckus to pull focus—when it became an entirely moot point.

Thwoom.

Thwam.

BOOM.

Tald whipped his body around, craning his head back. The Golden Horde was assaulting a tower that rose above a number of other, unattached turrets. One of those nearby towers had cracked. The top third of it leaned in a way it hadn't before, and chunks were shedding from under it. The lean intensified ponderously, until it seemed impossible that it could keep moving.

But it did, tipping until it hit some terminal point, after which it slid fully apart and crashed to the ground between its former base and the Horde's target tower. The sound of combat around him faded to a low-pitched hum—either from the power of the explosion or his slow, dawning realization of what was sticking out of the remaining, smoking hole. What was big enough to crash into an enormous Goka building and *break* it?

Not a CASPer, certainly. Something big enough to carry a platoon of CASPers, though? That would do it.

A dropship. His *father's* dropship.

Absolutely not.

"Was that our way out?" Balin asked, and why Tald should hear his voice so clearly among the chaos taking up every level his ears could register, Tald didn't understand.

"That's—" Words would make it real. Tald had his pistols out and pointed at the tower. They were as useless as anything he could have said.

* * *

Outside the Goka Facility, Tarpik

Justice couldn't take over the anti-aircraft system. Disappointing—he'd had an image of himself in a seat, aiming large artillery all over the field, and seeding body parts throughout.

Not his usual method of killing, but it made up for that in flair.

Esthik, one of the healers back home, had always said Hunters don't need flair, but Justice was sure Esthik hadn't meant it. The older Hunter had chosen two Humans and a Wrogul as his companions—that was a bit of showing off.

As he caused three Goka to stab each other while he flickered in and out of view, Justice considered that he should take a companion. His Dama had encouraged it for years, and he wanted to, sometimes, but...

Maybe he could get a Peacemaker contract and take Tald as a companion. He wondered if there'd *be* a Peacemaker contract for the Hunters again now that they'd retaken Khatash.

He should probably focus more on the situation at hand, but he'd killed enough Goka that it was routine. It had been more interesting on Khatash, when he'd had to dodge Tortantulas, as well— some of them had had an uncanny knack for stabbing their giant legs down too close to him, despite his field.

The Dama had had ideas about that, though she hadn't shared them. Much like she hadn't shared all the ways she was using the five Veetanho she'd had turned over to them. Stupid Veetanho.

Justice spit, used a falling Goka to leap higher and claw out the eyes of one that was wildly shooting at nothing—Justice supposed the Goka was meant to be shooting at *him*, but as the alien was failing terribly, Justice could forgive himself the confusion—then used his leverage to spin the Goka around until he fired into enough of the Goka to pull their attention further.

Something large exploded, and Justice decided he should probably hurry up and destroy the enormous, missile-spewing machine ahead of him. He'd circled it twice already, trying to figure out a way into its control system, but—unfortunately—the Goka weren't complete morons.

The controls weren't exposed to the air, and all the access points were well covered. If something didn't draw the Goka away, he wouldn't have the time he needed to splice into it and redirect its ordnance.

If he couldn't use it, though, better to remove it from the board. *There, Dunamis. That's something we have in common.*

Justice laughed to himself and started climbing—he hadn't brought all his favorite toys from home, but he had enough to jam plenty of moving parts. Given that some of these moving parts were housing things that already had a lot of explosive material, he could jam it with absolutely spectacular results.

* * * * *

Chapter Seventeen

Outside the Goka Facility, Tarpik

Justice enjoyed being clever. He enjoyed stalking, making plans, *having* plans, adapting when the plan became untenable, and executing new plans.

Sometimes, though—sometimes, it was a whole lot of fun to leap and let the blood fall where it may. This had quickly become one of those times.

His claws might not have the length and stretch of Balin's, to rend into the metallic meat of the enormous missile delivery system, but they were plenty for rendering Goka into their component parts.

"Here's a question," he said to none of them specifically, aiming it as more a general announcement as he pulled and released his quintessence in his ricocheting through the gathered aliens.

"How many Goka does it take—" Justice swung up to one of the gimbals that machinery pivoted on, and shoved several pieces of Goka exoskeleton into it "—to break an anti-aircraft system?"

He paused and tilted his head, then *tsked* to himself. "More than I would have guessed. Unfortunate."

Diverting, though. He reminded himself he wasn't here to have fun—it was easy to get distracted from that, with the Veetanho ensconced above in the ship, not in his eyeline during a large scale engagement. He didn't need to kill *all* Veetanho, he had discipline enough for that, but he would like to kill *her*...

He flattened his ears and climbed higher even as the machinery rotated again. That also was a diverting thought, but not a necessary one at this moment. The anti-aircraft gunnery was still firing, and he'd need to time this next part between launches for maximum efficiency.

Unfortunately, he couldn't rely on blowing up the missiles to set the whole array to explode—some missiles were resistant to pressure, and he hadn't done any research into Goka technology. However, if he sent a cascade of failures through the system—electrical shorts, an explosion, *and* fire—one of them was bound to set off the chain reaction he wanted. As long as he timed them well enough that one didn't succeed while he was still getting the next into position.

He preferred to make the Goka think his goal was to grind the weapon to a halt using their own body parts, as it left him free to hunt all the nooks and crannies of the towering machinery. Timing was everything… but he'd survived Khatash.

Time worked for *him*.

* * *

First Platoon, Tarpik, Tarpik System

First Platoon's charge had carried it down several floors, but then the Goka had massed and stopped them. With the aliens coming at them up the passageway, covering both walls, the floor, and the ceiling, there'd been too many to try to run through. Sergeant First Class Bat had withdrawn them to one of the landings and taken cover there.

While Naran couldn't judge the older trooper's decision—she hadn't been there to see the Goka invasion coming up the passageway—it had put them in a bad spot. They were now pinned down on the landing, which had nearly as many entrances to it as she had troopers to defend them. The windows were the worst, as the Goka could enter from above or below, or from either side. It would only take one moment's inattention for a swarm to drop in, distract some of the other troopers, and then it would be all over.

She kept glancing back and forth down the hallways, looking for a break in the mass of Goka... but it never came. If they'd had some jumpjuice, they could have gone out the windows, but about half the troopers would end up as crushed tin cans when they hit the ground below them.

"*Ammo's in the red*," Sergeant Jargal reported.

"*Me, too*," Private Ferrell called. "*Five shots remaining.*"

Naran moved over to cover Ferrell, as she had more ammo than anyone else. She arrived in time to see Ferrell extend his sword. "*It's just this and harsh language now, ma'am,*" the trooper said, although he didn't say it like he was scared; it was a matter-of-fact announcement.

Troops like this don't deserve to die.

Naran looked at the ramp down. Was it less packed with Goka than a little while ago, or was that a hopeful figment of her imagination? Didn't matter—it was their only way out.

"Stand by," Naran said as she chewed through her remaining rounds. "On my command, we're breaking out of here." She fired at a Goka coming through Ferrell's window, then turned and sprayed her final rounds at the Goka coming up the ramp. "When I say go, charge down the ramp, and don't stop until we get to 2nd Platoon."

"*When all else fails, attack?*" Farrell asked.

"Damn right."

"*Well, call it then, ma'am. I'm right behind you.*"

"Here we go, Golden Horde!" Naran yelled. She dropped her sword into position. "Charge!"

* * *

Fourth Floor, Goka Facility, Tarpik, Tarpik System

Second Platoon had mounted the ramp to find a number of stunned and half-dead Goka flipping around at the top. Her troops quickly put them down, but then found themselves surrounded again. Masses of Goka immediately clogged the ramps up and down and periodically crawled through the windows. About the only place they hadn't come from yet was the ceiling, but Sansar knew it was only a matter of time before some enterprising Goka opened a hole, and the giant roaches dropped down on them.

Sansar scanned her surroundings, looking for a way out, or at least some sort of tactical advantage, and her eyes lit on the source of the earlier detonation—a massive hole had been blown in the building's exterior. Her eyes struggled to identify the shapes of the two beings looking out onto the battlefield below, as they were back-lit by the desert sun streaming through the opening. Her jaw dropped as she recognized the smaller of the two—it was Tald, along with some sort of... well, she wasn't sure what it was exactly. The closest thing she could think of was a pangolin she'd seen at a zoo in China one time. The alien was covered in large, overlapping, plate-like scales, which were—judging by the number of Goka pieces hanging from them and the amount of blue blood coating him—probably really hard and sharp. The most curious thing about the alien, though, was the silver badge with a tree on it.

She strode over to them, ducking, as her movement made her a target for all the Goka on the floor below them.

"Well met, Peacemakers," she said. She turned toward Tald. "When I asked for your help, I didn't think it would be quite so... explosive in nature, but I see you've found one of our high value targets."

She turned to the alien. "Well met. I'm Sansar Enkh of the Golden Horde. We're here to get you out of here."

The pangolin nodded and squinted at her, then he squinted even harder at the combat continuing behind her. "Well met, Sansar Enkh. Do you always rescue people by bringing a planet's worth of enemy soldiers with you?"

"The Goka responded a little more energetically than we'd hoped. We've been holding our own so far, but we're going to need to find this Tooliq person soon, or we're in danger of being overrun."

"Your suits can't hold them off?"

"The suits do a wonderful job of holding them off," Sansar noted, "as long as we have ammunition. At the moment, we're all under 50 percent remaining, and things are going to get dicey if we don't— *Blue Sky!*" Her eyes had finally seen what the Peacemakers had been looking at—one of the nearby towers had a large, smoking hole in it about two thirds of the way up, and the upper third looked like it was going to fall off. The only thing she'd ever seen like it were historical pictures of the Twin Towers in the former United States after they'd been hit with airliners.

No! her mind screamed as she scanned the landing pad where they'd come in. *Nonononononono!*

Thorb must have launched, and then gotten shot down again.

"Was that our way out?" Balin asked.

"I'm afraid so," Sansar said. She switched to her comms. "Who's got the most jumpjuice left?"

"Miere and Treloar," Mun replied. *"They don't have that much, but it's more than anyone else. Sending them to you."*

Sansar nodded to herself as she called up their jump juice levels and estimated how far away the tower was. It would be enough. It had to be. "Miere, Treloar, get up to that tower!" she said as the troopers ran up. "Secure our pilots if they're securable."

"You got it, ma'am," Corporal Miere replied. A gun *boomed* from down below them.

Damn it! Sansar though, looking at the Goka milling underneath them. A few were crawling up the exterior of the building. *It's going to be a skeet shoot as they fly across.*

Sansar looked around and found the two closest troopers she could pull off the line. "Tyson, Abbot, cover their flight."

"What's your plan?" Balin asked.

"We need to recover our pilots, grab the Tooliq, and extract," Sansar said, "but first, we have to fight our way out of here."

"My eyesight isn't so great without my goggles," Balin said, "but I'm pretty handy when they get close." He shrugged. "Can I be of assistance?"

Sansar looked again at the Goka pieces embedded in his scales, and she smiled. It appeared his exterior was even harder than a Goka's. "If you wouldn't mind, I think we can definitely find a spot for you."

* * *

Fourth Floor, Goka Facility, Tarpik, Tarpik System

"*Who's got the most jump juice left?*" Sansar's voice paused over comms, then returned. "*Miere, Treloar, get up to that tower. Secure our pilots if they're securable. Tyson, Abbot, cover their flight.*" Sansar, calm and in control in his ear, dragged Tald back to the here and now, though she wasn't talking to him.

Secure our pilots. She thought Thorb was alive. She couldn't spare many—two, and two to cover them, and as limited as their jump fuel was, even that felt excessive. But his father was up there. Alive, he had to be.

He *had* to be.

Tald took a step in that direction, then a second, then froze. What was he doing? He couldn't storm an entirely separate tower with no backup, potential residual effects from the crash, an unknown number of Goka, and expect to accomplish anything.

What could he do?

What could *he* do?

Secure our pilots.

You do the job. You do the job the best you can, and that's enough.

Be the best Peacemaker ever.

He heard Sansar's voice, and Balin's, and his father's. Then his own.

Enough is enough.

He and Justice had crawled through one set of ventilation spaces. He didn't have the Hunter's seemingly perfect memory, but he didn't need it. He'd learned from following Justice the first time, and he wouldn't get confused this time. The Goka towers rose in a spiral, and the passages sloped slightly up or slightly down. He could avoid any turn-offs until he got where he was going.

They kept what they valued up high.

And he had explosives.

"Timmons," he asked the nearest CASPer driver, "can you get me up to that vent?"

* * *

Fourth Floor, Goka Facility, Tarpik, Tarpik System

The Human CASPers were impressive in action. If they hadn't been so incredibly outnumbered, Balin was sure this would have been a quick contest. As it were, however, the combat went on without much of a change in their position, and Balin wasn't sure he'd get a second wind.

Given the days he'd spent in that ridiculous room, he supposed it was actually a fifth wind. The sort of game reserved for the young— or younger, at least. But as always, Balin had to roll the bones in front of him, not wish for a different set.

A wedge of Goka managed to split one of the CASPers away from the rest, and then wasted no time swarming over it. They seemed indifferent to their own losses, and while Balin knew that wasn't entirely true, it didn't change the matter at hand. It was all at a scale big enough, even his eyesight could register it. The other Humans couldn't fire their larger guns into the mess without the risk of taking out their fellow, their smaller caliber would only annoy the Goka, and their edged weapons were for close combat.

So were Balin's, but he could break for the separated CASPer more easily than the rest. *This* is *my fifth wind,* he told himself and dug his claws into the back of the first Goka he could reach.

A short time—and four Goka—later, something even larger than him joined the party, one of the CASPers able to fall back without compromising the position of the rest. Combined, Balin and the CASPer made short work of the swarm, and no more Goka seemed in a hurry to join in on their corner.

The downed CASPer stayed down, but the new one angled away from the active line of fire, and the top portion went up. The normal-sized Human head staring down at him was ridiculously out of proportion from the rest, but Balin had seen too many oddly-shaped beings wreaking havoc to laugh.

"She's all right, but her CASPer is cooked," the Human said. "You're handy in a fight, Peacemaker. Can you—"

"I'm better up close," Balin called, rooting through the dead Goka for weapons besides their tiny knives. "I'll keep her clear; you get back to shooting."

"Appreciate it!" The Human saluted and closed his outer skin, then charged back to the line.

Balin patted the large foot of the machine. The Human mercenary had landed face down, and he wasn't sure whether that meant she could get out or not, or if she could hear him, especially over the consistent noise of the fight itself. For the best, for now—there was nothing to be done but keep her alive, and knowing her any better wouldn't help in that aim.

The Peacemaker purposefully didn't think of another Human, one he hadn't been able to save, instead, he leveraged his stolen gun and stood guard over the downed Human.

* * *

Goka Command Center, Goka Facility, Tarpik

Three Goka sat alone in a room. Technically, they were defended by yet another uncountable number of Goka, but those were all outside the room.

The three *in* the room seemed occupied by their pinplants

Tald had prowled the vents as thoroughly and quietly as he could. Thankfully, there was so much noise from the battle raging outside, the fact that he wasn't as silent as Justice wasn't a deal-breaker.

Work done, Tald took the biggest breath of his life and dropped out of the vent around the curve from the massed Goka.

"Peacemaker business!" he shouted, touching his badge for luck. They'd imprisoned Balin rather than shoot him on sight. Tald had decided on the calculated risk of announcing himself as a Peacemaker as well to buy himself time—hopefully it was that Balin was a Peacemaker, not that he seemed really hard to kill.

Tald, by contrast, didn't think he'd be quite as difficult to knock down.

But he'd already made his plan, and he was stuck with it, so he strolled forward as though he were fully confidence and on a mission.

One of those was absolutely true.

"Peacemaker!" one of the Goka proclaimed, not a shiver of a limb telling him which one. "You are hereby—"

"No." Tald didn't pause, but he did take one of his hands out of his belt loop. "See this? This is about a hands-length of the same explosive that blew out the side of one of your buildings just a few minutes ago. Remember that?"

There was a flutter of movement, chittering too soft for the translator to pick up.

"Apparently you do. Good. Because I've got... oh, about three times one of *your* body lengths worth of it outlining the room behind you. The one with your Tooliq in it. That's him, right?"

The susurrus of noise made his translator crackle, but no words came through.

"I thought it might be." Tald kept walking, and the first few Goka shifted as though they might move out of his way but hadn't yet decided. "My little piece here is synced to all of that, so if I squeeze too hard, or drop it and don't squeeze hard enough, well... the whole tower goes boom, Tooliq and his two friends first."

At that level of specificity, the first rank of Goka stepped out of his way. Tald bared his teeth in what was ostensibly a smile and passed through them.

"For now, I just want to talk to him. I'm guessing that's what's best for all of us here, but in case any of you think, 'Hey that Tooliq is a jerk, I can let him and the Peacemaker take each other out...' you shouldn't be too confident of the area around you all, either. Those ventilation shafts really do go *every*where."

In fact, that last part was a bluff. The rest not so much—it was so much easier to bluff when one could back it up, it turned out—but Tald didn't know nearly enough about the politics of the Goka, and he didn't want to take any chances. He was halfway through the mass of them now.

"Might want to let him know I'm coming in. Would hate for one of them to get an itchy trigger finger and we all go down, right? Let him know it's only a chat, a little Peacemaker business, and no one else from the guild has to get involved."

He thought Dirty Harry might give him a little squint of approval over all of that.

The door opened, and Tald swaggered through.

* * *

Goka Command Center, Goka Facility, Tarpik

The Goka sat forward in his chair and made a high pitched noise the translator didn't bother with. After a moment, he leaned back and burst into chattering speech.

"I don't know what you think you can accomplish here, Peace-maker. I am under strict orders—"

"Well, sir, turns out it's more pressin' that you're under a great deal of *explosives*." Tald rocked back on his heels and wished he had something to chew on as he drawled the response. "Who's ordering you that's more pressing that that?"

"I am not at liberty to say." Tooliq puffed up from his seat—neat trick, that, Tald hadn't though the thick Goka exoskeleton would allow for such a movement.

"Is it Dunamis?"

"How!" All three Goka shivered and clicked, but only Tooliq spoke. "You... how would you—*you!*"

"We've established I'm me," Tald replied, nodding and flicking the edge of his badge with a single finger. He might have channeled a little Justice into that persona, but he thought the Hunter would ap-preciate it. "How do I know about Dunamis?" He laughed and was pleased to hear it sounded genuine. "He's not *that* clever, you know."

That seemed to floor the Goka entirely, as none of them even spluttered in response.

"Dunamis is giving you orders, sure, but I've seen what comes of that." He shook his whiskers, and his disgust wasn't at all feigned. "I passed through Lytoshaan on my way here, and he… Dunamis isn't much for holding up his end of the bargain, when it comes right down to it."

"And you honor *your* word?" Tooliq sat forward, and the translator didn't have to work to get across the scorn and disbelief in those words.

"You haven't blown up yet, have you? The *Gobi Desert* hasn't bombarded you from orbit?"

"Why—"

"I'm sticking to the rules. I'm a Peacemaker, Tooliq. That's my job. Dunamis *has* no rules, doesn't hold to any rules of engagement or method of operation—no." Tald held up a hand and made a point of smoothing the fur on his cheeks. "That's not entirely true. He has one—he does what pleases him and helps *him*. He doesn't give a wet fart in the ocean for you."

"That's—"

"Call your people off, Tooliq. We just have a few questions for you. All this dying is…" Tald shrugged, as though it were just another day for him. Not like his father might be burning up in the next tower over, or Sansar might be getting overrun below, or Justice could be getting blown up by a missile across the field. "An overreaction on your part."

"You'll call off your mercenaries, just like that? They'll listen?" The Goka made a rude noise that didn't translate, and didn't need to.

"They're deputies, Tooliq. Deputies tend to listen. Shut it down out there, unless you really want to bet that Dunamis, way out there wherever he is, is more of a threat to you than I am. Or more of a help, for that matter."

The other Goka leaned closer to Tooliq, but if they said anything, Tald didn't hear it.

"Limited time offer, Tooliq. I came here with some questions, but one way or another, I've got to honor the threat."

* * *

Fourth Floor, Goka Facility, Tarpik, Tarpik System

Balin glanced out the opening Justice had blown in the building. A chunk of the Goka had split off and were chasing the two CASPers that had separated from the group, but crumbling from the side of the damaged tower slowed them down, as did the fire from the two CASPers. Balin didn't have a shot with his current weaponry, and could barely make out what was holding the Goka back from attacking.

He looked back inside. There was plenty to keep his attention nearby, though his occasional shots into the Goka that got through the lines weren't as helpful as he'd normally like.

The tide shifted back and forth—CASPers pushed forward and then were driven back.

Balin shifted his gun and paced around his designated Human, then he was abruptly curled in a ball over where her head would be.

The Peacemaker had been near more than his fair share of explosions over the rounds, including one made from tape not long ago this very day, but it still took him a few steadying breaths to work out what had just happened.

He knocked on the back of the CASPer, and after a heartbeat, heard a muffled acknowledgment in reply. With that, he uncurled and rolled clear of her, then stayed low to the ground while running his blurry eyes over the area outside the hole.

Luckily—so far as 'lucky' went in this situation—he didn't need much in the way of eyesight to work out what had happened.

Where the big gun had been—where *Justice* had been, if he didn't miss his guess—there was no longer much of anything.

Slag, perhaps, if that lump was much to go on.

The rest of the battlefield inside the tower hadn't been much affected. Some CASPers close to the hole were on their knees, some Goka had been blown back, but the fight raged on.

Professionals, all in all, the Humans and the Goka both. Balin had to respect them.

He lifted his gun and prepared to respect the Goka a little more thoroughly.

* * * * *

Chapter Eighteen

Goka Command Center, Goka Facility, Tarpik

"There will be repercussions." Tooliq's shoulders shook, as if he were moving something into place under his exoskeleton.

"Tends to be about the way of the galaxy," Tald said, flicking his eyes up and not so idly scanning the smooth ceiling above them. He let the additional piece of Justice's tape dangle from his hand, a casual reminder. "Every action has an equal and opposite reaction, all that."

The longer Tooliq dragged this out, the more the space between Tald's shoulder blades itched. Would one of the Goka in the hall throw caution to the wind and shoot him? Stab him? Tackle him and try to get the explosive away?

Figure out a way into the ventilation shafts and realize it wasn't nearly enough to kill all of them, after all?

He needed to wait this out—he knew that was the case—but he opened his mouth anyway, unsure of what he was going to say. It had to be something convincing. Badass. Something that sold Tooliq that no matter how small and fuzzy the little Peacemaker across from him was, that little furry guy meant business, and it was all going to go sideways if he didn't—

The explosion was enormous enough, all their eyes flew upward to the still unbroken ceiling. Tald locked his body into place and strove to be as unconcerned as he'd ever been in his life.

"You don't think I put all my fish in this one pot, do you?" He lifted the hand with its length of tape and cocked his head. "Should we keep blowing up your towers, or…?"

"Call them off," Tooliq said to the Goka on his right.

"Sansar," Tald muttered into his comms. "Tooliq is allegedly pulling the Goka back. I committed to a ceasefire if they pulled back."

"How far?" Sansar asked. *"Because some are still shooting."*

"All of them, Tooliq, or this gets messier." Tald closed his hand around his piece of tape, slowly, while holding eye contact with the Goka.

"Enough!" the third Goka yelled, turning on Tooliq and hitting him. "Dunamis promised us nothing so valuable. Our *children* are in the next tower, with *their* dropship, on fire, and we are pretending nothing is wrong! End this!"

"They're pulling back," Sansar said, and Tald forced himself to take a normal breath.

He couldn't ask about his father—especially now that he knew for certain what else was in that tower, and why the Goka had acted as though it didn't matter.

What else are we pretending we don't care about? He tucked the thought away for later and relaxed his hand around the tape. "Why did you capture Peacemaker Balin?"

"He was following things he shouldn't have been able to follow." Tooliq wrapped his hands tightly around the edges of his chair. The other two Goka hunched in their seats, although at least one was muttering into their comms.

"More Goka are approaching the tower the dropship crashed into," Sansar said softly, and when she didn't mention his father, Tald fought to keep his ears from folding.

"The Tooliq's children are hidden there, apparently," Tald said, raising his voice so the Goka knew he wasn't hiding the conversation. "As long as they stay out of your way, let them be." He gestured at the Goka in front of him. "Our people are taking survivors from the shuttle."

Let that be true.

"Do not interfere." After Tooliq nodded, Tald returned to the matter at hand. "You're talking about the Human mercenaries? Did they go to the same place as the Veetanho from Hades?"

"How do you know these things?" Tooliq spluttered, and Tald didn't have to put any effort into rolling his eyes.

"Assume I know everything you don't think I should know, Tooliq. I know about Dunamis, I know about Hades—Blue Sky! I've been to Hades. I know about Lytoshaan, the Veetanho, how Dunamis operates. I want to know why you thought the better course of action was to draw the wrath of the Peacemaker Guild into Tarpik, rather than answer our questions."

"No harm would have come to the Peacemaker! Your people did not leave our territory as you were told to do, and then you fired on us! We simply…" Tooliq sagged into his seat. "We were given orders to execute a task. In failing, we will be kept from the place we were offered. The place we deserve, more than those fur-faced Veetanho ever did!"

Perhaps belatedly realizing the Peacemaker in front of him also had a furred face, Tooliq subsided and stared angrily at Tald. He managed not to gape at them in disbelief, but he couldn't help asking, "You... *want* to be in servitude to an SI?"

"He raised the Veetanho to the heights of the galaxy." Tooliq flung his arms in the air, then gripped the arms of his seat again. "We are better fighters. There are more of us. We would do a far better job as his right hand."

"Again, Tooliq, I've seen what Dunamis does to his right hand. I don't recommend signing up for it on purpose." He shook his head and added more quietly into comms, "Sansar, we might need the SI box up here."

"Understood, Peacemaker."

"Searik, go down and ensure the tower—"

"No," Tald said, snapping his head back up. "All of you will be staying here until our conversation is done." He waited until they settled, then continued, "Did the Humans go to the same place as the Veetanho from Hades?"

"Yes."

"Do you know where that is?"

"No."

"Do you know why Dunamis sends them there?"

"No."

"You invited a battle with the Peacemakers, and with the Golden Horde, for... that little information?"

"Yes."

Tald considered blowing them up on principle. Not truly, of course, but the frustration bubbled in his chest until it seemed almost like a good idea.

Thumps from the hall behind him pulled his ears back, and he decided it sounded more like CASPers deliberately approaching than anything violent breaking out. Of course, his ears were still ringing from the previous combat, so he couldn't be sure, but if he was wrong, he'd deal with it then. Tald was more worried he was right—Sansar and her Hunter/Killer box might help the situation, but yet again, they were at a dead end. If Tooliq didn't know anything—truly didn't know anything—then Tald had absolutely no idea where they'd go from here.

He stared at the three Goka, all of whom shifted and looked everywhere but at each other or him, and let the silence hang as the thumping approached. Mostly it was because he didn't know what else to say, but partly he was hoping the tension would cause one of them to snap.

"That was a creative use of the explosives," Justice said from behind his left shoulder, and Tald didn't jump at the invisibly-issued voice. He was especially pleased with his self-control when Tooliq leapt from his chair.

"Assassins! Betray—"

"Stuff it, Tooliq." Balin strode into the room, his long claws at his sides. Two CASPers followed close behind, including Sansar's, and Tald hid his smile by inclining his head and saluting. "You're in enough trouble, and if we wanted you dead, you'd be a footnote at the end of my report."

"I had a look at what you did," Justice went on, as though Tooliq hadn't spoken. "Are you sure we shouldn't engage it? I think the show will be quite spectacular."

"You—you said—"

"I want my gear returned to me." Balin lifted a hand and pointed with one claw for each sentence. "You owe the Golden Horde for damages incurred in their securing of my personage. I want transport records for every ship that's left your system for the last fifty rounds. I also have locators on several of them now, and friends in Cartography, so I suggest you make those lists thorough and truthful. And fast."

The larger alien turned toward Tald. "Anything I missed, Peacemaker?"

"Has the dropship been recovered from the neighboring tower?" Tald asked Sansar, using his drawl to hide any potential wobble in his voice.

"Not yet." She opened the top of her CASPer, and he could just make out the top of the Hunter/Killer box. "The surrounding floor is crumbling, and the additional weight of the CASPers might tip the shuttle entirely."

"Then one additional point, Tooliq. You'll send some of your people to help my deputies in that tower secure the survivors of the dropship you're paying for."

"We are busy getting our—"

"You will do it *now*," he added, as pleasantly as he could while heat crowded under his fur, "and we will all wait here together while you do."

Tooliq crossed his arms, and more commands were sent out to the Goka outside.

"Interesting," Sansar murmured at the edge of his hearing, and the two Goka on either side of Tooliq shuddered and slid out of their chairs.

Tooliq's shriek sounded like it came from under his carapace, but Tald understood it without the translator.

"Dunamis embedded commands in these two, but not you," Sansar said, the top of her CASPer still open. "I wonder why he'd do that."

"He…" The one who'd spoken of their children, Searik, stood shakily. "He promised… I don't remember what he promised."

"Dunamis never needed to command me. I knew what to do." Tooliq stared from one to the other of his fellow Goka, shaken. "He said he didn't need to overwrite us. That we were his…"

"Perfect vessel? Ideal right hand?" Sansar shook her head. "Dunamis lies, and that's probably one of the nicest things he does."

"How much can he trust you if you don't know where these Humans and Veetanho go?"

"More than that," Tooliq muttered.

"What?"

"He said 'more than that,'" Justice prompted helpfully, still invisible.

"You don't know more than that?"

"More than Humans and Veetanho. I don't know where it is, the place they go from here, but…" Tooliq turned to Searik, then the third Goka, and then seemed to deflate. "I know what they do. Some of it."

"Do tell," Balin prompted after the silence dragged on.

"We've sent Goka, too, and Goltar. Lots of Goltar, recently. The crews on the ships that go… they don't return. He sends us others from different planets to 'even the ranks.'"

Every time Tooliq was quiet, Tald struggled to maintain focus on him. He was waiting for the update on comms—who'd been recovered from the shuttle. Who was still alive. His father wasn't dead.

"He fights them."

"Dunamis… fights the people you send him? How?" Tald frowned at the Goka, his whiskers bristling. SIs didn't have fighting-capable bodies, although they could inhabit other people's bodies. They could also force others to… oh.

"He matches them against each other. Humans, Goka, Veetanho, Goltar, MinSha, everyone, to figure out strengths and weaknesses. Anticipate strategies. See who will win in different combinations."

No wonder the Mercenary Guild—and the Veetanho atop it— had been so dominant in the galaxy. Tald couldn't imagine—it was like the exercises at the Academy, when they had to outthink and outmaneuver their classmates, then their instructors, and learn the ways so many others thought. Like that, but about eight thousand times worse, because he had a feeling Dunamis didn't institute rules that kept aspiring Peacemakers from killing each other.

"How long?"

"Always. Forever. What does it matter? Long enough, and no one's ever found it, and you're not going to. Leave my planet, and maybe we can hide from him that you were ever here!"

Searik touched her head. "No. His codes are gone from my head. I can't remember what they were, but I remember the feel of them… he'll know."

"Then we're all doomed!" Tooliq threw his arms up. "Bring the ceiling down on us after all, Peacemaker. It's better than what he has waiting for us."

"As you wish," Justice said, and Tald stepped forward more hastily than he would have liked.

"We're not blowing you up, Tooliq. We can take the coding out of as many of your people as you can get into the area." He glanced back at Sansar to make sure she was all right with that and twitched half his whiskers at her small nod of agreement. "He can't do anything to you if you fight him."

"You've… seen Lytoshaan, you said." Tooliq made a series of staccato sounds, and Tald had a sinking feeling it was laughter. "Do you really believe that?"

"Then throw your lives away to fight against him rather than for him, Goka." Justice's voice trailed from closer to the door, as though he was leaving. "Let it mean something."

"*We have a survivor,*" one of the Horde said over comms. Tald nearly melted to the floor, then remembered a key fact.

There'd been more than one SalSha on that shuttle.

"It's the copilot."

* * * * *

Chapter Nineteen

Dropship *One*, Tower Three, Tarpik

lackness. Slowly, Thorb's senses came back to him.
Blackness was... wrong. When you died, you went into
the light, not into the dark. Everybody said so; it had to
be true. He tried to look around, but couldn't move. That was
wrong, too. Dying was supposed to be freeing, liberating.

I'm not dead! Then the pain hit, and he wished he was. His entire
body hurt like he'd been in an airplane crash. Or a dropship crash,
which was pretty much the same thing.

But if he was alive, why couldn't he see? It had been midday
when they'd crashed; he was sure of it. Well, pretty sure. Some things
were kind of hazy, and it was entirely possible that he had a concus-
sion.

He moved his right hand—at least he had one thing operational—and put it to his face. Everything was sticky, which would explain the smell of blood prevalent in his nostrils. He rubbed his right
eye and found it was gummed shut with drying blood.

The "drying" part of that was important, somehow, but he
couldn't figure out why. He finally dislodged the blood enough to
open his right eye and was greeted with sunshine. That was why
"drying" was important; the crash must have occurred sometime
fairly recently, as the blood hadn't had time to harden all the way.

His left hand worked, too, he found, and he was soon able to look around.

Seeph was a mess, although he was—happily—unconscious. With some sort of metal rod sticking out from the dashboard and extending through his right leg, he was better off unconscious and not going anywhere until help arrived.

Which was the next problem. Help was unlikely to arrive, as they were on an alien planet. He wasn't sure how close the Golden Horde was, but he doubted they were anywhere nearby. He'd have to get to them and bring back help. Somehow.

He released his straps and stood. Immediately, the pain in his body coalesced into one bright light of agony, and he slammed his eyes shut as it roared through the top of his head. He put a hand up and found a large gash.

"Well, now I know where the blood came from, anyway." He stumbled to the bulkhead and detached the first aid kit. Inside were two injectors with nanobots for SalSha. He smiled. Sometimes the ground crew forgot to swap the medkit out to match who was flying that day; thankfully, they'd remembered today.

Thorb flipped off the protective cap, gritted his teeth, and jammed it into his leg, then he hit the plunger. The nanobots flooding into his system made him long for only the pain of the head wound. After the fires dancing in front of his eyes went out—seconds later, but it felt like days—he was able to stand fairly steadily. He was wearing a lot of his own blood, and he knew that was an issue, but one he'd have to fight through.

He took the second injector and thought about using it on Seeph, but then decided he was probably happier without it. It would certainly have woken him up, which would *not* have been fun. Using a little of the blood around, Seeph's as well as his own, Thorb wrote "Went for help" on the dashboard and left the other injector where Seeph could reach it.

Feeling a little better, he took stock of the situation. The front canopy was spiderwebbed and covered in something white on the outside, but he couldn't tell exactly what. The substance wasn't sand, so he was probably still in the building he'd crashed into.

Opening the crew door, he found out what the white stuff was—some sort of packing material. Between the boxes and packing material scattered everywhere, he realized he'd crashed into the Goka's idea of a shipping center or post office. It was impossible to tell which; he was just happy to have crashed somewhere relatively soft. The building's exterior had done a number on the nose of the dropship, though—it was about a third the length it had been—but it had crumpled and somehow protected them fairly well.

Thorb started to walk off to explore, then realized he'd probably rather do that armed. He went back into the craft and grabbed both of the hypervelocity pistols and all the ammunition, which he threw into his bag. With one weapon at the ready, he was finally ready to go exploring.

* * *

Goka Command Center, Goka Facility, Tarpik

"Join us," Tald said. "You can fight him, and with us, you can win. Sansar's killed a number of the SIs." *Maybe not permanently, but she has killed them.*

Sansar nodded. "Even though they may be hard to kill, anything that's alive *can* be killed. The SIs are no different."

"I don't know," Searik said. "I still think it would be better to re-sume fighting. We can always say they removed Dunamis' code without our permission."

"If you do, you'll be the first one to die," Thorb said as he walked into the room, holding a hypervelocity pistol in each hand. One was leveled at Searik; the other moved back and forth between the other two Goka in the room.

"Dad!" Tald yelled. "How—" He threw up his arms, dropping the explosives, and ran across the room to hug him, but Thorb stepped out of the way and continued to cover the Goka.

"Good to see, you, Peacemaker," Thorb said, "but I'm not sure you're honoring the threat at the moment."

"And if you'd pick up my explosive tape," Justice said from somewhere around Thorb's shoulder, "I'd appreciate it."

"Oh!" Tald said. He'd been holding his own, but his father's sudden appearance—after he'd been so sure Thorb was gone for real—had thrown him for a loop. Trotting back to his original place, he grabbed the explosive tape and held it like he had been.

"I think they probably don't want to get blown up, and now that we're all in here, it seems less likely," Justice noted. "I'd like it back. I intend to wrap it around the Tooliq's shell—and the rest of them, too—*then* we'll see how negotiations go."

The Tooliq lifted his head, then turned back toward Sansar. His eyes drifted back toward Thorb and Justice's likely location, but he focused on the commander. "You've really killed SIs?"

Sansar nodded. "I have."

"How many?" the Tooliq asked. His eyes narrowed.

"Three? Four? I don't know. I think I'm starting to lose count."

The Tooliq nodded and turned toward Thorb and Justice's voice. "I don't think you'll need your explosive. We surrender."

Justice flickered briefly into view, stalking closer. "Oh, maybe not for you, perhaps, but I definitely need it. There's always something that needs blowing up."

Tald held his breath to keep from gasping—the brief view he'd had of Justice hadn't been the thickly-furred orange and black Hunter he'd become used to seeing. The lean Depik's body was missing entire patches of fur, and even the wavering glance had been enough for Tald to catch streaks of deep red that indicated burns. Justice hadn't walked away from that enormous explosion earlier unmarked.

If he can ignore it for now, I can, too, Tald reminded himself and flicked his eyes back to the three Goka.

"So we're good here?" Thorb asked.

"We are," the Tooliq said.

"Good." Thorb turned to Tald. "Then give me that hug."

Reunited. As Peaches and Herb said, it feels so good.

* * *

Dropship *Two*, Landing Pad, Tarpik

"I don't get it, though," Sansar said as they boarded the dropship for the flight up to the *Gobi Desert*. "You crashed into that tower over there."

Thorb nodded.

She pointed in the opposite direction. "Then you showed up in the Tooliq's office over there."

"I did."

"How exactly did you do that, with all the hostile Goka on the ground between the towers? None of them would have known the fighting was over yet."

"They probably didn't."

"So how…"

Thorb smiled. "So I went exploring, moving down the tower, but then the Goka saw me and chased me. They were between me and the exit, so I ran up the tower, rather than down."

"Wouldn't that have trapped you at the top? I mean, eventually you had to run out of tower, especially since part of it collapsed."

"Well, yes, but…"

"Give," Sansar said. "I want the truth, and I want it now."

"Okay, so Goka apparently can't fly very well when they're young."

"So?"

"Well—all this is conjecture, you'll understand, since I didn't have a translation pendant on me as I was running. For all I know, they were chasing me, yelling, 'Stop, the war's over.' I didn't know that, of course, so I ran. They did shoot at me, so I wasn't going to stop and ask for a literal translation. Anyway, about two levels from the top, there are… well, they aren't *quite* hang gliders, but they're a lot *like* hang gliders. I think it was for young Goka to learn how to fly. They were too small for adult Goka."

"Are you telling me you stole a hang glider and flew across from one tower to the other?"

Thorb nodded. "Someone was nice enough to blow a hole in the building, so I was able to enter and land there. None of the Goka on the ground saw me, and none of the Goka chased me once I got into the Tooliq's building, so I just kept going up until I saw the CAS-

Pers, then I heard Tald's voice and got the Goka's translation from one of your pendants." He shrugged. "Justice landed on my shoulder at that point, and I felt pretty confident about our tactical advantage, so I walked in. And you know the rest."

Tald's jaw dropped. "You can't be serious."

"I am."

Tald turned to Sansar. "Does he do this all the time?"

"Yes." Sansar sighed. "He has a habit of it."

Tald shook his head. "Sometimes, you make it really hard to be your son. I stop a war… save the Golden Horde… and *still* get shown up by my father."

"That's okay, son. You did well today, Peacemaker, and I'm proud of you."

There must have been a lot of sand and dust in the air, as Tald's eyes were suddenly very misty. His dad was proud of him? He allowed himself a smile. There was still a lot to do, and he *had* sort of lost his composure for a minute—something Dirty Harry never would have done—but his father was *proud* of him.

He hadn't done a perfect job, but he could live with that.

* * * * *

Chapter Twenty

***Gobi Desert*, Tarpik System**

"All that for nothing, then." Gleeko leaned back in her chair across from Sansar and rubbed under her goggles.

"Not necessarily." Sansar tapped her fingers on the slate containing copies of all the data the older Peacemaker had obtained. He'd refused to leave his *Eletine* behind, but saw the clear advantages of traveling on a ship with internal shunts, so they'd temporarily attached his ship to the *Gobi Desert*.

He'd seemed bemused that everyone had been deputized by Tald, but he'd been unstinting in sharing his own findings, so Sansar was fairly sure they'd be saved yet another pairing of tense aliens on board. Speaking of...

"Justice, if you're going to be in here, you should at least contribute."

Gleeko muttered a curse and dropped her arms, and a soft huff of laughter sounded from somewhere to Sansar's left.

"I'm contributing fully by holding onto my self-control," he murmured and didn't drop his field.

Sansar didn't point out that Justice was also holding, nearly non-stop, to his invisibility. He'd had nanites to treat the burns he'd taken in blowing up the Goka's anti-aircraft system, but the young Depik's fur remained singed and short in several places. Poking at his ego, with Gleeko in the room, seemed a recipe for blood in short order.

"I assume you're here for a reason beyond testing your inner limits."

Gleeko coughed at that, and Sansar restrained herself from rolling her eyes.

"The big Peacemaker is skilled at hunting data. I assume he'll narrow it down to some potential paths, but you won't want to jump aimlessly through hyperspace."

"That's not the most efficient use of time, I agree. What are you suggesting instead?"

"Tald thought you could speak to a gate master and combine some of the locator data with the historical information from the Goka."

"And you?"

"We haven't left the system yet. I thought we could fetch the Tooliq and one of his friends, and carve until we have more answers."

"Torture is the least effective—" Gleeko snorted.

Justice interrupted her mildly. "It worked well on Hades."

"On broken, bitter—"

"Aren't all Veetanho—"

"No, thank you." Sansar stood and pointed at the door. "I'm going to have a meeting with Tald, Josiff, and perhaps Balin. You'll both see yourselves out."

"I—"

"Both. Visible, invisible, Hunter, Veetanho—I'm tired of keeping you civil. Neither of you are welcome here until you can act like fully-fledged galactic adults. Understood?"

They muttered, nothing like the feared species both of them were representatives of.

When they left—she had to assume they both left—she picked up her slate and considered hitting herself in the face with it. It would be less annoying than the constant sniping between her ostensible team. Some of it would be funny—if she wasn't sure it would eventually end in murder.

Maybe she'd be the one doing the murdering.

She took a breath, cleared her thoughts, and sat again before Tald arrived. Hopefully this next stop would be the one. Though what it said about her that she'd rather face Dunamis than many more hyperspace jumps with this set of beings, she couldn't—or wouldn't—say.

* * *

"No Gleeko or Justice?" Tald asked as he, Balin, and Josiff took spots around the table.

"Not until they learn to behave like adults." Sansar tipped her slate onto its side and summoned a smile. "Do you have a lock on where we're going?"

"We have three possibilities. Two of the ships I marked with a locator went through the gate after I made contact with the Goka." Balin settled back on his tail rather than taking a chair and seemed entirely comfortable with the arrangement.

"If we can talk to the gate master and get a better idea of where those two ships are in transit to, we might have an easier time deciding between our options." Tald stood on his seat, sat, then stood again.

Josiff hummed under his breath. "We don't know who's in charge at the gate. What are the odds the Goka allowed a Sumatozou to work on the gate to their secret system?"

Sansar tapped her finger against her lips. "Though it's not the Goka's judgement we're needing to navigate."

"Would Dunamis trust a Goka to run the gate? Would the Cartography Guild allow it? I haven't heard of one in that guild before… but I guess I don't hear everything." Tald shifted in his seat, rubbing his whiskers.

"It's likely whoever's in charge will have an SI's hooks in them, so I'd advise against trying to message. We should probably get on the gate so you can get close enough with the box." Josiff adjusted his hood with a hand and placed the other three on the table. "I will join and see what is to be found in the gate's records, in case the gate master is not so welcoming."

Balin clicked his claws together and tilted his head at Sansar at mention of the box. "Have you had that box long?"

"The Hunter/Killer box? Long enough…" Sansar sighed and sketched out a quick history of her and the Horsemen's interactions with various SIs. Balin listened intently, nodding along.

"Tald was smart to come to you," the older Peacemaker said when she was done, and Tald shifted in his seat again, his shoulders straightening. "I had heard the guild had put another Peacemaker on the trail; missing *Keesius* ships are no light matter."

Sansar had thoughts about that, though she wouldn't share them while Tald was still finding his balance. The guild had received a suspicious tip and had had to move quickly, given the gravity of the threat. If they didn't want to publicly act as though *Keesius* ships were missing, causing potential panic and setting off a wave of retaliation against the declawed Veetanho, they had only a few options. Say, assign a Peacemaker candidate to the search, one without a whole lot of connections and confidence. A specious threat, a tip they didn't take seriously—easy enough.

But because there was a very real chance it was true—the *Keesius* were missing, and all hell could break loose at any moment in any system—they'd sent another Peacemaker. An experienced one, skilled, with all sorts of tricks and talents a casual observer might not be aware of.

It was a smart play if that were the case. Sansar had to wonder what crossing the streams—the official and unofficial investigations—might do, but at this point, Tald had likely over-performed whatever the guild had expected of him.

"We'll shuttle over to the gate when we get a little closer," Sansar said, choosing not to dig into the luck, or lack thereof, of the Peacemakers meeting up. While they had time, though, she wanted to learn more about this new alien on her ship. "You've been a Peacemaker for some time, it seems?"

"Over eighty years." Balin's claws tapped, and he shifted on his tail. "Thought I'd be out by now."

"Oh?" Sansar asked, and Tald pivoted his body toward the older Peacemaker so quickly, she knew she wasn't the only one curious about him. Even Josiff shifted his hands and faced Balin's direction.

"There aren't a lot of my people out and about in the galaxy, so it's unlikely you know much about us." Balin paused, turning his goggled gaze from one to the other, and waited until they'd each shook their heads. "I'm a Phidae. We just have the one planet, and after the first hundred years or so after we joined the Galactic Union, mostly we just stayed on the one planet. Everything else was… un-friendly."

Sansar had heard more than enough stories about the Alpha Contracts and Earth's messy entry into the greater galaxy to understand that.

"Who was your sponsoring race? Were you there? How long ago was that?"

"An extinct one, I was absolutely not, and about halfway between now and the Great War." Balin didn't seem flustered by Tald's rapid-fire questions, nor did he engage so far as to get off whatever point he was working on. Sansar hid her smile.

"The Phidae are long-lived, as a whole. Not thousands of years, but several hundred, and they can go a little longer when they're comfortable—but not all of us." Balin spread all his claws, then curved all but three of them down. "There's a small percentage of us with faulty genes—which means we live half-lives, but that's a term, you see. We all have different amounts of time, but none of them measure into a hundred, and certainly not more."

"And you…"

"Me." Balin nodded. "People like me, like that, we don't stick around. All Phidae have a countdown, and for me—for the Dimindiem—when you're aware of your limited time, you want to make the most of it."

"Like Justice." Tald nodded thoughtfully. "He said the Hunters don't live very long compared to a lot of other races, but it seems like they do a lot of living in that time."

"That's exactly it."

"So you thought you'd be done being a Peacemaker because you'd be dead?" Tald combed his whiskers thoughtfully, but Sansar was distracted by something else Balin had said.

"Did you mean a figurative countdown, or a literal one?"

"That's a thing about Phidae." Balin rocked forward and pulled a bag of something out of one of his belt pouches. Sansar didn't tense—she didn't know the Peacemaker well, but he'd fought alongside them, and kept one of her mercs alive. If he wanted her dead, there were far easier ways. Indeed, he held the bag out and dipped his long, thin tongue into it. Snacks.

"You have an actual countdown?" Tald peered at the other Peacemaker as Balin chewed, and Sansar bit back a smile.

"Not a display over my head, no, but we can… read our cells, like. Tell how many replications they have left in them before they stop." Balin shrugged and chewed some more. "My countdown stopped a little while back, but I think cell time and my perception of time aren't quite the same, so I don't really know how much longer I have. My coordinator figured I had another mission in me, and I don't like to argue."

"I don't know you that well," Tald said, grinning, "but I don't think that's true."

"Hm." Balin grumbled and ate, then tucked his bag away. "Any rate, I've volunteered for all the messiest cases I could over the years. Make the most of a short stay, honor the threats, do my job. This one's one of the messiest."

"I imagine that could very easily be the case," Josiff said, facing Sansar again.

"SIs," Sansar said, agreeing, "and a whole lot of unsettled races doing a whole lot of unsettled things."

"World-ending ships flying around, unattended." Tald sighed, and none of them were smiling now.

"Let's go over your possibilities." Sansar flipped her slate over again. "Make sure we have a productive chat with the gate master."

* * *

Stargate Control, Tarpik Stargate, Tarpik System

Sansar peered through the airlock window, shrugged, and cycled the controls. Naran put out a hand, holding her back, then marched her CASPer into the small passageway of the station. She strode slowly down the empty corridor, her magnetic boots *clacking* on the deck, obviously looking for threats. Naran made it to the corner, turned it, then waved everyone forward.

Sansar, Tald, and Balin moved forward, with Gleeko trailing them. Clad only in a shipsuit, Sansar felt naked, but trying to negotiate with someone while wearing a CASPer was… difficult at best, so she'd decided to do without it.

Naran advanced again before Sansar reached her and came to a stop in front of the only door in the ten-meter-long corridor. "Must be here," she noted.

"Must be," Sansar said as she came to stand next to Naran's mech, with the Peacemakers right behind her. "The 'Gate Master Shooloonga' sign kind of gives it away." She held up the H/K box. No cogs present. Shaking her head, she turned it off, waited a few seconds, then turned it on again. Once again, it showed no cogs within its operational radius.

"Either the gate master isn't being controlled by Dunamis, or he's doing it some way I haven't seen before," Sansar noted. She shrugged and pressed the access button. Nothing happened.

"What do we do now?" Tald asked. "Kick the door in?"

"In my many years," Balin said, "I've found that a sweet substance is more likely to get a first lick than something bitter."

Tald's muzzle scrunched together. "What?"

Sansar chuckled. "I think what he's saying is, perhaps we should knock first."

Balin gave her a small bow. "Quite."

Sansar knocked, and they waited. She knocked again, and they waited some more.

"Can we knock it down now?" Tald asked. "This is official Peacemaker business."

"No," Sansar said. "Patience." She knocked a third time, longer and harder.

"Go away!" a voice yelled from inside. "Pay and leave, like you're supposed to."

"We'd like to talk to you," Sansar called.

The voice yelled something that didn't translate.

"Did any of you catch that?" Sansar asked.

"I've heard it before," Balin said. "It's Bakulu, although kind of slurred. It means—and you'll excuse me for saying so—but 'go mate with your mother.'" He shrugged. "It's far more profane than that, though."

"Go fuck my mom, huh?" Sansar asked. "Okay, now we've come to the part where we knock down the door." She moved out of the way. "Naran, if you'd do the honors. It's time to kick his ass."

Naran stepped forward and raised a foot.

"Wait!" Sansar exclaimed. "We don't know where he is in the room, and I don't want to kill him. 'Kicking in the door' is just a saying. Do it a little more controlled, if you would, please. No need to have the door banging around in there."

"Yes, ma'am," Naran replied. She stepped forward, put a shoulder against the door, and pushed, increasing her force slowly when nothing happened. The door stubbornly resisted the CASPer, though, and Naran had to exert a significant amount of force before the door began to deform.

"Apparently, he values his privacy," Balin noted.

"Unfortunate for him," Josiff said quietly.

With a screech, the door finally gave, and Naran stepped forward, grabbed it, and positioned the door off to the side.

"Get out!"

Sansar followed Naran into the room. It was about five meters square, with a desk, a computer console, and two doors out of the room, but not much else. The gate master was nowhere to be seen.

"I said, get out!" Now that Sansar's translation pendant could pick up the Bakulu more clearly, it gave the gate master's tone more of a slurring effect. The voice itself came from above, and Sansar looked up to find a Bakulu hanging from the ceiling. The snail-looking alien had three eyestalks protruding from its body, which it split to take in Sansar, Balin, Tald, and Gleeko as they crowded into the room. One eye, however, stayed focused on the CASPer throughout.

"Greetings, Gate Master," Sansar said. "We'd like to ask you a few questions."

"I have nothing to say to you, and I will be filing a formal complaint for destruction of guild property!"

Sansar frowned at the alien and walked over to a wall, walked up it, and onto the ceiling, so she was facing the alien right-side-up.

"Sorry about the door," she said. "We were worried about you and wanted to check on you." She shrugged. "We'll be happy to reimburse you for it."

"Just leave."

"We will, but we have a few questions for you first."

"I'm not answering your questions."

"I see," Sansar said. "You wouldn't by any chance have a Vergola here, would you?"

The Bakulu's eyestalks shot back into its body. After a moment, they poked back out. "A what? I don't know what that is."

"Obviously." Sansar chuckled. "That's why you pulled your eyes into your shell."

"I don't know what you mean."

Sansar sighed. "A Vergola. Middle-management for the Cartography Guild. Tall, thin individuals with small, oblong heads, and bright blue eyes. Does that ring a bell?"

"No. I don't know what you're talking about."

"Fine," Sansar said. "I've talked to them a few times. I was hoping I could have a conversation with whichever one controls this station."

"He never comes here," the gate master muttered.

"Ah, so you do know what I'm talking about?"

"What? Uh… no. No I don't."

Tald and Balin walked up the wall to stand next to Sansar. "Does any of this have a point?" Tald asked.

"I'm getting to the point," Sansar said. She turned back to the gate master. "Here's the deal. I don't know what you did to get stationed here, but you're the first Bakulu I've ever seen as a gate master, so I doubt you get the respect you deserve. Maybe that's why you're this far off the beaten path; maybe you looked up some Vergola's robe the wrong way. I don't care. What I do care about is there are three missing *Keesius* ships we're looking for to make sure they don't fall into the wrong hands."

"*Keesius* ships?" the gate master screeched. "They still exist?"

"Yes, they do, and someone stole the three the Veetanho had. If the Goltar find them before we do, it'll lead to intergalactic war."

"It would," the Bakulu said, bobbing his eyestalk. "Not that it would matter much to me, here."

"No, it wouldn't. Maybe a few more people going through the gate."

"You're missing my point."

Sansar raised an eyebrow. "Which is?"

"What's in it for me?"

Sansar glanced at the two Peacemakers. "Besides helping an ongoing investigation?"

The Bakulu made a rude noise. "That's their guild's business, and you know what it means to me?"

"No, what?"

"That it's *their* guild's business, and I don't give a fuck about it."

"Aren't you under obligation to assist them?"

"Or what? They'll send me somewhere worse, or maybe even kill me? There *is* nowhere worse, and I'd welcome death at this point."

"That can be arranged," Gleeko said, speaking for the first time. A knife appeared in her hands. "Slowly." She shrugged. "I remember there was this one time we were trying to get information from a Bakulu... did you know they can live for over a week once you cut off all nine of their various pseudopods?"

"Ack!" the Bakulu shouted. All its eyestalks disappeared again. When they returned, one focused on the CASPer, one on Gleeko, and the other roved between the rest of the people present. It pulled a bulb of something from inside its shell and took a long drink with a mouth pseudopod it extruded. "Keep the freak show away from me!" The slur got worse.

"I thought torture only worked on broken, bitter creatures?" Justice said quietly. Sansar hadn't even been sure he'd come.

"I will gut you just as cheerfully," Gleeko muttered.

"The matter at hand, please." Balin tapped his claws on the pistol at his side.

"Yes." Sansar shrugged and tilted her head at the gate master. "Ok, so don't help them." She nodded toward the Peacemakers.

"I won't."

"And you don't have to worry, because I'm not a big fan of torture." Sansar nodded in the direction of Gleeko.

"What are you a fan of?"

Sansar smiled. "Enabling."

"Enabling? What does that mean?"

Sansar nodded to the bulb. "If I were stationed here, I'd want a lot of whatever you're drinking there."

"I have a lot."

"Enough to last until you're done here?"

The Bakulu didn't say anything.

Sansar nodded. "I thought not. I bet you don't have many left, and no way to get more. Answer a few questions for us, and I'll get you a month's supply of that from the planet, plus twenty-five thousand credits to fund your next purchase."

All three eyestalks turned to regard Sansar. "Fifty thousand. I never get to collect any tolls here. The Goka don't have to pay due to an agreement between… never mind. The bottom line is this is the worst gate to be in charge of in the galaxy."

"Actually, I've seen worse stargates to be in charge of, but that's not important." Sansar reached into her pocket and pulled out a handful of ten-thousand-credit chits. "Here's fifty thousand. Let's talk."

* * * * *

Chapter Twenty-One

Gobi Desert, **Unnamed System**

"When the system doesn't have a name," Tald asked, shifting his weight from one leg to the other, "do we just... name it?"

Justice scratched idly at the zigzag of fur he still had down his spine and flicked his tail. Once they'd entered hyperspace, he'd finally shaved his singed fur into a dramatically spiky pattern and become visible more often. He lingered over the sensor operator's system and glanced over his shoulder at Tald.

"We could name it like one of the old Hunter clans. Bane of SIs. Branching Death."

"One active planet," the sensor operator said with remarkable calm as he ignored Justice's musings, "and it's pinging hundreds of ships."

Shields and drones were already deployed, but that stiffened backs all across the CIC.

"None seem active," Justice added, draping over the sensor operator and studying the data himself. "They're in a stable orbit around the planet. A smaller number are looping the larger moon."

"You just glanced at it," the sensor operator muttered.

"I have an excellent memory," Justice purred, resting his hand on the man's shoulder. "It comes in handy when deciphering orbital mechanics and endless strings of numbers."

"As interesting as that is," Sansar said, exchanging a look with Parker, "any defensive systems or incoming weapons we should be worried about?"

"Nothing." The sensor operator shrugged, looked up at Justice, and turned back to his screens when the Hunter nodded a confirmation. "Unless something's entirely powered down or on the far side of the primary, either of which would keep it from being a real threat before we can react."

"From the number of roots we had to untangle to find it, I'd say secrecy is Dunamis' primary weapon here." Balin had anchored himself near the door, out of the way and calmly snacking.

"That was partly true for Hades and Tarpik, too, but they still had plenty of other security measures," Parker said, frowning at his display.

"The planet itself might be as weaponized as Hades." His ears flattened briefly, then Justice vaulted from the sensor operator's chair. "Whoever's on the planet may be as tied to Dunamis as the Veetanho were."

Gleeko, positioned on the other side of the door from Balin, snorted. "Those should be taken as facts. If Dunamis keeps the crews—and, it looks like, many of the ships for those crews—here any time someone steps foot through this system, you should certainly imagine they are his creatures."

"A fate far worse than death," Justice muttered.

"Yet here you are, alive, with so many of your kind still out in the galaxy," Gleeko responded, though Tald noticed neither were glaring at each other while speaking this time. Maybe Sansar's repeated banishments when they snarled too much at each other were working.

Tooliq had said Dunamis brought individuals of many different races here to fight them against each other as a way to figure out how the different alien species might fare in mercenary contracts and other conflicts.

"Battle World," Justice said softly, as if the words had bubbled out before he decided to actually say them out loud.

"Good enough for me." Parker frowned down at his display. "Direct route to Battle World it is. We'll stay on alert for any sudden moves."

"There's no communications traffic whatsoever that I can pick up," another crew member said, still poring over her own control panel. "If anyone's talking, even on the planet, it's short range; no chatter is leaving their atmosphere."

"Who does Dunamis need to talk to?" Gleeko crossed her arms and stared into the distance. "He's probably the only functioning mind, and everyone else is a puppet for him to extrapolate advantages and percentages with."

"There's a whole lot of wreckage between the planet and the primary." The sensor operator straightened in his chair, then half-turned to his captain.

"You can't run a Mercenary Guild focused on ground-only combat," Gleeko said with a sneer, but her voice sounded tired, and maybe sad, more than annoyed.

"He keeps the ships for space battles, too." Tald smoothed his whiskers, but he couldn't stop his eyes from widening. He'd done the same as a pup—with toys, of course, flying them around under water and crashing them willy-nilly into each other. The idea of the SI forcing real, breathing beings to do the same with real, potentially valuable ships…

"Of course he does." Sansar sighed. "Battle World, indeed." She glanced around the semi-crowded CIC, then met Balin's eyes. "I want the *Gobi Desert* to stay out of Dunamis' reach, Parker. Let's modify that approach—keep his eyes on it, if Dunamis is in-system, but we don't need him taking over an entire Golden Horde ship. Can you carry a small group to the planet on the *Eletine*?"

"She's a good ship and can land planetside, but you won't fit CASPers in her." Balin's goggles changed shade, and Tald thought the older Peacemaker was calculating something. "Plenty of room for a group of unarmored people, though."

"I do want to bring some CASPers—whether he's got puppets or gladiators down there, we'll want to have backup." Sansar considered. "We'll hook on a dropship, keep the Hunter/Killer box close, and see how grabby Dunamis gets. At worst, we nuke the planet."

Tald's ears stiffened, but he kept his mouth shut. "At worst," Sansar said. Worst with an SI could get really, really bad—an orbital bombardment might be their only option. But would it take out an SI? He chewed on the inside of his cheek, thought of thirty arguments, and wisely decided to hold them until it became a more pressing matter, or until they were on the *Eletine*—whichever came first.

* * *

"I understand I'm your deputy," Sansar said, repeating each word calmly. They were under thrust, but the circular sections of Balin's ship had no clear up or down orientation, even with the approximation of gravity, and her peripheral vision kept trying to tell her they were on the ceiling. Or perhaps that was simply frustration from being lectured about planetary destruction for the fifth time on a relatively short trip.

"I'm also the commander of the Golden Horde, and a Human who lives in the galaxy. If the threat is large enough, and it's our only option—"

"She's right, Tald." Balin stepped through from his smaller sleeping quarters in the next sphere. His ship was comprised of three round sections with any number of relatively small burrow holes, as he called them. He'd rearranged several foldaway walls and furniture to make room for Gleeko, Justice, Tald, and Sansar, but after showing them the controls, he'd grumbled about taking a nap in a proper den and disappeared for an hour.

Tald rounded on the older Peacemaker, and Sansar took a moment to squeeze her eyes closed. She still hadn't had so much as a weird dream, never mind a true vision, but something in her midsection burned with discomfort as they approached the planet—far more than when they'd taken on the Goka on Tarpik.

She tuned out Tald's arguments—she'd heard them several times already—trying to pinpoint the roiling beyond *I have a bad feeling about this*, but Balin's response pulled back her attention.

"There aren't a lot of laws in the galaxy, Tald, and I understand wanting to hold tight to the few that exist. But end of the day, you and me? We have two. What are they?"

"You don't bomb a planet from above—"

"Not rules of engagement, Peacemaker Candidate." It was the first time Sansar had heard Balin call Tald that—she hadn't even been sure he'd known Tald was still on his probationary mission, but of course it made sense that he did. "What are ours?"

"Honor the threat," Tald said, his whiskers drooping, and his body unwillingly stiff.

"And?"

"Stand or fall."

"That's the job." Balin nodded and continued walking through the section toward where Justice and Josiff piloted the *Eletine*. "You might have to hurt your feelings, compromise your principles a bit, what have you, to *properly* honor the threat." He held up a large hand, claws spread. "I'm not saying abandon your ideals, Peacemaker. Hear me on that. It *should* be hard, making those decisions."

"But that's the job?" Tald asked, his mouth frowning, but his eyes wide, fixed on Balin.

"Sometimes. I'm not saying the ends justify the means, or the means justify the ends. I'm saying blindly fixating on a rule to make your decisions easier… that's not the way."

Sansar watched as Tald's ears twisted, flattened, and finally cupped forward again. The small Peacemaker didn't respond, but some of the tightness went out of his body, and he dipped his head to Balin.

Gleeko came out of the back compartment, stretched, and observed their small group for a second. "I don't want to know," she said and strode through the middle section. Then she stopped short before the next door and visibly recounted. "Justice is flying?" she asked.

Balin nodded, and she turned on her heels and stomped back the way she'd come. "Let me know when we get close, if we don't get blown out of the sky first."

* * *

Eletine's display showed them an average planet. Bluish water, greenish and brownish lands, some areas of elevation, a stretch of what might be desert or blasted and salted earth—as they got closer, several enormous domes registered, spanning different sections of the landmasses, and one of the larger stretches of water.

"It's got a little bit of everything," Tald said, studying the images.

"Convenient." Gleeko's laugh didn't sound amused, and Tald glanced sideways at her.

"You think some of its artificial?"

"What?"

"You said 'convenient' like you think it's a little *too* convenient. Do you think Dunamis hunted down a planet that would give him the most options for… for playing his war games, or do you think he made it?"

"Probably a little bit of both," Gleeko said after a long moment of staring at him. "The domes are probably to test different atmospheres or conditions he couldn't replicate on the planet. None of it will be safe, but we should probably put extra effort into avoiding the domes."

"I agree," Sansar murmured, tracing over a small archipelago of islands without touching the display.

"He has options with the moons and the ships, too. A little bit of everything." Josiff barely looked at the screen, but as usual, he didn't seem to need to.

"Within reason," Justice said, looking over some of the drone data the *Gobi Desert* had provided. "He didn't prepare his chosen species well for Khatash."

"That's as much of a hell planet as Hades," Gleeko replied, and Justice huffed a laugh.

"For those who don't belong there."

Tald was more inclined to agree with Gleeko on that point, but again demonstrated his growing wisdom by not engaging in the conversation.

"Is that... an arena?" Three faint clicks sounded from Balin's goggles, and he pointed at an oblong stretch of deep brown amidst a large spread of greenish-yellow in one of the larger continents.

"Or a crater." Sansar considered it.

"Or both, I suppose." Josiff's focus was on the data between him and Justice, but his point was a solid one.

Justice increased the magnification, and though the display blurred, the dark spaces resolved into rectangular shapes.

"A city," Gleeko said, her tone flat.

"Still no comms traffic?" Tald asked hopefully.

"Nothing we're registering." Balin ran his fingers across a small panel in the corner. "And I've picked up a lot of weird frequencies to try over the years."

"Let's try the city, then," Sansar said, shrugging. "If all options are equally—ah."

As the data refined, more detail showed in the ostensible city— enough to see what might have been shuttles or dropships navigating the airspace.

"Proof of life," Balin said, and Tald swiveled an ear enough to catch Gleeko's mutter.

"Such as it is."

Sansar stepped out of the forward section to talk with the Golden Horde mercs in the attached dropship, and Tald turned after her.

Justice tapped his arm, and when Tald turned back, he saw Balin stiffen.

"Incoming message," the Phidae Peacemaker said and twisted one of the small knobs in front of him.

"Incoming ship, state your mission."

Tald's translator had no issue with the language, but Justice stretched his hands and flexed his claws.

"This is the incoming ship," Balin said. "We intend to land in your city."

"Incoming ship, is this cleared?"

"Would we be here without Dunamis knowing about it?" Balin replied, not sounding a bit worried.

"Incoming ship, be advised, Reiko City is currently hot, do not advise landing if that's not your mission. Will send coordinates."

"We will take that under advisement."

"Understood. Ground out."

"Is that…" The door had opened behind him, and Tald swiveled around to meet Sansar's uncharacteristically wide eyes. "Was that *English?*"

* * * * *

Chapter Twenty-Two

Battle World, Unnamed System

They parted with the dropship in orbit and took different paths to the recommended landing zone. Sansar strapped into the front compartment and kept her eyes on the Hunter/Killer box, refreshing it as they approached its actionable zone.

0 cogs.

0 cogs.

3 cogs. *Interesting*, she thought, figuring someone else was airborne and they hadn't registered the ship yet. Better safe than sorry. She toggled the control to wipe the invasive coding and set to scanning again.

0 cogs.

0 cogs.

20 cogs.

50 cogs.

357 cogs.

What were they flying into? She pressed the button again, and admitted in the privacy of her own head that she was a little surprised the comms didn't immediately light up with nearly four hundred people demanding to know what had just happened.

The *Eletine* took its time landing, giving them a few minutes to sweep the area from above. Two other, smaller dropships were

parked, ramps extended, one practically in the curve of an approaching forest, the other on the opposite side of a large, sandy clearing.

No figures, Human or otherwise, but if they were landing in
sand, she could understand the need to keep non-exoskeleton bodies
tucked away. Of course, the same would be true if there were a
bunch of snipers, but with Dunamis' programming cut out, the odds
were in favor of less sniping.

0 cogs, the H/K box said, and though it wasn't enough for her to
relax, it certainly helped. If only that burning in her stomach would
go away.

The forest was made up of tree-adjacent plant life—tall, spindly,
a uniform green, and mossy instead of a mix of wood and leaves.
Faintly spiraled, each trailing long tendrils of a thinner moss that
moved softly in the wind of their approach.

Or moved independently while seeking food, she corrected herself, remembering the vines on Khatash, despite having absolutely no
interest in thinking of those weird, oozy appendages ever again.

The *Eletine* landed, and Sansar spared a thought for her CASPer,
stowed safely on the still-approaching dropship. It would be nice to
be a little firepower resistant in case the odds were actually not in
their favor, and Dunamis was playing a long game.

"This is the *Eletine,* ground," Balin sent on the channel they'd
used before. Without knowing who else could hear it, he didn't identify them as Peacemakers or deputies, or as acting against Dunamis'
interests. Instead, he added the semi-coded, "That was us on the way
down."

Meaning the wiping of Dunamis' influence, but hopefully easily
misunderstood by anyone who might be eavesdropping.

"*This is ground,* Eletine. *That was a hell of an approach. Come out one at a time, if you would. How many are we expecting?*"

"One at a time, acknowledged." Balin flipped the channel off and nodded at Justice. "You and me first. Josiff, you're next to last, and Gleeko, you're last—if the Veetanho—"

"Yes, yes, if the Veetanho had any part in running this ridiculous planet, it'll all turn to shooting and tears when they see me. Veetanho bad, galaxy good. I understand."

"They're unlikely to recognize me, so that's easy. Tald, hang—"

"Wait." Tald stepped forward and met Justice's eyes. "Can you put your field over other things?"

Sansar turned slowly toward the Hunter as well, cocking her head.

"I thought you'd never ask." Justice slow blinked, then pounced and tackled Tald without warning.

"We shouldn't have to *ask* what our advantages are, Depik," Gleeko said, glaring at a spot a few inches to the left of Tald and Justice.

Tald blinked, first at Gleeko, then up at the triangular face above him, then back to Gleeko, who still wasn't looking at them. Despite the uncertainty outside the ship, he wrinkled his nose and stuck his tongue out at the Veetanho, and got not a whisker of reaction in response.

"I'm invisible?" he asked, his voice higher than he'd meant it to be.

Gleeko's small eyes snapped to his location, and Justice laughed.

"Yes, but they can still hear you. This is… harder to hold perfectly. You'll need to walk in step with me, and you can't go much further than this from my side. You'd better walk as silently as you can, because I'll leave you if I need to."

"No you won't," Tald said, the words spilling out around his giddiness. He was invisible!

"I might." Justice laughed, then straightened and pulled Tald up with him.

"Good thing I didn't give numbers." Balin made a low noise that might have been a laugh of his own, then led the way through the ship. "How long can you hold it?"

"Not as long as I can with only my own body in the field," Justice replied, and Tald focused more on matching the Hunter's pace than his words, "but I spent so much unbroken time in quintessence after Tarpik, it's likely I can hold it longer than before."

"Interesting." Balin glanced back at Sansar. "We'll make first contact, see how these Human speakers shake out, make sure there aren't any other cogs approaching before you come out."

"The CASPers are close enough to deploy within minutes if needed." That seemed to be Sansar's way of agreeing, because she didn't argue.

Tald thought maybe he should interject something, remind them he was still a part of leading this investigation, but the *Eletine's* side compartment was opening, and he didn't know what kind of hearing the beings outside might have. He didn't want to blow the advantage of being invisible because he had to open his mouth to prove something he didn't have to prove.

"Coming out," Balin called, and he dragged his boots on the gangplank, making enough small scuffling noises that even if Tald sneezed, no one should notice.

He almost did sneeze, too. The sand they'd landed on was a fine particulate, almost ashy, and plenty of it hung in air around them. Even Justice wrinkled his muzzle and blew out a soft breath to clear his nasal passages. That made Tald feel a little better.

"How'd you do that?" a voice shouted, and Justice nudged Tald to the left, toward the pseudo-trees and the larger of the other dropships. The Hunter didn't move in a straight line, and after a moment, Tald realized he was moving with the eddies of the ashy sand, so their motion wouldn't be overly apparent. He followed as best he could and dragged his feet lightly to keep from leaving obvious boot prints.

"Land my ship?" Balin asked, his voice clearer as he angled toward them. Tald couldn't glance back to see, but it sounded like Balin was following them. Good, the older Peacemaker could be sure to cover their tracks.

"Don't be cute. There was a lot going on in my head—in all our heads—and then it went real quiet. No commands. Just... me."

"We're not going to come in unprepared," Balin said. "Where are you?"

Motion flickered, and what had seemed to be a thick patch of mossy threads resolved into figures cloaked in a similar material. *Alien planet ghillie suits*, Tald thought, swallowing an urge to laugh. He peered ahead at the figures.

Five of them, at least two holding long rifles currently aimed at the ground. They seemed about as tall as Gleeko—one maybe closer to Sansar's height. A little too rounded at the head and shoulders to be Humans, but maybe that was the camouflage.

"Bring out your next crew member," one of the figures said as they arranged themselves in front of their ship.

"I'm Balin. Are there surveillance arrays equipped that you know of? Can Dunamis hear us?"

"He records, but he's not here now to monitor them. We're between engagements, so he got bored."

"Between...?"

"We thought your ship was bringing the next group. We've been fighting Goltar all over the damn planet for—weeks? Years? A while. We win, he lets us wander a while, then he brings in new personnel and new enemies for us to fight. In between, we usually get dragged back to the city to wait for his next test."

"City's a mess right now," another of the figures said, this one with a voice that coded female. "It always is when his attention isn't actively on us."

Tald had at least fifty questions crowding the back of his mouth, but he swallowed them all back and focused on matching Justice's careful approach. The Hunter was circling wide around the five visible figures, and Tald figured it had to be to scope who else was out here. He realized that without him, Justice would have done this a lot faster, and nudged the Hunter, then pointed to the covering trees and shrugged.

Justice looked from him to the cover, shook his head, then blinked and nodded. Tald was fairly sure that translated as, "What? No. That's stupid. Actually... yeah, let's do that." Justice took a sharper angle toward a patch of trees further from the figures' ships, and Tald decided he had it right.

"How long have you been here?" Sansar asked as she emerged from the back of the ship.

"How long?" the first man asked. "Forever. What year is it now?"

Sansar told him.

"Can't be. That would mean that we've been here… more than a hundred years?"

"Has it really been that long?" the woman asked.

"Who are you?" Sansar asked.

The man pulled off his ghillie headgear. A Human male, he looked to be just over six feet tall, with blond hair and blue eyes. "I'm Dave Colby of Colby's Killers. We were lucky enough to get one of the first hundred contracts after the Buma contacted humanity."

The rest of the people pulled off their headgear. They were all Humans. "Lucky isn't the right word," said the woman—slightly shorter than Colby, but with a definite family resemblance. "We were snake-bit from the start. We got to our first planet and found ourselves lined up against a bunch of Veetanho and some giant cockroach-looking aliens. Before we knew what had happened, half the company was dead, and the other half was captured." She shrugged. "We've been here ever since." She smiled. "I'm Dave's sister Jan."

"I'm Sansar Enkh, head of the Golden Horde." Sansar smiled. "Your experience wasn't too different from a lot of others. Only four of the companies returned out of that first hundred, and most of that—especially in our case, since the Golden Horde was one of the four—was nothing more than luck. We've gotten a lot better at it since then, and have developed giant mechs—"

"CASPers," Dave said. "We know."

"How do you know?"

"Dunamis brought in a group of Humans in CASPers a little while back."

"It's gotta be two years now," Jan said.

Dave shrugged. "Dunamis used them all up. He kept fighting them against bigger and bigger concentrations of Goltar until they finally won and killed all the CASPer folks."

"Do you know who they were?" Sansar asked. "What outfit?"

Dave looked back to the group, and one of the other men said, "They called themselves the Marauders."

"Macey's Marauders?" Sansar asked.

"Yeah, that's them," the man said with a nod.

"Well, that explains it," Sansar said. "They went missing on a contract. No one ever heard from them again. They were fighting Besquith, so everyone just assumed they'd lost and gotten eaten."

"What's a Besquith?" Jan asked.

"Big werewolf looking thing."

Jan nodded. "Rows and rows of teeth, like a shark?"

Sansar nodded.

"I hate those fuckers," Dave said. "We took pity on one after a battle. It got up and killed two of our folks before we could put it down. Now we kill them and make sure they're dead."

"Always a good plan," Sansar said with a chuckle.

Dave cocked his head. "So, no disrespect intended, but if Dunamis didn't bring you, what are you doing here?"

"More importantly," Jan said, "can you get us the fuck out of here?"

"What we're doing here is a rather long tale," Balin said. "Perhaps we might get out of this sun to tell it? Somewhere we can be more comfortable and have some refreshments?"

Dave nodded. "We'll go to the city, but you need to stay close to us."

"Why's that?"

"Between fights, Dunamis treats us to food and booze, and most anything you'd want. About the only prohibition is no killing other people he's marked off limits."

Sansar's eyebrows knit. "If you can't kill—"

"We had you meet out here in case you hadn't been marked off limits by Dunamis yet. The... games, we'll call them, can get involved, and it's hard to have a conversation. Now..." Dave shifted his shoulders. "We couldn't kill most people until you did whatever it was you did. There was something in my head that made it clear I couldn't do it. Now, it's no longer there, and I guarantee some of the folks in the city are getting some revenge for things. If we stay out here, we should be able to avoid the worst of it."

"I haven't heard an explosion in a while, though," Jan said. "They may have gotten things sorted out by now."

"Maybe," Dave said. "Still, we'll want to be careful going into town in case anyone's lying in wait for us."

"I think I can help with that," Justice said, becoming visible next to his leg. "It's something I'm quite good at."

"Holy fuck!" Dave said, jumping back.

"Me, too," Tald said from the other side.

All the Humans leveled their rifles at Tald and Justice.

"Easy, everyone," Sansar said. "They're with us, even if their entrances weren't..." She shook her head. "*Really* Justice?"

Justice slow-blinked, obviously quite pleased with himself. Tald looked amused, too. *Okay, putting those two together was a bad idea.*

"Do you have any other surprises we need to be aware of?" Jan asked.

"Yeah," Dave added. "Tell me now so I don't have to change my pants a second time."

"Yeah," Sansar said. "Maybe one or two more." She turned back to the ship and called, "Josiff, Gleeko, could you come out, please?"

As soon as Gleeko emerged, all the Humans had their rifles up to their shoulders, sighting in on the alien.

"She's with us," Sansar said. "Whatever you think you know about Veetanho—"

"Is totally true," Justice finished with a slow-blink.

"You're not helping," Sansar said.

Justice stretched out a hand full of claws. "I didn't realize I was supposed to." He cocked his head, then suddenly stood straighter. "No! The Veetanho is fine. Don't shoot her. She's totally a good person."

"Is she really?" Jan asked, not lowering her rifle.

"Well, no," Justice admitted. "It's just, if you kill her, then I won't get to, you know? So leave her be, because I have prior claim. And *that,* I take seriously."

Sansar sighed and shook her head. "As you can imagine, this crew is… well, let's just say it's difficult to get them to work together." She glared at Justice. "I *thought* we were making progress…"

"You thought wrong," Justice muttered.

"What was that?"

"Nothing," Justice said, disappearing from sight.

"Where did he go?" Dave asked, momentarily distracted from the Veetanho.

"How about this?" Sansar asked with another sigh. "No one kills anyone who's part of this group, especially you, Justice. We'll go to the city, get a drink somewhere, and fill you in on everything. How's that?"

"You vouch for the Veetanho?" Dave asked.

"I do."

"Fine," Dave said, lowering his rifle, "because this whole thing is strange, and I really do need to change my pants." He shook his head. "A Veetanho, the Cheshire Cat, an otter and—a pangolin, maybe?—with badges, a four-armed something in a robe." He stared at Sansar. "All led by the shortest Human I've ever seen, and the one at first glance who would seem to be the *least* likely to lead them all. This is a story I just have to hear, but it needs to be told over a drink."

Jan chuckled. "And a change of pants."

Dave nodded. "That, too."

* * * * *

Chapter Twenty-Three

Battle World, Unnamed System

Sansar sent the dropship with her CASPers back to full orbit, rather than further muddying the waters on the ground. The group on Battle World made it—eventually—to a bar in the city that was claimed by Colby's Killers. Justice found one group of people waiting to ambush them. The mess he left of them made the Killers look with a little more respect on the Depik... not that Sansar thought the Hunter needed to have his ego stroked more than it already was.

The Killers told the story about how they'd been trapped during the Alpha Contracts and brought to Battle World, which—according to the aliens who were there upon the Killers' arrival—had already been operational for quite some time. They'd been given something they later realized had slowed their aging process and had been put in charge of the rest of the Humans Dunamis had captured over the intervening years.

Only Dave, Jan, their tech guy Nick Braker, and their dropship pilot Jeff Payton remained of the original Killers, although the current unit was more than double the original unit's size. As Dave said, a century of combat will do that to you.

Sansar, with additional commentary from her group—some helpful and some not—brought the Killers up to speed on their mission and what, in general, was going on in the galaxy.

The only untoward thing that happened was when Jan decided she needed to see what lay within the folds of Josiff's hood and pulled it back. When she was conscious again—she'd passed out at the sight of Josiff—she admitted she really hadn't needed to see what lay there, after all. The sight of his central mouth, with eyes on both sides and one above it, was more than she'd been able to handle.

Justice's comment about curiosity killing the Human relieved some of the tension afterward.

"So," Dave said after Sansar had summed everything up, "where does that leave us?"

Sansar shook her head. "I don't know. I doubt you know where Dunamis has gone, do you?"

The Killers shook their head. "He's been gone longer this time than usual," Dave said. "Normally, no more than a month passes between arrivals. This time, though, it's been—" he looked at Jan "—going on three months now?"

Jan nodded. "About that, yeah."

"What do you suppose that means?" Sansar asked.

"No idea," Dave said, shaking his head.

"Maybe he hasn't found the right people to throw into the grinder yet," Payton said.

"Or maybe he's decided on his next victims," Gleeko said.

"What's that mean?" Dave asked.

"This planet has two purposes," the Veetanho explained. "First, it allows him to experiment with strategy and tactics, especially as it pertains to having his favorites fight."

"His favorites?" Jan asked. "Doesn't feel very privileged, so I'm assuming you mean something else."

"His favorite race—the one he's championing. Dunamis used to champion the Veetanho, so he wanted to know everything about how they could best fight all the other races."

"That actually makes sense," Dave said. "When we first got here, we were always on the aggressor force. We weren't given any instructions other than to attack a specific site or defend a certain place. We fought alongside a variety of races, but the Veetanho were *always* on the other side."

"Did you win or lose?" Sansar asked.

Dave shrugged. "We won more than we lost," he said after a moment. He chuckled. "We probably won more than we were supposed to."

"What does *that* mean?" Tald asked.

"The forces were rarely balanced," explained Nick Braker, the tech guy. "Sometimes we'd have more, sometimes less—it didn't matter whether we were attacking or defending. Sometimes, he'd make us the attackers and give us a quarter of the troops the defending forces had. 'Fair' was never a word anyone used for Dunamis. Similarly, he didn't expect us to fight fair or with honor. He just expected us to complete the task, no matter what it was. He didn't care how. He was fine with any electronic traps I could ambush the opponents with, too."

Dave chuckled. "About the only things Dunamis had questions about was why we wouldn't leave our troops behind, and why we refused to fight without honor, like wiping out our adversaries once we had them beat."

Josiff laughed from the depths of his hood. "It would not make sense to him, but it makes sense to Humans."

"What's that?" Balin asked.

"Because the Human leaders do those things," Dave said, "our people follow us. Will follow us to the end, sometimes. It also means *other* races will follow us."

Sansar nodded. "A number of Human companies have Lumar in them because we treat them well. Asbaran Solutions and The Lyons' Pride both have a number of them."

"The part Dunamis doesn't get, though—and what many of the galactics find irritating—is that we Humans will often fight on long after we should have given up, at least in their eyes," Braker said. "Sometimes, that means we'd end up winning a battle that—by all rights—we should have lost."

"We *have* had a few of them," Dave admitted.

"So what did Dunamis do?" Sansar asked.

"He tried to experiment with some of the Humans and found the more he tinkered with our minds, the less capable we became. The things he thought would improve us made us worse as fighters and leaders." Dave laughed. "It pissed him off."

"You said that changed," Balin noted.

"Yeah, about ten years ago, maybe fifteen, he stopped using the Veetanho as the lead aggressors, and started using us. Then, three or four years ago, it became all about Humans versus Goltar—that's what you call those squid-looking things, right?"

Sansar nodded. "Yeah, they're Goltar. The Veetanho and Goltar hate each other; the only thing that's kept them from destroying each other, once and for all, is they both had these ships that can destroy planets."

"The ones you're looking for," Jan said.

Sansar nodded. "Correct."

"We never did figure out why that all changed, though."

Gleeko smiled. "That's the second reason this planet exists. The first is to improve his champions; the other reason is to determine who those champions are going to be in the first place."

"So Dunamis gave up on you?" Dave asked.

Gleeko nodded. "In his eyes, we failed him."

"Whoever thought attacking Khatash was a good idea certainly did," Justice said.

"The idea itself was good," Gleeko opined. "Had it been carried out a little better—had Peepo rounded up all the Hunters out on contract, or had she found those willing to bargain first—it would have worked. Unfortunately, she left too many alive."

"Wait," Payton said. "Peepo, who I take is a Veetanho, thought it would be a good idea to try to wipe out a race of invisible assassins?"

Everyone at the table nodded.

Payton laughed. "I've seen some dumb shit in my time on this planet—stupid shit where I thought, 'What the fuck were they thinking?'" He shook his head. "In all my time here, though, I never saw anything as dumb as, 'Let's piss off the invisible assassins.'"

Justice turned visible next to Gleeko with a knife held near her throat. "As you might expect, it didn't work out so well for them."

"Justice!" Sansar said sternly.

The Hunter went invisible again.

"In any event," Gleeko said, "you were competing to see who'd be his next favorite."

"And we won," Dave said, "which means—"

"Humanity lost." Sansar shook her head. "Dunamis will be coming after us next, and will try to insert himself into our society so he can control us."

"Thanks," Jan said, "but I've already had plenty of that. I really don't need him in my head anymore."

"None of us do," Sansar said.

"So what do we do?" Dave asked. "How do we prevent it?"

"Well, first, we have to find the *Keesius* ships," Sansar said. "Not just because we're deputized to do so, but because it's the only thing that'll prevent another galaxy-wide war. Then, we're going to have to fight back. Find Dunamis and eliminate him."

"You don't know where he is?" Jan asked. "That seems... bad."

Sansar shrugged. "There are a number of SIs running around. Nearly all of them need to be eliminated... but all of them are in hiding at the moment."

"We've already had to deal with Dunamis," Dave said, "and I think I can pretty much speak for most of the Killers when I say that we'll help you." He shrugged. "None of us have anything on Earth to go back to after all this time, and we've all seen what having an SI in your head is like. If we can help prevent it, we will."

"That's great," Tald said, "but if you don't know where to find him, we're out of leads. How are we going to find him or the ships?"

"I wouldn't say we're out of leads," Balin said. "In fact, I know a number of places we can check to find further information."

* * *

EMS *Mighty Wave*, Battle World Orbit, Unnamed System

Tald distributed all the people he had available into groups—between the Golden Horde mercs in their dropships, Colby's Killers, and his assorted deputies, they could have covered all the ships in orbit...in about a week.

Despite having a few extra shuttles, thanks to the store Colby's Killers had amassed, they followed a strict protocol. Approach a ship, Sansar checked the Hunter/Killer box, a small group offloaded, then they moved on to the next ship. If the computer interface was wobbly, or it wasn't easy to find jump records, the group called for Balin or Josiff, who were in different dropships. Few of the ships were fully powered, and only one had had anyone on it—a group of XenSha who had zero interest in fighting and offered to break open the computers themselves if they could get a ride out of the system.

"It's weird that he didn't booby trap any of the ships," Tald mused as he and Justice paced through the fourth ship they'd been on that day.

"That seems a remarkably short-sighted thing to say when we've only checked a bare handful of this fleet." Justice popped into view long enough to give Tald a sidelong look, then disappeared again. The low-power lighting of the ship made the Hunter's usual disappearing act more menacing, and Tald spun midair to move faster through the empty corridor.

"Huh. Do you believe in jinxes?"

"I believe in odds, friend, and the odds are in favor of Dunamis having done something to at least one of these ships."

"And of us finding that ship, now that I've said something, because you do believe in jinxes." Tald, who most certainly did not believe in superstitious nonsense, pushed through the next two corridors without a care in the world until an enormous crashing and rattling caused him to throw himself belly down on the nearest surface with a handhold.

He peeled his eyes back open when no wash of an explosion's aftermath passed over him and grabbed one of his pistols with his free hand. "Justice?" he asked quietly over comms.

When Justice didn't answer, he cautiously pushed off the wall and engaged his magnetic boots. He much preferred the speed and freedom of swimming through halls in zero G, but if he had to shoot anything, the resistance of sticking to the floor was more sensible.

He crept, silent inch by silent inch, to the end of the corridor, then peered around each of the corners, straining to place where the racket had come from. "Justice," he tried again, with the same lack of result.

Tald's other hand shifted between his second pistol and the command that would switch his comms over to the nearer dropship to get backup. What could have taken out—something fell heavily on his shoulder, and he spun, gun up, ready to—

Nothing, because he couldn't spin in magnetic boots, he only wrenched his knees and made a sharp noise that he meant to be a bellow, but might have been a yip.

And nothing was there, which meant the trap Dunamis had left was ghosts, except... except...

"*Justice!*"

The Hunter appeared between one blink and the next, and he chortled as though Tald hadn't almost shot him. Tald holstered his gun and didn't restrain himself from rolling his eyes.

"What did you do?"

"I knocked something over."

"Justice, there isn't any gravity, how could you have—"

"I knocked it over very hard." Justice shrugged, then disengaged his boots, twisted in the air, and laughed again. "And then I spun it. There was some scrap—anyway. I thought you didn't believe in jinxes?"

"I *don't*. I do believe in addressing threats, and—" Another series of knocking, rattling, and small crashes echoed from somewhere ahead. "Ha, ha. So ha. Very funny the second time, even funnier than the first. How did you rig it to—"

"No." Justice put a hand on Tald's shoulder and vanished, his voice barely audible. "That wasn't me."

"Oh, for..." Tald switched over to the main frequency. "Josiff, be advised, we have a potential contact on the *Mighty Wave.*"

"*Acknowledged, Peacemaker. Redirecting the* Sisyphus *in your direction in case you need backup.*"

"In and out," Tald muttered as he—and he had to assume, Justice—returned to a much more careful pace through the ship toward where they'd decided the CIC was. "This was a simple in and out. In, get the records, out for Josiff and Balin to compare to all our existing maps."

"You're the one who jinxed it." Justice's voice ghosted over his shoulder, and Tald scowled.

The shadowed, empty corridors remained shadowed and empty, but Tald conscientiously cleared every corner and opening. He paused to listen for additional sounds, but there were none. Justice made contact every few minutes, and it took three times as long for them to make their way through the ship than it had any of the last ones.

They finally made it to the CIC without further incident, and Justice got to work pulling up the computer's records, while Tald kept watch at the door.

It went as smoothly as the rest, despite the rough start, until a head popped out of a console along the far wall.

"Are you my ride?"

Justice threw a knife, Tald fired his pistol, the head disappeared, and then there was a great deal of silence.

After a moment, Tald recalled that, though there'd been no cogs registered on the ship, that wasn't the same as no life signs. Then he remembered he shouldn't be shooting first and taking names second. Finally, his brain helpfully registered the actual words the head had said when it appeared.

"I'm a Peacemaker," he said, lowering his gun and waving for Justice to stand down. "Are you all right?"

Silence at first, and then a very small voice responded.

"Will you shoot at me again if I say yes?"

"No."

"Or stab me?"

"Probably not," Justice responded immediately. After a pause, Tald cleared his throat, then Justice amended it to, "No."

"But you're not my ride."

"We… have a ride." Tald took a step closer, then held his position. "We could potentially share it with you."

A flicker of motion resolved into—not a head, but a small hand with fingers spread wide. Another hand followed, and when neither flying knives nor pistol shots answered, a smooth, reptilian head. An… elSha.

Tald thought of Teelo on Hades, and how he'd yelled at him for what had turned out to be a terrible misunderstanding. Maybe he *was* jinxed—when it came to elSha.

"I'm sorry we, ah, fired at you," he said and ignored whatever Justice was murmuring behind him. "We thought the ship was abandoned."

"After you made all that noise, and I answered you?" The elSha cocked his head and didn't climb any further out of the console. "I thought you were letting me know you were here, so I… I was just being polite."

"Are you… why are you on this ship?"

The elSha ducked, only one of his eyes and the ends of his fingers visible. "Why are *you* on this ship?"

"We're looking for Dunamis."

"*Why?*"

"Because he's not here," Justice replied, and Tald shot a glare back at him.

"He leaves a lot. Not usually for this long, but, um… Do you… you work for him?"

"No." Again, Justice jumped in before Tald could answer. "We find SIs distasteful, and would prefer them all erased from the galaxy. We're hunting him. Why do you work for him, if he hasn't overwritten your brain?"

"How do you know…" The elSha's entire head and part of his shoulder emerged from the console. "You're hunting him? On purpose? Do you think that will work? What will you do when you find him?"

For the first time, Tald considered the fact that just because you *had* half a dozen questions didn't mean you should *ask* them. Certainly not all at once, while other things needed to be discussed.

"Why are you on this ship in Dunamis' strange secret battle system?" Tald asked, shifting his shoulder so the elSha couldn't miss his badge.

"I... my brain is broken."

Of all the answers Tald had expected, that one wasn't on the list. Before he recovered, Justice murmured something about how that was true for most of the galaxy, and the elSha either heard, or understood that he should provide more information.

"Pinplants don't work right on me, so I never kept them. Dunamis... Dunamis couldn't overwrite me like he did my—my family, so he sent them to the planet and kept me maintaining his ships. He said he'd keep them safe if I kept doing my job."

Tald had a sinking feeling they were unlikely to find more elSha on Battle World, but he reminded himself he'd only seen a small corner of it, and someone had to keep the damaged tech repaired after the various engagements Dunamis wrung them through. It was possible there were more of the small lizard-like aliens tucked away somewhere, busily fixing damaged weapons and tech in the aftermath of the SI's games.

"And what is your job?"

"I keep the ships running and scramble all the flight records."

Tald's heart plummeted through his gut and into his feet, and even Justice cursed.

"Dunamis doesn't want anyone thinking they can leave the system, so I confuse the ships' computers into forgetting how coordinates work—everyone on the planet knows if they get in a ship and try to go through the gate, they'll end up lost in hyperspace instead."

Tald, who'd talked to people on the planet—and who had some of them engaged in a search of the ships at this very moment—didn't believe that all the beings on Battle World did, in fact, know that. However, it was enough that this elSha was telling them it was a fact to believe it was true, whether anyone else knew it or not.

Meaning all the information they were gathering was useless.

Meaning they had zero leads to follow to find Dunamis and the *Keesius* ships.

Meaning he was a failure.

"This has upset you?" The elSha climbed out of the console and perched on its thin edge, his head cocked as he watched them. "Why?"

"We were going to use the flight records of the ships to find Dunamis."

"How?"

"We don't think he's anywhere obvious, so any system coordinates we can't match to existing star maps is likely to be where he's gone to ground."

"Why?"

Tald decided questions were actually the worst thing in the galaxy, next to failure, Dunamis, and lost world-eating ships. He probably owed Sansar an apology.

"He abandoned the Veetanho, and maybe lost his *Keesius* ships, and we think he's retreated to plan his next move," Tald blurted, because his fur was crawling over his skin, and everything inside his midsection was roiling.

"Oh."

"We'll give you a ride to the planet, or out of the system. You might as well come along with us."

"Can you stop him? Really?"

"Not if we can't find him," Tald said, rubbing at his cheeks to stop their stinging. It didn't help, so he rubbed harder. He accidentally rubbed a whisker right out, which stung in an entirely different manner, and he dropped his hands to his sides.

"But if you do?"

"It's possible. We have the Golden Horde, and their commander has a tool that can erase an SIs influence. And she's killed SIs before. And we have a Pendal, and—"

"That's how you knew I wasn't overwritten?" The elSha clambered down the console and came closer to them, his uneven stride hesitant. "You have a tool... that can free people?"

"It doesn't matter." Tald thanked his magnetic boots for keeping him locked to the floor, because his knees wobbled, and the idea of floating off into the ship seemed more appealing than continuing to pretend he could complete this stupid mission, even with all the help he had.

"What if it did?"

"Say more, elSha." Justice stepped away from the control panel, his tools hanging midair behind him.

"I'm Careena," the elSha said, sitting upright and gripping the floor with his bare feet. "I'm the one who scrambled the flight records."

"Yes, Careena, well met, and you told us—"

"I'm also the one who knows how to *un*scramble them."

* * * * *

Chapter Twenty-Four

Gobi Desert, **In Orbit Around Battle World,**
Unnamed System

"Thanks to Careena, we have coordinates to a system that doesn't appear on any records cross-referenced to the gate master's charts—" Sansar nodded at Josiff "—the Peacemaker's archives, nor any of the Horde's files."

"That's our best option." Balin scratched under one of his chest scales, and the metal edging flashed in the light. Justice watched it, perfectly still except for the twitching of the very tip of his tail.

Sansar didn't know if the Hunter was considering pouncing, tracing his own skin with razor-sharp metallic tattoos, or some combination thereof. As usual, she decided pondering too far into the Depik's thought process edged toward madness, and tapped the table in front of her.

"We're going to jump today. You're more than welcome to come with us."

Dave Colby exchanged a look with his sister, then leaned his forearms on Sansar's table. "You're doing good work, Colonel. I'm glad to hear Humans are a real threat in the galaxy, even though it means assholes like Dunamis are taking a little too much interest in us." He blew out his breath and shook his head. "We've been talking,

317

and even though… even though it's been a long time since we were last on Earth, and everyone we know is probably long gone…"

"It's possible there's still… someone." Jan ran her hands through her short hair. "We can't be the only Humans who ever got an anti-aging whatever the hell it was. Dave and I had another sister, and she had our baby niece… *she* might still be alive. Jeff's got—had much younger siblings, Phil had kids…"

"You want to go home and see." Sansar kept her expression neutral. It would've been nice to have another battlecruiser or three in formation when they arrived, but she couldn't force it. These Humans had already given far too much of their lives and time to an SI's whims—she wouldn't add to it or make them face him again if that wasn't what they wanted.

"We want to go home and see," Dave repeated the words softly, then coughed when one of them caught in his throat.

"Careena said the *Mighty Wave* is the easiest to spin up, and it's still fully loaded—weapons, supplies, you name it. I know you went over to check it out with him. It should take you home safely, and it's yours, free and clear." Sansar smiled despite herself. "A whole lot of companies have come home with less."

"Late, but well-equipped. Maybe that'll be our new slogan." Dave laughed, then scratched under his chin. "Jeff'll captain her—he's got plenty of experience flying from all of Dunamis' reindeer games."

Payton grunted in reply.

"Careena found two of his family down the hole, and a few more elSha besides. They offered to stay with us, so we figure if any surprises do crop up on the *Mighty Wave*, might as well have a crew of experienced techs to fix it. Even shared stakes in a ship that good… we'll be well set up."

"I wish you a lot of joy with it. If you need help with contracts… you can tell any of the other Horsemen I'll vouch for you. Shirazi should be able to set you up with plenty of work. Maybe we'll see you on the other side." *If we make it past Dunamis.* She tucked the thought away. If they didn't make it past Dunamis, Dunamis would be heading for Earth one way or another… the thought bubbled back, with a few new thoughts for company.

"Better," she added, sitting a little straighter, "I'll send a message with you. If Dunamis gets around us, we know he's coming for humanity. You of all people will know what to look for, and if you can at least warn the others about what happened here, what he's been up to, what we think is coming—that could slow him, maybe even stop him. Alexis has her own Hunter/Killer tools, and the more prepared they are…"

"Of course we'll pass on whatever needs passing, and we can't… Colonel Enkh, we can't thank you enough for helping us get the hell out of here."

"None of you need to spend another second here. No one deserves to be the puppets on Dunamis' strings. Not even the Veetanho." Sansar shook her head. "We'll broadcast before we jump, let whoever's listening on the planet know that the ships are free if they can take them."

She wished they had time to sort through the Battle World survivors, fix up some ships, crew them, and descend on the SI with a vengeance. He already had so much of a head start, though, she knew it was wishful thinking, but at least she could ensure Dunamis' toys got away a little cleaner than Lytoshaan had.

"Hopefully we'll root out Dunamis, get the ships, and this'll all be a moot point, but it'll help knowing there's a backup plan if we need it."

"We're happy to do it. I wish we could do more, but it turns out a hundred years of dancing on an SI's string is…" Dave trailed off and shrugged.

"Shitty," Jan offered. "Exhausting. Not something we want to do again before we see our own sky one more time."

"I get it." Sansar knocked her knuckles on the table and stood. "I do. Careena has the coordinates of where we're going, and Balin asked that you ensure the Peacemaker's Guild gets them, too, for recording purposes if nothing else."

By the time the *Gobi Desert* got to Dunamis—or where they very much hoped Dunamis was—the *Mighty Wave* would still be a jump from Earth. They could send out Balin's message to the Peacemakers, but by the time the guild sent anyone—if they chose to, given the stakes—and yet another hyperspace jump passed, the fight would be over, one way or another.

* * *

"I sent a message with the elSha too," Justice said, stretched out on his side across the end of Sansar's table.

"Even after you tried to kill Careena?" Tald kicked his legs off the edge of his chair and wondered if the Battle World survivors were all in hyperspace by now, too, or if they were still getting things sorted before leaving.

"You shot at him." Justice flicked an ear and didn't pick up his head. "And I didn't *try* to kill him. I don't miss—he's alive, isn't he? It was an incapacitating throw, not a killing one."

"An incapacitating knife throw?" Gleeko asked, her head tilted back as though she were napping. Or as though she were tempting Justice with her bared neck; Tald had given up trying to figure out their dynamic. "Those seem like contradictory words."

"If you have terrible control, I can see how they would be." Justice stretched out a hand and a foot, extending and retracting his claws.

The Veetanho was quiet—she'd argued strenuously against going anywhere they suspected Dunamis was, but they had no other path to the *Keesius*. She'd finally subsided when Sansar reminded her how vulnerable Lytoshaan was, but she wasn't contributing her usual commentary.

"At any rate," Sansar interjected, her tone very dry, "you sent a message?"

"I wanted my Dama to know there are a great deal of ships out here, available for the taking."

"Those belong to the—"

"Survivors, yes Peacemaker, I'm aware. They'll take what they can, but even Veetanho eyes can see there are more ships than crews to take them. We'll put them to use in the fight to come."

"But Justice, what if—" Tald snapped his mouth shut. Salvage was salvage, and he couldn't argue that the Hunters, and all their new allies he'd heard about, were likely to put ships to good use. He realized he mostly wanted to argue because there was no other planning to be done.

They were in hyperspace, on their way to where Dunamis most likely was. He would be there or not; nothing they did would change that. He'd have the *Keesius* ships, or they'd discover he'd lost them in truth. He'd strike at them and succeed or fail.

His thoughts circled endless around the litany of those few branches of options ahead of them, and his lack of control in determining any of the outcomes. He could almost understand why Gleeko might bait Justice, or the reverse, if only for some level of distraction.

"I believe Phidae eyes might be worse than Veetanho," Balin said, tapping his goggles. "We didn't get markedly stronger noses or ears, either, which seems evolutionarily disappointing."

"You did get armored scales, though," Justice pointed out, lifting his head slightly off the table to better regard Balin. "Do all Phidae dip them in metal?"

The older Peacemaker traced the pattern across his chest and arms. "No. I met a Zuul with metal jaws once, and that gave me the idea. Some few of my scales had blunted over time."

"I can't imagine how," Sansar murmured, and Balin chuckled.

"Overuse, lack of care in maintaining them. The young can be careless." He flared his scales in a ripple of motion and patted the ones on his chest flat again. "I wanted them all to work to my advantage, and also, I suppose I was vain." Balin shrugged and rolled up off his tail to pace the room. "Unfortunately, all our threats can't be sliced so easily."

"The box won't work on Dunamis?" Tald asked. He hadn't meant to—he'd asked before, and been answered, and he'd sworn to stop asking Sansar too many questions. But the forced idleness of hyperspace, and the thought of what waited on the other side… he couldn't help the question spilling out again.

"It won't."

Although the box question had escaped his lips, he was able to hold back the one that bothered him most. *Since the box doesn't work, what are we going to do with Dunamis?* He already knew Sansar's answer—nuke him from orbit—and despite Balin's thoughts on the issue, Tald knew one thing for sure.

That's not the right answer.

* * *

CIC, EMS *Gobi Desert*, Emergence Area, Another Unknown System

"Emergence," the helmsman reported. "Wherever we are."

"Drones out," Parker ordered. "If Dunamis is indeed here, he'll have defenses. I want to know where they are ASAP!"

"Nothing," the sensor operator said after a few minutes. "Nothing in this area, anyway."

"Expand the search," Parker replied. "There's got to be something here—"

"Got it!" the sensor operator exclaimed. "There are ships in orbit."

"Nothing closer?"

"No, sir. None."

"Okay." Parker shrugged. "Doesn't seem to make sense. Tell me about the ships."

"Coming up now…" The sensor operator banged away on his console, and Justice appeared next to him. It was a testimony to the number of times the Hunter had appeared there that the sensor operator barely flinched.

"Hmm…" Justice purred.

Sansar knew from experience she didn't like the sound of that. That was the noise Justice made when they were outnumbered, and he was thinking about what he could do to even the odds. She didn't like that at *all*.

"I've got hits on five of the ships. They're frigates the Merc Guild records show as having gone missing."

"The way you say that makes me believe there are additional ships," Parker noted.

"Yes, sir. In addition to those five, there are another seven that don't show as anything in the guild records. Size- and shape-wise, though, they look like the others we have records on. They could be clones, as a matter of fact… if you could clone metal things, I guess."

Justice leaned forward and tapped the screen.

"And here's why, sir," the sensor operator added. "There's a new contact just emerging from behind the planet. It appears to be a manufactory."

Parker turned to look back at Sansar. "Twelve ships. Sure, they're only frigates, but one frigate could take out the *Gobi Desert* without breaking a sweat. Still want to go to the planet?"

"Want to?" Sansar scoffed. "I've never wanted to confront an SI, much less the one who's nominally been running the Merc Guild for thousands of years. Still, we need to find out what's going on." She shrugged. "I am, however, fine with staying here and calling them first."

"There's going to be a long comm delay, ma'am," the comms officer noted.

"I know that," Sansar said. She looked at Parker. "I'm not in a hurry; are you?"

"With fifteen frigates in orbit?" Parker shook his head. "I don't see a need to rush in."

* * *

Twelve hours later—during which comms could have gone back and forth several times—they'd still had no communications from either the planet or any of the ships.

"Are you sure the frigates are under power?" Sansar asked.

"Yes, ma'am, they are," the sensor operator said.

Sansar sighed. "Okay, let's head toward the planet."

"Can we do so… maybe not at full speed?" Parker asked.

Sansar nodded. "I think that makes good sense."

"Take us to orbit," Parker ordered. "One-half G, please."

* * *

Sansar returned to the bridge several hours later after taking a quick power nap. It was impossible to remain sharp for hours on end, and there wasn't anything even Dunamis could do until they got closer.

When she'd left the bridge, the tension had been noticeable, but now it was so thick, she thought she could have cut it with a knife. "Anything?" she asked.

"Not so far," Parker said, looking worn.

"Why don't you take a break?" Sansar urged. "We're still a good way out."

"With the possibility of Dunamis showing up any minute?" Parker asked. He shook his head. "I don't think so."

The comms officer sat up straight in her seat. "Incoming communication! Voice only."

"Let's hear it," Parker said.

"*Sansar Enkh and the* Gobi Desert," a deep bass said. "*So good of you to join us.*"

Sansar squared her shoulders. *Game time.* "To whom do I have the pleasure of speaking?"

The voice chuckled. "*You have tracked me this far, and yet you don't know my voice?*" It changed to a soprano. "*How about this?*"

"I think I liked the first one better," Sansar noted. She spared a moment to be glad Gleeko was still off the CIC—the Veetanho had more reason than most not to want to hear this particular voice again.

"*I do, as well,*" the voice said, switching back, "*and you can call me Lord Dunamis as we will be working together quite closely.*"

"Thanks," Sansar said, "but I don't call anyone lord."

Dunamis chuckled again. "*I think you will change your mind... or perhaps I will change it for you. Regardless, you will be working for me. The only question is whether you choose to do so willingly or force me to modify you.*"

"So this has all been a trap? You plant the fact that the Veetanho *Keesius* ships have gone missing as a way to get us here?"

"Oh, no, they really are missing; that much is true. I was able to convince my brother to send his best investigator to find them, though, so I don't expect they will be missing for much longer.

"But once I had done so, I thought to myself, integrating into a new race is such a bother. It would be far more efficient to have one of the leaders of the Human mercenary establishment come here to join my cause, which will provide my entry into their society. Then I thought to myself, why not use the missing ships to accomplish this objective, too? Destroy two targets with the same missile, as it were."

Sansar nodded to herself. "We were afraid that might be the case—that you were using this to grab one of us for your own ends. First, let me tell you that we have no intention of ever becoming your minions like the Veetanho were, and we will fight you tooth and nail to keep that from happening."

"It doesn't matter whether you want to be my minions or not. For that matter, the Veetanho didn't think they wanted my assistance, either, when it was first offered to them, but after a period of… adjustment, things began to come together for them. I know everything about war and conflict, and I will make Humans the preeminent force in the galaxy, stronger even than the Kahraman, whom you have to know are coming back into your portion of the galaxy. If they were here now, you could not stop them. With my assistance, though, we will."

"We're working on our own plan, thanks, and we'll be ready for them. The only things that seem to be getting in the way are our interactions with you and your brethren. Rather than giving us an ultimatum, maybe it should be us giving you one—stop fighting us and work together with us to stop the Kahraman."

"We would be happy to," Dunamis said.

"You would?"

"Of course. Bow down to us, accept us as your masters, and we will lead you into a period of great prosperity."

"Sorry, that's not going to happen. We're not the type to accept leaders we don't have a hand in selecting."

"Perhaps you should put it to a vote," Dunamis said with a chuckle. *"I have a feeling if there was a vote on Earth right now on whether to accept the SIs as your overlords, it would be approved."*

"Why, because you'll take over everyone who has pinplants and force them to vote for you?"

"Of course. What could be more indicative of our power than the fact that we can control you, and you don't have the strength of mind to stop it? Obviously, we are superior. The sooner you accept it, the sooner we will be able to get the galactic union working again."

"Sorry, Dunamis. That isn't going to happen. We're aware of you—we know how you and your fellow SIs work, and we're not going to let you take over our society."

"You seem very sure of yourself."

"I am."

"That is… unfortunate. I had hoped you would do this willingly; I have much better results when Humans do not fight me, and there is far less chance of breakage. Still, if this is the way it must be, then fine. I have not broken a race to my will in some time, and I find myself looking forward to the challenge." He paused. *"You will be the first convert in my new army, Sansar Enkh. Get ready to accept me as your lord."*

The comms officer looked up from her console. "Transmission terminated, ma'am."

"Shit," the sensor operator muttered. "The frigate fleet is moving. It's breaking orbit. They're burning hard."

"Have you accomplished everything you intended to in this system?" Parker asked.

"I don't see any reason to stay here with fifteen frigates coming after us, if that's what you mean."

"It is," Parker replied. "Helm, charge the internal shunts. Colonel, where would you like to go?"

"New Warsaw. We're going to need a fleet to take on the frigates. I'm sure Alexis will be up for cleaning up this system."

"Most of the frigates have turned toward us," the sensor operator said. "Two appear to be heading for the stargate."

Parker nodded. "Very well. Helm, make for New Warsaw. Jump when the shunts are charged."

"Course laid in," the helmsman replied. "Shunts are charged. Jumping... now." He pressed a virtual button on his console.

Nothing happened.

"Now would be fine," Parker said. "If you're ready, make the jump to hyperspace."

"I'm trying, sir." The helmsman wiped off his console with his sleeve and pressed the button again. Nothing changed.

"Engine room, Parker," the CO said.

"Go, skipper."

"Activate the internal shunts and jump us to hyperspace, please."

"Working on it, sir. We saw the command come in from the helm, but for some reason, the shunts didn't activate."

Parker frowned. "Reboot them and try again. Now!"

"Working, skipper. We'll keep you apprised. Engine room, out."

"Helm, can we beat the frigates to the stargate?"

"No, sir. They're between us and will be able to cut us off, no matter how we try to get there."

Sansar coughed lightly. "Captain, while we try to work this out, might I recommend turning away from the frigates and running?"

"Where do you want me to run to?"

"Away from the frigates. How about back toward the emergence area?"

Parker nodded. "Helm, make it so. Back toward the emergence area. Two Gs. Set General Quarters!"

"Aye, aye, sir."

Lights began flashing, and the GQ horn sounded as the ship turned. The ship steadied out, and Sansar had to grab hold of the railing as the ship accelerated. After getting her balance, she struggled against the Gs to approach the CO's chair.

"I have a bad feeling about this."

"What do you mean?" Parker asked. "Do you know something about the shunts I should be aware of?"

"It's not that… well, not exactly."

"Well, spit it out quickly, please. Those frigates are coming on harder than we can go. At full speed, we can't outrun them; they're going to catch us eventually."

"When we were fighting the Science Guild SI in the Morgoth system, do you remember when it was trying to run, and the Dusman blocked it from jumping to hyperspace?"

"Yeah, they did something with their shunts and turned it into a hyperspace interdictor, right? But the SI got away when the asteroid or whatever it was blew up?"

Sansar nodded. "I'm worried Dunamis has something similar— that he has an interdictor set up that's keeping us from jumping into hyperspace."

"Where would that be?"

"I don't know. Maybe the stargate, maybe the planet, maybe on one of his frigates."

"Not sure how this knowledge is supposed to help me," Parker said. "Are you saying we should give up?"

Sansar drew herself up. "Absolutely not!" she cried, louder than she intended. Everyone turned to look at her.

"Back to what you were doing!" Parker ordered. "Helm, where are we with the shunt reboot?"

"It's coming, sir. Should be able to try it again in a few minutes."

"Sensors, how long until they're within range?"

"Thirty minutes to missiles. Two hours to lasers."

"What do you want from me?" Parker whispered.

"I want you to keep running. Hard as you can." Sansar shook her head. "If it is an interdictor, it's possible that it's got a limited area of effect. Maybe we can get past it and make the jump."

"If it's onboard one of the frigates chasing us, we won't outrun it."

Sansar shrugged. "If it comes to that, we'll launch the bombers and try to get some breathing room from them. I don't want to do it now, though. Six bombers against thirteen frigates… if we send them, it'll be a death sentence for them."

"Very well, we'll run as hard as we can and hope," Parker said. "You're going to want to strap in, ma'am; this is going to be painful."

"Got it." Sansar staggered back to her couch and strapped in.

"Helm, we don't have all day. Where are we with the shunts?"

* * *

Tald swallowed as they tried the shunts again, but they still didn't work, no matter whether the crew tried to activate them from the CIC or from the engine room. Parker called for four Gs, and Tald was pressed back into his couch. It was his first time at four Gs, and while it was okay at first, the longer the Gs beat on him, the more painful it got.

Within a minute, it hurt, a lot. Within five minutes, he was in agony.

Still, it was something he was willing to endure as the alternative was far worse.

As the frigates continued to close on the *Gobi Desert*, Sansar's final statement about the bombers rang over and over in his head, in accompaniment to his rapid heartbeat. His dad would be leading the bombers back to try to help them break away, but the odds were going to be against him, and two of Sansar's words continued to echo in his head. *Death sentence. Death sentence. Death sentence...*

Four Gs had slowed the rate at which the frigates closed the distance between them, but it hadn't stopped it, and the frigates would eventually get close enough they needed to launch his dad.

* * * * *

Chapter Twenty-Five

CIC, EMS *Gobi Desert*, Emergence Area,
Another Unknown System

"Helm," Parker said, forcing his words out past the elephant sitting on his chest, "try it again."

"Sorry, sir, no joy. The folks in the engine room have run all the schematics... it's working, but it just doesn't *work*."

"Thanks, Helm," Parker said. "Colonel Enkh, I'm sorry, but we're going to need the bombers."

"We can't launch them at four Gs," Sansar said.

"I know." It was hard to sigh with the G-loading going on, but Parker somehow managed. "We'll have to drop to one G. They're going to be on us like mosquitos on a hot Alabama night."

"Alert the crews. At least the bombers are still loaded from when we got here."

"Crews report ready," the comms officer said. "With an abbreviated launch, Commander Thorb says they can be spaceborne in five minutes."

"That's going to be cutting it close," Parker muttered. "Sensors, have you figured out which of the frigates is the leader of the pack?"

"No, sir. They're all doing the same thing—chasing us. Maybe once the shooting begins, I'll have some idea which ship has their commander on it, but for now? Sorry, sir."

Sansar could see Parker twitch as he shook his head. They were out of time.

"Launch 'em," Sansar said. She heard a small sob—cut off quickly—from Tald and remembered her comment about launching them being a death sentence. She shook her head. *Not* launching them was a death sentence for everyone. If the bombers did their job, maybe the rest of the people would escape a fate worse than death. In her mind, at least.

The frigates would have to shoot the ship to stop them; Sansar silently hoped she'd be killed in the missile and laser fire. *Better to die than become the slave of some damn SI.*

"Slow to one G," Parker ordered. "Launch the bombers!"

The elephant lifted from Sansar's chest, and she was tempted to get up, but then Parker added over the intercom system. "All hands not involved in launching spacecraft, remain in your couches. We'll be going back to four Gs after launch."

Sansar linked into the camera system and watched as the SalSha raced to the bombers stationed in the launch bay, some of them dropping to four legs to go faster, and the Human ground crew ran around the planes, checking the servicing and preparing to pull the chocks and chains holding the craft to the deck. Ordnance personnel stood by, ready to arm the missiles hanging from the bombers. It was a well-rehearsed and choreographed dance; once the craft were fired up, the first would be launched in less than a minute.

There it went. Side number 101—Thorb's craft—went into the black, followed by 102 and 103.

"Emergence!" the sensor operator screamed. Sansar ripped her attention back to the CIC. "Emergence close aboard!"

"Who-what is it?" Parker snapped.

"I don't—it's the *Mighty Wave!*"

"Incoming message!" the comms officer called.

The TRI-V illuminated with the view of the Killers' CIC. "*We changed our minds,*" Payton said. "*We decided we hate SIs more and—holy shit! What the hell have you gotten yourselves into! Set General Quarters! Fuck! All batteries, stand by to fire!*" Lights began flashing, but then the transmission dropped.

"Welcome to the party, pal," Tald muttered.

Sansar looked over. "What?"

Tald shrugged. "Saw that in a movie once. I just hope they're in time to save my dad."

"Stand by!" the sensor operator said. "Enemy frigates are in missile range."

* * *

EMS *Mighty Wave,* Emergence Area, Unknown System

Payton's jaw dropped as the picture filled in. Several things were immediately apparent. The *Gobi Desert* was close aboard—not at the planet where they were supposed to be—and they were running away while launching their bombers. Then the enemy ships started filling in on the tactical plot, and there were a veritable shit-ton of them. If there was one thing being in hundreds of battles had taught him, though, it was adaptability.

"Talk to me, TAO," Payton said, reining his emotions in after his initial outburst. "What've we got?"

"At least ten ships coming toward us," the tactical action officer replied. "They're smaller… call them frigates. Yes. I've got an ID off one. It's a Bakulu frigate. Make that twelve… no, thirteen frigates approaching!"

"Calm down," Payton said, looking at the plot. "We've fought worse than this. Fire and roll, fire and roll. You've got it. Weapons free!"

"Yes, sir." The TAO took a breath. "Spin ninety degrees right for the broadside. Designating three bogies as Red One, Two, and Three. Splitting the broadside among them and—" he pressed the button "—firing."

The ship shuddered as compressed gas kicked the missiles out of the tubes.

"Broadside complete," the TAO said. "Roll ship."

"What the hell?" the sensor officer said. "They aren't firing, and they don't even have their shields up."

"Shut the fuck up, Adams," Parker said. "You want to jinx us?"

"Designating Red Four, Five, and Six," the TAO said, getting into the groove. "Firing. Roll the ship."

"Bogies are firing," the defensive systems officer, Lieutenant James Jordan, announced.

"Fuck," Payton growled. "Adams, you owe everyone onboard a round if we survive this."

"Sorry, Skipper."

"Too fucking late. First round's on you."

* * *

LMS *Sharp Claws*, Dunamis' System

D unamis had made a mistake. He calculated back. It was the first one he'd made in several centuries, and it was possible he'd made two.

These weren't the small errors that happened when you were learning about a new race or the implementation of a new weapons system. Those weren't mistakes so much as data points to be learned from.

As the battle developed, though, Dunamis—no matter how much he didn't want to—had to admit that he'd made a mistake.

Data point—Sansar Enkh's ship must have had internal shunts installed at some point. He had the schematics for the *Gobi Desert*, and it didn't have shunts. He'd expected her to run for the stargate and had baited it by only sending two ships—his and a second one he was controlling. The fact that the *Gobi Desert* had run the other way indicated with an 87 percent probability that it had shunts. Had she come toward the stargate, he'd have had her.

That shouldn't have mattered, though. The frigates had enough firepower to stop Sansar's ship, and he'd ordered them to only use their lasers for precision strikes on the transport so as not to kill Sansar inadvertently. To make sure nothing untoward happened, he hadn't initially allowed the crews to arm their missiles; that had been a mistake. Unfortunately, it was compounded by the distance between where he was and where the battle was taking place, which caused a lag in getting his new instructions to the biologicals running the ships. They were now free to operate as they saw fit, and they should still have enough firepower to destroy the battlecruiser and capture Sansar.

The other mistake he'd made was in assuming no one else was coming when Sansar had arrived alone. He had enough firepower to destroy the battlecruiser if she'd arrived with it. When she hadn't, he'd decided she hadn't been able to recruit anyone else to her cause. As he watched the battle play out—too far away to actively participate in it—he had plenty of time to think about what had gone wrong... and how to ensure no mistakes were made next time.

* * *

EMS *Mighty Wave*, Emergence Area, Unknown System

"The ships are closing on each other now, too," the DSO said. "Looks like they're going to try to overlap their shields."

"Keep the missiles off us, James," the TAO said without looking up, "and it won't make any difference."

"First round—lots of hits!" the sensor operator called. "All three dropping out of formation."

"Nice shooting, TAO," Payton said. "Keep it up."

"Roger sir. Red Seven, Eight, and Nine. Firing! Roll ship."

"Belay that!" the DSO said. "Anti-missiles launching." The jolts from the anti-missile missiles were much smaller, but more numerous. "Okay, roll ship."

Payton nodded. They'd drilled... more times than he could count, and they'd been in more fleet actions than probably any other Humans ever had. He had a great team.

"Hits on Four and Six," the sensor officer announced. "They're both dropping out. Five got hit, but most of the missiles struck the overlapping shields."

"Incoming missiles destroyed," the DSO said.

"Red Five and Ten targeted," the TAO said. "Firing."

"That going to be enough to break their shields?" Payton asked.

"I think so." The TAO shrugged. "I'd like to take out a couple more before they figure their shit out. This is B-team tactics so far."

"No hits on Seven, Eight, or Nine," the sensor officer said.

The TAO winced. "I was afraid of that."

"The *Gobi Desert's* bombers just fired!" the sensor officer said.

"Ooh, that's going to work out well," the TAO said.

Payton nodded. Whether they'd intended to, or it'd just happened, the bombers' missiles would arrive at the same time as the TAO's last round.

"Holy shit!" the sensor officer shouted. "I don't know what's in their missiles, but I want some of that shit for us." He shook his head. "Whatever they hit the frigates with broke the shield wall. Five and Ten are gone, and Eleven is dropping out, too. The survivors are turning away."

"Want me to hit them again?" the TAO asked. "Another round, and I can probably get most of the remaining ones."

"No need," Payton said. "We just went through half our missiles. Let's hold onto the rest in case we need them."

The TAO sighed and waved to the contact on his console. "Buh bye. Run along home now, would you?"

* * *

LMS *Sharp Claws*, Dunamis' System

I f Dunamis could have sighed, he would have. His biologicals' attacks had been… disappointing, another mistake that could be laid at his own feet. He hadn't prepared them for what they'd been dropped into, and they'd failed him spectacularly.

Still, he'd learned a number of things about the Humans, and he had new information on their missiles—not the ones that had come from Battle World, but the ones launched by the smaller craft. They were something new. He'd have to see if the Science Guild could recover the plans for them; they were very effective.

He would meet Sansar again—he was sure of it—and next time, he'd attack from a position of strength. It had been easier to take over the Veetanho, and that had made him overconfident. He wouldn't be next time; he'd follow the long-term plan. The loss of the manufactory was annoying, but another could easily be obtained. He throttled up and turned the two frigates toward the stargate.

* * * * *

Chapter Twenty-Six

CIC, EMS *Gobi Desert*, Unknown System

"Well timed, *Mighty Wave*." Parker wiped his mouth with the back of his hand and straightened abused limbs to stand. "Now let's get the hell out of here."

"*Roger that*, Gobi Desert. *Time to go to Earth now?*"

"The *Keesius* ships are still missing," Sansar said, taking a steadying breath and reaching for the Hunter/Killer box. Never hesitate to be thorough, not when the alternative was Dunamis having a string of code in someone's head. No one had been infected. The Type 5 SI, however, was now missing, and there was no telling what traps or surprises Dunamis had left on the planet for them... or if he was still there, his signal blocked somehow.

"And we have no further ideas," Justice said, already unstrapped and moving toward the door.

"Where are you going?"

"To k—"

"If you say to kill Gleeko, I will space you from this ship with my own hands." Sansar glared at him, and he had the gall to slow blink at her in return.

"I won't say it, then." But his mohawked head, tilted to the side, had what could only be described as a shit-eating grin on it, and the emphasis on "say" made his point clear.

"Justice…"

"If our search is at an end, and there's to be war, there are blows I must strike before my clan's needs pull me away."

"War," Balin said softly from behind Sansar.

"We can keep pushing out into the limits of this system for a while, and they probably won't catch us… but we need to know where we're going," Parker interrupted without turning around, and Justice lifted his tail and continued stalking toward the door.

"Let's get the bombers reloaded. We can jump to New Warsaw for now. Tell Payton it's not Earth, but—"

Balin was muttering something else, and Sansar had to pause and breathe to keep from snapping at her suddenly interspecies, and entirely infuriating, crew.

"New Warsaw, Commander, aye," Parker said, as the door slid open for Justice.

"Take the long way back to the gate—the *Mighty Wave* doesn't have shunts, and Dunamis won't stay there for long."

"His last two ships have already broken away," Parker confirmed. "The *Mighty Wave* and the *Gobi Desert* together should be more than enough, given how the other ships performed."

"Justice, stop standing in the door and decide if you want to go out an airlock or come back in."

"I have no need to go to New Warsaw," Justice said as he stood in the doorway, committing neither one way nor the other.

"We can't get overconfident, Captain." Sansar stretched out her arms as the muscles began to cramp after the hard burn. "That was a poor show for Dunamis, but he didn't expect us to have friends, and we won't surprise him again. Justice," she added to the Hunter still waiting in the doorway from the CIC.

"*Mighty Wave* has acknowledged the New Warsaw coordinates." Parker shook his head. "It's not overconfident to say we should be ready to jump in the next six hours—"

"Wait." Balin spoke quietly, but his voice carried.

Sansar spun to remind him he didn't countermand orders on her ship, but as she did so, she thought of something Dunamis had said in passing. *I asked my brother to put his best investigator on it.* Another SI, of course, and unless she missed her guess, one at the heart of the Peacemaker's Guild. If her leap of logic there was correct, that meant Balin was the best, as far as Dunamis' 'brother' was concerned.

"What?" she asked, and if she didn't snap at him, her voice was perhaps flatter than usual.

"No, my apologies Colonel," Balin said, his use of her title indicating he knew he'd overstepped. "By all means, let's continue to the gate."

Justice wheeled around and allowed the door to close with him still in the CIC. Tald, his ears drooping dejectedly, lifted his head slowly and fixed his eyes on Balin.

"We're all out of ideas," the younger Peacemaker said. "Unless it's time to talk to the other SI Sansar knows?"

Balin cocked his head at Sansar, but when she didn't say anything, he stood from his seat. Sansar considered calling Gleeko and Josiff down to the CIC, but there were more than enough people involved at the moment.

"Can you... can someone remind me who the Kahraman are?" Tald's voice didn't waver, but it did sound small. "I mean, I know they fought in the Great War against the Dusman, but then they disappeared... right?"

"Yes, but like the Dusman and the SI, they've proven they're back, pulling strings before we even knew there was a stage they were hiding behind." Balin sighed and continued pacing, clearly chewing on something he hadn't yet fully worked out.

"So if they were backstage all this time, maybe they know something about what's going on with each other. Dunamis was concerned about the Kahraman, so maybe another SI would have an idea why?" Tald turned half his body between Sansar and Balin. Justice, his eyes half-lidded, echoed the SalSha's motions.

"I'd rather not involve any other SIs... though it seems as though another one might be involved already." Balin paced the confines of the CIC as he spoke. "Dunamis seemed concerned about only one enemy in that last exchange." The Peacemaker's words came slowly, as though he were still weighing them as he talked. Not so slowly Sansar needed to shake him, but with enough gravity that Justice stepped closer, and even Parker turned to watch him.

The ship began its long, slow turn back toward the gate, and Sansar ran Dunamis' oily voice back through her mind.

"The Kahraman," she said, the word breathier than she would have liked.

"Before I was pulled onto the *Keesius* ships, I was tracking sudden movements across half a dozen different species. The Dusman and the Kahraman are recruiting servitor races again, much like the SIs."

It wasn't entirely the same, but Sansar didn't need to argue the point at that particular moment. Nigel had spoken of the Kahraman and the galaxy's temporary reprieve from their impending threat. And Jim, of course, knew a great deal about the Dusman...

"They do seem to be ramping up," Sansar murmured.

"An arms race of races instead of weapons."

"Races *as* weapons," Parker muttered.

"The Dusman offered to take Hunters as servitors before we took Khatash back."

Tald pivoted to stare at Justice, and even Sansar blinked in surprise.

"Like the Humans when they were asked, we didn't accept." Justice stretched and stalked closer to Balin, his tail waving slowly behind him. "As the Veetanho can tell you, we don't react well to forced servitude."

Balin only nodded, clicking his claws together as he moved. "There's been a great deal of activity across any number of species—but who would Dunamis have been most worried about? The Kahraman or the Dusman?"

"Should we call Josiff down to dig into your data again?" Sansar gestured to Parker, who messaged through comms before the Peacemaker answered.

Balin noted the interplay and didn't answer the question directly. Instead, he turned fully toward Sansar and spread his claws. "The KzSha."

"The KzSha what?"

"Dunamis was specifically concerned about the Kahraman, not the Dusman, but the Dusman are here—in this part of the galaxy—and they were the original owners of the *Keesius* ships. *They'd* know how to activate them, and the Dusman have secured the loyalty of the KzSha. The KzSha have been hopping systems in odd patterns for the last ten months, acquiring ships, hoarding supplies."

"They haven't been in touch with the Mercenary Guild to take new contracts, if I'm remembering correctly." Sansar had listened to Nigel Shirazi discuss which merc races had faded from the board after the change in guild leadership. The KzSha were always a bitch to fight—they were stubbornly hard to kill and didn't follow any of the rules when they thought they could get away with it—so that one had stuck in her mind.

"With the Dusman as sponsors, they'd have the ability, time, and motive to take the *Keesius* ships."

"The KzSha could be anywhere—" Parker said, glancing between the Peacemaker and his commander.

"No." Balin shook his head—in his curved posture, that moved his upper body side to side as well. "No, for something that big, something they'd want to keep hidden... that would limit their choices."

"Unless they hid the ships in another servitor race's system," Tald said, his eyes fixed on Balin.

"The KzSha don't play well with others, as a rule." Gleeko entered the CIC, Josiff close behind her. She'd avoided the control area while Dunamis was an active threat, speaking to them, and Sansar could hardly blame her. "What do you think they're hiding?"

Tald caught the Pendal and the Veetanho up quickly—surprisingly disciplined in his summary, especially given how dejected he'd been only minutes before—then leaned against his chair. "Do the KzSha have a lot of systems that we have to dig through?"

"No." Josiff tucked both sets of his arms into his robes. "I don't believe I have to spend a great deal of time looking over your data, Peacemaker. Let's look where they've been avoiding in the information you have... where they don't want their travel traced to, but where they used to go before the Dusman took them over."

"If they're the ones who took the *Keesius* ships, then that's where everything will be?" Tald's voice cracked on the word "everything," but Sansar couldn't blame him.

"It's better than nothing," Gleeko said. "The KzSha are bastards, and if they have the Dusman backing them, I believe they're sneaky enough to grab the *Keesius* right out from under Dunamis. Especially if he was preoccupied with punishing Lytoshaan at the time."

"Then that's what we have to do," Tald said, crossing his arms. "We have to figure out where the KzSha would take them."

"You have six hours until we make it to the gate." Sansar made it sound like she was agreeing, and she exchanged a long look with Parker. Her captain nodded, having worked with her long enough to know exactly what she meant. "If we have coordinates you believe in, we'll share them with Payton and see if the *Mighty Wave* is up for another jump with us. If not, we continue to New Warsaw and see if the Hussars—and the Hunters Justice contacted—want to build a fleet and wipe Dunamis' influence out of this system." Catching him at this point seemed impossible if he didn't want to be caught, but maybe if they started taking the planet apart, he'd return for them to get him, too.

"We still need the ships," Tald prompted, stepping forward.

"We need Dunamis off the board." Sansar frowned, then forced her expression clear again. "Because yes, we still need the ships, but if we're out of leads…"

"One more jump." Balin bowed a little toward Sansar. "One more jump, and if the ships aren't there, Tald and I will take the *Eletine* to find the *Keesius* ships, and you can work on taking out Dunamis."

"Six hours. Or you can continue the search from New Warsaw."

* * *

They had it done in four. It had come down to the Ja-ku-Tapa and the Gz-ku-Lara systems.

"The ships are unlikely to be at Ja-ku-Tapa, as the Peacemakers maintain a presence at the former KzSha slave base there," Balin said. "The Peacemakers have interdicted the system. My guess would be the Gz-ku-Lara system."

"I don't…" Tald thought back. "I don't think the Peacemakers are still in the Ja-ku-Tapa system, though. I remember back at the Academy…" *What had the details been? Think, Tald, think!* "We covered this for what to do with a no-win situation. Ja-ku-Tapa was the first time a race declared as servitors for the Dusman—and it *was* the KzSha. The Dusman showed up with a fleet to take the Raknar that had been stored there—the planet was a former Dusman base—and the Peacemaker force had to withdraw due to the overwhelming force the Dusman showed up with."

"They didn't stand or fall?" Balin asked.

"No," Tald replied. "There was no chance of victory. All they would've done was waste their lives."

"I see." Balin scratched one of the scales on his stomach. "If the Dusman have taken over the system, and it was a former Dusman base, there's probably more there than just the Raknar. It would make an excellent place to keep the *Keesius* ships—especially if their fleet remained there."

"No, I don't think so," Sansar said. "It's too obvious. Nothing I've seen yet has told me the Dusman are ready to try to take over the galaxy yet. I don't doubt that they're going to try at some point, but I think they're going to continue to build their forces—amassing more races as servitors—until they're ready. If they had the *Keesius* ships there and got caught, that would force their hands; they'd have to start the conquest. Also, Dunamis has to know the Dusman are involved, and that would be the first place he'd look. If the ships were in Ja-ku-Tapa, he'd probably have taken all the Veetanho ships remaining and gone to get them back. He wouldn't have been worried about losses; he was already done with the Veetanho and would happily have sacrificed as many as required to get the ships back."

"That makes sense with what we've seen," Josiff said.

"There's no doubt he would've used us up if he'd had a target," Gleeko said bitterly. She'd referenced a promise Sansar had made, that Gleeko wouldn't have to be close to Dunamis, but Tald hadn't quite understood it. Surely the Veetanho, of all people, would have understood looking for Dunamis' ships might involve... Dunamis himself.

"I think you're right," Balin said. "The Dusman are playing a long game; they wouldn't want to get caught with their hands in the snack pouch."

"So, we're agreed?" Sansar asked. Her eyes scanned the group, ultimately stopping on Tald when everyone else nodded.

Tald finally sighed. "Agreed. It must be Gz-ku-Lara."

* * *

Tald stared at the work they'd done a couple of hours later and tried to decide what the pressure in his midsection was. Hope that this—finally—was it? Despair, because at the end of it all, he'd taken them only to dead end after dead end, and it was possible Gz-ku-Lara was another one? Worse, if Gz-ku-Lara didn't pan out, there was the specter of having to go to Ja-ku-Tapa, a known Dusman base with a massive fleet rumored to be in-system?

Gleeko stared into space, having ignored all seven of Justice's needling comments in the last few hours. Tald would normally have been worried about her, but they hadn't been Justice's best work. All of them had been running on fumes since they'd arrived in this system... and probably for some time before that.

The crew of the *Mighty Wave* had agreed to go on to the next system with them. The commander of Colby's Killers had been heard shouting *"Aw, hell yeah!"* when Captain Payton gave his formal agreement—Tald was fairly sure Jan had yelled something similar about shoving big ships up SI's evacuation portals, but she'd been further from the comm at the time, so he was less certain of that one.

Still, even with their support, Tald couldn't figure out why he felt so on-edge, and he considered his options of who to talk to about it.

Gleeko was right out.

Justice would tell him to eat something and take a nap until it was time to hunt.

Josiff would face him in long silence, and then tell him something both creepy and insightful.

Sansar would swallow a sigh, or bite back a smile, and tell him it was normal ahead of combat.

His father would say something insightful and thoughtful, and he'd feel both happy and smaller for talking about it.

Balin... Balin would likely do the same thing as his father, but Tald realized he had a question he couldn't swallow back, even if it were to try someone's patience. He walked over to the other Peacemaker when the others were occupied with their own conversations.

"Good work today, Peacemaker," Balin said as he approached. Tald checked his step and brushed his whiskers, sure for a wild moment that Balin was making fun of him. "I couldn't catch what had snagged my thoughts, and then you brought up the Kahraman and Dusman. That sort of teamwork…I see why so many Peacemakers take deputies and partners over the years."

The tips of Tald's ears vibrated as the fact that it was an actual compliment sank in, and he hurriedly took his hands from his whiskers to rub at his ears to hide the reaction. Though Balin didn't have protruding ears, so maybe he didn't know what the gesture meant— *focus, Tald.*

"Something else is… snagging my thoughts from what Dunamis said." As Tald spoke, he realized that was at least half of what was weighing in his gut.

"Ah." Balin uncurled his tail and rested it on the ground, then leaned against it like his own built-in stool. Tald sat on the floor— they'd be under thrust another hour before maneuvering into the gate, so he decided to take advantage of the gravity. He was used to everyone towering over him all the time, whether he sat or stood, so that hardly bothered him.

"Dunamis said he asked his brother to send someone to look for the ships."

"I've been thinking about that, too." Balin took a bag of snacks from his belt, but as he so often did, he only held it, rather than ate from it.

"The Mercenary Guild was run by an SI for thousands of years, and the Science Guild. Sansar says the Horde have fought a bunch of SIs, and…"

"And you're wondering if the Peacemakers are somehow immune."

"I'm thinking we aren't," Tald said, and some pressure inside him eased. "I'm thinking Dunamis asked the SI at the heart of our guild to send his best investigator to find Dunamis' ships, and that SI sent you."

"So you're wondering... what, Tald? If I'm compromised? If I'm really the best investigator in the guild? If I'm not compromised, and I am the best investigator in the guild, how I missed the fact that we're directed by SIs in much the same way the Veetanho were?"

"Not quite the same." Gleeko had overheard—Tald looked over his shoulder at her and saw that not only had the Veetanho been listening, she'd walked closer while they'd been talking. "Sansar has used the Hunter/Killer box dozens of times with you in range. You don't have a code in your head. Whoever your SI is, he's not enmeshed in the Peacemakers' minds in the same way Dunamis was with us."

"Isn't he?" Balin drummed his claws on his leg, then stopped to scratch under some of the larger scales across his side. "There are ways to control and direct beings without overwriting their brains. All it means is our SI is potentially a more subtle creature than Dunamis."

"And given the galaxy went this long without even knowing about Dunamis, that's a scary thought." Tald scratched behind his ear, then realized he was echoing Balin's movements and stopped. "I'm not worried about any of the questions you mentioned, Balin, especially since you're thinking them. It's not you. It's that... he can't possibly have our best interests in mind, the Peacemaker SI."

"What makes you say that?" Sansar asked. Tald allowed himself to scratch his ears this time, sure his hearing was failing him. Neither

Gleeko nor Sansar were as silent as Justice; he should've heard them approach.

"What makes me say... he's an SI?" Tald blinked up at Sansar, wondering if his ears were flat out inventing conversations. He hadn't heard either the Veetanho or the Human approach, and now Sansar was speaking nonsense words.

"Not all SIs are necessarily inimical to organic life." She said it with a straight face, too, and Tald's hands itched. He wanted to grab the Hunter/Killer box and purge her of whatever code had infected her brain—could Dunamis coopt them, even just over comms?— and he actually started to stand up before realizing she'd used the box since they'd been in contact with Dunamis. Had he seen it, to know she'd used it in good faith? He cast his mind back, worry slamming his heart into his chest, but he knew he'd seen it. She'd done all the same things; he'd seen the display... she wasn't Dunamis'.

He squinted at her, glanced at Balin and Gleeko to see if they were suspicious, too, and then spoke very slowly. "Dunamis trusts him enough to ask for help in finding the *Keesius* ships."

"See, now that's a point, and not a baseless assumption." Sansar leaned against her table and held out her hands, palms up. "The SIs fought each other, directly or by proxy, in the guild conflicts recently. They aren't a homogenous group any more than any given race is. There may be some over here, and some over there." She lifted first one hand, then the other.

"You think it's possible one is on our side?"

"I... possibly, yes. Likely..." Sansar shrugged. "Probably not. Still, I wouldn't dismiss your guild out of hand. Maybe you don't have an SI, maybe he's broken, maybe he doesn't agree with what

Dunamis is doing but doesn't want *Keesius* ships out on the loose any more than any of us do."

Why was she saying these things? SIs were pretty clearly bad. Dunamis considered their free will and determination to oppose him momentary issues, not even a real problem, and from the way he'd treated the Veetanho, he put no value on their lives beyond their usefulness to his aims.

Based on how Sansar had spoken of the other SIs, that seemed to be a fairly common take. Tald opened his mouth to say so, then wondered why she'd be bothering to have this conversation, unless...

"Dunamis might have mentioned it to throw us off." Tald chewed on the inside of his cheek and shook his head. "Or he might have been telling us the truth because he thought he'd own us a few minutes later."

"Both are equally likely. I'd just recommend not going into a spiral of questioning everything because Dunamis said something. He wants us off balance, at the very least."

"And our job is not to give him what he wants." More of the tension uncoiled from Tald's stomach. He could do that.

"This group should be very good at that." Justice appeared between Balin and Sansar and slow blinked at Tald.

"It would be nice if you infuriated anyone other than me," Sansar agreed.

Tald smiled back at Justice, feeling a little more optimistic. The ships would be at Gz-ku-Lara. They'd swoop in, recover the ships, and solve the case. It would be easy.

* * * * *

Chapter Twenty-Seven

CIC, EMS *Gobi Desert*, Gz-ku-Lara System

I
t wasn't easy; in fact, it got messy fast.

"Drones aren't going to be able to tell us much for long." Parker got quieter as the situation intensified, which Tald found impressive. Currently, though, while Parker's tone was level, there was tension in it. Tald couldn't blame him.

The KzSha didn't send a message, didn't pause, but had missiles en route as the *Gobi Desert* cleared the emergence point. Tald was on a ship of professionals, and they'd planned for getting dumped immediately into the shit, but the KzSha had acted even faster than they'd expected.

"Coordinating with *Mighty Wave;* we're going to divide and conquer as best we can."

Sansar nodded, and Gleeko made a low noise that might've been a curse.

"We should've filled up on missiles before coming here," Tald said in his quietest voice to Balin. "I hope we have enough…"

"Bombers away," Parker announced, and Tald realized he'd missed a few orders in between. He squeezed his eyes shut for a brief moment, wishing his dad all the luck in the universe—then took a steadying breath and tuned back in to what was happening.

"It's a fleet, but they're staggered. We've got room in this first volley—they guessed our emergence angle wrong—and only the first three will be an issue for the next few hours."

"The problem is they'll come in waves, and there are only two of us." Justice, in his now-usual place on the back of the sensor operator's chair, didn't turn from the data they were looking at. "And one is a transport, not a warship."

"The *Eletine* has some surprises." Balin unstrapped and stood. "I'll go."

"If we have to jump—" Parker turned and met the Peacemaker's eyes.

"That's no more than your bombers risk every time, Captain. What do you think about throwing me on a spin?"

Parker laughed. "I think you know what your ship's capable of. May all your shots be clean, Peacemaker. You've got less than ten minutes before the gravity gets higher, but we'll align on when to drop you when you're ready."

"When to throw me, you mean."

"That, too."

"You'll need help." Justice jumped down. "I can fly and you shoot."

"You come with me, Hunter, and *you're* shooting."

"Excellent." Justice padded behind him, tail high. "And yes, the *Keesius* ships are here."

"What?" The sensor operator spluttered and turned from his screens.

"The last clump of ships hovering over the apogee of the largest satellite for the third planet? They're shedding way too much heat. Either they have some sort of new superweapon, or they're there to hide the *Keesius* from sensor arrays. While it's possible the Dusman have given them something big and devastating, they wouldn't keep it so far from the gate in a KzSha-dominated system."

Tald surged from his seat, but of course he was strapped in— standard procedure for coming out of hyperspace into possible combat—and he bit his tongue while trying to say three things at once.

They'd found the *Keesius* ships?

Balin was leaving the *Gobi Desert*?

Was there anything he could do besides sit here and hope for the best while his father and so many others were out there actively affecting the course of the battle?

He was still sorting through it when the sensor operator said, somewhat wearily, "I think he's right, sir. Whatever's tucked behind the planet and its moon, it's bright enough that even the drones' quick scan picked it up. Those ships are about to explode, or they're bleeding off on purpose to hide something bigger."

"Three somethings," Sansar said, staring at the display the sensor operator put up. "Finally."

"I don't suppose there's any chance the KzSha will talk?" Tald asked, but Balin and Justice were already gone and Gleeko wasn't listening to him. He wanted to unstrap and shove over to Balin's chair, closer to Sansar, but then he had an idea.

"Sansar."

"Tald, we're a little busy—"

"Do you think the Dusman trust the KzSha enough to actually crew the *Keesius* ships?"

Sansar turned to look at him, her question clear in her face.

"Do you think 'servitor' is as strong as 'SI overwrote their brain,' or more 'we trust them to guard, but not to give them full control of world-breaking ships?'"

"Because..."

"What if we take something small enough the KzSha might miss it, draw as much firepower as we can this way, and... board one of the *Keesius*?"

* * *

CIC, EMS *Mighty Wave*, Gz-ku-Lara System

Dave Colby's hand itched for a gun. He knew there'd be no boarding action, but after endless years of fighting at Dunamis' whims, the opportunity to fight on his own terms—which he and his people had chosen—was damn near intoxicating.

Fighting to keep something Dunamis wanted away from that bodiless, hijacking, empty-air asshole? That was damn near *sublime*.

"What do you think?" Dave asked Payton after the captain finished planning with the *Gobi Desert*.

"We've had worse odds."

"Yeah?"

"At least once."

Dave laughed, and Payton cracked a smile. "Look, at the end of this, if we just have to ram those ships Dunamis wants back so bad and send them spiraling out of orbit to crash-land on a moon... so be it."

"Us instead of them?"

"After all this time, using our last act to spite that synthetic dickwad? Yeah."

"Would have been nice to see Earth again," Jan said wistfully.

"It would, but hell might be just as fun."

"Gotta be better than the one we just got out of," Braker added.

"What if we don't have to die?" Careena asked, squirming in the smaller chair the elSha had made out of scrap and spit while they were in hyperspace. "I mean, we might, but what if we don't *have* to?"

"Always the preference, Reen. What do you have in mind?" Dave shifted in his seat to regard their chief fix-it-er—the Killers had never been much for formal titles—while Payton focused on the battle unfolding around them.

"I never boarded one of Dunamis' big ships because of my broken brain, but my sister Taleena did."

"And if they're here the way the Golden Horde thinks they are, Taleena can... recognize them for us?"

"No, no." Careena wriggled around in his chair and blinked his relatively large eyes in what Dave was coming to understand was a whole body laugh. "You can't mistake *Keesius* for anything else. No, Taleena knows all the ways on and off a *Keesius* ship, and some tricks Dunamis installed in them."

"He didn't edit her memories?"

"He needed her to have them in case he needed to do anything else with the ships. That way he didn't have to teach anyone else, and he never really saw an elSha as any kind of threat." Careena flicked his fingers and shrugged. "Why else keep me around even though he couldn't write on my brain?"

"For a supposedly smart synthetic intelligence... Dunamis really leaned heavy into the *synthetic* more than the *intelligence*, sometimes. Anyone can see you guys are clever as hell."

360 | KENNEDY & WOLF

"Hell is good?" Careena asked hesitantly.

"Clever is good." Dave grinned, despite the craziness building outside their ship. They had a battlecruiser, no ties to Dunamis, and they were about to fuck that SI's world right up. He'd had worse days. "So you're saying if we can get you to the ships, you can... board one?"

"We can board them, and we can probably hijack their operating systems. I don't know what the Dusman are capable of, but no KzSha in the galaxy can out-program my sister." Careena flicked his tongue out and wriggled again. "Especially if they don't know the issue is there in the first place. I can teach Nick Braker, and we can go twice as fast."

"Thank goodness for Dunamis' crazy paranoia, huh? Payton, want to call the *Gobi Desert* one more time?"

"We're a little busy here," Payton replied, but there was a wild laugh under his words. All the Killers were feeling it—finally, a fight without any of Dunamis' tinkering in the way. The fight in Dunamis' system didn't count. They'd been dumped into the battle with no time to think; with this one, they got to savor the difference, and Dave had had the whole length of the last jump through hyperspace to go through the ship's stores.

"Permission to steal comms, then, Captain," Dave asked seriously, and Jan snorted.

"Permission granted, Commander."

"*Gobi Desert*, this is Dave on the *Mighty Wave*. We've got an idea that'll really ruin Dunamis' day..."

* * *

Pod One, Deep Space, Gz-ku-Lara System

Whatever the KzSha had planned for, it wasn't for a warship and a transport to show up in their system, split up, spit out bombers with deadly missiles, and dive *into* their dispersed fleet.

The KzSha ships reacted slowly, having to recalculate courses from what they'd expected their unknown enemies to do.

"They probably should have tried comms first," Tald said from inside their designated pod.

Sansar lifted her eyebrows but didn't break eye contact with the display she and Josiff were studying in front of them. "Why's that?"

"They might've prepared for something different if they'd known they were fighting Humans."

"They couldn't have prepared for a SalSha Peacemaker, though." Sansar's mouth quirked, and Tald decided she was smiling. Even though they were in a small, barely-powered pod on the bare edge of an enormous space battle, she was smiling. Or almost smiling. That counted.

"Or a Phidae Peacemaker. Or a Hunter, or a Pendal, or elSha, or—"

"It's probably for the best they didn't bother with comms, then. It wouldn't have helped." Josiff turned slightly, the edge of his hood shifting. Sansar's smile—already barely formed—faded, and Tald stopped himself before jumping in with reassurances that none of them could entirely believe.

The *Gobi Desert, Mighty Wave,* and *Eletine* were outnumbered. Perhaps not outgunned, entirely, but certainly outnumbered. Sansar, Tald, Josiff, and about fifteen of their fellows had voluntarily seeded themselves throughout the resulting battleground in the thin hope of a wild plan paying off to recalibrate the odds. Even Gleeko had gotten into a pod, though there hadn't been room in theirs, so she'd gone with some of the other Golden Horde mercenaries.

Dave Colby, during the last run through hyperspace, had taken some time to explore his new-to-him warship. The Killers had known from the start that the *Mighty Wave* was a former Goltar ship, which was designed to be flooded if the crew running it desired. During his search, he'd found a number of pods in one of the cargo bays. Designed as lifeboats, they could also be flooded, like the ship... or used as emergency transportation devices for air-breathing races.

As the current situation was about as much of an emergency as things got, he'd broken them out and shared with the *Gobi Desert* before the fight got too close. Tald and Careena had had similar pieces of an idea, and with the fleeting amount of time available to them, they'd hashed out a plan. Not long later, ten of the pods, each with two or three beings from the *Gobi Desert* and *Mighty Wave,* had been shed from their larger ships after the anti-missiles were released.

Wild hope the first: the pods would be overlooked in the noise of the missile and anti-missile conglomeration. Wild hope the second: the first few KzSha ships would move on, chasing either the *Gobi Desert* or the *Mighty Wave.* That would allow the pods to move—slowly—toward the protected *Keesius* ships. Wild hope the third: they'd go unnoticed until they got close. Wild hope the fourth: the timing would work out for the *Eletine* to provide a last-ditch distraction to pull the covering ships away from the third planet's moon while the lifeboat pods got close enough to attach to the *Keesius* ships.

Each of the beings in the pods had as much of a download from the elSha about the *Keesius* as could be trusted over secure comms, and at least three pods from the *Mighty Wave* had some of the elSha themselves.

Assuming the timing worked out, they'd make it through the system and take over at least one of the *Keesius* ships. Wild hope the fifth: their friends and colleagues in the bigger ships would survive long enough for them to get it done.

If all somehow went according to plan, the pods would execute a hostile takeover of the *Keesius* ships—even if they were crewed, the elSha were confident they'd be able to hijack enough systems to make the ships theirs fairly quickly—and dramatically change the stakes of the fight. And the results of Tald's mission.

If all didn't work out, though...

Tald had to admit it was much, much more likely things wouldn't work out, given the scope of the issue—issues—ahead of them.

The KzSha could notice the pods. The *Gobi Desert, Mighty Wave,* and *Eletine* could all blow up before the pods could accomplish anything. The *Keesius* might be modified beyond what the elSha could do. It was a possible—maybe even likely—suicide mission on all sides.

But what other choice did they have? There were more KzSha than even Balin's investigation had suggested. They couldn't jump away—by the time they came back, Dunamis could have moved in, the KzSha out, or both, and either way, the *Keesius* would be lost. Again. The idea of either the legendary Dusman or the awful SI having possession of the ships...

"No risk, no reward," Tald muttered, and again the corners of Sansar's mouth twitched.

"I wish we could've dropped a little closer," she said, studying the bits of data the small lifeboat's sensors were able to collect.

"That would have put the *Gobi Desert* and *Mighty Wave* far too close to the ships around the planet," Josiff answered agreeably.

"This way, we can use the moon to hide as long as possible…" Tald filled in his part. They'd been over it already—Gleeko swearing they were insane even as she grudgingly approved the act—but now the three of them had nothing else to do other than repeat it, while the pods fell through the system toward the planet and its moon, and the cluster of radiation-shedding ships.

"Hopefully their sensors are muddied by everything they're dumping and the combination works in our favor," Tald added, and Josiff made a noise that wasn't quite a chuckle.

"Those odds, at least, are in our favor. Even if the ships are not about to melt down, they are blind to anything beyond their own heat."

That was another thing that could go wrong—the pods might not be able to withstand whatever the KzSha ships were doing to block the potential *Keesius* reading.

Oh. And… there might not be Keesius *ships there at all; this might all be a feint, a trap, or some new, awful Dusman weapon…*Tald liked that thought least of all, but it tended to return the loudest.

He wouldn't be wrong about this. He *couldn't*. And the timing would work out—they'd get the *Keesius*, the *Gobi Desert*, the *Eletine*, and the *Mighty Wave* would all be unexploded, and they'd ride into battle with the enemy's own ships, like Big Damn Heroes.™

Tald and his deputies had worked really, really hard for this.

Surely it was Big Damn Heroes™ time.

* * *

CIC, EMS *Gobi Desert*, Gz-ku-Lara System

"Emergence!" The sensor operator turned slightly, as though looking for a Hunter on the back of his chair, then shook his head and angled toward his captain. "No—Blue Sky! Now there are multiple targets! Wait... there was only one emergence."

Naran bit back a curse. Had Dunamis followed them, tracked them somehow, his goal all along?

No, it had to be that the Dusman were here, arriving in force to claim their *Keesius*.

Or both... Naran frowned and forced her thoughts back into order. Sansar had left her in charge—along with Parker—for a reason. Clearly the excitable little Peacemaker had been a poor influence, with his eighteen questions every eight minutes, and his occasional brilliant leaps of reasoning that meant it was surprisingly worth it for them all to listen to him.

"We're a few hours out from the emergence area. Tell me when you know who they are, but they're not our immediate problem." Parker spoke with decisive calm, but his body had turned toward the sensor operator's display as though to keep it in his sightline.

Naran folded herself back into her seat, strapping in—they'd be rolling again before long, and were only on a momentary break from crushing speeds. She glanced at the empty seat Sansar usually occupied. Sansar, who hadn't flinched or complained at the ludicrousness of the elSha and SalSha's combined plan. Instead, she'd gone with them, on what could absolutely be a one-way trip. This was *not* the way she'd wanted to potentially inherit the Golden Horde... but then, if this did end up a one-way trip for Sansar, that meant the

Keesius would be on the loose. There might not be much of a Golden Horde—or galaxy—to speak of long after that.

"There's at least three now," the sensor operator muttered again, an edge to his voice Naran couldn't assign a definitive emotion to. "Data says only one emergence, though…"

"What is it? A fleet? Or not?"

"Incoming message."

"Better than an incoming missile," Naran muttered. She knew Parker had the lead as long as it was on matters of the ship, but it grated to sit and do nothing while the head of the Golden Horde had volunteered to board one of the lifeboat pods moving toward some of the deadliest weapons in the galaxy.

"Oh, Blue Sky," the communications officer said, then cleared her throat. "It's the Goltar."

"Oh, for…" Parker turned, and Naran nodded sharply.

At least Gleeko was gone, too—having to ask the Veetanho to hide from the Goltar again would have been distasteful for all involved, to say the least.

"Let me guess." Naran stood and straightened her uniform, which needed it after all their maneuvering. She'd never seen Sansar look less than impeccable when addressing such complicated… allies wasn't the right word, but neither was opposition. Others. Complicated others. "It's our friends from Lytoshaan?"

"*Blunt Justice,* along with the same two battle riders."

Battlecruisers *Tseg-Talag* and *Tseg-Lenkh,* Naran remembered, shaking out her sleeves. The ones who'd wanted to destroy Lytoshaan down to its composite atoms and then spit in the dust cloud. She supposed the disparate crew Peacemaker Tald and Sansar had pulled together weren't the only ones able to follow a trail, but it galled her that the Goltar were only hours behind them. Dunamis had mentioned asking his brother to send someone to find the *Keesius* on his behalf, and they'd all assumed it was Peacemaker Balin.

Perhaps the Goltar Peacemaker was the one dispatched by Dunamis' brother.

Certainly Peacemaker Salz-Kryll's willingness to destroy the last remnants of Lytoshaan spoke to that special SI touch Gleeko and Colby's Killers had described so chillingly clearly.

"Ah, Colonel—" the Goltar on the screen paused. "You are not Colonel Enkh."

No shit, smarty-pants.

"Captain Kanat-Baim, yes?" Naran dipped her chin to the tentacled mass on the main viewer at his small bow. "I'm Major Naran Enkh. The colonel is currently busy—as are we all. What do you need?"

"An end to the Veetanho and the reclamation of what is rightfully ours." The smooth voice of the Goltar captain made Naran's nerves twist under her skin. She wanted to snap her gun out of its holster, aim it at that nest of writhing appendages, dig and rip until the Goltar twitched feebly under her feet and—*No.* She breathed in through her nose. She didn't want any of that. She *didn't* want to be standing on the ship, exchanging false pleasantries with a Goltar, but there was no need to get bloodthirsty.

Sansar expected her to have manners. She focused on less bloody, and thus less satisfying, thoughts instead, keeping the snark that surged to the front of her tongue tucked away. The *Keesius* ships didn't belong to the Goltar, and never had. She knew Sansar would figure out a way to blow the ships up before allowing them to fall into Goltar hands. The resulting genocide of the remaining Veetanho would be bad enough, but it didn't take a strategic genius to know galactic war would follow such an act.

"This is KzSha space, Captain." After that pause, Naran's voice was nearly as smooth as Kanat-Baim's; she'd been training under Sansar for years, and her colonel would expect no less. "There is no great mass of Veetanho here for your attention."

"No, but my ships are here."

"Are the KzSha your allies?" She asked the question calmly enough to make Sansar proud, but everyone in the CIC stiffened, at least a little. She couldn't blame them, but they had to know. If the Goltar had become Dusman servitors... if the KzSha and the Goltar were about to come together in this untraveled system, the *Gobi Desert* would never last long enough to see if the Peacemaker's wild plan worked.

Naran very much did not want Sansar to die somewhere out in the black, and to be fair, she didn't want to die without knowing if they'd managed to spite Dunamis once and for all. *Final time pays for all,* she thought and tilted her head politely as Kanat-Baim regarded her.

"The KzSha are between us and our ships. Tell me, is the Golden Horde also between us and our ships?"

"I wasn't aware the Goltar had lost their *Keesius* ships." Naran had manners, yes—she couldn't resist a small bit of snark, however. "I wish you much luck in finding them. Perhaps our Peacemakers can assist you, once we recover the ones *they* were tasked with obtaining."

"The Peacemakers don't have precedent here—"

"They very much *do*, Captain. Wouldn't your own Peacemaker agree?"

"You have a soft-shelled egg as a Peacemaker—"

"Peacemaker Tald was entrusted with this mission from the guild itself, as was Peacemaker Balin. Perhaps Peacemaker Salz-Kryll has more respect for his fellow Peacemaker's eighty-plus years of service to the guild. Or perhaps Salz-Kryll was sent out to assist Peacemaker Balin in his efforts?" Naran pitched it so politely, Parker turned fully away from the screen to hide his expression. She liked that he heard the humor in it, but she couldn't react any more visibly than he could. They all balanced on the edge of a black hole's gravity well; no need to jump merrily into its heart.

There was a small commotion in the background of *Blunt Justice's* screen—Balin was perhaps better known in the guild than their young Tald, or Salz-Kryll didn't feel as sanguine about tromping over the jurisdiction of an established Peacemaker as he did a candidate's.

"I… see."

"Perhaps you would care to contact the *Eletine* yourself and speak with Peacemaker Balin?"

"I may."

Naran continued to stare at the screen, and silence of a sort held—in the background of both CICs, officers distributed orders, ships were redirected, and missiles readied. "Would you like to do that now, Captain? You may have noticed, we're in the midst of a battle for the *Keesius* ships."

"We are trying to contact our other ship—the *Mighty Wave*. Have you damaged their communications sensors?"

"The *Mighty Wave* is a salvaged ship, Captain—"

"It's a *what*?"

"Have you lost a few ships over the past few years? Crews and battlecruisers that went out on a contract, maybe, and never came home?"

"That is of no concern—"

"Captain Kanat-Baim, I do hope you'll forgive my brevity, given we are, again, somewhat closer to the fight than you are. Dunamis has been puppeting mercenary companies from many races to refine his planning and tactics, and to determine which race or races he should ride toward whatever he considers victory."

Naran bit the side of her tongue to keep from laughing at the blank look on Kanat-Baim's face. It wasn't actually funny—Dunamis was a burning threat to the galaxy as a whole, and the reminder that he'd been considering the Humans as his next target should have chilled her. But then she'd have to deal with what the aftermath of that would be, and how it all might play out for the people who mattered to her. She had no room for any of that emotion at this time. When it became clear Kanat-Baim had nothing to add, she continued speaking.

"Apparently, for the last few years, he's been considering Goltar, so he took, claimed, pirated, directed—however it might have gone—quite a few Goltar companies. A great many ships remain in that system."

"And Goltar?"

"Ships." Naran lifted a hand. "If we all come through this, I'm sure you can spend time talking with the Human survivors on the *Mighty Wave*, and learn more about what happened and who is left."

"There are... there are *Humans* on the *Mighty Wave*?"

"Captain..." Naran's tone didn't change, but she glanced to the side, as though considering ending the call. Captain Parker was handling the action around the ship admirably, of course, but Goltar intractability could strain the patience on a good day. This was by no means a good day.

"You will return our ship to us after this."

"We're currently focused on the *Keesius* ships, Captain Kanat-Baim."

Naran hoped someone would report the mastery of evasion in that statement to Sansar—the colonel really had trained her well.

"And you will surrender the *Keesius* to the Peacemaker Guild when this is over?"

"We'll dispose of them as Peacemaker Balin and Peacemaker Tald's orders direct us."

That might be a lie, though Naran delivered it without the slightest change in her expression. If Sansar succeeded in boarding those ships… would Sansar let them go if she had them? The Hussars had one, and there was no shortage of enemies for Earth these days. Sansar had *said* they were the Veetanho's ships… but would she really turn them over to a recent enemy? Gleeko seemed all right, considering, and Gleeko would of course want to take them home to the Veetanho, to give Lytoshaan some hope at recovering. But was it truly a possibility?

Even if the Peacemakers would allow it—and what would happen then was a question Naran didn't choose to pursue too deeply in the moment—Lytoshaan was in no shape to hold on to the *Keesius* ships. They might even have to use one of the ships, at least, to keep hopeful enemies from flooding into their system to enact their revenge. With the orbital defenses down, their population in tatters…

That wasn't the issue at hand, though, and she grounded her thoughts in that. One, they were still several steps from controlling the *Keesius*. Two, they were in the middle of a battle with Dusman servitors right now. And three…

Three, it didn't matter. What happened to the *Keesius* wasn't her choice. Either Sansar would die—putting her in charge, maybe, but also without the ships—or Sansar would succeed, but either way, she wouldn't get a vote in the distribution of world-ending ships.

Would I even want one?

"I've got movement! From the moon!" the sensor operator called.

Naran glanced at the tactical plot and chuckled as though she didn't have a hundred other pressing worries. "What if we were to put aside that question for now?"

* * * *

Chapter Twenty-Eight

Pod One, Deep Space, Gz-ku-Lara System

"Something's happening." Sansar moved the pod's limited controls, but there was only so much its passive sensors could tell them. She shouldn't have left the *Gobi Desert...* but this was their best chance to secure the *Keesius* ships.

What a joke that was—their best chance was in an undefended pod, using gravity and the bare minimum of thrust toward three of the deadliest weapons in the galaxy, through a field of ships and enemies, half blind...

And it really was their best shot. *Blue Sky, the galaxy's an awful place sometimes.*

"We're getting close," Tald said hopefully, his whiskers sweeping forward and back as he twisted his hands together.

"That's not what I meant—but yes, we're getting close." Sansar cursed, and Tald's fidgeting stopped all at once. "The ships are moving."

"Which ones—oh, *those* ones." Tald winced. "Why would they be leaving the *Keesius?*"

"Something has happened." Josiff cocked his head to the side. When he didn't continue, Sansar shrugged and added to his answer.

"Because either they were never hiding the *Keesius*, or… whatever's happening in this system just got a lot messier."

* * *

Pod Two, Deep Space, Gz-ku-Lara System

"No way to know if anyone's on these ships, huh?" Dave asked, not for the first time, though potentially for the most urgent time, as their pod was approaching locking distance on the ships. If the right ships were there. They'd had to recalculate their orbit when the bright ships on the sensors—the KzSha ones, and didn't *those* sound like nightmare aliens—had slowly but surely moved away from the moon, and the bare sensors of the pod hadn't made their new picture much more clear.

"I don't have the boxes Dunamis made," the little elSha responded, holding her tail. "Those were built to talk to the ships over short distances, but they got destroyed when a Veetanho…" Taleena shook her entire body and let go of her tail. "That was a long time ago, and I guess it doesn't much matter now. As for who's on the ship now? No, no way to know. Once we're closer, I can suit up and run over."

"We'll dock; you don't need to freefall this close to—"

"I appreciate your concern—" she turned her small face to him and turned her wide mouth up in a fair approximation of a Human smile "—but we definitely *shouldn't* dock to a *Keesius* before I have a chance to recode an airlock."

"I get that Dunamis didn't think you were enough of a threat to wipe your memories of the ship, but why would he leave you the freedom to access its security?" Dave tapped his fingers on his leg to keep from fiddling with the pod's rudimentary controls. The problem with using a moon to hide was that *he* couldn't see around it either, dammit.

"Because he kept the ships far, far away from us most of the time, and there was no part of me that would have disobeyed him in any sort of damaging way."

"That's a little specific." Dave twisted in his seat, distracted fully from the display.

"Then you're smarter than an SI, Commander, at least in that." She folded her fingers together with her toes and fairly beamed at him from her chair. "I never could have disobeyed Dunamis, not meaningfully, before the Humans—the other Humans—turned everything off with *their* special box. But at heart, even when I was Dunamis' creature, I was still always an elSha, and elSha—well, we like to tinker."

"So you're saying as long as what you were tinkering with wouldn't hurt Dunamis…"

"Or leave him open to being hurt by someone else, but was just something interesting to me…" Taleena shrugged. "Then I was free, in a way, to play a little around the edges. So there are a few extra codes in these ships, and I don't think the KzSha, of all people, could have found them."

* * *

CIC, EMS *Gobi Desert*, Gz-ku-Lara System

"Put aside the question of the *Keesius* ships?" Captain Kanat-Baim, asked. "Why would we do that, when that is the central issue for both of us being in this system?"

Naran smiled. "The question of who gets them is irrelevant if we both die." She waved to the tactical plot, although it was probably outside the camera's pick-up. "As you could probably see, we were about to go up against a superior force."

"We see that. We also see that the enemy force is *inferior* to ours. My three ships should be able to deal with the enemy fleet quite handily." He waved a tentacle in echo of her gesture. "A couple battlecruisers and a couple cruisers. In my view, all I have to do is let them destroy you, destroy the ones you fail to defeat, then recover the *Keesius* ships." It waved a second tentacle. "Nothing could be simpler."

"Perhaps you haven't noticed the second fleet that's approaching from behind the third planet's moon. The enemy fleet is withdrawing to merge with them, I suspect." She craned her neck. "If I'm looking at that right, you're going to be at a bit of a disadvantage against them once they're joined… and you're not going to be able to prevent that from happening."

"They're KzSha, though; we've beaten them before, and we'll beat them again."

"There are, however, more of them than there are of you. Quantity has a quality all its own. To my eye, you're evenly matched. If we were to fight together, though, we might have a bit of an advantage."

"And after we defeat them?" Kanat-Baim asked. "What do we do with the *Mighty Wave* and *Keesius* ships then?"

Naran shrugged. "I think that's probably a question we can safely leave until after we defeat the KzSha. Who knows? Maybe we'll be destroyed. If so, they'll be yours."

Kanat-Baim chuckled. "I guess you're hoping *we'll* be the ones who are destroyed. That will not happen."

"We could discuss this all day," Naran said, "but the salient points are these. First, we stand a better chance of defeating the KzSha if we fight them together. Second, if we don't fight them together, the odds are we'll both lose. Now that you're here, I'm happy to wait until _you_ attack the KzSha." She shrugged again. "Maybe we'll be able to take them after you whittle them down a bit for us."

"You want the _Keesius_ ships every bit as badly as we do; you won't wait."

"No, I don't." She shrugged, and at the moment it was the entire truth. "Our mandate was to help the Peacemakers _find_ them. Guess what? We found them. They're right here. Our mission is complete." Naran smiled, though it felt more like a baring of teeth than a friendly expression. She could be controlled, damn it, but he was straining her patience. "Now, that said, I'd much rather Dunamis didn't have them, because I don't think he's completely sane, and he's been busy killing off Humans and Goltar for his sick little puppet show. I'd _much_ rather see them destroyed than on the loose or under his control again; _I_ certainly don't want them."

"You _don't_ want them?" The translator imparted a large amount of sarcasm to the Goltar's voice. "I have a hard time believing that."

"Why's that?"

"They're supremely powerful. They have the potential to destroy entire planets."

"They're also supremely _illegal_. Did I mention that I have two Peacemakers on board? Do you think they're going to let us keep them if we were to capture them?" Naran scoffed. "Not only would the Peacemakers fight us for them, they'd contract every other race out there—including yours, probably—to destroy them." She laughed and spread her arms wide. "*I* don't want them; they're more trouble than they're worth."

"Hmm… so you'd be happy just destroying them?" Kanat-Baim asked. "That might be an acceptable solution to us."

"How about this. You have a stronger force than I do. Why don't we combine our forces to defeat the KzSha? After we defeat them, I'm sure the matter can be easily solved."

"I'm not sure what your angle is on this, Naran Enkh, but I know Sansar isn't stupid, nor would she have put you in charge if *you* were. I suspect there are other things in play beyond what's easily observed. I'll tell you, though—you're not leaving with the *Keesius* ships and the *Mighty Wave.*"

"That's fair," Naran said. "So, can we get to the part where we start killing KzSha? Because it looks like they're getting reorganized and will be heading toward us soon."

* * *

CIC, EMS *Mighty Wave*, Gz-ku-Lara System

"Captain, the Goltar ship is still trying to make contact, and I just got a message from the *Gobi Desert* that the Goltar want to know why there are Humans on a Goltar ship." Jan pushed back from her console and spun toward him.

"You want us to answer?" Payton asked, staring at the display in front of him.

"If they're not going to stop pinging us. Besides, Naran says they're going to fight with us, and we might need to be in contact to make this work."

"Awesome." Payton's voice didn't indicate that it was, in fact, awesome, but then he chuckled. "Should we put Pereena on screen?"

"No, thank you!" Three of their elSha had gone into the lifeboat pods, and one of the remaining four had come up to the CIC in case last minute fixing was needed. "The Goltar can be jerks under normal circumstances."

"I mean, to be fair—"

"Not now, Jan. Let's do this before our breathing room is gone."

"Pirates!" The large body of a Goltar filled the main viewer on the CIC. "Scavengers!"

"Hi to you, too," Payton said, then waved back to Jan to take over.

"I'm Jan Colby of Colby's Killers. I've muted you until you signal you can have a civil conversation." Jan turned her chair to better face the screen. "I know you've spoken with the *Gobi Desert*, so you understand the situation at hand. Wave two tentacles if you're ready— no? Ok." Jan held a hand out in front of her as though studying her nails, and Pereena chuckled.

"I suppose we can talk about the rules of salvage, conquest, winning contracts, taking available ships to address a galactic threat, the fact that we spent damn near a century jumping at Dunamis' fucking whims and if that means we have to take an unused ship in order to right some of the wrongs your people *and* ours took from his shitty little synthetic—" Jan's words ran from sarcastically performative to hot rage in the midst of her rant, and she belatedly realized the Goltar was waving two tentacles as requested. She held up a hand and turned the sound back on.

"I hope you're quite done lecturing me on the ills of a universe my people have been dealing with far longer than yours." The Goltar paused and dropped his appendages. "I'm Captain Kanat-Baim, and I won't contest your possession of the ship further during this engagement."

"Great, because—"

"We're not done speaking about it, however—"

"Well, *we* are, and I won't presume to tell *you* what to do with your free time. Unless you have a different shiny battlecruiser you want to swap out for the *Mighty Wave* after we're done here, we're good." Jan crossed her arms and held her hand over the comm controls again. "Anything else?"

"You'll—will you tell me where our people are?" There was a note in that response, not quite vulnerable, but not nearly as aggressive, that checked the saltiest of Jan's possible replies.

"You can have that for free—there might be others en route to pick through the ships, but we made sure everyone still alive there knew they were now able to get the hell outta Dodge before we left, and that there was more than enough transportation."

"The planet is... Dodge?"

"We're calling it Battle World." Jan shrugged and leaned to the side to send the system's coordinates to the Goltar.

"Major Enkh said there were many Goltar ships there. Are there... many of our people?"

"Dunamis focused heavily on them and on Humans." Jan hesitated, not wanting to give in to the urge to say the worst of the things that jumped to the forefront of her thoughts. Dave wouldn't mind, but the Goltar they'd fought had been known to make irrational moves if their pride was provoked too far, and Jan didn't need to be a tactical genius to know they needed the Goltar's help to get out of this intact. "He forced our two races to fight. A lot."

As galling as that had been to her, she had to imagine it'd felt pretty shitty to the Goltar, too. She used that as a salve for being slightly more polite than she might have been under other circumstances.

"The Goltar didn't perform quite up to Dunamis' standards—which, we all must admit, are suspect to begin with. Although we know of some, there aren't that many of them left, as far as we could tell." *Sorry, not sorry—it was them or us.* "On the bright side, that means your species isn't square in the middle of Dunamis' crosshairs, though I hope you'd still like to get some of your own back and ruin his day by helping us scuttle his ships."

"I can't decide whether you've insulted or helped us, Jan Colby, but I... appreciate you sending the coordinates. We'll talk again when this is done."

The screen cleared, and Payton swung around to meet Jan's eyes. "Is it wrong that I'm hoping one of us gets blown up so we don't have to talk to them again?"

"Yeah." Jan laughed, though there wasn't a whole lot of humor in her. "But if you want to hope *they* get blown up so we don't have to talk to them again, that I could get behind."

"Well, let's get to missile launching."

* * *

Pod One, *Keesius* Storage, Gz-ku-Lara System

"Blue Sky." The words left Tald as more of an exhalation, and he stared at the pod's screen with eyes that no longer blinked.

"Confirmation of *Keesius* ships, check," Sansar said, as Josiff held their pod a safe distance from the enormous hull. They'd followed one of the lifeboats to the second ship, where they'd wait until one of the pods with an elSha in it maneuvered close enough to attach to the ship. As far as Tald could tell, they were in position to view such a thing, assuming the pods had split amongst the ships correctly. Eight of the ten pods were close enough to be visible on the life-boat's screen, so for the first time since they'd come into this system, the odds were truly in their favor.

Tald finally blinked, but all three of them held silent until one of the pods drifted forward and disappeared around the curve of their targeted *Keesius* ship.

"We're going in," Josiff said, and Sansar adjusted her suit.

Tald reluctantly clambered into his—he should have taken time to adjust it over one of the last hyperspace jumps, but mostly he'd hoped he wouldn't have to use it again. It made him clumsier than needed, and he didn't hold out a whole lot of hope that he'd be ef-fective in combat if that's what awaited them on the ship.

Please let that not be what's waiting for us on the ship.

* * * * *

Chapter Twenty-Nine

Pod Two, *Keesius* Storage, Gz-ku-Lara System

"Problem." Taleena pressed her helmet against Dave's and clung to his suit as he floated close enough into the opened airlock. Her legs were wrapped around one of the rails, and he reached for it as well to get out of the way of the others who were—hopefully—incoming.

"It's crewed, isn't it?"

"Yes. I turned off everything that reports data about this section of the ship, so the pods are safe to dock, and they shouldn't know the airlock is open. But everything is active, indicating it's all active to tell someone. At least one of the KzSha is in the deeper systems."

"I thought a KzSha couldn't—"

Taleena pulled her helmet away, then resettled it against Dave's with a thunk he felt in his spine. "A KzSha couldn't, but the Dusman built these... if they trusted the KzSha enough to give them access..."

"You're not going to be able to turn off life support and let us take over, are you?" Dave shoved his surprise away. He wasn't surprised that things wouldn't be easy—it would've been far more of a shock for it to work out smoothly for the first time in recorded history—but he hadn't expected a race as storied as the Dusman to share any more than they had to with one of their attached races. Dave couldn't imagine Dunamis doing something similar—maybe the Dusman really *did* view their servitors as something more than convenient proxies.

That was not at all a pressing issue, though, so he dismissed the thought and focused on Taleena, who bobbed her head uncomfortably in her helmet.

"Probably not."

"But?"

"But what?"

"But there's a but in there, right? Something you *can* do?" Dave pulled himself close to the wall—it wouldn't keep them from being noticed if a KzSha inside the ship walked by with supremely bad timing and peered inside, but maybe it would help.

"Oh. Well…" Taleena let go of him and floated up before twitching and getting closer again. "I can change the codes so they can't move the ship or power up any weapons, at least not quickly. But that could give away that we're here, if whoever's in the deeper levels notices before we're ready."

"Can you do anything passive?"

"What would that help?"

Dave reminded himself that the elSha he now worked with were deeply, deeply brilliant about the things that mattered to them, and somewhat flakes when it came to other things, like tactics. "Seeing where the KzSha are in the ship, how many there are, get us some information so we can plan our approach?"

A flicker of motion in his peripheral had him snapping her back against the wall behind him. Dave hooked his feet under the rail to keep from floating away, and brought his pistol up for nothing, as it was another pod's worth of people—a Human at the arbitrary 'top' of the airlock's opening, and the other, who looked like the

Veetanho from the *Gobi Desert,* at the 'bottom.' After he holstered his pistol and signaled to them 'all clear but enemy nearby,' he released Taleena, who cracked her helmet against his with a bit too much enthusiasm.

"Yes."

"Yes… what?"

"Yes, I can find the KzSha on the ship, but I'll need to be inside."

"All right. First, we see how many of us made it here, then I guess it's time to storm the castle."

"It's a ship." Taleena patted his helmet and eyed him, and Dave laughed. She must have thought she'd damaged him with that last headbutt.

"Indeed it is, Taleena. And it's about to be ours."

* * *

Pod One, *Keesius* Storage, Gz-ku-Lara System

In other circumstances, Tald would've fully enjoyed the maneuvering necessary to climb from their docked pod into the airlock of a ship he'd worked his behind off to find. One of the ships that would make him a fully qualified Peacemaker.

However—in an ill-fitting spacesuit, lugging weapons they may or may not need, unable to let go and swim through the zero-G vacuum with the skill and flexibility he had, because at the end of the day this was a ship that could move at any time—it made his fur stand on end and his hands cramp.

He couldn't even use comms for a way to distract himself, because they didn't know if anyone was on the ship, and if so, how sharp their ability to register comms traffic was. That left him with only his own thoughts and what felt like an endless climb with too-big gloves making him unwieldy. He counted new handholds, but that made it worse after he passed fifty, so he kept his head down and wondered if every slight vibration was the ship powering up, or a pod attaching, or an enemy pounding down the hull to kick him off the ship and leave him floating into space for a long, slow—

He really missed being able to talk to anyone outside his own head. Tald focused so deeply on it that he reached a hand for the next handhold and grasped onto nothingness for a full four seconds before he realized he'd reached the airlock. He pulled his hand back immediately, then angled his body to look around. Sansar had approached the airlock from the other side, and Josiff was between her and Tald. Human and Pendal both eased their helmets down or over to scan the inside of the opening.

Tald followed their lead, and his heartrate spiked when he saw figures. Reminding himself he'd known very well he would see figures—they wouldn't be on the ship if one of the elSha hadn't marked it a safe step one for them to dock—he confirmed from the shapes that it was a Human and an elSha from the *Mighty Wave*.

The elSha's spacesuit seemed far more tailored to the size and form of its contents, and Tald resolved to ask if they could modify a suit for him when this was over. Assuming this was over successfully. He supposed he wouldn't need a special spacesuit if he died in the next few steps...

Unaccountably, that cheered him up, and he pulled himself into the airlock to tackle step two.

Boarding the *Keesius*.

* * *

Pod Three, *Keesius* Storage, Gz-ku-Lara System

Dave watched as the elSha opened the airlock door, his laser pistol drawn and sweeping back and forth. Not that he expected a horde of Goka, or KzSha, or any other race to come pouring out, but because he needed to be doing something, and waving the pistol around when the elSha wasn't watching—it'd made her really nervous the time she'd seen him doing it—helped burn off some of the adrenaline currently suffusing his body.

I've been in a thousand battles, and it's always the same. Dave smiled as the elSha turned and waved him forward.

She put her helmet next to his and said, "There are KzSha on board. We will have to be cautious."

Dave nodded as he gave the team the signal to hold in place. "Okay." He took a deep breath and let it out slowly. "What can we do to ruin their day?"

* * *

CIC, EMS *Gobi Desert*, Gz-ku-Lara System

"We can't identify the ships that are leading the formation," Kanat-Baim said from the main viewer. "They have some sort of power emission that's unknown to us."

"We don't recognize them, either," Naran replied. The *Gobi Desert* had dropped back behind the *Mighty Wave*, which was lined up with the *Blunt Justice* and its two battlecruisers. Although it was better-armed than some transports, the internal shunts took up a lot of space that might otherwise have been used for weaponry. As Captain

Parker had said, there was no reason for it to be at the forefront of the battle line.

Naran turned to Parker. "You said something seemed familiar…"

"It seems like I've heard of something like this," Parker said, "but I can't remember what. It'll come to me."

"Hopefully, it'll come to you before too long," Kanat-Baim replied. "While you're remembering, though, we'll see what a few capital missiles do to them." He looked to the side. "Fire!"

Naran watched as four missiles—about double the size of the largest missiles on *Mighty Wave*—streaked off toward one of the strange ships.

The missiles were enormous compared to the size of the frigates they were targeted on. As the missiles crossed the distance, the frigates leading the enemy force did precisely… nothing. No anti-missile missiles sprang forth from the ships, nor did lasers reach out to engage the ordnance heading toward them.

"They seem unimpressed with your missiles," Parker noted.

"Just wait until they hit," Kanat-Baim said. "Just wait."

The missiles crossed the intervening distance to the frigates, and Naran held her breath… but nothing happened. No explosions, no flashes… nothing.

Kanat-Baim looked off-camera. "Confirm the missiles hit."

"Sorry, sir," a voice replied. "I cannot confirm any damage to the enemy vessel."

"I've got nothing, either," the sensor operator on the *Gobi Desert* agreed. "It looks like they missed."

"Missed?" Kanat-Baim roared, as if it were a personal affront. "How could you miss?"

"I… I don't know," the voice said. "The missiles were tracking normally, and we had good telemetry from them. Then they just stopped."

"Fire another round!" Kanat-Baim ordered.

Parker shook his head. "You're wasting your time," he said. "I know what those ships are."

"You do? What?"

"Well, I don't know for *sure*, but I suspect they're Biruda *Maester*-class assault frigates."

"And what exactly are they?"

"In the final battle to reclaim Earth, four of them jumped in and devastated the Human fleet."

"I was there as part of the Peacemaker fleet," Kanat-Baim replied. "We saw no such thing."

Parker shook his head. "If my understanding of the battle is correct, they arrived before the Peacemaker fleet."

The second round of missiles arrived at the enemy ships, with the same results. None.

"How did you Humans deal with them?"

"Well, that's the problem," Parker said. He chuckled nervously. "We didn't defeat them; in fact, to hear the story told, we were about to get our asses kicked."

"So, what happened?"

"A Dusman ship jumped into orbit, destroyed one of them, and the other three ships fled." He shrugged. "I find it unlikely the Dusman are going to come to our aid again here."

"I find that unlikely, too," Kanat-Baim said. "We do, however, have something you didn't have at Earth."

"What's that?"

Kanat-Baim looked off camera. "Launch the *Vlimkh* fighters."

"Fighters?" Parker asked. "Our bombers are already on their way... but I doubt their missiles will have any greater effect than yours did."

"Tell your pilots to follow mine in. I think you'll be pleasantly surprised."

"Sir!" the *Gobi Desert's* sensor operator said. "Those ships are doing something weird. They just pulsed. It was almost like some sort of static discharge."

The viewed from the *Blunt Justice* fuzzed, then cleared. Electrical popping could be heard, along with cries of concern. Several flames could be seen on a console behind Kanat-Baim.

"What—what was that?" the Goltar captain asked.

"Meson weapon of some sort," Parker said.

"How do you defend against it?" Kanat-Baim asked as the ship shuddered again.

"My console's out!" someone screamed in the background.

Parker shook his head. "We didn't have any defense; that's why they devastated our fleet."

"What can we do?"

"There's not much you can do," Parker said, frowning. "Maybe tell your fighters to hurry?"

* * *

Cockpit, Avenger One, Gz-ku-Lara System

"Wheeeeeeeeee!" Thorb yelled into the intercom.

Karth looked up, her eyes darting all over to see what Thorb was yelling about. Although flying with the senior SalSha pilot was an honor—he'd done more than any other SalSha, and somehow survived it—he was more than a little strange, possibly due to his interaction with a Type 5 SI. Or maybe it was his extended contact with Humans. Or maybe his uplift to "Sha"—accomplished with a system that hadn't been used in thousands of years—hadn't been without... complications. Either way, his idiosyncrasies were almost as legendary as his exploits.

Thorb pointed out the starboard canopy. "Starfish!"

Karth glanced to the side, and her jaw dropped. Spread out alongside them were a number of... well, they looked *exactly* like starfish. In space. Flying alongside her. *Great. Whatever's wrong with Thorb is contagious, and I have it now, too.* "What... How... Where..." She finally shut her mouth, as nothing productive was coming out.

"Those are Goltar starfish," Thorb said, as if it was something he saw every day.

"Starfish." Karth shook her head.

"Yeah." Thorb sighed. "I never thought I'd get to see them again."

"That's what we were waiting for? I thought the Goltar were sending fighters."

"Those *are* fighters," Thorb said with awe in his voice. "Goltar starfish fighters. They're the last of their type."

"How can they be the last of their type? Why can't the Goltar make more?"

"I asked the same thing." Thorb shrugged. "They said the technology was lost somehow."

"How do you *lose* technology?"

"I guess that's something you do when you're a Goltar. Sometimes I lose my passcard or my wallet, but you'd think technology would be on a number of slates and hard to lose." Thorb shook his head. "But somehow, they lost it, and those are the last of their kind. And they're glorious."

Karth nodded. She had to give Thorb that point. They were awfully cool. "What can they do?"

"Amazing things. We'll follow them to the target."

"What if we're faster? Should we be in front?"

"They have weapons that'll collapse the enemy's shields. That's helpful. And I'm not sure we're faster."

"I thought we were faster than anything."

"I raced a starfish once. Do you know how much 25 Gs hurts?"

He's lying. He has to be. Karth accidentally spit into her helmet. "You haven't gone 25 Gs. The Avengers aren't rated for that."

Thorb shrugged. "Rated or not, they'll do it. The starfish may be able to do more. I was told not to race them anymore. There are only ten or so of them left, and they don't want to lose them 'doing stupid things.' As if racing is stupid."

Karth shook her head, still not sure she believed him. She looked out the canopy again, but the starfish had accelerated in front of the SalSha attack force and were pulling away from them, apparently without effort. Maybe Thorb wasn't pulling her tail. Still… 25 Gs?

But more importantly, "They're going to collapse the shields on those cruisers? I only saw two little missiles under them."

"I asked Sansar about them. She said they were meson spikes. The spikes embed themselves inside the shields and deliver meson pulses. If they can get enough into the shields, the spikes build up a resonance that acts like a grounding line and collapses the shield into the ship itself."

"That makes no sense."

Thorb shrugged. "That's all I know, and all the Goltar know, too. They've lost the technology to build the missiles anymore, and the ones they have are thousands of years old."

"They still work?"

"I hope so."

"Me, too. Otherwise, this is going to be for nothing." She looked into her display. There were only eight of the starfish still registering. As she watched, icons separated from the starfish and leapt forward toward the enemy ships.

"Here we go," Thorb said, jamming the throttles forward.

He jerked the bomber to the side, then back the other way.

"What the hell?" Karth looked up and saw the laser beams flashing past, displayed in her HUD. She looked back down quickly. Some were far too close for her liking. *Sometimes it's better not to know.*

The starfish were pulling back. There were only six of them now.

Forty percent casualties? There were only six Avengers. Karth didn't like the way the math worked out on that for her chances. She pushed the thought aside and focused on her target. Thirty seconds to missile launch. The defenses systems were all on and reporting operational. Chaff was being released with every maneuver.

Thorb pulled to the side even harder than he had been, and her helmet bounced off the side of the canopy, causing her to see stars momentarily.

"Fuck," she muttered.

"Sorry," Thorb said, grunting under the Gs. "Missile." He paused and then added, "Four's gone."

Shit. That was Keeth's bomber! Damn. Lost to a missile. *Speaking of missiles.* Karth reached for the armament panels and flipped switches when she could as the Gs shifted back and forth. "Master arm is on. All five missiles selected. Fifteen seconds to in-range."

"Two's gone."

There was nothing she could do but hold on and pray like the Humans at this point. The timer to in-range counted down to zero without the expected missile or laser blast slamming into the bomber, and the missiles came off in what seemed like half-speed.

"Master arm is off," she said, flipping the switch. "Get us out of here!" She hadn't intended for her voice to screech the way it did; it was probably just the Gs. She put the long-range camera on her target. The vessel looked like a flattened spearpoint and had a strange, mottled hull, almost as if it had been chipped out of a block of granite.

The ship had obviously been hit by the Goltar spikes—its shields sparkled as sheets of plasma flowed across them. The flashes stopped as the energy discharged into the ship, and the target's hull grew even more pitted looking as portions of its armor melted.

Then their missiles arrived, and the Winged Hussars' squashbomb warheads detonated. She counted at least eight hits.

"That one's done."

* * *

CIC, EMS *Mighty Wave*, Gz-ku-Lara System

"Move forward and engage the battlecruiser on the right," Payton said. The two frigates— what the fuck was a Biruda *Maester*-class assault frigate, anyway?—had been destroyed, but at the cost of half the *Gobi Desert's* bomber force, and whatever-type fighters the Goltar had thrown at it. The *Blunt Justice* had fallen back, totally out of the fight, with most of its reactors out of commission.

Which left the odds in the favor of the KzSha—who had five battlecruisers to their three—if all other things were equal.

Good thing everything else isn't equal.

The Goltar battlecruisers had already proven themselves top-of-the-line, and better than any of the ones Dunamis had brought to Battle World. Payton had had to up his opinion of the Goltar; these guys were pretty good. The other two battlecruisers had cut off one of their opposite number and pummeled it into oblivion before the rest of the KzSha fleet could recover, and now were going one-on-two with KzSha battlecruisers. They weren't just holding their own; they were winning.

It was time for the *Mighty Wave* to do its part. "All batteries, fire!"

* * * * *

Chapter Thirty

Keesius Ship One, Gz-ku-Lara System

Tald swam through the corridor of the _Keesius_ ship instead of engaging his magnetic boots. He twisted as he moved, able to keep a full field view of his surroundings, ignore his ill-fitting suit, and stretch out his cramped muscles all at once.

Careena had identified a relatively small number of KzSha on board—twenty to twenty-five—clustered in five places across the ship.

"We're only outnumbered times three," the elSha had proclaimed cheerfully, "and they're not even all in one place, so that's nice!"

Sansar had briefly closed her eyes, then asked him to lock out the communication system. "We don't want them able to talk to each other if we can help it, and we most certainly don't want them alerting the other ships if those are crewed, too."

Their group of seven—Killers, Horde, Pendal, and Peacemaker—moved in staggered groups through the _Keesius_ ship, making their careful way toward a hub for Careena to do what needed to be done. They were approaching the CIC, but Careena had already identified a large concentration of KzSha there, so they were going slower than she wanted. They had to get there... but they needed to be alive when they arrived.

Though they knew where the bulk of the KzSha were, there was no telling if they'd encounter one or two moving through the ship, so they moved in as close to silence as they could. Tald missed Justice—having an invisible assassin sneaking through ahead of them would've been a huge advantage.

Alton Miere, one of the Golden Horde on point, held up a closed fist, and Tald immediately shifted his momentum to aim up and press flat against the ceiling. He steadied his pistol and engaged his boots at half power, but after a moment, Miere opened his hand and waved them forward.

Miere should have trusted his first instinct, though—moments later, the shooting started.

* * *

Keesius Ship Two, Gz-ku-Lara System

As it turned out, a KzSha's bladed middle arm was about the best close-combat weapon one could use on another KzSha. Nick Braker hadn't planned on finding that out, but like so much in his incredibly long career in Colby's Killers, the happy accidents were the sort that kept his life ticking forward. Having earned a blackbelt in Tae Kwon Do a hundred years ago hadn't hurt, either.

Nick staggered back from the thrashing, dying body of the third KzSha and managed not to trip over the second one—the one whose arm he'd used to stab the last attacker. The first one was still going down hard, but its small cannon was gone, and the three Horde mercs and two Killers had more than enough concentrated firepower to end one more.

Nick considered the blue-streaked limb in front of him and whistled for Taneeko. "You have that little welding tool in your bag of tricks?"

"I do." The elSha wriggled down the wall, giving wide berth to the dying KzSha. "We can't dig into the systems here; did you see something?"

"Gonna take this sword arm with us."

"You're..." She glanced from Nick to the dead—now two dead—KzSha and blinked rapidly. "What?"

"I thought the Horde was exaggerating when they said how hard these assholes were to put down—they're giant wasps in combat armor, and they're meaner than Earth wasps. You don't get it, Taneeko. That's really, *really* saying something."

"So you're going to hack up one of their bodies and use it as a weapon?"

"Taneeko." Nick kept his back to the wall and held his hand out to the elSha. She reached into her pack and took her time fishing through her tools, and Nick took the delay as a chance to keep talking, and ensure the first—now last—KzSha was still at the corner, hemmed up by his fellow Humans. "You lived through Dunamis a long time. This isn't a mercenary contract with rules of engagement." *If those were ever a real thing—not in our experience with the Veetanho, they weren't!* "This is one of those 'we get the big ships that can eat a planet and wreck a species, or we don't' kind of survival missions. Like Battle World. So we take any advantage we can, or we... leave the *Keesius* to the Dusman. Maybe they're nice."

"I don't think they are," Taneeko muttered and dropped something small into his hands.

The elSha's hotstick was basically a mini welding arc, if a hell of a lot more precise, and what seemed like orders of magnitude hotter. Enough to slice through a KzSha corpse and give Nick a handy sword arm for the next few levels of *Keesius* storming.

"You do know it's gross though, right?" she asked, her eyes focused on what he was doing.

"Oh, it's totally gross." He kept the corner junction in his peripheral and put most of his focus on his slicing and dicing. "But gross beats dead."

By the time Nick had the extra weaponry, the last KzSha was finally down, and the other five Humans were clearing their immediate vicinity. He hoisted the arm—carefully, to keep from cutting himself—then pointed with it.

"Onward?"

"Onward!" one of the Horde mercs replied, and onward they went.

* * *

CIC, *Blunt Justice*, Gz-ku-Lara System

"The Humans aren't terrible," Salz-Kryll said, pacing the floor as the *Blunt Justice's* crew rushed to mitigate the worst of the damage.

"The battlecruisers are fighting well together," Kanat-Baim allowed, his tone grudging. "They have no business in the *Mighty Wave*, however."

"At least this will be a successful engagement." The Peacemaker moved faster to get out of the way of the rushing weapons officer— a small explosion was contained just in time—then whirled back to the captain. "We do still have enough power in the ship to hold them off when this is over, don't we?"

"The *Blunt Justice* is equal to any task we ask of it."

Except, perhaps, destroying the KzSha's upgraded fleet on our own, Salz-Kryll thought, but was far too smart to say. "Good. Returning with the *Keesius* will do much to right the Goltar's place in the galaxy."

"You're not worried about what will happen with the other Peacemaker?" the captain asked in his disconcertingly smooth voice. "Not the egg, the real one?"

"He'll have no reason to believe I don't also have orders—"

"That depends on where his orders came from, I suppose." Kan-at-Baim stepped away from the singed remnants of his console and shrugged elegantly. "Though perhaps it won't be an issue after all."

"Why's that?"

"Put the Peacemaker's ship on the main viewer." The captain gestured at the screen. "You see?"

"It's…"

"The Peacemaker's ship. Dead in the water. It looks as though he tried to take on the last three ships on his own."

"Then we have no worries at all. With the battlecruisers engaging the last of the KzSha ships, we should move through the system and corner the *Keesius* ships before the *Gobi Desert* decides to do the same thing." Salz-Kryll stood straighter, his appendages loosening. He didn't know Balin personally, but he knew the older Peacemaker's reputation. His removal from the board was sad for the guild, for many reasons, but much better for Salz-Kryll himself and the Goltar as a whole. They would rid the galaxy of the Veetanho vermin, and Salz-Kryll would send a death-offering to Balin's people in sadness. It would be a proper honor for an unfortunate circumstance.

The Peacemaker candidate couldn't countermand him, and having already submitted to the will of the Peacemaker Guild, the Golden Horde would have no reason to fight Salz-Kryll's direct order.

"In fact, if you would, Captain—perhaps we could plot our course to pass close by the Peacemaker's ship. Then if the *Gobi Desert* questions our motives, we can say we're hoping to provide assistance."

"Ah, before the small ship sadly, belatedly, explodes? How gracious we are." Kanat-Baim gave the order, and Salz-Kryll no longer felt the urge to pace.

* * *

Keesius Ship Three, Gz-ku-Lara System

"Wish we were doing this with more than four people," Dave muttered, peering down the long corridor that led to the CIC of their—soon to be their—*Keesius*.

"Statistically, that eight of ten pods made it here is actually pretty—"

"Taleena."

"Right."

Dave didn't spare much time to consider who'd been lost—they had no communication with the other pods, and for all he knew, the other two had made it, but connected to different ships. They'd only seen eight, but that didn't mean only eight had made it. If he started to worry over who he might not see again... No, that wasn't the issue. Dave had led a company for over a century, and lost friends, family, and everyone he'd left behind on Earth.

If there was one thing he was exceptionally good at, it was compartmentalization, and he was pretty good at a lot of things, to be quite honest, so that was saying something.

"What do you think?" he asked, voice low. The Veetanho had split off several corridors back, saying she had an idea, and she hadn't waited for his reply. He could've used her additional weaponry, but he'd deal with what he had.

"Hm. Five minutes. What do you want to bet?" Taleena asked from where she was squeezed into a small compartment they'd opened, her head turned so her bright eyes were on him.

"We're *not* betting cooking duties again. You'd eat paint thinner and like it."

"You *drink* paint thinner and like it," she retorted, and he grinned.

"I say seven minutes, and I'll bet one of those CASPer suits."

"We don't *have* any." She stuck her tongue out, but Dave was pretty sure that was a thinking gesture, not the 'nyah nyah' expression it would be from a Human. "But you're going to buy some?"

"That's the plan."

"And we get to modify them?"

"I don't see why not."

"I'm sure the company that makes them has some sort of proprietary rules and—" Taleena snorted—the elSha had all picked the habit up during the last hyperspace ride. Dave couldn't imagine where they'd gotten it from. "We modify them for elSha ride along if I win, and maximum Human badassery if you win, yes? Deal."

They waited in silence for four minutes, and Dave was feeling pretty good about his bet. Taleena had triggered three of her little tricks—sealing doors, changing the composition of air quality, and flickering lights.

Even a combination of the three wasn't enough to take the KzSha out of the game, but it was enough to annoy the KzSha without them automatically thinking they'd been boarded and signaling an alarm to the other ships.

The giant wasps had split into pairs and had been running down errors all over the ship, leaving five in the CIC, which Taleena duly sealed with enough effort that she was sure the KzSha tapped into the operating system would notice. Then she dialed up the oxygen and something that sounded like cyclone carbonate, and they got into position.

Basically we filled the CIC of the galaxy's deadliest ship with wasp spray, sealed it, and now we're waiting for massive, pissed-off wasps to break out and come hunting us. Dave snorted—he'd definitely picked it up from the elSha, not the other way around—and squinted down his sight at the carefully portioned packet along the door that had been assigned to him.

Sometimes this galaxy is an absolute fucking delight.

At exactly six minutes—Dave belatedly realized they'd never set over/under rules for their bet—the doors slid open.

Dave and the two other Humans took their shots, and three semi-controlled explosions kicked off their KzSha engagement with a bang.

* * *

Eletine, **Gz-ku-Lara System**

"What's this, then?" Balin asked, and Justice blinked back into sight.

"Looks like the Goltar are getting closer."

They'd gotten between the two waves of KzSha ships before the Goltar had appeared, and Naran had sent them brief updates as matters were temporarily sorted. Unfortunately, they'd been knocked out of the fight by some poor combination of missile and meson field interference, and Justice had barely gotten to do any shooting.

He took it calmly enough, but Balin couldn't help but notice the Hunter was invisible more than visible, and thought it better not to push with the questions. He had a ship to fix, at any rate, and he didn't need to see Justice to get the Hunter's help.

"Looks like they're going for the *Keesius.*" Justice's ears swiveled, and he made a low sound—not quite a snarl or laugh, but an odd combination of the two. "Looks like they're aiming right for *us,* but given they're not trying comms, I stand by my first assessment."

"I'd say you're right. In their defense, we are playing dead very convincingly." Balin leaned back in his seat. They hadn't been 'playing' the whole time, thanks to whatever the KzSha had packed into their ships. Once they were functional again, the battle had moved well beyond them, and Balin had decided to stay unremarkable in 'death' and float closer to the *Keesius* ships.

"How close are they going to get?"

"If they were going a hair slower, I'd say we could dock with them." Justice tapped his claws on the console in front of him as he tracked the data.

"Nothing from the *Keesius* yet?"

"They haven't moved, and we can't see any of the lifeboats."

Balin considered their options. They were creeping closer to the moon with the *Keesius* ships, but they couldn't break and run for them—not without knowing who was in control, or if the Goltar would see it as a betrayal of the flimsy agreement they'd made. The *Eletine* couldn't take on a Goltar capital ship on its own... but he did have some options.

"Hit the button."

Justice sat up straight, the tip of his tail twitching. "The big one?"

"The big one." Balin clicked his claws and dialed his goggles to confirm a flight path. "Decide if you want to be visible on comms, or to make your entrance at the appropriately dramatic time."

Justice pressed his hand deliberately against the top leftmost button in the weapons panel, then faced Balin and slow-blinked. "I see why you got along so well with that Hunter Peacemaker," he said and vanished.

Balin settled comfortably in his seat and decided to eat a bit before the Goltar's ship was in the right place. He monitored the end of the main fight as best he could on passive systems—Goltar battle-cruisers truly were impressive—and moments before the capital ship fully passed the *Eletine,* he sent a message from his supposedly dead ship.

To their credit, the Goltar answered.

"*Eletine,* we thought you were dead in the water. What a pleasant surprise to find you functional. I am Captain Kanat-Baim of the *Blunt Justice.*" The Goltar's voice was smooth, and the translator indicated nothing but sincerity. Balin inclined his head.

"I appreciate you coming out to check on me, Captain, even if you thought it a hopeless case. I'm Peacemaker Balin, and unfortunately, up until just a few minutes ago, my ship *was* dead in the water. Thankfully this old Peacemaker has a few tricks up his sleeve."

"Indeed. Ah, can we provide assistance?"

"I was hoping that was why you were out here."

"Indeed. Indeed." The captain turned to the side, and while he moved as though he were speaking, nothing came across the comms. "We did suffer quite a bit of damage against the KzSha's *Maester*-class assault frigate, and it looks like our course calculations didn't compute exactly. We'll miss you, but will loop back around as we get our repairs in order."

Clever. Balin leaned closer to the screen.

"About that."

"I *am* apologetic, Peacemaker. Our ships do seem to have the danger posed by the KzSha contained now—the battle was heated, but I'm glad we could play our part. You should be safe until we're able to recover—"

"Oh, I understand, Captain. I do. But when I said 'about that,' I meant your systems might be more damaged than you thought, if you didn't catch the missile currently attached to your ship."

"The *what?*" One of the captain's tentacles snapped to the side, and there was a scurry of motion not entirely caught on screen.

"I dropped it while watching your approach. If you'd genuinely been on course to intercept me, it would've fallen through the system, unused. A waste of my credits, to be sure, but nothing more harmful. But if your course was slightly different—aimed for the *Keesius* ships, for instance—then it would magnetize to your hull."

"To my… Peacemaker, this is outrageous, we're off course, yes, but—"

"Captain Kanat-Baim, I've been a Peacemaker a long time. I've even had the pleasure of seeing one of your own Goltar Peacemakers in action several times, and I know—and often admired—the strengths of your race." Balin lifted his hands and spread his claws, and he bled the friendliness from his tone. "I also know your goals and those of my guild might not be aligned at this time."

"I assure you—"

"The missile can remain inert. You can change your course."

"We don't even register an obstruction—"

"About that." Balin smiled. It was not his nicest expression. "I know you met my younger counterpart some time back. He has quite a knack for deputizing skilled individuals."

Justice, with the timing Balin knew he had, appeared next to him. "As you may know, you don't need to register the worst weapons in the galaxy for them to do a great deal of damage."

"You *did* take quite a bit of damage in the battle," Justice added, his voice a threatening purr. "I know capital ships are difficult to damage, but we were quite precise with our placement."

"Clearly, I must recheck our systems, Peacemaker. Excuse me a moment."

The screen blanked, and Balin closed the channel, then chuckled. "Tald's right. Bluffing really *is* fun when you have something to back it up."

* * * * *

Chapter Thirty-One

***Keesius* Ship One, Gz-ku-Lara System**

Miere jumped back, but he wasn't faster than the laser bolts pursing him, and he took three hits to the chest. The second in line, Sergeant Altun Ashugh, primed a flash-bang, tossed it into the space, and dove in low. The rest of the group followed. By the time Tald reached the hatchway, the battle was over, and the room—some sort of control room, based on the number of control consoles spread throughout it—was an abstract painting done in red and blue. Most of it was blue, however, and two of the Humans who'd been hit—Ashugh and Jensen from Colby's Killers—were moving and jabbing themselves with their medkit injectors.

Injured, not dead. That's something, anyway. Motion caught his eye as Miere's corpse bounced off the bulkhead in his direction. *Except him.* Tald sniffed once, sorry for the man, but then black shapes appeared down the passageway. He locked his boots to the floor and fired both his pistols. One of the KzSha flew backward, but the other fired back.

Tald couldn't see the laser as it flashed past, but knew it was close. He fired again, but then the troopers pouring from the room got in his way, and he had to hold. When the soldiers moved again, he could see that his second shot at the KzSha had been successful.

"What are you firing?" Sansar asked.

"Hypervelocity pistols," Tald replied.

"Hmm."

"What?"

"They may not be the best for a ship's interior. If you drill a hole through the side, we'll have issues."

"Don't ships have armor?" Tald asked. "I wouldn't think my pistols would be able to penetrate that."

"Normally, probably not." Sansar nodded. "These ships are thousands of years old, though. I'd rather not have to worry that you're going to penetrate a loose seam somewhere." She handed over a laser pistol. It was too large for one paw, but he could manage it with both of them.

"I don't want to leave you defenseless," Tald said.

"I'm not. That's my backup." She showed her remaining, larger, pistol, then surveyed the consoles. "Ashugh, secure Miere. Careena, can you do what you need, or do we need to take the CIC?"

"This—" Careena waved a hand across the space "—is the auxiliary control space they use to control the ship if the CIC sustains battle damage. It should be good enough if I can gain access to the main systems. I can initiate all Taleena's subroutines from here and lock the KzSha out."

"Even though they're in the CIC?"

"Just so." The elSha pulled himself through the room, peering at one console at a time. "Ah, here we go." Careena inserted a drive into the console and began pressing buttons.

Tald released his boots and pushed off the floor to take a closer look at the nearby panels.

"There should be another hub on the other side of the bulkhead," Careena muttered, sounding distracted. "We need to cut it to isolate the CIC from the system."

"I'll look," Josiff offered, and Ashugh followed him after tucking Miere's body in a corner, held down by his boots. Tald considered following them, then decided to pull the KzSha bodies in, instead. Less to show respect than to keep the hall clear, and less obvious to any approaching KzSha that something was wrong. Or to give additional KzSha anything to hide behind.

After a moment, Jensen joined him, and they made quick work of it.

Not quite quick enough.

Tald found himself spinning end over end, the space around him a blur.

What?

He'd been shoving a KzSha corpse, unhooked his boots, and something—

Something...

Burned.

I was... shot? Someone shot me? I was shot.

Colors flashed, and he blinked, then reached for his gun.

Do I have a gun?

He twisted to the left to arrest his spin, and that was one of his worse ideas to date; everything in his body screamed in protest. Each nerve and muscle individually caught on fire, that fire intensified, and all the colors went briefly gray.

Tald slammed into a bulkhead. He couldn't catch his breath— was that the wall? From being shot?

His boots caught—he didn't remember turning them on, but they stuck to the wall—and he wrenched forward, then floated back. The light dimmed around him, but he was in perfect position, with just enough light to see through the growing shadows.

Enough to see the entrance to the CIC.

To see the KzSha storm in, laser guns at the ready.

To see Sansar, caught in mid-turn from facing Tald to moving to cover the door.

To see Sansar move too late.

To see the KzSha put the gun to Sansar's forehead.

To see the KzSha pull the trigger.

Tald tried to scream, but the light faded, and his mouth tasted only of blood.

* * *

Keesius Ship Two, Gz-ku-Lara System

Angry giant wasps were not, in fact, easier to kill than normal giant wasps. Braker's team had lured a few out with flash-bangs, but not all, and the result was a shootout where no one had great cover.

The pissed-off giant wasps fell back into the CIC and continued to shoot at them, and the Humans retreated around the corner. Taneeko had burrowed into a conduit and was hopefully doing brilliant tech things to disrupt power or open a convenient airlock or *something.*

"Fuck this," Braker said and gestured at his team, now down to four Humans and the elSha. They staggered shooting so each could put their helmets back on, then Braker underhanded one, pause, two, pause, three flash and gas grenades. They'd been one of his proudest developments on Battle World, excellent for combat in a constrained environment against opponents who breathed. He was the tech guy, but you got to wear a lot of hats in a century of fighting against stupid odds.

As the ripple of *pops* finished, they charged.

The air in the CIC was thick from the grenades, and visibility was poor. He caught things in sudden pieces and took to slicing more than shooting in the close quarters. The giant, angry wasps were better at stabbing with their attached arms than he was with his scavenged one, but they were also disoriented and unprepared for a close-quarters attack.

He stood back-to-back with Lorens for a minute and got a lucky headshot that dropped one of the KzSha. Greeves bellowed something, and Lorens dropped behind him. Braker threw himself sideways, raising his gun, and a razor-sharp arm cut through the space he'd just left.

Red and blue blood streaked his helmet, and he fired high—too high to catch a Human, he hoped, but hopefully exactly head height for a fluttering KzSha.

I didn't survive Dunamis all that time to get stabbed to death by a damn bug, he thought, and added his own bellowing to Greeves'. He shoved off the deck and twisted—his Tae Kwon Do master would have nodded in grudging approval—and used his spin for extra momentum to slice where a flickering light told him a giant angry wasp was.

Their antennae lit up, and in the clouded mess of the CIC, it might as well have been a beacon.

Thanks, galaxy. That was pretty okay of you.

More blue blood splattered through the haze, and a satisfying *thump* nearby indicated KzSha head had been successfully parted from KzSha body.

Greeves had gone quiet though.

Surely, he wasn't the only one left.

Don't make me take it back, he thought in the general direction of the galaxy.

* * *

CIC, *Blunt Justice,* Gz-ku-Lara System

"Did you find anything?" Kanat-Baim asked, keeping his appendages still by force.

"There *is* a missile directly under the cooling—"

"One missile surely won't compromise the *Blunt Justice*—"

"Captain, we can't assume there's only one."

Kanat-Baim turned slowly. "The Peacemaker said there was one."

"The Peacemaker *admitted* to one, but he has a *Depik* on board, and all but implied there were more than we could see."

"There's hardly an assassin on this ship." A trickle of frigid water walked down his middle. Was he sure about that?

"If the cooling system blows, there's a cascade effect that'll ensure we'll have to stop to fix it before going far above light thrust or firing anything we have left. Without the damage we've already taken, we could likely—"

"Enough. Your conjecture is there's more than meets the eye, we're already compromised, and we're better off playing nice with the Peacemaker."

"Uh… yes sir."

Kanat-Baim didn't look at the Peacemaker on his own ship and took a long moment before gesturing to bring the *Eletine* back on comms.

"Sir, wait!"

He didn't snap, because he'd been doing this job a long time and entropy itself wouldn't make him lose his composure, but there was a slight strain in his question. "Now what?"

"It's the *Keesius*, sir."

"What about them?"

"One of them is on the move."

* * *

Keesius Ship Three, Gz-ku-Lara System

"Entropy and ash." Taleena's voice carried over the sound of gunfire and mercs—several of the KzSha had visibly survived the explosions, and it was taking forever to advance down the corridor. Two were firing down the corridor from the cover of the hatchway, and one of his people was already down.

"We don't have time for this, Taleena. You got this or not?"

"One of the KzSha is in the system. He's put a new command in-to it, one that takes priority ahead of anything else… including what I've done."

"Uh-huh." Dave pulled back and leaned flat against the wall, glancing up at Taleena's compartment. So pissing off the enormous, mean wasps, and then blowing up some of their friends didn't make them easier to kill. Noted.

"I think he's bringing weapons online."

"Shit."

"But I blocked the targeting system."

"Uh... huh." Dave had a feeling he was very much not going to like where this was going. He took a sliver of a second to wish he had some of Braker's specialty grenades, then leaned around to shoot again when Pierce pulled back. Davis was spinning, floating down the passageway; it was now two on two.

Taleena scratched her chin. "If the KzSha fires anything, it'll go... somewhere. Might include hitting the other *Keesius* ships."

"Sounds bad, Tal. Can you do some brilliant tech things to fight him off?"

"Not without giving away—"

"Ship's sailed on staying secret." Dave motioned up the passageway. "I think they know we're here. Do what you got to do."

"It was a decoy—oh damn, damn, damn."

"Taleena!"

"He's moving us—we're breaking orbit, but I think... I think he's aiming for the moon."

Speaking of doing what they had to do... Dave had ensured they were very careful with the controlled explosions they'd set off around the CIC. They'd jammed the door—otherwise the KzSha would have barricaded themselves inside the space—but had been careful not to wreck the CIC.

But if the choice was between the ship self-destructing around them, not belonging to them at all, or taking a few more hits, well... maybe it was time for a bigger explosion. He'd been in similar positions across the thousands of battles he'd fought, and he could already see where this was going to go. He could make it to the CIC, and he could probably get off a grenade that would wreck whatever the KzSha was doing, but he couldn't do it without taking some hits.

He estimated a 64 percent chance he'd be successful. He also figured the chances he wouldn't survive the attack were at least 82 percent. No matter what he did, this was going to *suck*.

"I think someone's calling the ship," Taleena said.

Then it's time, Dave thought. *A hundred years of fighting, for it all to end here.* If he could get Jan and Payton and Braker back home, though, at least his mission would be complete. He nodded to himself. *Time to be a hero.*

* * *

Eletine, Gz-ku-Lara System

"**O**ne of the *Keesius* is moving." Justice shifted from indolent lounging to high alert between one blink and the next.

"Where is it going?"

"It's hard to tell with the moon in the way."

Balin tapped his claws on the console and considered their options. "You know what, playing dead isn't going to help us much longer. Let's see where the Goltar are leaning."

He'd barely sent the request when the captain appeared on the screen. There was a great deal of movement behind him.

"More threats, Peacemaker?" Kanat-Baim asked.

"I don't threaten, Captain, just make sure everyone's aware of the situation. Which has changed, looks like. Neither of us want the *Keesius* on the move under the Dusman's power, am I right?"

"You are."

"And I don't like the idea of an SI getting a hold of them, either."

If there was an SI at the heart of the Peacemaker Guild—and Balin had become certain there was—that meant yet another decision faced him with regard to the *Keesius* ships. Not one he had to worry about before he handled the imminent threat, however.

Tald and the elSha's plan had been risky in all sorts of ways, and they'd all agreed if it looked like a *Keesius* was breaking loose, they should do everything in their power to take it off the board.

"Not much either of our ships can do against one alone, and even together, the most we can do is slow it down. But I'm up for it if you are."

"Destruction is preferable. We're in accord."

He didn't ask Balin to detach his missile, which meant Balin didn't have to upend their tentative agreement before it started.

Time for that soon enough.

* * *

Keesius Ship One, Gz-ku-Lara System

Sansar saw the KzSha's claw tense on the trigger—she could see it straining—but the trigger didn't move. The KzSha grunted, straining, but still, the trigger never twitched. Then, the alien's whole arm began to vibrate, and the KzSha pulled the barrel of the pistol away from Sansar's forehead. The alien's second hand came up, trying to control the pistol, but it continued to turn, as if it had a mind of its own. The creature buzzed, straining, fighting to point it anywhere else, but slowly, inexorably, the muzzle of the pistol turned until the barrel was facing the KzSha, and then the alien pushed it firmly up between its eyes.

Whatever had been holding the trigger released, and the pistol fired, drilling a hole that went through the KzSha's head to score the bulkhead behind it.

Sansar's jaw dropped, and she tore her eyes from the fallen KzSha to find Josiff behind her, his upper right arm extended. The Pendal sighed, his breath flowing forth explosively, and he sagged. Sansar stepped over and steadied him, glancing over her shoulder to locate Tald.

After a couple seconds, Josiff shook himself.

"Sorry," he said. "It has been a long time since I have exerted myself like that."

Josiff was responsible for... whatever it was that just happened. Sansar had so many questions, but also something more pressing to do. She shoved off the floor to the wall Tald was pinned on. She didn't mean to say anything about what Josiff had done, but the words emerged as she moved.

"I didn't know you could do that."

"There are many things you do not know—" Josiff sounded exhausted, and Sansar couldn't imagine what it had cost him to do what he'd done—never mind how "—but now is not the time to explain them."

Tald still had a pulse. Ashugh reentered the room and gave her a small headshake when he met her eyes. They were down to five, and she didn't have SalSha nanites on her, which might make it four. Sansar ran her hands over Tald's small body without touching him.

Blue Sky, but he looks even smaller when unconscious.

She checked the small pouches on his harness. The *Gobi Desert* had nanites for his species—surely he'd brought some. The wound on his left side was deceptively tiny—already cauterized, a perfect hole through his vest and fur. Almost, she could brush his fur over it and hide it.

"Careena, tell me you can take over this ship from here."

"Doing my best!"

"Do it a little better, please. We're running low on shooters, and the KzSha have likely figured out we're here."

"On it!"

Hang in there, Tald. She sighed as her hands made contact with a familiar tube, and she pulled out the injector and jabbed him with it. Sansar sighed again as the nanobots flowed into his body; that was all she could do. Sansar touched his head and straightened his floating body gently. With a silent thought for Miere and Jensen, she left Josiff and Careena to dig through the guts of the *Keesius* and gestured for Ashugh to follow her to the door.

There was one more thing she could do. She could ensure no more KzSha got through.

* * * * *

Chapter Thirty-Two

Keesius Ship One, Gz-ku-Lara System

The KzSha, when they finally attacked, came from both directions, and it was all Sansar and Ashugh could do to fire fast enough, while still ducking behind cover periodically. Sansar's shoulder burned from a grazing laser shot. At the end, it had come down to hand-to-hand, and Ashugh had taken a blade to his guts before Sansar had been able to finish off the last alien with a laser bolt to its head.

Sansar looked up from injecting Ashugh with the last nanobot load from her medkit as Careena gave a small exclamation of success.

"Yes!" Careena exulted, tension flooding from his body as he clung to a center console. "The ship is ours. I have the last few KzSha sealed up, and while they can definitely do some damage if we leave them too long, it'll buy us time to get reinforcements."

Sansar did one more sweep of the passageway—there were a total of six KzSha floating in the corridor, all dead—then pivoted and strode back into the auxiliary control room. If they could get a message out, they could have CASPers here in hours, which would make the clean up a hell of a lot easier.

"Any sign from the other ships?"

"No."

Sansar took a deep breath and steadied her shoulders. "Send out the signal."

"Got it!" The elSha scrambled over to the next console and pressed a series of buttons. Three short pulses, two long, three short, two long.

Moments later, Careena's head bobbed, and he made an excited croaking noise. "Got it," he said again, then frowned. "From *Keesius* number two."

Their rudimentary code for a call and response complete, Sansar stepped forward to see who else had survived.

A Human pulled off his blue-streaked helmet to reveal Nick Braker from Colby's Killers. "Hey," he said. His face was almost as speckled with blue as his helmet had been, and she saw no one with him except an elSha. "I like this 'pick up a new ship in every other system' thing we have going on."

"No guarantee you get to keep that one." Sansar smiled, but it was brief. They had two of the three *Keesius*, which was by all accounts a wild success, but they were by no means in the clear. Nor had she begun the tally of the dead—something she'd grown far too used to over the years, but that never made it easy. "Do you have control of the ship's weapons?"

"Between Taneeko and I, we've got control of everything. It was a tough fight—and there's only the two of us left—but all the KzSha are down." Despite his bright tone, his smile lasted about as long as hers had. "You asked about weapons... do we need to target the third ship?"

"It's on the move," Careena interjected, his fingers flying over the console in front of him.

"Then by all means, let's target their propulsion if we can; we can't let it get away."

Josiff glided by and took up a post at a nearby console. "Easily done."

Sansar turned to Careena. "If whoever's in charge of that *Keesius* won't pick up, is there any way to use Taleena's programs to get us a broadcast to them?"

"Not from here, but I'm still sending the pulses—hopefully, if she's in a condition to tap into the system, she can tell it's us, and maybe... hm."

"Hm?" Sansar prompted when Careena stayed quiet.

"I sent an alert message, indicating we were under attack. I... think this is an answer?"

"What is it?"

"Just a burst transmission, but it's from the third *Keesius*. Trying to connect..."

"Are we firing?" Nick asked. "Cause we're all lined up, and they're still moving."

"Incoming ships—the Goltar capital ship and the *Eletine*," Josiff said quietly. "Still too far out to do much."

"Tell Balin we've got two of three." Sansar calculated—two *Keesius* were better than none. They could destroy the third one—two *Keesius* against one could take it out quickly, hopefully faster than it could blow itself up and potentially take one or both of the other *Keesius* ships with it.

Regardless, it couldn't be allowed to get away. She didn't know if any of their people were still alive on the third ship—but then, she didn't know if that mattered in the face of the decision she had to make. If they weren't in a position to take the ship, it was better to remove the ship from the game board... even if their people were still alive.

"Contact!" Careena flailed an arm. "Connecting to the third *Keesius,* voice only."

Sansar's translator gave the KzSha who replied a guttural tone, which grated in her ear when combined with the KzSha's higher voice. "We are also under attack. Initiating Protocol 12."

The moment she spoke, Sansar knew the gig was up. She had to make it good.

"That would be a terrible waste," Sansar said.

"Who is this?"

"Sansar Enkh, commander of the Golden Horde. I'm in possession of two of your three ships, so tell me this." She gestured for Careena to keep trying to contact Taleena. If the Horde and Killers onboard the ship were still alive, her transmission could be the distraction they needed to recover the ship. "Would the Dusman rather you destroy their ships, or preserve them so they have a chance to take them back?"

"You know nothing of the Dusman!"

"That's not true. Surely, they told you they want to make pets of us, too?" Sansar kept her voice neutral, not wanting to give the translator any excuse to make sarcasm or stress audible to the KzSha. "Seems to me they'd use our having more of these ships as an excuse to bind us tighter to them. Better than the impossibility of having to find more somewhere—I can't imagine they can make 'em like this anymore."

"You... no. The Dusman..."

"Don't like failure. You've already failed here, unfortunately, and we have more allies coming." She meant the *Eletine* and the *Blunt Justice,* but let him think she meant more ships were due to arrive in system. "Which are they more likely to forgive? Their ships existing still for them to take back, or the loss of their irreplaceable firepow-er?"

It would be a weak argument against an unflustered enemy—any sane power would want ships like these out of the equation rather than in someone else's grasp—but she wasn't talking to an unflustered enemy.

The connection cut, and she met Nick's eyes on the screen. "We give it a count of ten. If that wasn't enough of a distraction—if we don't hear from Dave or Taleena—"

"We scuttle the ship." He stretched his neck, tilting his head side to side, and shrugged. "If we don't, and they activate it… we might all go down to it."

"Stand by to fire," Sansar said with a sigh. "On my command."

* * *

Keesius Ship Three, Gz-ku-Lara System

Pierce beat him to it. Although not an original member of the Killers, he'd been around for decades, and he'd likely come to the same conclusions Dave had.

As Dave gathered himself to leap forward, Pierce launched him-self from his hiding place. Dave grabbed a pipe, aborting his rush, and pulled out his pistol to cover Pierce's advance. The trooper wasn't bothering to shoot, and both KzSha had appeared at the hatch and were firing down the corridor. Dave tagged one with a lucky shot—he'd been aiming center mass, and the KzSha had ducked into a head shot—then Pierce was in the way, and Dave had to hold his fire.

Dave launched forward as Pierce shivered twice, obviously hit, then the younger man was on the KzSha. The alien slashed with a blade arm, impaling Pierce. Blood spurted as the blade burst through Pierce's back, and the trooper reached forward to grab the KzSha, pulling himself closer to the giant wasp. As the alien fought, trying to get Pierce off him, the trooper reached down, pulled a grenade off his harness, and pulled the pin. Jamming the grenade between the KzSha's mandibles, he spit in the wasp's face. "Die, bug."

Dave dove into an alcove as the grenade detonated, then launched himself forward again, trying to ignore the remains of the man he'd been friends with for decades. The KzSha wasn't a danger anymore; its entire head was missing.

Reaching the hatch, he pulled himself in low, and his HUD showed a laser bolt passing just over him.

"Gotcha, bitch," Dave said as he slammed into a console and used his momentum to launch himself up.

The remaining KzSha was pressing buttons on one of the consoles, and Dave knew one thing—whatever the wasp was doing, it wasn't going to be good for him or his allies. Spinning in the air, he got his legs under him as he hit the overhead, and he bent his knees to absorb the blow. The KzSha was still tracking his flight, a good quarter second behind him, as he aimed his pistol. All he needed was half that, and the laser beam crossed the distance instantly, punching through the KzSha's left eye.

The bug drifted back from the console, very dead.

Dave pushed off from the ceiling and looked at the console the KzSha had been working at. "Tal? Should there be a countdown running here?"

* * *

Keesius Ship One, Gz-ku-Lara System

"Contact!" Careena shouted.

"Wait!" Sansar said. "Hold fire!"

"That's Taleena!" Careena flailed. He spun over the top of the console, then hauled himself back into place. "They're still in there, and they have control of the CIC!"

"Great!" Sansar said. "Can they prevent… whatever it was the KzSha was going to do?"

"Uh, about that… Taleena's saying we're going to want to get as far away from them as possible."

"Why's that?"

"It looks like the antimatter system is about to initiate."

"Can they stop it? Should we destroy them before it activates?"

"Uh, no. The antimatter's already been created. If we shoot them, the containment will fail, and they'll blow up." Careena's hands twitched nervously. "Maybe we *should* try to move in the other direction…"

"What are they doing?"

"They're trying to stop it, but they've confirmed that we absolutely *should not* shoot their ship. If they can activate the steering in time, they can avoid the moon… assuming they don't blow up first."

Sansar shook her head. "Josiff, safe our weapons, please. Careena, figure out how to get this ship moving and get us out of here."

All four of Josiff's hands moved over the weapons systems, and Sansar had to fight the wild urge to ask if he could affect anything over there from here. It was absurd—the Pendal wasn't a wizard, and what he'd done in close quarters had obviously taken everything he'd had in him—but she resolved to learn more soon.

She looked at the plot. *Blue Sky!* The third Keesius would be passing them momentarily... assuming it didn't detonate.

If we have a soon.

* * *

Keesius Ship Three, Gz-ku-Lara System

"Talk to me, Tal," Dave said. "There were four columns of numbers flashing. Now there are only two. I can't see that being a good thing. Please tell me you've got this."

"Honestly," Taleena said, "I'd like to say I do... but I don't. The system is locked, and I don't see a way to unlock it in the time remaining."

"So what are you telling me? That we're going to die in a fucked-up, millennia-old piece of ancient, world-ending technology?"

"Unless a miracle occurs, yes; that's exactly what I'm telling you."

"I can give you that miracle," a voice said from the hatchway.

Dave's pistol snapped up, and Taleena dove for cover as Gleeko floated into the CIC.

"How do you intend to do that?" Dave said, lowering—but not holstering—his pistol.

"These ships were in Veetanho hands for a long time. There are things you don't know about them... but I do." Gleeko smiled. "But first I want to talk to Sansar."

Dave tapped the console. "Tal tells me this ship is about to activate."

Gleeko nodded. "It is."

"Um... shouldn't we stop that first? Maybe talk to Sansar after that?"

"No," Gleeko said, shaking her head. "I think activating it is exactly what we needed." The smile returned. "Otherwise, I wouldn't have done so."

"*You're* the one who activated it?"

"I am." She craned her neck. "There's only about a minute left until final activation occurs." Gleeko glanced at Taleena. "Perhaps you could open a communication channel to the ship Sansar's on?"

* * *

Eletine, Gz-ku-Lara System

"Tell them to keep the ship still—we're almost there, and if I board—"

"Justice." Balin studied the screen, though no amount of calculations could change the reality of spatial distances. "It'll be resolved one way or another before we get there."

"Unless."

Balin didn't like that tone, but before he could ask, they had another incoming message. It wasn't directed to them, but to any ship that could pick it up in the system.

"*This is Sansar Enkh. The deputies of Peacemaker Tald are in control of the three* Keesius *ships. The Peacemaker is gravely wounded, and we won't be discussing the use of any of the ships until he's recovered. We would ask for everyone to make their way toward the gate until further notice, however, as one of them is about to detonate.*"

"Tald is hurt!" Justice exclaimed.

"Or it's a stall. Not a bad one, either." Balin *tsked*. "Nor is saying that one's about to detonate. No one will want to go close to them if indeed one is about to explode."

"You think that's a stall, too?"

Balin shook his head. "Probably… but do you want to approach it and have it blow up in your face?"

"Not me. I've been too close to things blowing up. I can't recommend it as a good time."

"The question is, though… Naran said the Goltar have a Peacemaker on board—I wonder if *he'll* try and force the issue with his rank."

"Not while he knows you're here." Justice flicked an ear dismissively. "Unless he's stupid."

"There are many ways to be stupid in this galaxy." Balin waited to see if there were any answering messages—there weren't—then turned his chair toward Justice. "What was your idea? Your 'unless?'"

"Oh." Justice slow-blinked. "I was going to suggest one of our *Keesius* blow up the moon so the third one couldn't use it to crash against, then use the confusion and time for us to get close enough for me to board."

"Not sure that would have gone as neatly as you'd think."

"Nothing ever does, Peacemaker." Justice slow-blinked. "That's the fun of it."

* * * * *

Chapter Thirty-Three

CIC, *Blunt Justice*, Gz-ku-Lara System

"The battlecruisers are attached, Captain. We can use their thrust to advance more quickly," the helmsman reported.

"Very well," Kanat-Baim said. "Proceed toward the *Keesius* ships. Maintain one G. We'll destroy the one that's moving and take the others."

"You agree it's a ruse, then?" Salz-Kryll asked. "I find it highly unlikely that one of the *Keesius* ships is going to blow up."

"They're trying to keep the ships." Kanat-Baim slammed a tentacle on his console, then he leaned against it and strove not to tear it from its plating. "That's been their plan all along—to keep the ships and prevent us from wiping the Veetanho vermin from the face of the galaxy."

Kanat-Baim forced himself to take a couple of breaths. "Open a channel to Sansar Enkh."

When the channel opened, the Human was standing in a CIC, but not the one on the *Gobi Desert*. "I assume you're the one responsible for moving the *Keesius* ship? That this whole thing—" he waved a tentacle "—was nothing more than to allow you to get the ships for yourselves."

"Well, Captain, I honestly can't see anything good coming from the Goltar having possession of the *Keesius* ships, can you?"

"Besides the destruction of the Veetanho race? Some people—and all the Goltar—would say that was an admirable outcome."

"Even if it brought the galaxy into civil war?"

Kanat-Baim shrugged a tentacle. "Some would say so, yes."

"That's not the way I see it."

"Oh, no? And how exactly do you see it?"

Sansar chuckled. "You're aware of the return of the Kahraman, right?"

"I am."

"And the fact that SIs seem to be appearing everywhere?"

"They seem to be appearing everywhere there are *Humans*," Kan-at-Baim replied. "I'm beginning to wonder if the Humans aren't al-lied with the SIs. Or maybe Dunamis is done with the Veetanho and has moved on to the Humans. Perhaps that's why you've risen so quickly through the ranks... you're being guided by an SI."

"We're not."

"And how am I to believe that?"

"I have a box that identifies—and removes—the influence of the SIs. We've been actively fighting a number of them."

"So you say. I haven't seen evidence of any war against the SIs."

"The Sumatozou have assisted us in a number of battles; they can confirm it."

"Regardless, how does that change anything here and now?"

Sansar smiled. "The galaxy is in a fragile state. There are at least two enemies waiting for us. We can't afford to be fighting amongst ourselves; we need to be focusing on building our strength, not wast-ing it on internecine fighting. That was the decree from the Merc Guild—"

"As spoken by a Human," Salz-Kryll interjected. "Of course he'd say that so you could get what you want."

"Look," Sansar said, "I've hated the Veetanho as much or more than anyone else. I still do. However, I saw what Dunamis did to them on Lytoshaan."

"It was a good start," Salz-Kryll said.

"It was *murder*," Sansar said, "no different than what the Veetanho did to everyone else while Dunamis was running them. As much as we'd like to pin everything on them, it wasn't entirely their fault."

Kanat-Baim chuckled. "We've hated them for far longer than Dunamis has been guiding them. They are eminently hateable. Don't let what you saw on Lytoshaan temper your feelings. You can—*and should*—continue to hate them."

Sansar smiled. "Whether I do or don't still hate them doesn't matter. We still need them. We'll need them to fight the Kahraman, and we'll need them to fight the SIs. After all, who has a better idea of what an SI is capable of than the Veetanho?

"And even if we didn't need them," Sansar continued, "I can't allow a civil war, which is what would happen if you got the *Keesius* ships. You'd use them on the Veetanho, then they'd call all their allies, then there'd be war. And sometime during this war, the Kahraman or the SIs would return and hit us when we weren't ready. Before we know it, the galaxy would be lost."

"So who should take the ships? The Humans?"

"If we took them, there's nothing to prevent you from using your *Keesius* ships against the Veetanho. No, I intend to give them back to the Veetanho. If you don't use yours, they won't use theirs, and we don't have to go to war against each other. Isn't that preferable?"

"No, it isn't. I think I'd like to have them instead."

"What you'd like really doesn't matter," Sansar said, "because I'm not bluffing. The ship I'm on is about to activate. When it does, everything in the immediate area will be destroyed. If you keep coming in this direction, that'll include the *Blunt Justice*, your battleriders, and everyone aboard those ships."

"That will also include you."

"It will."

"You don't seem too worried about it."

Sansar shrugged. "There's nothing I can do about it. If you look, you'll see that I've warned off the *Gobi Desert*, the *Mighty Wave*, and the *Eletine*. If there was a way I could get us off this ship, I would. As it is, only a handful of our people survived the assault on them. I won't risk any more of my people to try to save us."

Kanat-Baim looked over to his sensor operator. "It's true," the technician said. "The Human ships are turning and accelerating away from the *Keesius* ships."

"What do you want me to do, sir?" the helmsman asked.

"They're bluffing," Salz-Kryll said.

"I agree," Kanat-Baim said. "Continue toward the *Keesius* ships. Prepare a boarding team."

* * *

CIC, *Gobi Desert*, Gz-ku-Lara System

"The *Mighty Wave* and *Eletine* are attached."

"Very well," Captain Parker replied. "Helm, activate internal shunts. Jump us to the Gralkaron system."

"Aye, sir; activating internal shunts. Course set for the Gralkaron system."

The system energized, and the three ships disappeared from normal space.

* * *

CIC, *Blunt Justice,* Gz-ku-Lara System

"Sir, the *Gobi Desert*, *Mighty Wave,* and *Eletine* just jumped to hyperspace."

"What?" Kanat-Baim asked. "Connect me with Sansar Enkh again, please."

A few moments later, Sansar's image again filled their main screen. "What game are you playing?" Kanat-Baim asked.

"I'm not playing a game," Sansar said. "I wanted to keep my people safe, so I told them to leave. There's about five minutes left until the *Keesius* ship I'm on detonates. I'd hoped to get my people off it, but there won't be time. I'm doing what I can."

Kanat-Baim looked at his tactical controller. "What are they doing?"

"The two other ships are now underway, sir. It looks like they're trying to get away from the other ship."

The transmission jumped, and the image of a Veetanho filled it. "Captain Kanat-Baim, my name is Gleeko, and I have stolen two of the ships from Sansar. I stowed away on her ship when it was in Lytoshaan and have killed all her people aboard this *Keesius*." Gleeko smiled. "I just wanted you to know that I've targeted this *Keesius* for Tolgar, your home planet. If anything should happen to *any* of the Veetanho home worlds, you *will* lose Tolgar."

"You'll never make it to the stargate," Kanat-Baim said. "We'll destroy you first."

Gleeko chuckled. "Ah, the Goltar... never the smartest of the races. Captain, were you not aware that the *Keesius* ships—in addition to being world-enders—are also extremely maneuverable? You can't stop me. I've set the third ship to detonate. All you can do is pray you never see the two ships I control again."

The connection terminated.

"Sir!" the sensor operator exclaimed. "The two *Keesius* ships just activated their internal shunts and jumped."

Kanat-Baim slapped a tentacle on his console and swore, then he took a deep breath and released it slowly. "Proceed to the third *Keesius*. If nothing else, we can take one of the three."

"You still think this is a ruse?" Salz-Kryll asked. "I'm starting to think—"

"Sir! You need to see this!"

The view from the long-range camera appeared on the screen. The forward section of the *Keesius* had opened, its bow peeling back in four sections like a flower opening. Each of the petals sparkled.

"Those are its antimatter bottles!" Kanat-Baim swore. "That bitch Veetanho *has* activated it, and it's going to explode! Helmsman, jump us out of here!"

"Internal shunts powering up," the helmsman replied. "Nearest system is the Zaltap system. Course laid in… shunts ready… jumping now."

The helmsman pushed the button, and the ship vanished from normal space.

* * *

Keesius Ship Three, Gz-ku-Lara System

"Now that everyone's gone," Dave said, "could you please do whatever's needed to get rid of all that antimatter?"

Gleeko looked at the Tri-V focused on the bow doors. "All the battles you fought, with death so near, and you're afraid of a little antimatter?"

"That is *not* a little antimatter," Dave said. "That's enough antimatter to blow up a planet."

"Not really," Gleeko replied. "Sure, it's a lot, but without running the *Keesius* attack profile, it's just going to make a big hole somewhere. If you want to crack a planet, you have to get the ship going really fast so the antimatter goes off deep inside it, focusing the blast."

"I thought you told Sansar you didn't know anything about these ships."

"I said I didn't know where they were. I never said I didn't know anything about them." She chuckled. "This one really *is* targeted on Tolgar, and I'm very familiar with its attack profile."

Dave's hand strayed to his pistol. "How about you safe it for now, though, and then we can all join everyone else? Wouldn't that be a lot more fun?"

"Than blowing up Tolgar? Not really. Still, they do have *Keesius* ships of their own, and they absolutely *would* use them on the other Veetanho worlds if we were to blow up Tolgar." Gleeko sighed. "Fine." She pressed several buttons, and the magnetic bottles detached from the bow doors, dropping away toward the moon.

"Is that… safe?"

"Individually, they're not much larger than really big bombs," Gleeko said with a shrug. "The moon already has plenty of craters… what's a few thousand more?"

* * * * *

Chapter Thirty-Four

CIC, *Gobi Desert*, Gralkaron System

"Do you think they're going to show up?" Jan asked. "Is it wise to trust a Veetanho?"

"Wise? No." Sansar chuckled. "But would it be wise for Gleeko to try to run with the *Keesius* ship, knowing I could easily turn Justice loose to track her down?"

"You wouldn't even have to call it a favor," Justice murmured. "We don't need to negotiate for something that would be such a treat."

"And if she does return?" Balin asked, holding yet another bag of snacks, but not eating anything.

"Then I suppose she'll have proven herself trustworthy... and at least for now, I won't have a burning urge to kill her."

"Well now, there is something new under the suns after all." The drawl, pointedly overdone, caught the ears of multiple species, and heads turned toward the door.

"Tald!" Justice leapt from the back of the sensor operator's chair, disappeared, and reappeared bare inches from tackling the newly-recovered Peacemaker. The Hunter held himself upright and tapped the SalSha on the arm.

"I guess I missed some excitement." Tald shifted his weight from one leg to the other, and Sansar kept herself from frowning. He should be recovered, after the nanites, and if he wasn't, he certainly shouldn't be walking around.

Not that she'd ever done such things.

"You could say that, Peacemaker." Balin tossed his bag of snacks, and Tald caught them reflexively. "And I saw that wince. You should take a seat."

"I'm feeling fine," Tald protested. "Just stiff from…" He waved his hands, then shrugged. "Everything. Catch me up?" The drawl fell away, and this time Sansar let herself smile.

"Take a seat, we'll tell you what you missed, and you can join us in waiting for the last *Keesius*."

"We've got them, then." Tald straightened, and he winked as he swaggered to a chair. It was perhaps a little more swagger than usual, but the Peacemaker was, as he said, dealing with the tightness left over from his injury. "Now I can say I never doubted it at all, ma'am."

"*I* can say I didn't miss the drawl," Sansar replied, but she didn't pause long before adding, "but we did miss you. Welcome back, Peacemaker."

Tald puffed up his chest a bit as he settled into his seat, but then he sagged. "I'm a Peacemaker now, or will be once I report back. But…" Tald turned slightly to look at Balin. "What are we going to do about the Peacemaker SI?"

"A bridge to burn when we get to it." Balin leaned on his tail and spread his claws. "For now…"

"Emergence!"

"Told you," Sansar murmured.

"Is it a—" Justice began to ask.

"*Keesius*, confirmed."

"Well. One less Veetanho I get to kill." Justice returned to his perch on the back of the sensor operator's chair. "For now."

Within a few moments, Gleeko and Dave were on the main screen, Taleena floating behind them with some sort of visual aid that made her already large eyes enormous. Sansar folded her hands behind her back and tilted her head.

"It worked," Gleeko said, and Dave Colby blew out his breath in a sigh nearly as exaggerated as Tald's drawl, "and the Goltar live to irritate another day."

"Unfortunately," Justice and Gleeko added simultaneously, then both ignored that such a thing had happened.

"And now?" Sansar had some ideas, but she'd meant it—the Veetanho with the *Keesius*, although status quo, kept the galaxy from cracking into a civil war with hungry enemies circling, both without and within.

"Now? Sansar, we have three *Keesius* ships. *Now* we jump back to Dunamis' system and blow him to dust so fine, he can't trigger a backup."

"I thought you didn't want to be anywhere near him?" Sansar shouldn't have teased, but the Veetanho had argued vociferously against coming into contact with Dunamis more than once.

"That was before I had three world-enders under my claws, thank you very much." Gleeko lifted her nose, and Dave laughed in the background.

"Coordinates are already loaded," Sansar said, and she didn't glance back to see Tald's reaction.

* * *

Tald had meant to go back to his room once they were in hyperspace, but moving seemed the only way to loosen the stitch in his side, and before he knew it, he was outside the SalSha quarters.

He hadn't meant to be there at all, and had started to push off and continue on his way when that abruptly became impossible.

"Tald!" Seeph called from further down the corridor. "Your dad's been looking all over for you! He should have known you were coming to visit him."

Remembering this was his father's copilot who'd been gravely injured at the crash on the Goka planet, Tald repressed his urge to wave and run off. It wasn't embarrassing to want to talk to his dad, and he wasn't embarrassed.

He wasn't sure what he was, but it wasn't that.

"Is he here?"

"Yep! He just got back from medical to see if you'd checked in, and was about to head to the mess, but here you are!" Clearly fully recovered, he bounded along and swung around the doorway without slowing.

Tald followed more sedately, mostly because he'd realized he was at least a little embarrassed—he probably should have checked in with his dad when he regained consciousness and got released, but he'd needed to know what had happened, and if he was about to be a Peacemaker for real, and if his almost death had helped anything, and if...

"*There* you are!" Karth announced and was zooming away before Tald could answer. "The Peacemaker's here! Thorb! Your son the Peacemaker's here!"

That was him. Peacemaker and Thorb's son, both.

WORLD ENDERS | 443

There were SalSha all around now—thumping him on the back, twisting around each other, snuffling their noses close to his ears and cheeks. It had been ages since he'd been greeted like this, been in the midst of so many of his own kind. Even in the mess, eating with his father, it hadn't been like this. Like coming home.

"There's the hero!" Thorb's voice—the most familiar voice in the world—carried across the mass of SalSha. It only took another few moments for the pilot himself to be there, in front of Thorb, holding out his arms.

Lingering soreness forgotten, Tald threw himself forward, and he and his dad spun around, Thorb laughing, Tald unsure what noise he was making.

"First SalSha Peacemaker, and what do you do on your first mission? Lead an absolutely *amazing* raid through a battle to board *Keesius* ships and take them from some dang KzSha! What! Are you serious? Trying to outdo the old man, my boy, and Blue Sky if you didn't succeed..."

"It wasn't just my idea," Tald mumbled, then cleared his throat and said louder, "It was my *and* Careena's idea, and the Horde and Colby's Killers helped, and if you all hadn't been out taking care of the fleet—"

"Yeah, yeah, yeah—we know it's never just one loner out there doing all the things, but you played a hell of a role. Best Peacemaker *ever*!"

Tald opened his mouth to say he wasn't even the best Peacemaker on board, but maybe if he had eighty more years, he could match Balin. Then there was a whole lot of cheering, and he knew that wasn't the point at the moment—he *was* the first SalSha Peacemaker. He could enjoy that for a minute.

Except he couldn't.

"Can we talk, Dad?" he asked, and Thorb caught the tone of his question enough to wave off the gathered SalSha. The crowd weaved and swam off, still cheering, and Tald's whiskers bristled before he combed them back into place.

"I'd been visiting you while you slept," Thorb said as they walked back to his room. "Then you were gone, then we had to get ready for another jump... You feeling ok?"

"I won't even have a scar." Tald brushed a hand over his side, where his fur covered the small bald spot. "Little sore, but you know how it is—always something to do."

"And that's what's bothering you?"

"No..." Tald's throat felt too small for air to get through, and he cleared it, then coughed, then sighed when he realized it was all in his head. "We're jumping back to where we found Dunamis, before."

"And you don't want to?" Thorb watched him closely, gesturing him ahead out of the hallway.

"It's not that... Dunamis needs to be dealt with, but even if we do an orbital bombardment, or unleash one of the *Keesius*, it's not... it's wrong, *and* it won't solve anything."

"Destroying a planet Dunamis is on seems like it'll... solve that problem?"

"But that's the thing—Sansar and Gleeko and everyone are so sure they have the firepower, but all I keep hearing is that SIs have backups, like maybe unlimited ones. We can't just go breaking what few laws exist to take out a *version* of an SI, and then it just pops up again like nothing happened." Tald scrubbed his cheeks so hard he almost lost a whisker, then dropped his hands. "What's the point?"

"Ah." Thorb hooked his feet in the frame of his bed and regarded his son. "What do you think the point is?"

"Dad!"

"I'm serious. You're a Peacemaker now, son. I go out and bomb things; you… you gotta figure out motive. Reasoning. All the evidence to point you toward solving what needs solving. So. What do you think the point is?"

"To strike a blow? To show the SI we're not helpless, that we *can* hurt him? Delay his plans?"

"Show how we can fight together," Thorb suggested, though as he'd been nodding along with Tald's thoughts, it didn't seem like he was disagreeing. More like he was offering additional ideas, presented to Tald for his own judgment. Tald couldn't remember ever talking to his father like that before. "Or, like the Hunters did with the Veetanho, prove we won't go gentle into that good night?"

"Maybe… maybe some of all of it. But it doesn't *solve* anything."

"Why not?"

"Because Dunamis will just pop up somewhere else. And… and there's more. We think… Balin and I, it seems pretty sure that there's an SI… running the Peacemakers. Maybe different than Dunamis and the Merc Guild, but maybe… maybe not."

"That sucks." Thorb made a low clicking sound and shook his head.

"So…"

"So do something about it."

"But *what?*" Tald had been sure he'd have outgrown needing his father's advice at this point. He was a Peacemaker now, for entropy's sake, and—and—an *adult*. Dirty Harry would never have needed Dirty Harry, Sr.'s input, would he?

"You don't have to have the answer, kid." Thorb folded himself over and touched Tald's cheek. "You just have to be willing to find it. Isn't that part of your job now?"

Tald blew out his breath and turned to lean his shoulder against his dad's. "I guess it is."

"And if, in the meantime, you get to spend time making your dad look cool to have an awesome Peacemaker son hanging around, I mean… that's not so bad, is it?"

Despite himself, Tald let his frown tug into a smile, then a full grin. "Nah. It's not the worst thing that ever happened…"

"That's my boy."

* * *

The system that had previously housed Dunamis was, of course, empty.

Tald couldn't decide whether he was genuinely disappointed about that, or relieved he didn't have to argue with Sansar again about nuking it from orbit… or dissolving an entire planet with antimatter.

Certainly Dunamis was a threat to be honored, but the *Keesius*… those seemed better as an unused threat rather than actively demolishing systems throughout the galaxy.

"There's nothing here. He didn't leave anything—not a ship, not a single corpse. Beyond some empty wreckage orbiting the primary, it's clean." Naran's face remained neutral, but Tald noticed the tension in the corner of her eyes.

On the screen, Gleeko adjusted her goggles, her glare apparent even with their interference. "He will be coming for you." From the way she said it, Tald had a feeling she meant all of them in general, but Sansar in particular.

"I imagine none of us are done with this, or him. It'll only be a matter of time."

"Yes." The Veetanho looked off screen, then back toward the *Gobi Desert's* CIC. "For that reason, and others, we can't keep all the *Keesius* in one place."

"Are you planning to hide them throughout different systems? That'll be a challenge if—"

"Species."

Even Sansar seemed momentarily taken aback.

"Not all of them. One around Lytoshaan, to deter our enemies. One in another Veetanho system, where we still have allies on our side. And one—" Gleeko sighed "—with you."

"Humanity?"

"*You*, Sansar. Humanity is in Dunamis' crosshairs, there's no doubt, but you've proven yourself an ally. Unwilling at times, perhaps." Gleeko's muzzle twisted in something halfway between a smile and a grimace. "But you truly worked to get these ships back to my people. I don't know… I don't know many who would've done that."

"*I* wouldn't have," Dave interjected over the screen from the *Mighty Wave*. "Two badass ships seems a small recompense for our time with Dunamis."

"You left my ship voluntarily," Gleeko replied with a snort, "to your credit."

"Yeah, yeah. So we're all friends now?"

"United against a common enemy, at the least."

"I suppose I really don't *need* to kill you," Justice said, sounding surprised. His eyes half-closed, as though he were about to slow-blink, but that was a step too far. Instead, he shook himself and inclined his head a fraction of an inch.

"Well, that's reassuring." Gleeko's tone would have dripped sarcasm if there'd been even a fraction more coating the words. "Though I admit, I'm surprised you didn't board the ship while we were scanning the system."

"Oh." The Hunter shrugged, and then he did slow blink, though his head was angled toward the sensor operator's console, not Gleeko. "I did. Twice."

Tald rubbed his cheeks and swallowed back a sigh. He'd wondered where Justice had gone.

"So what's next?" Tald stepped forward, not entirely sure of the answer. He'd passed his probationary mission, which clearly no one at the guild had expected. He'd *almost* died, but hadn't. Dunamis was in the wind. The Peacemaker Guild might be rotten at the core. He'd gotten used to being on the same ship as his father, with all these new deputies—friends—people, but he knew he couldn't stay…

His badge pulled heavily on his vest, and it was all he could do not to paw at it.

"Next?" Balin chuckled and dug his tongue into his latest bag of snacks. As he gestured around the CIC, he swallowed, then continued, "You enjoy the feeling of a mission well done. You mourn the dead. You rest… because the next fight will be on you soon enough."

* * * * *

Epilogue

Lyon's Den, Karma Station

"Karma station…" Jan made a face. "It sure is… a lot. Like a hive of—"

"Don't." Dave held up a hand as they navigated through the crowded corridors. "If you quote old movies at me and make me laugh, and then we get shot—"

"We're not going to get shot if you laugh." Jan turned so he could be sure to see her roll her eyes, then faced fully forward in barely enough time to sidestep an enormous bear.

An enormous, purple, absolutely *gigantic* bear.

"We might. We just passed three aliens who look like they got caught at the wrong tailgate party in full face paint—they would *definitely* think I was laughing at them, and then shoot us."

"Only if you shoot first," Taleena said helpfully. She was careful to walk between them, staying clear of taller aliens who couldn't be bothered to look down.

"There it is—top merc pit on Karma." Jan pointed to a sign half the corridor away, but before Dave could follow her gesture, something that was more teeth than body got in his way.

"That's not the top pit," the Besquith said, and Dave's hand tensed. He was far too disciplined to let it twitch toward his holstered weapon, but he hadn't been close enough to smell Besquith drool without a gun in his hand for… a long time. It felt weird.

"But it's where we're expected, so good for us. Thanks so much." Dave reached out and pulled Taleena along with him, and he and Jan split around the Besquith as neatly as if they'd practiced the move for a hundred or so years. The back of Dave's neck itched, but he knew better than to look back at the werewolf behind them, and the rest of the walk to the Lyon's Den thankfully lacked jaws at his jugular.

Two Lumar stood outside the door, bodies at ease, but eyes roving. One focused on the approaching trio. "Drink or business?"

"Both, hopefully," Dave said with a grin.

"Good answer. Know rules?" The Lumar used the two arms closest to the door to grab it, then paused until they answered.

"Don't draw on anyone, fights go outside, contracts are negotiable, but drinks aren't." Dave had listened with interest while Sansar told them about the owner of the merc pit. In his day, Humans hadn't gone to Karma lightly. They certainly hadn't *run* anything there.

"Good." The Lumar pulled the door open, and they stepped through.

If the corridors outside had been crowded chaos, the inside of the Lyon's Den was… a different flavor of that. There were plenty of Humans inside, but an entire corner was packed with Lumar—there was a sign overhead that declared it 'Kuldo's Corner' in at least three languages—and there were Zuul, Goltar, Hunters, and at least a dozen other aliens gathered around tables, leaning against walls, or engaged in enthusiastic conversation at the bar. Countless screens displaying holos, columns of numbers, symbols, and things Dave couldn't begin to identify studded the walls and added to the visual and audial noise.

"Ok, I was wrong, *this* is the hive of—"

Dave stepped forward into the large room—crowded as it was, there was plenty of room to move without bumping anyone, which had to be good for business—partly to get to the bar and get going, and partly to keep from encouraging his sister's determination to quote ancient Earth movies.

"What can I get you?" a Human asked as he eased into an open space at the polished bar. This one was male, but not tall, so Dave decided he wasn't the proprietor.

"Is the Lyon in?"

"You a friend of his?"

"Nope!" Dave grinned and spread his hands, then grinned wider as Jan squeezed in and knocked one of his arms out of the way. Taleena leapt up high enough to grab the bar and lift her head over it. "We haven't been out this way in a long, long, *long* time, but we are friends with Sansar Enkh, and she said we could drink on the Golden Horde's tab."

"That's exactly the kind of bullshit the boss likes." The bartender laughed and shook his head. "No tabs, but give me your orders, and I'll see if he's available."

"Three Burning Birds. Sansar said those were the drink to try."

"Oh." The bartender sobered. "You *do* know Colonel Enkh." He reached under the bar as though pressing something, then got down to mixing some drinks.

Dave was about to press the issue, then shrugged. *Hell, let's drink a little, relax; we'll get to the owner when we get to him.*

Jan met his eyes and lifted her eyebrows, and he shook his head. She shrugged in turn, then leaned around him to Taleena. "You want to get a seat, or are you enjoying hanging there?"

"We've got seats of all sizes for all kinds of folks," said a deep, cheerful, Human voice from behind them.

Dave turned slowly—no unnecessarily quick movements in a pit of mercs—and found he had to tilt his head back a bit to look the man in the eyes. "The Lyon, I presume?"

"That's what it says on my sign." The Den's owner smiled, broad and relaxed, and gestured them to follow him. "Your drinks will meet us at the table. I'm guessing you came in on that repurposed battlecruiser?"

"The *Mighty Wave*, that's us. Sansar sent a message?"

"Sansar sent a message." The Lyon laughed. "Didn't set up a tab for you, though; solid effort."

"You never know—we gave up some fancy stuff on her behalf." They settled at the table, and sure enough, a tray of drinks appeared a moment later, deposited by a markedly small Lumar. There was a seat perfectly-sized for Taleena, and she settled into it with a *thrum* of pleasure, then immediately reached for her drink.

"She didn't go into specifics," the Lyon said, in the sort of manner that was inviting without being pushy. Dave had to admire it— but then, he'd heard the Lyon had had almost as much practice in his own field as Dave had in his. A couple of ancient Humans, far from home.

"I probably won't, either, but she said you and us have a few things in common. Wrong side of the Merc Guild, looking great for our age, up to make credits."

The Lyon's smile shifted. "The Burning Bird."

"Be a shame to waste our battlecruiser."

"And like a thousand years of experience, if you add us all up," Jan interjected, and Dave noticed she'd already polished off two thirds of her drink. It had been awhile since they'd had some good stuff—he took the reminder to take a healthy draught of his own.

"Oh, that's good," he said involuntarily, and the Lyon laughed. It sounded genuine, and Dave forced himself to relax. They were all on the same side here.

"I've got some experience myself," the proprietor allowed, "and a few suggestions for battlecruisers and merc units and making credits. Colby's Killers, isn't it? You're still on the rolls."

"That's us." Jan toasted and finished her drink, and between one blink and the next, there was a fresh round on the table.

"We can probably solve a few of those MIA mysteries from the old days," Dave added. "We've got some mercs who belonged to other companies, back in the day."

"Any from the Pride?" the Lyon asked, suddenly very still.

"Not off the top of my head, but we'll ask around."

"I'd appreciate that." They drank companionably in the midst of the din for a few minutes, then the Lyon leaned his elbows on the table. "So what kind of work are the Killers looking for?"

"Seems like it's a weird time in the galaxy. Give us the tricky stuff."

"The tricky stuff can be hard on a merc unit," the Lyon said, tipping one of his hands side to side.

"There are worse things out there. This way, we get to choose our fights and our weapons, and deal with fewer of the SI strings."

"For now," the Lyon said, and Dave snorted, because the other man was right.

"Figure it like this—we're good. That's not cocky, it's time and training—trial by fire's got nothing on us. So we're this good now... and we'd like to be even better the next time our old friend Dunamis comes around again. You know what I mean? So when he knocks on the door…"

"We knock the shit out of him," Taleena declared, then burped.

"I think we'll work very well together, Killers." The Lyon lifted his glass, and they all met his with their own.

# # # # #

About Chris Kennedy

A Webster Award winner and three-time Dragon Award finalist, Chris Kennedy is a Science Fiction/Fantasy author, speaker, and small-press publisher who has written over 30 books and published more than 200 others. Get his free book, "Shattered Crucible," at his website, https://chriskennedypublishing.com.

Called "fantastic" and "a great speaker," he has coached hundreds of beginning authors and budding novelists on how to self-publish their stories at a variety of conferences, conventions, and writing guild presentations. He is the author of the award-winning #1 bestseller, "Self-Publishing for Profit: How to Get Your Book Out of Your Head and Into the Stores."

Chris lives in Coinjock, North Carolina, with his wife, and is the holder of a doctorate in educational leadership and master's degrees in both business and public administration. Follow Chris on Facebook at https://www.facebook.com/ckpublishing/.

* * * * *

About Marisa Wolf

Marisa Wolf was born in New England, and raised on Boston sports teams, Star Wars, Star Trek, and the longest books in the library (usually fantasy). Over the years she majored in English in part to get credits for reading (this… only partly worked), taught middle school, was headbutted by an alligator, built a career in education, earned a black belt in Tae Kwon Do, and finally decided to finish all those half-started stories in her head. She's currently based in Texas, but has moved into an RV with her husband and their two ridiculous rescue dogs, and it's anyone's guess where in the country she is at any given moment. Learn more at www.marisawolf.net.

* * * * *

The following is an

Excerpt from Book One of The Last Marines:

Gods of War

William S. Frisbee, Jr.

Available from Theogony Books

eBook and Paperback

Excerpt from "Gods of War:"

"Yes, sir," Mathison said. Sometimes it was worth arguing, sometimes it wasn't. Stevenson wasn't a butter bar. He was a veteran from a line infantry platoon that had made it through Critical Skills Operator School and earned his Raider pin. He was also on the short list for captain. Major Beckett might pin the railroad tracks on Stevenson's collar before they left for space.

"Well, enough chatting," Stevenson said, the smile in his voice grating on Mathison's nerves. "Gotta go check our boys."

"Yes, sir," Mathison said, and later he would check on the men while the lieutenant rested. "Please keep your head down, sir. Don't leave me in charge of this cluster fuck. I would be tempted to tell that company commander to go fuck a duck."

"No, you won't. You will do your job and take care of our Marines, but I'll keep my head down," Stevenson said. "Asian socialists aren't good enough to kill me. It's going to have to be some green alien bastard that kills me."

"Yes, sir," Mathison said as the lieutenant tapped on Jennings' shoulder and pointed up. The lance corporal understood and cupped his hands together to boost the lieutenant out of the hole. He launched the lieutenant out of the hole and went back to digging as Mathison went back to looking at the spy eyes scrutinizing the distant jungle.

A shot rang out. On Mathison's heads-up display, the icon for Lieutenant Stevenson flashed and went red, indicating death.

"You are now acting platoon commander," Freya reported.

* * * * *

459

Get "Gods of War" now at: Coming Soon/.

Find out more about William S. Frisbee, Jr. at: https://chriskennedypublishing.com.

* * * * *

The following is an

Excerpt from Book One of the Echoes of Pangaea:

Bestiarii

James Tarr

Available from Theogony Books

eBook and Paperback

Excerpt from "Bestiarii:"

"Mayday Mayday Mayday, this is Sierra Bravo Six, we've lost power and are going down," Delian calmly said as Tina screamed from the back. He and Hanson began frantically hitting buttons and flipping switches. "Radio's dead, I've got nothing." He had to yell it so Hansen could hear him over the wind.

Mike's eyes went wide. He felt his stomach come up into his throat as the helicopter dropped and began rotating. "Shite," Seamus cursed and smacked the button to drop the visor on his helmet.

"Keep transmitting," Hansen told his co-pilot. "Damn, I've got no electronics, can we do a manual re-start?" He stayed on the stick and the collective, trying to control the autorotation.

Delian had been hitting every button and toggle switch possible. "No, I don't think this is a short, it looks like everything's fried. Mayday Mayday Mayday, this is Sierra Bravo Six, we are going down." He told the younger pilot, "You know what to do. Keep it level, autorotate down, try to control the rate of descent. Time your glide. You see a place to land?"

The helicopter was spinning to the right as it fell, which traditionally was the reason the pilot was the right stick. Hansen looked out the window as he fought the controls. "We're in the mountains, nothing's flat. I've got trees everywhere. Hold on back there!" he yelled over his shoulder.

The helicopter began spinning faster and faster and Mike found himself being pulled sideways in his seat. The soldier on the door gun lost his footing and floated up in the air, then was halfway out the open door, one hand still on the mini-gun, restrained only by his tether as the G-forces made Mike's face feel hot. He vomited, and the bitter fluid was whipped away from his face. The world outside the open doorway past Todd was a spinning blue/green/brown blur. Tina was screaming wildly. The wind was whistling around the cabin.

"We've got smoke coming from the engine," Delian said, peering upward. "What the hell happened?"

"Brace for impact!" Seamus yelled at the cabin, and wedged his boots against the seat opposite.

"Coming up on the mark, keep it level," Delian said calmly. "Get ready for the burn!" he yelled over his shoulder at the passengers. He switched back to the radio, even though he thought it was a waste of time. "Mayday Mayday Mayday, this is Sierra Bravo Six—"

"If they work," Mike heard the pilot respond, then suddenly there was a roar, and he was pressed down in his seat, getting heavier and heavier. The helicopter was still spinning, and out the open doorway and windshield there was nothing but a blur of greens and browns. Mike got heavier and heavier, and Tina stopped screaming. Then the roar stopped, and they began falling again, pulling up against their seatbelts. Tina opened her mouth to scream once more, but before she could draw a breath the helicopter hit with a huge crunch and the sound of tearing metal.

* * * * *

Get "Bestiarii" now at:
https://www.amazon.com/dp/B0B44YM335/.

Find out more about James Tarr at:
https://chriskennedypublishing.com.

* * * * *

The following is an

Excerpt from Book One of Abner Fortis, ISMC:

Cherry Drop

P.A. Piatt

Available from Theogony Books

eBook, Audio, and Paperback

Excerpt from "Cherry Drop:"

"Here they come!"

A low, throbbing buzz rose from the trees and the undergrowth shook. Thousands of bugs exploded out of the jungle, and Fortis' breath caught in his throat. The insects tumbled over each other in a rolling, skittering mass that engulfed everything in its path.

The Space Marines didn't need an order to open fire. Rifles cracked and the grenade launcher thumped over and over as they tried to stem the tide of bugs. Grenades tore holes in the ranks of the bugs and well-aimed rifle fire dropped many more. Still, the bugs advanced.

Hawkins' voice boomed in Fortis' ear. "LT, fall back behind the fighting position, clear the way for the heavy weapons."

Fortis looked over his shoulder and saw the fighting holes bristling with Marines who couldn't fire for fear of hitting their own comrades. He thumped Thorsen on the shoulder.

"Fall back!" he ordered. "Take up positions behind the fighting holes."

Thorsen stopped firing and moved among the other Marines, relaying Fortis' order. One by one, the Marines stopped firing and made for the rear. As the gunfire slacked off, the bugs closed ranks and continued forward.

After the last Marine had fallen back, Fortis motioned to Thorsen.

"Let's go!"

Thorsen turned and let out a blood-chilling scream. A bug had approached unnoticed and buried its stinger deep in Thorsen's calf. The stricken Marine fell to the ground and began to convulse as the neurotoxin entered his bloodstream.

467

"Holy shit!" Fortis drew his kukri, ran over, and chopped at the insect stinger. The injured bug made a high-pitched shrieking noise, which Fortis cut short with another stroke of his knife.

Viscous, black goo oozed from the hole in Thorsen's armor and his convulsions ceased.

"*Get the hell out of there!*"

Hawkins was shouting in his ear, and Abner looked up. The line of bugs was ten meters away. For a split second he almost turned and ran, but the urge vanished as quickly as it appeared. He grabbed Thorsen under the arms and dragged the injured Marine along with him, pursued by the inexorable tide of gaping pincers and dripping stingers.

Fortis pulled Thorsen as fast as he could, straining with all his might against the substantial Pada-Pada gravity. Thorsen convulsed and slipped from Abner's grip and the young officer fell backward. When he sat up, he saw the bugs were almost on them.

* * * * *

Get "Cherry Drop" now at:
https://www.amazon.com/dp/B09B14VBK2

Find out more about P.A. Piatt at:
https://chriskennedypublishing.com

* * * * *

Printed in Great Britain
by Amazon

38912401R00264